ER DOC'S FOREVER GIFT

SUE MacKAY

CHRISTMAS WITH HER BODYGUARD

CHARLOTTE HAWKES

MILLS & BOON

First Published in Great Britain 2018
by Mills & Boon, an imprint of HarperCollins*Publishers*
1 London Bridge Street, London, SE1 9GF

ER Doc's Forever Gift © 2018 by Sue MacKay

Christmas with Her Bodyguard © 2018 by Charlotte Hawkes

ISBN: 978-0-263-93385-7

MIX
Paper from
responsible sources
FSC C007454

Printed and bound in Spain
by CPI, Barcelona

ER DOC'S FOREVER GIFT

SUE MacKAY

MILLS & BOON

To all those amazing people who fly the rescue helicopters and to the medical personnel on board, whether in easy situations or dangerous locations. You rock.

CHAPTER ONE

LIFE COULD BE so damned unfair.

There were days Sienna Burch hated being a paediatrician, today being one of them. Maybe she should bow out at the end of her contract, go buy a patch of land in a sleepy backwater and grow tomatoes and wear a long, billowy skirt.

Like hell.

While colleagues had warned her she'd been on a hiding to nowhere from the moment young Caleb was admitted with meningitis, she also knew parents trusted her to do all she could for their adored child. She always did that. But they also expected her to win, and unfortunately, that outcome wasn't achievable every single time.

Another yawn pulled at her. It would be too easy to shuffle further down the SUV's seat and drop into a deep sleep right here in her garage. Far too effortless. Elbowing the door open, she gathered her handbag and jacket up from the passenger seat before staggering upright.

Bed? Or food? She needed both. And a shower. Food took time because she'd have to clean up afterwards. Unless she went for the easy, not so healthy option of a toasted sandwich and only one pan to rinse out. There was ham and cheese in the fridge. Her tongue lapped her lips. Yes, she did allow herself a few semi-healthy treats.

Sighing, she headed for the kitchen, flicked on lights, dropped the blind.

Boom, boom, boom.

'What the——?' Music loud enough to wake the dead thumped through the walls. 'Great. Why tonight?'

The new guy next door nearly always had music of some genre on the go when he was at home, but rarely was it loud and intrusive. In the living room she flicked on more lights. Hopefully he'd notice she was home and cut the volume. That was when she heard laughter and voices. 'He's having a party. Wonderful.' How did that happen when he was new in town on a temporary contract at the Rescue Helicopter base, temporarily replacing her real neighbour for three months?

Not that Sienna had met the guy, only caught a couple of glances of a well-honed body filling out jeans in a way that should have him a modelling contract with the manufacturers. Not her type at all. *Oh, yeah, then what is?* With her crazy schedule she rarely had civilised hours to have fun in.

The guy seldom seemed to be home either. Not unless he liked permanently closed windows and doors. Another blast of music slapped her. If only he had the place shut up tight tonight. How was she going to sleep with that going on?

Forget toasting a sandwich. Bread and cheese while tugging clothes off and getting under the shower was the way to go. Her bed was beckoning with relentless persistence. Only thing was, her mind couldn't blank out the anguished cries of Caleb's parents as they'd switched off life support. From past experience she knew there were no shortcuts getting through this anguish, that it took time and looking after herself—which meant getting adequate sleep.

Thump, thump, thump. And she'd thought the volume was at its max. Sliding right down her bed, covers up to her neck, pillow over her head, Sienna closed her eyes and counted sheep. Not that those dumb animals ever helped her out, but she needed to zone out, find oblivion.

Then her dad piped up in the fog filling her head. Of course he did.

'Relax. Enjoy life and all it's got to offer. What's happened to my girl who loved to track butterflies? Who wanted to grow wings and fly?'

His words taunted her whenever she was too tired to fight them.

'Not tonight, Dad. Please.'

An hour later, Sienna tossed the pillow and covers aside to swing her legs out of bed. The headache pills she'd taken with her bread were not working as the drums in her head were louder and harsher than ever. Those weren't the worst beats. Next door there had to be a whole band of drummers competing with each other; the noise level was so unbelievably high. The voices had also increased in volume.

All she wanted was eight hours straight being comatose. Hours where Caleb didn't feature, where his parents' sobs didn't break her heart. Hours in which she couldn't think about her promise to her father to lighten up some by Christmas. She'd settled here, in this city, bought this apartment for a reason and nothing or no one could be allowed to change it. Yet it seemed everyone was trying to.

Click, click. Her vertebrae pulled her straight. Time to confront her neighbour. Her muscles began to soften. She didn't do conflict, unless she was fighting for a patient's life. Yes, well, her patients needed her to get some sleep so she could think straight. *Click, click.* That music was going to shut down. Now.

* * *

Harry sat on the edge of the deck, a warming bottle of beer swinging from his fingers. Midnight had been and gone. If only he could say the same for his visitors. Unfortunately they all seemed intent on burying their raw grief in loud music and lots of shouting and talking.

A tight-knit group, they'd naturally turned to each other today when they heard the news of the loss of their top pilot after the helicopter he was flying back from having the machine serviced went out of control and hit the ground. The cause of the crash was as yet unknown, and likely to be for weeks, if not months, but the mechanics were on high alert. Bet the crews would be too, come tomorrow.

Lights came on in the apartment next door, then the deck was flooded in a yellow glow.

Oh, oh. Trouble on the horizon? Harry shrugged and sipped the beer, not really enjoying it yet reluctant to set it aside. His hands always had to be busy. If only he had something to do to fill in the hours before this lot were ready to head home in the taxis he'd order, and pay for. Being the new boy on the block, he hadn't known Gavin Bradley well, but the guy was a legend in the emergency air service—his reputation for spot-on retrieval in difficult conditions ran the length of the country. He would be missed very much.

A shadow crossed the end of the drive, turned in his direction. The shadow became human, walking with confidence and yet at the same time almost with caution, like a young girl with little care to burden her. Then she came into the light, making her way up towards him, an opposing grim expression on what might be a beautiful face if she wasn't carrying the weight of the world on her back. Apparently this was the girl next door. Only he could see now her girl days were long gone, morphed into someone who stole the breath away from him and tightened his groin without any input from his brain.

Harry slowly drew another mouthful of beer—it really was foul—and put the bottle down on the deck beside him. 'Hello. So we finally get to meet.'

That delicious mouth flattened further. 'This is not a social call.' Her voice was husky—and laden with barely contained anger.

'That's a shame.' In more ways than he cared to admit, even to himself. Close up, she was even better looking than he'd first thought. Her flawless skin covered perfect facial bone structure. 'I'm Harry, by the way.'

That startled her. 'Sienna Burch,' she snapped. Hadn't she expected to be introducing herself?

'So what can I do for you, Sienna?' Though he kind of had an idea what was getting her knickers in a twist. It was late on a working night, and the guys inside were a little loud.

'Could you please turn the music down? Or preferably off? I need to get some sleep.' Her expression wasn't softening, but that didn't quieten his pulse. A bit of a challenge in the making?

Over the past weeks he'd been vaguely aware of her coming and going at all hours, but hadn't got around to introducing himself. Nothing unusual in that when he was on a short stint in a town he was unlikely to return to. His breath caught. He had to be slipping—because behind whatever was tightening her face this particular woman was a stunner, and he was partial to stunners. Fess up, he liked women, full stop. Especially hot, shapely, downright beautiful ones. If that made him shallow then he could live with that. It suited his mantra: keep moving on.

'Excuse me. The music?'

'I'll give it a go, certainly.' Now he could hear one of

the girls crying behind him. That'd been a while coming. Apart from initial tears everyone had been stoic, but he'd known it was only a matter of time before they showed their grief in the teary form. And he was supposed to charge in and turn the music off and make like everyone should go home?

'I'd prefer that you actually did it, not make a half-hearted attempt. I've had a long, difficult day and I need to sleep.'

Bet your day was a breeze compared to the one these guys are dealing with.

'I'm sorry about that. I will do my best, but I have to warn you my colleagues are suffering an enormous shock and this is their way of letting off steam.' It wasn't as though he had the sound turned up to full volume every night of the week. This was a one-off.

That tight mouth wasn't giving an inch. 'I see.'

No, she didn't. 'Have you seen the news today?'

'As if.' Finally that mouth softened a fraction, and Sienna lifted her chin slightly. Definitely beautiful in a classic way. 'What did I miss?'

'One of the rescue helicopters went down this morning.'

She gasped. Now that tightness was taking a backward step. 'With serious consequences I take it.'

'The pilot died and the other pilot on board is in a serious condition in the ICU at Auckland Hospital. Fortunately they didn't have medical crew or a patient on board or there'd be more casualties.'

Another gasp, and Sienna moved closer. 'I'm sorry. That's terrible. I didn't hear about that.'

What did she do for a living? Take gym classes in a cave? That tee shirt and those fitted leggings highlighted a well-formed body with muscles in the right places and soft curves to add a sensuality that teased him. Like he needed this right now. But it seemed certain parts of his body were out of sync with the sadness roiling in his mind. *They* wanted action. *They* weren't getting any.

Then Sienna added, 'I'm sorry to hear that. Really sorry.' Another step and she was beside the deck.

'It's been a huge shock for everyone. You understand I'm filling in at the helicopter rescue service?'

'Yes.' She leaned her tidy butt against the handrail post. 'I haven't been very neighbourly, but I'm hardly ever at home.'

'Don't worry about it. I'll be gone in a month.'

Sienna straightened again. 'Anyway, I do need to get some shut-eye. My day wasn't a lot better.'

Her frostiness did nothing to detract from her looks, but however much she needed some quiet his loyalties lay with those inside his apartment. 'Maybe, but I'm giving these people the chance to de-stress before making sure they get home safely. You could join us and wind down from whatever upset you with a wine and some music.'

'It would take a lot more than that.'

He had to ask. 'What happened?' Damn it, why couldn't he just mind his own business? Now he'd have to listen to some story that barely registered compared to the crash, as well as be sympathetic.

'I lost a patient. A six-year-old boy.' Her bottom lip trembled.

Damned if he didn't want to haul her into his arms and hold her until the trembling stopped. His fingers gripped the beer bottle as if his life depended on it. 'That's terrible. You're a doctor?' Not a gym instructor, then.

'A paediatrician. The best, and the worst, job out there.' Her voice was low and slow.

She's a doctor?

That explained the hours she was away from home. Who'd have thought it? But then, why not?

We don't all come with labels on our foreheads proclaiming our medical knowledge. And why can't doctors be beautiful, and have stunning figures?

Just because he'd never met one quite as attractive as Sienna Burch, didn't mean they didn't exist.

Then she yawned.

Which got to him, made him want to soothe her to sleep. 'The kids are the worst cases. They always get to me, even if only for a greenstick fracture.'

'And the parents. They're hurting as bad. They want to take the pain into themselves so their babies don't have to suffer, and it's torture when they can't.' Sienna lifted her head and stared at him, her own pain obvious.

She took her job seriously, but it was hard to find a good doctor who didn't. Impossible. Thoughtlessly he reached across with one hand to touch her arm. So much for hanging on to his bottle as a shield. 'I totally understand.' Squeezing lightly, he hurriedly pulled away. But it was too late. Warmth trickled from her skin through his fingers and up his arm.

Sienna was upright—and uptight. 'If you can't turn the music off then at least lower the decibels.'

Sarah, one of the pilots, appeared on the deck. 'I think everyone's ready to head home now.'

Harry stood up and found his neighbour's head came up to his chin. Not often that happened. 'There you go. You should be able to get that kip soon.'

'I appreciate it.' Sienna turned and stumbled down the path, not so youthful in her movements now.

He couldn't take his eyes off her. Somehow she'd woven her way under his skin while being the antithesis of the open, cheery women he usually went for. She hadn't effused sympathy, nor had she been cold about what had happened, just contained. But then, she was used to other people's pain. 'See you,' he called after her, the temptation to goad her just a little way too hard to ignore. If she could shake him up, then he could return the favour. 'Maybe we'll both be at home at the same time one night this week.' Unlikely since he was rarely here and then mostly only to eat and sleep.

There was no reply, just a lengthening of the strides taking her away.

As he was unused to being ignored, his interest was piqued. Had it been entirely her bad day at work putting that exhaustion in her face, her eyes? Or was there more going on in her life causing problems? Harry huffed a bitter breath. Why did he even want to know? He didn't do getting to know women beyond the obvious, yet within minutes Sienna Burch had got under his skin like a serious itch. Not a good look. Best he didn't scratch. That was going to take some serious effort, for sure.

'I'll start ordering taxis, shall I?' Sarah nudged his arm with her shoulder. 'For most of this lot anyway.'

Sarah had been trying to get his attention, as in up close and personal, from the day he'd started at the rescue service, and he'd been putting out the thanks-but-no-thanks signal to no avail. It would do wonders for his tired soul to lose himself in a woman tonight. Which was blatantly on offer, if he was reading Sarah correctly, and he had no reason to think otherwise. But he had a hard and fast rule—no sex with colleagues.

Sienna isn't a colleague.

His gaze tripped sideways to the other drive leading up to the adjacent apartment and the woman stepping onto an identical front step. Short-tempered, not overly concerned for others needing an outlet for their grief, a different kind of woman. Intriguing. Irritating. To be ignored, forgotten about. If that was possible. *It had better be.* He turned to his co-worker. 'Make sure everyone gets a ride home. Everyone,' he repeated in case his message hadn't got through. Boy, wouldn't he like to scratch that itch with Sienna.

His temporary neighbour had ruffled his feathers. He couldn't remember the last time a female had done that. Probably when he was fifteen and keen for just about any girl willing to join him in a bit of fun. His gaze remained on the neighbouring apartment, noting lights turning off, another going on—in the bedroom. Bedroom, bed, sheets, or not. Go, damn it. Just focus on that temporary bit and he'd be fine, wouldn't succumb to the sudden craving filling him.

I won't. I really won't.

Would he? Could he call her a colleague because they were both doctors? It'd be a stretch but something to hang on to if this itch got too strong.

CHAPTER TWO

'WE'VE LANDED ON the roof of the hospital, Felicity,' Harry told his young patient. 'You'll soon be inside where the doctors can take good care of you.' He checked the belts holding her on the stretcher.

She pushed the face mask aside. 'I don't want to be here. I wanted to stay on the island.' Petulance didn't suit her.

Gently putting the mask back in place, he said in his best friendly doctor voice, 'You need checking out by the specialists.' He could understand that petulance but she'd nearly drowned. With lungs in the condition of hers because of the cystic fibrosis, that was bad. 'You coughed up a lot of water.'

The mask was again shoved away. 'You don't get it,' griped the fifteen-year-old. 'This was the end-of-year trip that all year tens in science have been slogging their guts out for. Me included. And on the first day you bring me back to Auckland. Thanks a bundle.'

His heart softened for this angry girl. People with her condition didn't get a fair bat at life. But as a doctor there was no way he could've left her on Great Barrier Island. They might've cleared the water from her lungs, but all of it? Secondary drowning was always a risk, especially with her condition. Close attention was required for the next twenty-four hours.

'Ready?' asked Connor, his off-sider, standing on the ground waiting to take one end of the stretcher.

'Sure am.' Harry nodded to Felicity. 'I'm sorry I had to bring you home.'

She blinked and tears spurted out of the corners of her eyes. 'It's not your fault. I shouldn't blame you. If Tony Wilcox hadn't leapt on my back I wouldn't have gone under water. *I* know not to. At least not for as long as I was down there. I got stuck on a rocky ledge for a bit.'

Again he replaced the mask, certain she'd remove it any minute. 'You give him a hard time when you both get back to school.' With practised ease he and Connor quickly had the stretcher out and rolling towards the sliding door decorated with red and gold tinsel that gave access to the hospital emergency lift. Staff in scrubs were waiting for them. Presumably a doctor and nurses. Wait. The serious demeanour on one face was familiar. The slam as his stomach hit his toes was not. 'Sienna? You work at Auckland Central?' Duh, obviously. It made sense, given that she lived not too far away.

An abrupt nod in his direction as though he was immaterial to this scene had his blood more than heating—it was boiling. Down, boy. Not the time or place. For confrontation, or getting friendly. What was it with her that already his body was reacting so blatantly? She really had worked a number on him. Bet she had no idea either. Damn it.

'Hi, Fliss. This is a bummer, isn't it?' Sienna was focusing on their patient almost as if she hadn't acknowledged him while everyone prepared to transfer the girl over to the hospital bed and change oxygen supplies.

'It's not fair, is what it is,' grizzled the once again maskless girl. 'You told me I'd be all right for a few days, Doc Sienna.'

'I'm sorry, Fliss, I guess I was wrong.' Nothing but compassion in her voice.

Sienna was taking the blame for something that was totally out of her control? Miss—make that Dr—Frosty? He really had read her all wrong last week. Or was it only in her medical capacity she managed to show warmth towards others? 'I take it Felicity's a regular patient of yours?' Harry looked to Sienna.

'Yes. We've been working towards this stay on the island for weeks now.'

Sympathy radiated out of those eyes he now saw were vivid blue, the colour of Lake Tekapo on a summer's day. A lake he'd spent a day on trying to catch trout the first time he worked in New Zealand. It had been a fantastic day and despite the lack of fish he'd never forgotten how relaxed the stunning mountainous scenery and the bouncing waters had made him feel. It was a place he intended to revisit, if he ever found himself with a couple of spare days. The lake would be warmer than Sienna was towards him. Why the chill? Could that explain this overreaction to her? She was a challenge? It couldn't be that he wanted to get to know her better, except maybe physically, and by the steely glint in those eyes *that* wasn't happening.

'Can I have the notes?' A hand with rose-pink, perfectly manicured nails highlighting long, slim fingers waved in front of him.

Harry shook his head to rid the thoughts his overheated brain conjured up of those nails tripping over his hot skin. This was his unfriendly neighbour. Doc Frosty would never be interested in running her fingers anywhere near him. Not unless she was going to use them to impale him for not turning down the music the moment she'd requested he do so. The following morning she'd barely managed a nod in his direction as she'd left for work when he'd gone out to the four-wheel-drive that came with the apartment.

'Excuse me, the notes?'

Focus, man. Passing over the required information, he explained, 'The school first-aid officer managed to get Felicity to bring up a lot of water before we arrived, but she's still coughing up fluid intermittently.' A lot of that had to do with the mucus clogging her lungs, but still there was danger in residual salt water wreaking havoc with her breathing.

'I'm glad the first-aid officer knew what to do.' The frost melted a little as she studied Felicity.

'I agree.' Harry nodded before filling Sienna in on more details. Then he crossed to Felicity. 'You take care, now; get back on your feet quick smart. Don't let Tony Wilcox win this one.' He got a watery smile in return.

'Who's Tony Wilcox?' Doc Frosty asked from right beside him in a not so chilly tone.

'The guy who caused Felicity to have her head under water too long.'

'He didn't mean it,' their patient interjected, with a red flush going on in her cheeks.

So that was how this went. Young Felicity was keen on Tony and didn't want to show it. 'I'm sure he didn't.' Harry grinned, then turned to Sienna, his mouth still curved upward. 'Might see you later, Doctor.'

As in, I could drop in to your place with a bottle of wine.

And probably get thrown out on his butt, because that had to be the dumbest idea he'd had in a long time.

Once again he didn't get any acknowledgement from Sienna as she headed into the lift, all her attention on their patient. He couldn't fault her for that. Felicity came first, but it irked that she hadn't taken a few seconds to give him a nod. Yet the woman had apologised to her young patient for her trip going horribly wrong. The doc did have a heart. She might keep it buried deep, but he certainly couldn't fault her for that. He did the same. It saved getting too involved and then having to bail when things got too intense. But still, he wouldn't have minded a smile: a warm, tender one like the smile she had for her patient.

Sienna held her breath until the door to the lift closed off the view of her neighbour. Her *very sexy* neighbour. It didn't make sense. Harry wore red one-size-fits-most overalls and he looked hot beyond belief. There again, she'd been out of the dating circuit for years so could be that a four-foot-nothing, overweight goat would look sexy in the right circumstances.

A hand was tugging at her sleeve. Drawing in air and shutting out Harry, she turned to her patient. 'Hey, Fliss, I hear you took seawater on board. That won't make your lungs happy.'

The face mask was snatched away and words spewed out. 'It's not fair. I worked so hard to go on the trip. It's the first time Mum's let me go away without her and now I'll be a prisoner in my own home again.'

'Put this back on.' As the lift jerked downward Sienna slipped the mask over Felicity's face.

It was promptly torn off. 'Why bother? I don't have a life anyway. Not one I like.' Tears were tracking down her sallow cheeks as she gasped in tight lungfuls of air. Short, sharp gasps that wouldn't give her anywhere near enough oxygen. 'What happens if I don't get home for Christmas, huh?'

To run with the physical problem, or the real issue behind this? Like other children with cystic fibrosis, Felicity had missed out on a lot over the years. 'Your mum only wants what's best for you.' Sienna drew a breath. Yvonne Little also had a son with the same condition and was raising the children on her own, her husband having thrown in the towel saying he couldn't cope. As if Yvonne cruised through everything. 'I know you want more than anything to be doing what your friends are, but we both understand that's not always possible.'

'Doesn't mean I have to like it.'

'No, it doesn't. As for Christmas, you'll be home well before then.' Fliss could also be back in here with yet another of the massive chest infections she was prone to, but Sienna wasn't bringing up that subject. The girl knew it as well as she did.

'My grandparents are coming in two weeks. I don't want to be in here then.'

This discussion could go round and round endlessly. Sienna gave her a smile. 'Let's get you cleaned up, and start monitoring your obs. If everything's all right, you should be able to go home tomorrow.' She'd been about to say 'go back to Great Barrier Island' but realised in the nick of time it wasn't her place, that Yvonne didn't need her adding to her problems.

'Whatever.' Felicity tugged the mask back over her face, closed her eyes and turned her shoulder towards Sienna.

Sienna made a mental note to talk to the children's clinical psychologist before leaving at the end of the day. Felicity needed help beyond her scope.

Early that afternoon Sienna hung seven-year-old Andrew Dixon's file on the hook at the end of his bed and turned to his parents. 'Andrew's responded well to his surgery. His bloods are back to normal, indicating there's no more infection.' The burst appendix had temporarily knocked the boy for six. 'As for his appetite, it's coming on in leaps and bounds.'

'When can we take him home?' asked his exhausted father.

Sienna smiled. 'Tomorrow morning after I've checked to make sure everything's still going how it should.' She loved giving out the good news.

Andrew's mother was on the verge of tears. 'Thank you so much for everything you've done. I hate to think what would've happened if we hadn't got him here in time.'

'Don't torture yourself with that. You did get him here, and soon he'll be creating mayhem at home and you'll be trying to shush him up.'

'Thank goodness for the rescue helicopter. The pilot's great and the doctor awesome. He was so calm even when it was so serious.'

Sienna's heart leapt. 'Who was your doctor?'

'Harry someone. I'm going to write to the head of the rescue base saying how good he was.'

'That's always a nice thing to do.' Harry won people over so easily, no doubt his charm and smile coming into play. He hadn't won her over. No, but she'd hadn't been able to stop thinking about him all week. Sienna studied these two in front of her. 'Andrew's going to sleep for a while. Why don't you take a break?' They'd sat at his bedside most of the past two days and nights. 'Go to a café and have a decent meal. Not a hospital one that's unrecognisable. I'll be here and the nurses will keep a close eye on your boy.'

'But what if he wakes and asks for us?'

'Your phone numbers are on file.' And the nurses were adept at calming upset children. 'Go on. Get out of here and have some couple time.'

'Couple time? What's that?'

Don't ask me.

'Remember you're about to return home to three boisterous kids,' Sienna said. She'd met Andrew's siblings yesterday, and the ward hadn't been quite the quiet haven it was supposed to be while they were here. 'Time to your-selves is what you both need.' Sienna all but shooed them out of the room.

Andrew's father nodded as he passed her. 'You're right. A short spell to ourselves will do wonders. We'll be at that café on the corner if anything changes.'

'It's not going to.' Sienna watched the couple walk away and for a moment wished there was someone special in her life to go have a meal and coffee with, to help her let go of all the hang-ups from a normal day on a children's ward. Someone like Harry? Definitely not. He was too sure of himself for her liking. So if she wasn't liking him, why this sensation of slipping on ice whenever she was near him? She'd seen first-hand how caring a doctor he was with Fliss, and that always scored points with her. He just wasn't such a caring neighbour. Was that a big deal? They might've got off on the wrong foot, and a simple con-versation could correct that. Did she want to fix it? She was single for a reason, wasn't prepared to risk the hurt of being dumped again. Her life was contained, probably too contained, but it was comfortable. Safe. Boring?

'Go home, Sienna. Take time out for yourself.' Dale ap-peared in front of her, refocusing her errant brain.

'It's just gone two. I've got hours to go. Anyway, I told Andrew's parents I'd be here while they take a much needed break.'

'I've got it covered.' The head of Paediatrics was study-ing her as if he'd never seen her before. 'You've put in ri-diculously long hours this week, as always.'

'That's how the job goes.'

'Most of us have a life outside these four walls that we actively try to participate in with family and friends, not spend our energy avoiding.'

But she didn't have family close by.

You do have friends in town.

Who were equally tied up with work as she was.

'Spread those wings, Si. Lighten up a bit.'

Yes, Dad.

'Take the whole weekend off. I've got your patients covered,' Dale remonstrated like a harassed parent. 'You're not doing yourself or anyone else any favours working all these ridiculous hours.'

I need to make sure I'm busy all the time.

But he was right. She had put in uncountable hours throughout the week, and even for her she was overtired. It was time to relax. And honestly, not to have to think about medications and results and children in pain sounded like bliss. It'd be a rare treat—if only she knew what to do with it. 'I'm out of here.'

Walking off the ward in the middle of the afternoon should've been exciting. Instead it was…worrying. Hours stretched ahead. Her father was right: she was far too ensconced in her life of all work and no play. But how to change? Where to start?

At home, standing on her narrow deck, Sienna couldn't come up with anything to do with this precious time out. It felt alien. The sun was still in the sky. The birds still tweeting. Had she really become so rigid in how she lived that she couldn't think outside the square?

Too serious, my girl. You need to relax sometimes.

Staring across her front lawn, Sienna noted the grass needed cutting. While the area was pocket-sized, the thought of hauling out the electric mower didn't excite her. Not that it ever did, but keeping the grass under control was one of those things she did to feel on top of her world. Pathetic.

Deliberately turning away, Sienna glanced across at the adjoining apartment. If Harry was at home she might be tempted to take a bottle of wine over and apologise for being such a grump last week. Her fingers tingled and she flexed them to relax the tension taking hold in her muscles. She did want more excitement outside of doctoring in her life, right? But with an attractive man who managed to get under her skin even when she was mad at him? Why not? Go for broke. Or go put her head under the pillow and not come out for a month. That should work.

Spinning around, she headed inside, away from that lawn, those shut windows, the car that needed a wash. In the lounge she automatically flicked a straight curtain straighter.

Stretch your wings.

Yeah, right. Like how? Picking up her phone, she checked for messages, pressed speed dial for her friend Anna. 'Hey, sorry I'm so late returning your call but it's been one of those days.'

Anna laughed. 'When isn't it with you?'

'Says the lawyer who never goes home before midnight. So what's up? Want to have a meal downtown tomorrow night?' Girlfriends united. Boring if fun. Why did she glance across to Harry's place? Nothing would ever happen between them.

'We can celebrate. As of this morning you legally own every last nail and tile in your swanky apartment.'

'I'd forgotten you were filing my petition today. So Bernie's finally paying up? After three years arguing? Unbelievable.' Sienna's heart stuttered. 'This is great news. I'll never have to think of him again.' The lying, cheating fiancé who'd decided he preferred to live with the woman he'd reconnected with at his school reunion than marry her when for years he'd sworn he loved her more than his high-end car and multi-million-dollar home.

'It's all wrapped up, plus there's a bonus. He's paying

your legal costs and money for half that rental property you bought jointly.'

'My shout for tomorrow night. Cortado's.' Their favourite place for major celebrations. Putting the phone down, Sienna again checked the time, but only minutes had passed. 'Now what?'

Go for routine.

In Titirangi over an hour later she pinged the locks on her car, swung a leg over her cycle and headed up the winding road leading to Piha Beach. Almost immediately the high humidity had her in a sweat. Good for the muscles, not so great for her breathing, but she kept pedalling hard. This would get whatever was eating her out of the system. She was not thinking about Harry, right? Not picturing that good-looking face or the smile that increased the speed with which her blood moved through her veins. Not at all.

A car swerved around her, the passenger jeering about her butt as it passed.

'Get a life, will you?' she snarled between breaths. Why couldn't people leave others to get on with what they enjoyed? What was so much fun about being rude to strangers?

Cycling was her time to relax, because she concentrated entirely on riding and often forgot what had got her on the bike in the first place. Except today it wasn't working.

What did Harry do for relaxation? Apart from hold noisy parties for upset colleagues, or stay out overnight maybe? Did she really care? Unfortunately she might. Though she shouldn't. He was on a temporary contract and would soon be gone again. It had taken months for her to trust Bernie enough to get close to him, not weeks, so she could forget all about getting to know this man. Hard to do, that. He just seemed to pop up in her mind whenever there was a free moment.

The front wheel wobbled in thick gravel. So much for concentrating on riding. Shoving the neighbour and the world out of her mind, she focused on getting to the top of the busy road without taking a break.

Harry had muscles in all the right places and made whatever he wore look superb. Of course she'd noticed. It would be rude not to. Some sights weren't made to be ignored. Bet he did some form of sport or worked out. Was she so desperate for changes in her life she was hallucinating about the neighbour? Except Harry wasn't a fantasy and her reactions to his physique were all too real. Oh, yes, real and solid and tempting. Damn it. Next stop, the library for a pile of books to keep her entertained until this feeling passed. Probably about when Harry left town.

Wheel-wobble. Again. Her cycling had taken a turn for the worse.

Deep breath, focus, right pedal down, left up. Left down, right up. That's it. Careful, sharp bend and steep decline. Squeeze the brake, change gear. Concentrate.

It worked. Until the road straightened and the incline lessened, giving her nothing to concentrate on so hard. Nothing except the man persisting in getting in her head space. What would he be like in bed? He exuded confidence in everything else that she'd seen so it followed that—

Toot-toot.

Sienna swerved abruptly, away from the centre of the road, and towards—over—the edge. Her front wheel dropped abruptly, alarmingly. Her body flipped forward, her hands gripping the now useless handlebars, her legs still pumping, even though she was in freefall; down, down, down. Bushes tore at her, twisted the cycle left then right, and on downward. The momentum compounded the speed. More bushes, bigger now, snagging at her, tear-ing across her face, her arms. Then she was upside down, slamming the ground with her shoulder, tossed sideways, with the cycle she still held on to with a fierceness she couldn't explain now twisted between her legs. Pain tore through her, then a thud.

Bounce. Bounce.

Slowing.

A tree blocked her path.

Thump.

Blackness engulfed her.

CHAPTER THREE

SIENNA BLINKED HER eyes open, gasped at the pain filling her body from every direction. 'What happened? Where am I?' There were dark clouds in her head, along with pulsing, banging symbols of pain. Dragging her eyelids up, she stared at the scene in front of her. Trees, bushes…

Darkness took over again.

'Hello?'

She was having a nightmare. Any second now she'd wake up and find herself on her bike heading down the hill towards the beach. Bike. Hill. Rolling over and over.

'Can you hear me?'

A groan escaped her constricted throat. She'd gone off the edge of the embankment, a sheer drop down to these bushes. The pain was really making itself known, as if her body had a grudge with her. In her legs and back, her arms, the left shoulder—sucking in a breath, she tried not to think about what that might mean. She needed to toughen up, check herself out instead of panicking. Work out what the damage was and make a plan for getting out of here.

Moving could be detrimental. Spinal damage is a real possibility.

'Are you all right down there?'

That persistent voice was annoying. 'Go away. I'm trying to think here.'

'I don't know if you can hear me but I've phoned for help.'

So the voice wasn't in her head. There really was someone up on the road. She wasn't alone. As she opened her mouth to holler a reply her lungs filled with air and her upper body moved. Pain splintered her and the blackness rolled in again.

Thwup, thwup, thwup.

The bushes flattened and the trees swayed. A helicopter filled the little view Sienna had of the sky when she next pulled her eyes open. A bright red-and-yellow rescue chopper. Gratitude swamped her. Whoever that man was who'd called for help, she owed him big time.

A figure attached to a thick rope was lowering in her direction. Help had arrived. In a pair of red overalls. She'd be out of here in no time. Then she'd be able to get patched up and back on her feet.

If my injuries aren't serious.

A shudder tripped through her, her tightening muscles sending warning signals of pain to her brain. It was tempting to move, to try to sit up, to prove she was all right. The doctor in her kicked in. *Stay still.* Let the rescue crew do their job. But waiting had become difficult. What if she'd broken her spine? She was a paediatrician. She didn't have time for learning to walk again, or never walking…

'Hello, this is becoming a habit.' A familiar, husky voice broke through her fear. 'Harrison Frost, your neighbour.'

Harrison. 'Not Harry, then.' Harrison was way sexier than Harry. Ah? Hello? Head injury talking? Sex while smashed up on the side of a hill? Why not? That'd certainly be creating a new norm for her. Don't forget, she told herself, that if she hadn't been thinking about him she wouldn't be lying here afraid to move.

'Good, you're cognitive. And yes, I go by Harry most of the time.' The guy was snapping open the hooks that held him to the rope and giving the thumbs-up to some-one above in the chopper, at the same time speaking into a radio. 'Take it away.'

What were the odds he'd be the one coming to her rescue? But then, nothing seemed to be going right for her lately, so those were as short as the two-year-old with pneumonia she'd treated this week. She could only hope Harry was more forth-coming in his attitude as a doctor than as a neighbour. 'You didn't bring the music.' Anything to keep from the pain get-ting stronger with every breath.

'I would've if I'd known it was you who'd taken to fly-ing off the side of roads.' Harrison shucked out of his back-pack. 'Right, let's check you out. You haven't moved since coming to a stop against the tree?' He began disentangling the cycle from her legs.

'Of course not.' Unless she'd moved while out cold. 'I need a neck brace first. My left shoulder is possibly broken. My right ankle is giving me grief, but as for internal inju-ries I'm certain I'm in the clear.' The pain throbbed up and down both legs. Bruising from the bike when she'd landed?

'Leave those decisions to me. Obviously nothing wrong with your head. You're stringing sentences together and enunciating clearly.'

'I am a doctor.' And it was his fault she'd ended up in this mess, tramping through her mind the way he had.

A small smile lifted one corner of his mouth. 'Right now I'm the doctor, you're the patient, and I get to make the diagnoses, starting with doing the ABCs.'

Her airway was fine, the proof in her relatively easy breathing when pain wasn't interfering. 'Might have known you'd be bossy.'

His smile hit her hard. 'It goes with the territory and stroppy patients.'

Putting as much indignation into her voice as she could muster, she growled, 'I'm stroppy?'

'Yep.' Harrison's eyes were focused on her chest, purely to check she was breathing normally.

A twinge of regret came and went. She didn't want him thinking of her as anything other than a patient. Not really. But it was nice to be noticed by a good-looking guy occasionally. 'Have you always worked on the helicopters?'

'No, I'm an emergency specialist so I've spent most of my time in emergency departments. Working on rescue choppers is different. It takes some getting used to not having a whole department filled with every bit of equipment I require.' He might be talking trivia but there was nothing trivial about the way he was checking her over.

She could get to like this man. If she didn't already.

'I can imagine.' He was right. She had to let go and trust him to look after her, but it was hard. She never gave control to anybody over even the most insignificant thing. And this wasn't insignificant. Thump, thump, went her head. Her mouth opened but she couldn't give him the go-ahead. She just couldn't.

As he carefully removed her helmet, Harry asked, 'Have you lost consciousness at any time?' Seemed he had no difficulty taking charge, regardless of what she thought.

As he's meant to.

'Twice. I think. Maybe three times.' And about to again if the clouds gathering in her skull were any indication. She'd been trying too hard to say what was needed without slurring or forgetting what she had to tell him and it was taking its toll.

'Pulse is rapid. I'd say you're in shock.' Firm yet gentle fingers touched her neck, her skull, her jawline. If only they could stop the pain.

She guessed she couldn't have everything.

Please let me be able to walk away from this.

Fog expanded in her head, pressing at her skull.

'Sienna, can you hear me?' Was that Harry? Harrison. 'Yes.' But there were drums in the background. The humming in her ears also added to the noise.

Firm fingers slid over her skull, pressing lightly, feeling for trauma. 'From the state of that helmet you hit something with your head. At least the helmet did what it was meant to. There doesn't appear to be any damage to your skull, though you probably have mild concussion.' Then he was listening to his radio, and confirmed what she heard loud and clear. 'The weather's closing in. The guys above say we have to hurry or we'll be stuck here until the storm passes.'

'What storm?' Come to think of it, she was feeling chilly. But that would be shock. Wouldn't it?

Come in, Dr Burch. You know your stuff.

'Am I cold or is the reaction to my crash setting in?'

'Both,' answered Harry, slipping a neck brace into position. 'This'll keep your head still.'

A male voice came through the radio in his shirt pocket. 'Sorry, have to back off now, Harry. Hang in there. I'll return as soon as viable.'

The tree she'd come to a halt against rustled and leaves dropped onto her. 'Don't let them go.' She had to get to hospital and sort out her injuries.

'Not a lot of choice,' Harry told her before easing her cycling shoes off. 'Can you feel me touching your toes?'

'Yes.' Relief swarmed through her.

'Wriggle them.' There was a reciprocating relief in his dark eyes. 'Good.'

Neck immobilised, tick. Feeling in feet, double tick. 'My shoulder?'

But Dr Harry was working his way up her legs, as in

how a doctor would, not a lover. As she'd said earlier, this just wasn't her day. 'Your ankle's okay. Lots of bruising would be about as bad as it gets.'

Those fingers… Sienna sighed. Gentle, and warm, and enticing. As if she could succumb to their hidden promise.

Where did that come from?

Had to be the bang on her head. Her brain had been derailed. Whatever, it was good to let these wonderful sensations take over. They relaxed her, made her forget a little of why she was here, and had her thinking one bottle of wine wouldn't be enough to take across to his apartment.

Dr Deep Voice continued. 'Unfortunately I didn't bring my X-ray machine to check your shoulder.'

Typical relax-the-patient talk. 'Funny…not.'

'For someone who's knocked herself out, bashed up her body and got into difficult terrain, you have a lot to say. But I can tell you the shoulder's not dislocated, and from the normal angle I'd hazard a guess it's not broken either.'

'I'll give that box a half-tick, then.'

Large, oh, so gentle hands prodded her stomach, moved up towards her ribcage. Deep concentration tightened his face.

'Ow!' She gasped as sharp pain struck. 'What—?'

'Take it easy.' He pressed her back against the ground with that firm hand she was beginning to recognise for its warmth and strength.

Sienna hadn't realised she'd moved. 'Tell me.'

But he'd turned away to talk into the radio that had crackled into life against his expansive chest. 'Yo… What's happening up there?'

'Weather bomb coming in fast. You're going to have to hang in on your own for a period yet. We'll be back ASAP.'

She mightn't know the voice but she sure knew that warning. ASAP meant 'in a while, even a long while'.

'Isn't there another way out of here?' There was a road just above them.

Harry was shaking his head. 'Afraid not. You picked about the worst spot on this road to fall off. The slope is all but vertical. Hauling you up it is not an option. We're going to have to wait it out. The thermal blanket will protect you from the wind and keep you warm.'

The wind had picked up, and now rain slashed at them, driving in sideways. Sienna shivered. Every part of her body hurt, some worse than others. She wanted to cry from it all but instead drew a deep breath and held on—just. Things kept going from bad to worse, and she only had herself to blame. 'But if there aren't any broken bones or internal injuries I can give getting to the top a crack. Better than lying here.'

'You banged your head, remember?' He was removing nasal prongs from a container. 'Do you remember what happened?'

'I—' lost focus and rode into the middle of the road then executed an abrupt dodging movement when a car came up behind her '—made a mistake.'

Thinking about my job. About you.

Really? She'd been thinking about Harry while riding? Yes. She had. Which went to show how easily she could be distracted. 'Are you giving me oxygen?' Of course he was.

'Your breathing's a little rapid. Best we get that settled.'

'Got an electric blanket in that pack?' Shivers were taking over.

'Sure have.' He locked that dark gaze on her. 'Relax. We'll get you out of here, and in the meantime I've got you. Don't worry about a thing.'

Had she been that transparent? Worry about her injuries despite his optimistic assessment was building like a volcano about to erupt. This could've been a disaster, might've been the end of everything, and she was afraid of tempting fate by accepting she hadn't been seriously injured before the hospital gave her the all-clear. With effort she hunted for something to talk about that might keep those concerns a little quieter. 'You're Australian.'

'Well spotted.'

'Where from?' Hard to concentrate when her mind was trying to shut down, but the longer she stayed awake the more she might learn about this man. Because despite— or was it because of?—being stuck on the side of a hill going nowhere in a hurry, she wanted to learn more about him, to make up for the weeks they'd been neighbours and strangers.

'Melbourne.' He wasn't making it easy.

'City or beyond?'

'City. The swanky part of town. Boys' college, box seats at the MCG, and all the rest of it.' A lime would be sweeter than that tone.

'Why Auckland now?'

Answer fast before I fall asleep.

'It's where the next job came up.'

That woke her a little. 'You move around a lot?'

Like my dad does?

'Depends on what turns up.'

If she could move she'd shake him, but then she'd already known how irritating he could be. Worse, he was sounding more like her father with everything he said. 'You ever just talk for the sake of it?'

To keep your patient distracted from her situation?

'I have been known to.'

She gave up. That darkness was pressing in, relieving her of any control. *Don't think about that.* Sienna groaned and slurred out a question that was totally irrelevant to anything. 'What time is it?'

* * *

'Five thirty.'

Harry continued tucking the thermal blanket around Sienna, all the while keeping an eye on her. It wasn't hard. Even injured and stranded out in the middle of a storm she was beautiful, and stirred his blood relentlessly. Once they got out of this mess he was going to have to do something about Dr Frosty, who wasn't as frosty as he'd first presumed.

She used it to cover real emotions. Emotions he'd noticed flitting across those stunning blue eyes during the time they'd been together on the hill. He'd seen how her decline into sleep had briefly halted when he'd answered her question about moving around a lot in the affirmative. Had someone important kept moving away from her when she needed them? A partner; husband; lover? He could keep guessing or get on with being the emergency doctor he revelled in being. 'Have you got an underlying condition I should know about?' he asked without any hope of getting an answer. The shock had caught up and she was that far gone now.

But, 'N-no-o.' Sleep slurred her speech.

He could relax on that one. 'Good. You're safe at the moment. Our pilot's one of the best and he'll return the first instant he can. We'll get you out of here in one piece, Sienna.' But only when it was safe to do so. Another helicopter crash was not on the cards.

'Safe?'

He nodded. As if she saw that. 'Very safe.'

Her eyes opened, surprise momentarily replacing the other emotions swimming there. 'Am I really—?' She swallowed, tried again in that slurred whisper. 'In one piece? You weren't feeding me the happy-clappy line to keep me calm until we're away from here?'

'I wouldn't insult you. Nor would I feed you expectations that could be stomped on once you're in hospital. You have mostly bruises,' he repeated his earlier diagnosis to shore up her failing confidence. 'Lots of them. I still don't think there's anything to worry about regarding your shoulder except severe bruising. Possibly some rib damage, but I'd say you've come off lightly.' When her eyes widened with hope, he rushed in. 'Not lightly enough that I'm about to haul you up the bank with a rope around your waist. We're still at the bottom of a precipice with a summer storm rampaging around our ears.' Was that hail? It wouldn't surprise him, given the ferocity of the wind and rain pounding them. Thunder backed him up; no lightning flashes but then the clouds delivering the icy pellets were hiding that. Auckland was known for its short, sharp seasonal storms. In this case, not what the doctor ordered, but then when did anything ever go completely right on a job? It was the nature of the urgent scenarios to throw spanners in the works. Big ones mostly. And often through weather.

Digging into the pack, his fingers closed around a concertinaed umbrella which he pulled out and opened to hold above his patient, shielding her from the worst, angling it so a gust of wind didn't turn it inside out. It would be best if Sienna slipped into unconsciousness again so she didn't feel discomfort and had no idea of the time ticking by as they waited for the chopper to return. He could only hope it was today. The weather reports had forecast more storms over the next twelve hours at least.

Beside him Sienna moved. Trying to roll over? Harry placed his free hand on her good shoulder. 'Easy. Don't move.' Their ledge wasn't as wide as he'd like. Sienna had been extremely lucky that that tree had halted her tumble.

'Mmm…umm…'

So she *was* out of it, unaware of where she was, and more importantly getting a break from the pain. Good. He tied the umbrella to the base of the tree so it sheltered her face before taking running checks again. Concussion seemed to be her most worrisome injury, and he could handle that. Relief that she hadn't fractured any major bones or suffered serious internal injuries spread through him, though from her reaction when he'd touched her ribcage it was possible she'd cracked one or two ribs, or torn cartilage from the bones. But she'd be able to lift a glass of wine when he took that bottle next door. Because he was going to. Without a doubt. It might be tempting a snub, but he'd risk it. Thanks to this accident they were inextricably linked, and he'd use that to his advantage. He wanted time with her that much. And after today she couldn't deny he existed.

On his haunches, hunched under the edge of the umbrella, Harrison studied the captivating face he'd first admired a week ago. Shock and pain had dimmed her raw beauty, but there was no denying the fine features and that classic facial structure sucking him in. 'So we're both doctors.' Was that attraction stirring his groin? No. Too weird, that idea. This was purely because Doc Not-So-Frosty had a figure that demanded attention from all working parts of a man's body, and a face to take the edge off anything she might say.

Again Sienna moved. Again he held her still. 'Shh, easy does it.' He kept his voice low and soft, sleep her best option for now. When she didn't relax he sat next to her, stretching his legs the length of her body so they were touching side by side, and began soothing her hand, making light circles with his fingers. Slowly, slowly, the tension fell away from her muscles and she stopped moving her hands and feet. Had she been unconsciously checking again to see that she hadn't damaged her spine? It had been her biggest fear when he'd arrived, and who could blame her? Cycling accidents were notorious for shoulder injuries, but spinal damage was up there too.

His radio barked into life. 'Harry, are you receiving? This is Ginger.'

Their pilot. 'Harry receiving loud and not so clear. What's up?'

'You're stuck there for a while yet, I'd say. What's the situation with your patient?'

'GCS four.' Not bad considering how rapid her descent must've been, and the bone-jarring—if not breaking—halt against the tree. But the score could change rapidly, dropping to a dangerous level if Sienna got too cold or there was internal bleeding going on he hadn't discovered. But all indicators said she was lucky there. He turned his back on her, just in case she wasn't as out of it as he believed. 'Don't let that fool you. I want her out of here ASAP. Her temperature has taken a dive since the hail came across.'

'Roger. Understood. I'm talking to the weather gods every few minutes but so far they're ignoring me.'

'Keep at it.'

'I'll get back to you in thirty unless the all-clear comes through. Hang in there and keep her safe, man.'

As if he'd do anything else. Keeping safe came first, especially for his patients. Not so much for himself. He'd always been a bit of a risk-taker, snowboarding off mountain ranges and deep-water diving in shark-infested waters; though with that one there'd been a team of experts at his back. Not that his parents would've noticed if things went pear-shaped. His brothers understood his apparent recklessness, though they didn't condone it, but to their credit they left him to his own decisions, something he appreciated almost more than anything. They weren't meant to feel guilty for him copping all the blame their mother had dished out for disasters big and small when they were young—and not so young. He was the cause of her disappointment with how life had served her, so his brothers had been spared the vitriol. Because they'd been wanted, planned for. Unlike him.

Harry swallowed the familiar bile. These days, since his mother had taken over control of the multinational company his grandfather had created, the family was more divided than ever. He and his brothers were together in their need to get on and make lives for themselves, while their parents fought endless battles between themselves over who was in charge of the company. His siblings had found love with wonderful women and dived right into their own families, putting distance between themselves and the parents who might've wanted them but didn't show much affection towards them. Finding a woman to love and have a family with was not something Harry planned on doing. His one and only serious relationship years ago had turned out to be as nasty as his parents' one, and confirmed his belief he did not want that for the rest of his days. Just as he didn't want to be told to try harder, become greater, aim higher. If someone couldn't love him for who he was then he wouldn't bother. He'd learned to be happy with his single status; he just wasn't always so careful with himself.

He reached for Sienna's wrist. What was her pulse now? Her wrist was slight and her skin satiny. If anyone around here had a high pulse rate it was him.

'So you're a doctor, and a cyclist. What else interests you?' he asked into the wind-tossed space in an attempt to distract himself from the heat tripping up his arm from where his fingers still touched her skin. Lowering her arm, he pulled back. 'I know loud music isn't one of your favourites, Doc Frosty.'

He barked a harsh laugh. Doc Frosty and Dr Frost stuck together on a hillside.

Ever since the night she'd stormed up his drive he'd been aware of her. Or rather, of how often she wasn't at home. It made sense now he knew her profession. Putting in long hours came with the territory. Which was one reason he loved his work. There was no time for anything else other than light, short relationships with women and easy-going friendships.

Those odd moments of longing for something he couldn't explain that came in the middle of a night shift when there was nothing happening but waiting in the tedious dark for a call that he always hoped wouldn't end badly for the victims were to be ignored. The unsettling need for something, someone, had to be banished. He was his own person and, once free of his mother's blame game and his wife's endless demands to be someone he wasn't, he'd vowed he'd never let someone else dictate how he lived, or where, or why.

His brothers lived the lives of their choice, and encouraged him to do the same, though they weren't always keen when he leapt off mountains with nothing more than a board strapped to his feet for safety. They and their families were his support system, the people he loved most. There wasn't room for anyone else. He'd tried once. Never again.

His eyes tracked across Sienna's exhausted face. Yes, she cranked up his libido something wicked. No, she wasn't going to become important to him other than as a patient at this point in time. Yes, he wanted to learn more about what made her tick. No, he didn't have any intention of spending time with her.

No longer than it took to share a bottle of wine, at any rate.

CHAPTER FOUR

'HOW LONG HAVE we been waiting for your lot to return?' Sienna stared through the semi-dark at Harry. His rugged face was in shadow while the lantern he must've had in his pack gave an eerie glow to their surroundings. He was so close it wouldn't take any effort to touch him. What would his skin feel like under her fingertips? Warm? Exciting?

Then he blinked and sat up straighter before reaching for her wrist, his finger instantly on her pulse. 'A little over an hour. Not long, considering.'

Definitely warm…and exciting. 'Hmmm…'

'What does "hmmm" mean?'

That she liked the spiky sensations going on up her arm from where he held her. 'Thank goodness you got here before the weather packed in or who knows what shape I'd be in by now? First thing I'm going to do once back on my feet is buy a lottery ticket. Who knows? My luck might still be running.'

His gaze cruised over her in a not-so-doctorish manner when she said 'shape'. A manner she could get to enjoy very quickly. His chuckle was delicious: more warmth, as well as comforting, and as if he was *with* her. 'I'll drive you to the shop when we're off the hill and the ED guys have tidied you up.'

Sienna shifted her numb butt and got stabbed with aches

throughout her body for her effort. Her head pounded but thankfully her vision was clear. All the better to observe this annoyingly interesting man. Sticking her tongue firmly in her cheek, she asked, 'You hanging around Auckland for a day or two more, then?'

'Up until Christmas.'

'Then where are you going?'

'I'm starting to doubt you've got concussion. Your recall is superb. Remind me never to tell you anything important.'

A smile accompanied his words so she remained relaxed. 'As we hardly ever speak that's not likely to happen.'

Harrison grunted. 'Here's the thing. We seem to keep getting thrown together so I'm figuring we might as well get to know each other a little. Only as neighbours,' he added quickly.

'Sounds like a plan as soon as I'm mobile again.' Fingers crossed that'd be tomorrow, not months down the track due to serious damage.

'We can share a bottle of wine on the deck.'

So he was okay with the wine idea. She must've talked in her sleep. They couldn't have been having similar thoughts about getting together for a drink. Could they? How soon could he visit?

Downplay this.

She hadn't said anything in her sleep about how he made her blood sing, had she? Better concentrate on staying wide awake from now on.

He went quiet, and the haze in Sienna's head began to rule despite her worry about what she might say next. But the fog didn't take over as it had earlier. Had she run out of puff? Or was it that she was awake enough that images of her neighbour were rolling in? Leading her into temptation?

As if. Stuck out here was so not the place for anything other than waiting to be lifted off.

Harrison sat beside her, his long legs stretched out, his hands relaxed on his thighs. Hard to ignore. He was more than attractive. There was something dependable about him that activated all her buttons when she stopped thinking how exasperating he could be. The pounding started up again in her skull. Not Harrison's fault. Not even thoughts about him were to blame. She was falling asleep.

Falling. Over and over.

Sienna awoke with a jerk, and groaned.

'Hey, easy.' That hand she was getting inordinately fond of touched her good shoulder.

Something niggled from her dream. 'What if no one had seen me go off the edge of the road?'

'Let's not go there. You were seen and here I am.'

She could have broken her back, been left for days till someone found her, or worse.

'You need to relax, my girl. Spread your wings and fly.'

Sienna's eyes flew open. Her father was right. She had been missing out on so much. What if she had broken her back? That would finish everything. This had been a wake-up call she needed to heed. 'Bring that wine over the first time we're both at home.' Then she'd return the favour a few days later. If they got on well enough to repeat the date. Date? Not likely. Calling that a date only underlined how sad her life had become. Whether or not they had anything else to do with each other afterwards, spending an hour with Harrison meant she'd be making a start on getting out there to do things she'd only ever thought about. How was this for another? 'I'm going to sign up for flying lessons.' Plummeting down a hillside had a lot to answer for. But if that had gone horribly wrong there wouldn't be any crazy ideas to put into action.

'You want to become a private pilot?' Bafflement dark-ened Harry's voice. Then he reached for her wrist again. Did he think she was slipping into gaga land because of that knock on her head? He could be right, but she didn't think so.

That tingling thing on her skin was going on under his fingers. 'My father keeps telling me to spread my wings and try different things. I'm interpreting him literally.' Then she shuddered. 'Only problem is I'm a bit afraid of heights.' Though flying on a commercial flight had never caused any problems. 'So this could be a bit of a challenge.'

Respect blinked out at her. 'You need to do a bungee-jump from the Sky Tower. That'll cure you.' He laid her arm down against her side. 'All normal.'

'Glad you weren't taking my pulse when you made that crazy suggestion.' To be honest, she was surprised it had been normal when all the nerve endings in her wrist had been on high alert to his touch. 'You ever done a jump?'

'I get my thrills regularly dropping out of helicopters, so no need.'

'That's feet first on a winch, not upside down on a rope.' Could she do it? Yes, she could. If she didn't she'd crawl back into her safe box, probably never to come out again. She'd survived today's crash; the momentum needed to be carried on. 'Do it with me,' she challenged before she could put her brain into gear.

His eyes widened and those full lips tipped into a tummy-twisting smile. 'You're on.' He held his hand up, palm out towards her. 'It's a deal.'

Did he have to look so shocked at what he'd agreed to? There was no getting out of this one. She wasn't sure whether to be pleased, or downright terrified. Only time would tell. Raising her arm and biting down on the stabs of pain from wrist to shoulder, she lightly hand-tapped him back, and tried not to think about that large hand making hers look tiny and feel…? Just feel. It had been too long since the last foray into men and sex, and not once had she known this sense of the ground slipping out from under her. More likely that came from her precarious position perched on a steep hillside. 'You didn't agree just to keep your patient happy?' She'd be gutted if he said yes.

'I never promise what I don't intend seeing through.' Harry's radio crackled into life. 'Yo, how's things looking?'

'We're coming in to get you. Ten minutes out,' was the reply.

Sienna sighed. Back to reality, and a challenge she'd initiated. Seemed if she was going out with a bang it was with someone sexy and good-looking and intriguing. And if she felt things were getting out of control too fast, Harry would be leaving in the not too distant future, so she wouldn't have time to make a dreadful mistake about getting too close to him. It took months for that to happen with her. Not weeks. Or days.

'You hear that?' Harry asked, already packing the kit.

'We're going home.' On some days hospital was as much home to her as her apartment, probably more. The only difference tonight being that she'd get to use a bed. Hopefully briefly.

'You'll be lifted up first. Do exactly what Connor says and you'll be fine.'

'That come with a guarantee?' Now was the time to find out how scared of heights she was. For one, she'd be totally reliant on other people, and she didn't do that very well. Hello? Bungee-jumping would be the same. She *was* going to be all right.

'Written? Or will you take my word for it?' Harry asked as he attached the harness that'd take her away.

'Get me out of here,' she smiled. At least she tried, but it was feeble. Now that the hill was about to be left behind she should be letting go of some of the restraints keeping her tense, but it didn't come naturally. She hadn't been in real danger of falling further, but she'd had no control over what happened to her. Still didn't, but she was headed to an environment she understood more than just about anything else. Time to find out every last detail about her injuries.

Then she was spinning in slow circles as the ground dropped away. A gasp escaped. That tree that mashed her helmet had saved her life. Beyond the pine was—nothing. A large, open space that didn't stop for metres, and then at a rocky outcrop. A shudder tore through her, another gasp drew air into her already full lungs. Definitely learning to fly. Or getting a pet cow or...

'Hello, Sienna. I'm Connor.' Already he was swinging her inside the helicopter. The clips keeping her harness and the rope joined were undone and dropped downward again, and she was lying on a stretcher, with tiredness seeping into every muscle, in her head, her mind.

Harry had barely clambered inside when Sienna felt the sway of the chopper as the pilot took them away from the hill.

'Last stretch.' Harry gave her a heart-warming smile. 'Soon you'll be back in control.'

He got that? This man was too good to be true. Or too risky. She didn't want anyone being able to read her so easily, or so accurately.

Harry leaned closer. 'I didn't ask. How did you get out to Titirangi to go cycling?'

See? She really wasn't up to speed. 'I drove out. Did we bring the bag from my bike with us?'

Relief nudged her when Harry nodded. 'We did.'

'Thank you.' She owed him. 'Maybe I should be the one bringing the wine.'

'Your keys in this?' He held up the small bag that had been around her waist when she'd gone flying over the edge.

Her turn to nod. 'And phone.'

'I'll sort something to retrieve your vehicle tomorrow.'

'You don't have to do that.'

'You're right, I don't. But I will.'

She had no energy to argue. Nor any better ideas. She could ask Anna, but she'd said something about finalising a case for Monday. 'If you take me I can drive it home. What about my bike? Is it worth trying to get that back?' It had cost a small fortune.

'And risk falling down the hill again? I don't think so. Best talk to your insurance broker.'

There was that. The pitch of the rotors changed. 'We're at the hospital already?'

'Yes. Let's get you inside to the warmth.' Harrison began preparing to disembark her. 'By the way, you won't be driving your vehicle tomorrow. If nothing else you'll be stiff and horribly sore.'

'That's for me to decide.' But he was right. Driving was out for a day or so.

'We'll talk about it later.'

She wouldn't be seeing him later, not even in ten minutes' time. Thank goodness. He had a habit of pushing her too far when he wasn't happy with what she said. Once she'd been offloaded he'd be back in the air, heading to base and signing off his shift, which actually finished at least an hour ago by her estimate, and she could arrange things re the SUV to suit herself.

An annoying grin came her way. 'Lost for words? I don't believe it.'

'Get me out of here.'

Within minutes she was being wheeled into the emergency department by one of the nurses and—Harrison. Seriously? The guy had a cheek. He'd told the crew to head back to base without him, that he'd sign off on line. He was chatting non-stop to the nurse, of the female variety, and reporting Sienna's obs and injuries, or lack thereof.

She'd be lucky to get any proper attention. The nurse was all but panting as she listened to every word he uttered.

Remind me not to let my mouth hang open next time I'm thinking Harrison is hot. It's so unbecoming. Not to mention embarrassing.

'That's it,' Harry wrapped up and handed the star-struck woman the notes he'd filled out throughout their time on the hill. 'Who's on tonight?'

'Amy Roberts and Josh Barrett, and there are two house surgeons. One of those two will attend Dr Burch.'

'I'll see about that,' retorted Harry as he took over pushing her bed into a cubicle.

A thrill of amusement made Sienna's eyes widen.

Don't open your mouth.

She wasn't the only one Harry annoyed just by being himself. This man who alternated between irritating and distracting was going to get her the best care available. Or he was going to try. She couldn't remember the last time anyone had looked out for her in this way. Her father had used to when she was a child, and Mum, even Bernie had in the beginning, but since the demise of her engagement there'd been no one covering her back. Probably her own fault, since she'd been so intent in standing tall and in control, to save getting walked all over once more. This felt…?

Good. Lovely.

Oh, give over.

It was exciting. Until she wriggled her legs to get comfortable and the throbbing that had been going on in her calves upped the tempo and the pain, reminding her there were more important issues at stake right now.

A large hand landed lightly on her arm. 'Take it easy. You're not ready to go dancing yet.'

'I wish.'

Don't take your hand away. It turns me to jelly, sure, but suddenly I'm not minding.

And the look of disappointment on the nurse's face was priceless. For once Sienna liked the sensation of coming first with a man, even if only for few minutes. By the time the doctors had poked and prodded her she'd be wishing to be alone with her aching body, and hopefully going to sleep. By then Harrison would be kilometres away, probably getting ready for a night on the town.

'You like dancing?'

She couldn't remember the last time she'd let loose on a dance floor. Looking up at him, she admitted, 'I used to.' She'd been nimble on the floor, had an ingrained sense of timing, and always lost herself in the music. Put dancing on the list. Suddenly the reason she was in the emergency department on a bed struck her, and she turned her face sideways into the pillow. Her spine was in working order, there didn't seem to be any serious internal pain anywhere, just around her ribs, her skull wasn't mushed, but what if they were wrong? What if—?

'Stop it.'

Her eyes blinked open.

'You're not doing yourself any favours concocting all sorts of scenarios where you can no longer cycle, work, or dance.'

'Damned know-it-all, aren't you?' Sienna snapped, but some of the knots growing in her belly backed off. Some of them.

* * *

Harry strolled into the general ward of Auckland Central Hospital at ten the next morning. Why he was going to visit Sienna was beyond comprehension. So much for thinking he knew himself well. Getting the keys to her SUV which he'd forgotten last night wasn't the main reason for being here, more of an excuse to see her. 'Morning, Sienna.' Damn, but there was little colour in those soft cheeks, and the sparkle hadn't returned to her eyes, the vivid blue now an overcast sky shade. He would not acknowledge the tightening in his chest, nor the urge to pick her up and hold her close until she smiled properly.

'Harrison. What are you doing here?' Flat-mouthed didn't suit her, even if he was more used to seeing that than the smile which tightened him in places best not remembered at the moment.

'Come to take you dancing.' One corner of that wide mouth lifted enough to know he'd hit the mark. 'Or we could book that jump off the Sky Tower for after lunch.'

'I won't be eating for hours before I go leaping off any building,' came her retort. And yes, a half-smile now.

Unbelievable how good that made him feel. How scared, too. 'So you've had a gourmet breakfast care of the hospital kitchen?'

'Something unrecognisable.'

'Any doctors been to see you this morning?' Highly unlikely, it being Saturday, but then everyone had fallen over backwards to attend to her last night. Seemed she was a very popular paediatrician. No serious injuries had turned up but Amy Roberts still insisted Sienna stay in overnight so they could keep an eye on her mild concussion.

'Amy just left. I'm allowed to go home whenever I'm ready.'

Phew. No ongoing problems from that knock on the

head, then. 'I came to collect the keys to your vehicle, so I can give you a lift before Connor and I go collect it if you like.' It hadn't taken any persuasion to get his offsider to go with him. Someone else who thought Sienna was the bee's knees.

'You've got this all under control, haven't you?' The smile had disappeared.

What'd he done wrong now? 'I'm only helping you out.'

Sienna glanced up at him. 'I know. Thank you.' A sigh rippled across her lips, and tightened his gut. 'I'm not used to people stepping up for me.' Shock registered on her face, as though she'd admitted something huge.

'It's no big deal.' He didn't want her thinking he might keep popping over the fence to do things for her. 'How were you planning on getting home?' So much for not putting his hand up to help further.

'I phoned my friend and left a message, but she'll be at the market, then going for a run, so who knows when I'll hear from her?' Again Sienna glanced up at him. 'I guess that's a yes, please. Thank you, I'd like a ride home. If it's still on offer.'

'Unless you want to stay in your hospital gown, you're going to have to squeeze back into those tight leggings.' Could hurt a bit, what with all the bruises she'd collected. By the time they'd got her to the ED she'd been black and blue from head to toe.

Her chin shot forward and he'd swear her teeth were clenched tight. 'No problem.'

'Then let's get this done.'

'You can wait outside.' More jaw-tightening going on.

'You're going to need help.' And he was a doctor. He'd seen it all before. Yes, but he hadn't seen Sienna, and he'd spent a lot of time fantasising about her in the early hours of that morning.

'Not from you, thanks all the same.' She swung her legs over the side of the bed, grimacing as those bruised muscles did their job. 'You can go find me a nurse.'

His hand lifted of its own accord, took her elbow. 'Let's make this as easy as possible.'

'Sienna, what have you done to yourself? I couldn't believe it when I saw your text. Why didn't you call me last night?' A tornado in the form of a tiny woman dressed in sports shoes, shorts and top spun into the room. 'Are you all right?'

Harry immediately stepped between the newcomer and Sienna to prevent those widespread arms slamming around her. 'Careful.'

'Anna, I'm fine.'

The woman skidded to a stop, her hands dropping to her hips. 'You look anything but fine. A cycling accident? What happened? Did an irresponsible driver cause this? Want me to talk to the police for you?'

A genuine, full-blown smile appeared on Sienna's face, lighting up her eyes, softening her cheeks.

Harry's stomach dropped to his toes. *I want one of those.* No, he didn't. Or shouldn't. They were dangerous. He'd be pulled under, have to fight his way back to the surface. Might never make it.

Sienna was talking. 'Take your law hat off, Anna. The accident was all my fault.' So why did she look sideways to him for a moment? 'I phoned to ask you to give me a lift home.'

'Seriously, Si, are you okay? No broken bones or anything?'

'I was very lucky.' Again she glanced at him.

Her visitor's head shot up and he was being stared at. 'I'm Anna McIntosh. Of McIntosh, McIntosh and Brown.'

She underscored her name. 'Who are you?' Like, don't fool with her friend or there'd be trouble.

'Anna, this is Harrison Frost, the doctor who came with the rescue helicopter.'

He presumed that was a law firm Anna had mentioned, one that everyone should recognise, and, being new to town, he didn't. He put his hand out. 'Pleased to meet you, Anna. While I work for the Rescue Service, I'm also temporarily Sienna's neighbour,' he added for a bit of mischief, not wanting to be fobbed off as the medic and nothing else. But what else was he? Apart from a man who got tight in the groin every time he saw Sienna? And the guy who'd suggested taking a bottle of wine over to her place?

Anna's handshake was firm for someone so slight, her scrutiny of him just as telling. 'Just when did you get Sienna to hospital?'

If he could have avoided answering he would have, because this woman was putting two and two together and he didn't like the accurate answer. But Sienna was as capable of answering as him, so he told the truth. 'Seven forty-five last night.' Now the questions would really start. Like why was he here this morning, did he have a wife and kids somewhere, was his job permanent? He knew them all and this woman most certainly had Sienna's back, which had to be good. Unfortunately for him, he didn't have a résumé covering his dating habits and status in his back pocket, because he too had Sienna's back—he just mightn't be as comfortable with that as her friend was.

'Enough, Anna,' warned Sienna.

'To put your mind at ease, Sienna fell about sixty feet through scrub and came to a halt against a tree which saved her life. And because she wore a helmet she got mild concussion, no major brain trauma.' Harry paused. In his haste to stop those questions he was speaking out of turn by mentioning Sienna's injuries, but a quick look to Sienna showed she had no issue with that. In fact she gave him a nod, so he continued. 'Apart from the concussion she has major bruising and the ligaments on one side of her ribcage are torn. That's very painful and only taking it easy will help.'

Anna reached over and gave her friend a gentle hug. 'I'm so glad you didn't do any permanent damage, Si. You don't need any more trouble.'

He knew it. He'd seen worry in her eyes last night as she evaluated the injuries she might have got. But he'd also felt there was lots more going on behind that frosty look she did so well and which no longer cooled him at all. The need to protect her rose higher, surprising in its intensity. He looked out for family and patients. Sienna didn't fit either category, no longer being a patient and never going to be anything remotely like family.

'Tell me about it.' Sienna looked around the room and back to her friend. 'My next consideration is, do I replace the bike or do I stop riding and play safe?'

'Thought we'd decided over dinner the other night you'd done with playing safe,' Anna answered.

So Sienna was a cautious woman. With her choice of sports, or was her heart overprotected as well? And why was he even wondering?

Sienna stared at Anna, confusion darkening her gaze briefly. 'No, you came up with that idea. I never agreed. Not totally.' Then she grinned. 'But you never take any notice of anything I say, so no surprise there. Since you're here, can you help me get dressed and then drop me off at home?'

A thoughtful look came over Anna's face and Harry found himself under a kind of scrutiny that had the power of a high-calibre X-ray. 'I'll help you get dressed, but I can't take you home, sorry. I've got something to do in the city and,' she waved a wrist encircled with a top-of-the-range watch, 'I'm going to be late. Since Harrison's your neighbour, he can give you a lift.'

'What have you got to do?' Sienna demanded in her annoyed voice.

So he wasn't the only recipient of that tone. Harry would've laughed if he wasn't getting edgy over Anna leaving her friend with him. Sure, he'd said he'd drive her home, but it was the scheming gleam in the lawyer's eyes that rattled him.

'See a dog about a bone,' Anna answered with a little smile.

'You don't have a dog,' Sienna snapped as it dawned on her she was being set up.

'Nor a bone,' the other woman laughed. 'Now, where are your clothes? Harry, can you leave us for a few minutes, please?'

He found himself out in the corridor without realising he'd moved. That was one powerful lady. Anyone on the other side of the bench when she was prosecuting stood little chance. Behind the closed door Sienna's voice had risen, only to be overridden by her friend's calmer one. Whatever Sienna wanted—he suspected a ride home with her friend and not him—it wasn't happening.

Harry's stomach sucked in, and his hands tightened. He had offered Sienna a lift, and meant it with every fibre in his body. To be told he had to do it rankled. But not as much as Sienna trying to avoid him. Now was when he should be running down to his four-wheel-drive and heading out of the city for the day.

Someone needs to keep an eye on Sienna for today at least. She's been discharged but even mild concussion can be uncomfortable for some time to come.

Sometimes being a doctor came with obligations. It was not possible to turn his back on anyone in need.

Sienna is not an obligation.

Then what the hell was she, apart from an annoying neighbour, a good patient, and an attractive woman who had him asking too many questions of himself about her? Was the petrol tank of his vehicle full? He could go to Taupo for the day. Stay the whole weekend even. He wasn't back on duty until Monday.

'I'm ready.' A soft but firm hand touched his arm.

Stepping back from that light but intoxicating touch, he growled, 'Let's go.'

'Anna means well.' Sienna was wobbling on her feet.

Putting his hand over hers to keep her there, and balanced, Harry said under his breath, 'Sounds like you believe that,' then louder, 'I'm sure she does.'

'We've been friends since university when she fell in love with one of the students in my class. Our friendship has lasted while her marriage didn't.'

Why was Sienna telling him this? It wasn't anything he needed to know. Unless she thought he was interested in Anna. 'Sorry to hear that.'

Have you ever been married? Got a brood of kids somewhere?

There hadn't been any sign of ankle-biters around her place, but she could be the career woman while the father took care of them—alone. 'You weren't attracted to anyone in her class?'

'No.' Tension rippled off her.

Best leave that line of conversation alone. 'Are you Auckland born and bred?'

'No.'

'Where are you from, then?' He'd go with ignoring the tension, try to lighten the mood that had overtaken her.

'New Zealand.'

Give me a break here.

'Right.' The lift doors slid open and he stood back to let Sienna in first.

'I was born in Whangarei, had my second birthday in Invercargill, my third in Christchurch, fifth in Pukekohe, ninth in Waihi. Went to high school in Napier, so that covered five more birthdays. University in Auckland.' There was no bitterness or joy in that statement. 'We lived in a house bus.'

She'd been on the move most of her childhood. What about other friends? A shudder rocked him.

There wouldn't have been any when she was young.

Nor things like sports teams to join and stay with year after year. 'You've stayed in Auckland ever since?'

'Oh, yes.' Sienna was staring at the floor, seeing something he could only guess at. 'Returning to the same place, the same things, every day, is important to me. Don't get me wrong. Being on the road all those years was fun, and I have some wonderful memories, but I prefer the sense of belonging that I get from my own home.'

Even he with his diabolical mother couldn't imagine not having some place to call home growing up. Not that he had his own home as an adult, but that was his choice and one he could change any time he chose. 'Your parents stopped moving around for you to go to high school?'

'I demanded they did—said I'd run away otherwise.' She suddenly looked very small. 'Mum had home-schooled me up till then, but she couldn't teach me algebra and physics and all the subjects required if I was going to become a doctor.'

Obviously it'd hurt her to make that demand. Determination must've been her middle name, though, if she'd stood up to her parents so adamantly.

Go, you, Sienna.

Now he understood her question to him about being a wanderer. Not that it mattered. His lifestyle suited him because he didn't want to settle down, be held in one place to make someone else happy. Sienna was safe from him. Now he understood he wasn't in danger of falling for her wiles because no woman was going to put her foot down and demand where he stopped, where he lived, what he did. Sienna had done that with her parents, she knew it worked, she'd do it again for something she believed in. She was absolutely the wrong woman for him—if he'd been looking for one, which he wasn't. Where was the relief of knowing that? It should be shoving aside these silly niggles of interest in who she was behind that professional façade she wore too easily, making him let it go. But he couldn't. 'Where are your folks now?'

They'd reached his four-wheel drive. Harry pinged the locks and opened the door for Sienna, helped her up onto the seat, saw her swallowing when she knocked her ribs. He also swallowed. When he'd taken her elbow to help her up he'd been hoping to save her from added pain.

It wasn't until he was on the road heading towards their apartments that she told him, 'Mum's still in Napier, living in her own home. She has a friend, Bill, to share occasions with, but not her house, while Dad's travelling all over the South American continent,' she said, sadness thickening her words.

'Last night you said he'd told you to spread your wings. He doesn't understand your need to be settled in one place?'

'He understands all right, he just doesn't agree. Says I'm missing out on too much. To some extent that's true, but I'm also winning in other ways.' She leaned her head back and closed her eyes, her hands tight balls on her thighs. 'I'm getting to watch my trees grow.'

'You have to do what's right for you, not live according to someone else's ideas. Not even your father's.'

Very wise, Harry.

But it was what he did. Lived alone, worked wherever a job came up, didn't have a house to call home, though he did own a string of properties he rented out. Didn't do anything to abide by his mother's edicts.

'Yeah,' was Sienna's answer to that gem of wisdom.

CHAPTER FIVE

SIENNA STOOD BY her kitchen bench, waiting for the kettle to boil, and wiped up splashes of water on the counter, rinsed and dried the teaspoon Harry had dropped in the sink when he'd made her a coffee earlier and placed it in the drawer, handle to the right. Now what?

There wasn't a part of her body that didn't ache, and downright hurt in some places. Especially the ribs, because she'd forget and put her arm out to reach for something, and ping, pain would stab her. Bed was the best place to be, but it felt alien in the middle of the day. Alien, and uncomfortable, and rendered her useless.

So here she was, wondering what to do with herself, apart from swallow some more painkillers. The problem with those were they weren't soothing what really ailed her. The accident had rattled her more than it had any right to do. It was all very well deciding it had been the wake-up call she'd unconsciously been waiting for. Quite another to know what to do with it.

Write a list.

What would a list of things to occupy her when she wasn't being a doctor, over-zealous house-tidy-upper person, or cyclist achieve? Apart from frustration at learning how insular she'd made her life? Her bike was now scrap metal, leaving two of those options to fill in her time. Doctoring was out for a couple of days. Not a week as Amy Roberts had recommended. Two days of hanging out around here trying to come up with ideas she didn't have a clue about would test every shred of patience she had. She wasn't familiar with relaxing in a sit-and-read, or do-a-jigsaw-puzzle, or cook-a-fancy-meal kind of way. This was her haven in that it was *her* front door that opened into *her* home filled with *her* furniture, and outside were *her* trees, but as far as doing random fun activities here? It didn't happen.

Her head ached enough as it was without her having to think. The short sleep she'd had on top of her bed after Harry left to go fetch her car hadn't improved her mood.

He'd out and out ignored her when she said she'd arrange for someone to get her SUV. At least she hadn't been stupid enough to say it could stay where it was until she was fit to drive. She did like having four wheels and all the windows intact. Titirangi was a good neighbourhood, but not all hooligans knew that.

Harrison. Her finger tapped her wrist. An enigma. Today he'd guided her not only to her door when they got back from the hospital, but had taken the key from her shaky fingers, unlocked the door and, hand on her elbow, walked her inside to the kitchen, where he'd pushed her gently onto a chair and proceeded to make coffee and toast. Who did he think he was? This was her territory. She got to decide who came through her front door, and what they did once inside.

Tell that to someone who believes you. You enjoyed every moment of it—couldn't find reasons to keep him at a distance.

True. All of it.

The moment he'd gone she'd tossed the toast down the garbage disposal and the coffee down the drain. The hospital breakfast was still firmly lodged somewhere between her mouth and her stomach and nothing was getting past. Or was that because of nerves about her neighbour? Harry had a cheek taking over as though he owned the place, but he'd also acted as a friend. Like Anna usually did, before she had a brain fade and decided Harrison Frost was the man to be seeing to her needs. Sienna had a clear idea what needs Anna was thinking about. It was *not* happening. Even if her skin tingled and her fingers warmed whenever he was near.

The kettle whistled, clicked off.

Sienna stared at it. What was she doing? Coffee was still the last thing she wanted. Reaching to put the mug back in the cupboard, she knocked against the shelf and gasped as pain tore through her ribs. The mug slid from her fingers and shattered on the tile floor. Sweat beaded on her forehead.

Great. Well done. It had been given to her by her mother on the day she graduated from high school. An English, fine china mug with blue daisies painted around it, it had once belonged to her Welsh grandmother. Sniff.

Toughen up. But she had precious little from her past to appreciate that wasn't in her head.

Write that list.

Start with finding a replacement mug.

The sun was streaming through the wide picture window in the lounge as Sienna hobbled towards the leather recliner chair, picking up pen and paper from the sideboard drawer on the way.

Buy Christmas presents for all the kids on the ward to take in on my first day back at work.

Really? She'd never done anything like that before, but now a frisson of excitement caught at her. Why not? The parcels would have to be generic as she didn't know each child personally, but kids were kids, and they'd enjoy getting a gift.

The leather was warm from the sun. The paper remained blank. Sienna grew drowsy. The events of yesterday were playing havoc with her mind and body.

Spread your wings.

Take flying lessons, she scrawled, and let the ennui flattening her take over.

Blink, refocus. Collect stamps. She shook her head and held her pen firmly away from the paper. Not her thing. Anyway, where did a person find stamps these days?

Buy a new bike. Learn to cook Italian food. Design pretty scrubs to wear on the ward.

This was silly. Who wrote lists of how to get on with their lives? Besides, she didn't want to alter her life too much. She liked knowing how each day would pan out. Like she'd seen yesterday's crash coming? That only went to show it was better to keep some form of control going on. She dropped the pen and pad on the carpet. Didn't lean down to align the pen with the edge of the pad.

Wow. Letting loose, Si.

No, just too tired and sore to move. Her eyelids drooped.

The sound of her SUV coming up the drive woke her. But Harrison didn't stop there. Oh, no; using her remote control, he opened the garage and drove in. No stopping the guy when he was on a mission.

A mission to help, Sienna.

True. But she wasn't used to someone wandering through her space as though they belonged there. Then he was coming right inside, calling softly, 'Sienna, it's Harry. How're you doing?'

'Fine. I'm in the lounge.' She wanted him to come in? For the first time in years it felt a bit lonely in here, but Harry wasn't the fix she needed. He was a good neighbour, he might even be becoming a friend, but she couldn't rely on him to be around forever. He was like her father, always on the move, and she would never go back to that lifestyle, not for anybody.

'Your car's back. I'm going to drop Connor home. Anything you need while I'm in town?' He came into the lounge and the room instantly shrank around her, the air filled with something intangible yet vibrant.

Talk about making it harder to push him away. Friendly, easy-going. It wouldn't be difficult to forget she wasn't in need of anyone else in her life. 'No, thanks.'

'You get any sleep?' He stood in front of her, those mesmerising eyes scanning her in a professional capacity. 'You still look exhausted.'

She supposed he was thinking medicine and nothing else. Why would he? A man with his looks and body could have any woman he chose, not some mashed-up doctor with chips the size of rocks on both shoulders. 'I got some,' she growled. 'I'm fine.'

Stepping back, he sighed long and loud. 'I'm sure you are. I'm going to the supermarket. If you think of anything I can get you flick me a text.' He reached down for the pen and notepad. 'Here's my number.' A quick scrawl and he handed the pad over and left the room without a backward glance.

When she looked down the annoyance he usually managed to crank up arrived in full force.

Stop sweating the small stuff, had been added to her list. *Her* list. Not his to play with. Bet he always knew what he was doing. Again she asked herself: Who did Harrison Frost think he was, coming in here like he owned the place, telling her what to do?

Snatching up her pen, she scribbled another line, just to remind herself she was in charge here. Not Harrison.

Then the pen fell from suddenly lifeless fingers as she stared at the pad. Oh, no. Big mistake her writing that previous left-field thought on her list. Now she was definitely on the back foot. Harry would be laughing so much he'd wet himself.

Find a man to have a fling with.

The words beamed off the page. She might as well have hung a sign at the front door. What had she been thinking? Stuck on Harrison, that was where her brain had been. The sooner she got back to work the better.

Swinging into his drive, Harry stared across at Sienna's apartment. All the curtains were wide open, so she hadn't gone back to bed when it was obvious she was dropping with exhaustion. Stubborn woman.

Find a man to have a fling with.

He hadn't been able to get the words out of his skull for one second. His body was sitting up, ready to play ball, if he was the man she was looking for. But he rubbed her up the wrong way too often for that to happen.

He grinned. He'd also be in trouble for adding to her list. Bring it on. Feisty was good, kept things interesting, and put the brakes on getting too friendly. The problem being the more he saw of her the more he wanted to find out what made her tick. He wanted to be that man on her list. But did she actually mean it? Compared to other women he'd known, Sienna had keeping to herself down to an art form. His grin faded. Come Christmas he'd be out of here. He hadn't decided where to spend Christmas yet. It depended on where the next job was and when he'd be required to start—if one came up. Right now there was a scarcity of vacancies, which was a pain in the backside. Never before had he had a problem finding his next position; sometimes he'd had two or more to choose from. If nothing came up he'd take a break and go on a short trip somewhere exciting. The fishing was supposed to be good on the Coromandel.

Out of his four-wheel drive, he rescued the groceries from the warm back seat and headed indoors, and couldn't stop himself taking another look over the fence on his way. No sign of Sienna.

Groceries unpacked and stored, Harry checked his phone. No messages. No jobs. He gazed around the apartment, identical to Sienna's if he didn't factor in his tee shirt on the table, shoes by the fridge and yesterday's breakfast dishes in the sink. There hadn't been a single thing out of place next door. Not a one. How did anyone live like that? He couldn't, not if his life depended on it. There wasn't any point to being über-tidy.

Right now he had time on his hands that had to be used somehow. Not something he was used to. The washing he'd put on before heading out to Titirangi needed hanging on the line. That'd fill all of five minutes.

The lawns. They were getting out of hand, grass halfway up his calves in some places. The electric mower wouldn't make enough noise to disturb Sienna if she was asleep. Her lawns could do with a tidy-up as well. Though the grass would barely reach his ankles, he'd observed how she liked to keep it immaculate. Might win some points along the way.

Joke, Harry, joke.

An hour later Harry switched the mower off, and immediately wished he hadn't.

Sienna was coming towards him in an odd slow, limping

kind of way with fire in her eyes. 'You didn't need to do that. I am quite capable of mowing my own lawns.'

'Thank you, Harry, for doing that job. I really appreciate it,' he snapped back, warning his heart to stop feeling quite so sorry for her. Heart? Didn't he mean head? Absolutely.

She stumbled, righted herself quickly. 'Yes, well, sorry. I mean, it was kind of you, but it's a bit of a mess.' She blushed.

Finally some colour in those cheeks he had to resist running a finger down. 'A mess?'

The red hue deepened, and the blue in her eyes glittered like that lake when the sun was going down over it. 'Um, it's just that I like to mow up and down in straight lines.'

And he'd started at the far corner and gone round and round until he reached the centre. He stared at this woman. What the hell difference did it make? The grass was cut, done for another week; two if they were lucky with the weather and the spring temps didn't encourage too much growth. 'Whatever,' he said in a churlish tone that he instantly regretted. He wasn't a child, didn't do spoilt. If she wasn't happy with him then she wasn't. Not his problem. 'I promise not to mow them again.'

She closed her eyes, drew a long breath before opening them to stare at him with something he thought might be embarrassment creeping into her face. 'I am ungrateful, aren't I? Thank you for doing the lawns. I deliberately went cycling yesterday so I didn't have to do them, and that's unheard of.'

His stance instantly softened. 'You'd have been better off now if you had got the mower out.'

'I'd still have gone for a ride, and I'd probably still have been distracted by...' Her voice petered out as shock overtook that embarrassment.

'By?'

'It doesn't matter.'

'I think it does if it was a big enough distraction to send you off the road.' She'd glanced at him twice when Anna had asked how the accident happened.

Those full, tempting lips clamped shut.

'What was it?' It couldn't be anything personal because they didn't have a history, not one that spanned even a week. He wouldn't count that night and the loud music. But he hadn't been able to forget her since then. Maybe he should be counting it. Ah ha. Was that it? 'You're still annoyed that I didn't instantly turn the music down that night?'

'Not at all.' Her eyes were fixed on something over his shoulder, giving nothing away. Because she *had* been thinking about him while pedalling up the road?

Yeah, right. Get a life, Harry. If that's the best you can come up with you need to get out of here.

'It must've been another shock for you when I turned up at your accident site, swinging down on a rope from the helicopter.' If she had been distracted by him while cycling that would've felt weird to her. He tried to recall what she'd said, the expression on her face, but only came up with her anxiety and pain. No, he'd got it all wrong. So why was she looking everywhere but at him?

'Believe me.' Her head lifted, her shoulders pulled back until pain must've struck and she let go again. 'My crash had nothing to do with you.' Her composure wasn't working. Colour streaked her cheeks, those eyes he was coming to enjoy watching were widening and blinking as if batting away the truth. 'But yes, I was surprised when I saw you unhooking from that rope.' Colour rose again in her cheeks and down her neck.

Laughter rolled up his throat and blistered the air between them. 'I bet you were. Your worst nightmare coming to save you.'

She swallowed. 'Your words, not mine. I was relieved that it was someone I knew. Okay, I didn't—don't—know you, but we had met, and it helped. Nothing to do with the medical side of things, though you were excellent, by the way.' Now she wasn't shutting up and would she ever regret that.

Harry interrupted. 'I'm putting the mower away. Then I'll come take your pulse and check your breathing.' And if they were fast? Would that mean she wasn't improving, or she was reacting to his touch? In reality it was his pulse that needed slowing.

'Don't bother. I'm going back to bed.'

Bed. If ever there was a word with too many connotations. But Sienna didn't blink, blush or look as if she'd made a mistake. Back under control? He hoped not. 'No problem. Just assure me you've taken your meds and are feeling as well as can be expected.' He could dampen down the heat that began expanding through his groin the moment she'd come out to blast him for doing her lawns. If she disappeared inside. If he concentrated really hard. Hard. Wrong word.

'I'm doing everything I'm supposed to, thank you, Dr Frost.' Turning her back on him, she hobbled back inside her apartment.

Harry couldn't help himself. She wound him up something terrible. 'I'll look in later to make sure you're okay and prepare a meal for us. Anything you don't like, Doc Frosty?'

'Harassment from neighbours,' she threw over her shoulder.

The laugh that shot up his throat and over his lips was sudden and real. Damn it. He liked this woman. Frosty, feisty, annoying. None of those attitudes had put him off—

instead they had ramped up his interest so much it could become dangerous.

Time to start ringing around people he knew and try harder to find a job that would take him away from here at the end of this contract.

A couple of hours later his phone rattled off a tune just as he was about to head across to Sienna's with a meal of steak, fries and salad to share. The tension that had been building since he'd left her earlier disappeared the moment he saw the caller ID.

'Hi, Lance. What's up?'

'Much the same as last time we talked. I'd swear the kids are growing a centimetre a day. Soon they'll be patting me on the head and asking if I've eaten my greens. What about you? Fallen out with those Kiwis yet?'

'Not through lack of trying.' Aussies and Kiwis loved to hate each other, but put a third party between them and they were always allies.

'This isn't because you've found someone of the opposite sex to keep your bed warm and other things on the go for longer than a day?'

'Not likely. No, I just like the country.' And his neighbour. But Sienna wouldn't budge from here. So? He wasn't asking her to. 'What's this about? You don't usually ring for a chat.'

Lance grumped, 'It's been a while since we shot the gap over a beer.'

'Eighteen months. Your wedding anniversary.' His mate had found his perfect match. They'd have no issues about not wanting the same things for themselves and their kids.

'One in a million, I know.'

The love in Lance's voice stilled Harry's heart, turned him a little green. What was that like, knowing someone put you first most of the time, cared what happened in your day? Didn't want to hold you responsible for everything the world threw up?

Lance's tone changed to serious. 'Have you got your next position lined up yet?'

'Funny you should ask. There's a bit of a drought at the moment. Not that I'm too bothered. Something always turns up somewhere.'

'I might be able to help.' Lance hesitated, then, 'It'd mean coming back to Melbourne.'

No surprise there. Lance was based in his home town. 'I can do that for a short stint.' He'd returned to Melbourne twice to fill in at emergency departments, staying with Lance and his family, while avoiding his parents except for an occasional meal on the South Bank.

'Yeah. I figured.'

Got it. Not for a few weeks. 'How long?'

'Melbourne General needs an ED head of department for at least twelve months.'

The city was right up there on his list of great places. It only had one fault. His parents lived there. But he needed a job, and twelve months was better than eight weeks here and three months someplace else. Huh? Since when? He liked moving around. Yes, but not all the time. It was becoming a bit of a drag living out of a pack. Not literally, but with the limited contents he found more and more he missed having personal possessions around him. None of his favourite books to indulge in, having to wear the same old clothes week in, week out, not even his squash racket for when he suddenly felt like banging around a court. When had this started? His gaze drifted in the direction of the adjacent apartment. Not in the last week, surely? Not since the advent of Doc Frosty? If that was the case then he needed out of here quick smart. 'Tell me more.'

He got a brief outline before Lance said, 'I'll email the details tomorrow. But what's your gut reaction?'

Did he want this job? A job with no end date? In Melbourne? He wouldn't be able to avoid his folks forever. They'd want more than dinners. Did that matter? His mother couldn't belittle him any more, couldn't blame him for the roof leaking or the company not doing so well. Instead she and Dad could go on handing out the blame to each other as they'd started doing the day he walked down the front path never to return. As for Celia, she was long gone, living the high life in Sydney with some other poor sod to boss around.

'You trying to think up reasons to say no?' Lance asked.

'Yes. And no. I need to read the conditions and think this through.' Not that Lance wouldn't make sure everything was good to go. It was just— Hell, he didn't know what was holding him back, especially when he needed to find another job soon. Yes, he did. Melbourne. His parents. Sienna. Huh? What did she have to do with any of this?

'I recognise stalling tactics when I hear them.' Lance didn't hold back. 'Thought you'd put all that behind you.'

'I have.'

'So what's the "but"?'

'None of yours.' But this was his mate on the other end of the call. The man who'd helped him set up a flat after he left home, who'd stood by him when his parents had a very public spat at his graduation. There wasn't much Lance didn't know about him. 'It's not the past that's a problem. It's the future.' There. He'd said it out loud. Now he waited for the roar of laughter.

It didn't come. 'At long last.'

'Don't go getting ideas of me settling down with a woman and kids and the picket fence.' He didn't like the taste of that. Too cloying. 'It's more about stopping moving all the time, finding one place to set up home. I can still take jobs in different locations, but having a place to call my own to return to is starting to appeal.' He could still remain single, unfettered.

'Melbourne won't be that place, will it?'

Again his gaze travelled the distance between apartments. 'No. Might be. Haven't got a clue. After a good night's sleep I'll probably have changed my mind again.'

This is all new to me, and takes some getting my head around.

His eyes were still fixed over the fence.

'Go have that sleep and let me know about the ED job.'

Harry stuffed the phone into his back pocket. That meal needed delivering before it got too cold to eat. Sienna should be up and about by now. Her sleeps were short, followed by aimless wandering around the apartment. Not so aimless that she hadn't been writing a note on what to do once she was properly back on her feet. A grin lifted his mouth, and his spirits. Bet she was spitting tacks at him over that. His grin widened. Then there was that fling idea. Did he want to take up the challenge? Hell, yes. But would he? Watch this space, he mused.

'Hello? It's your pain-in-the-butt neighbour, bringing dinner,' he called softly from the doorway.

No reply. Placing the plates on the table, he contemplated the merits of going to check on her for all of two seconds. He was a doctor and had promised Amy Roberts he'd keep an eye on Sienna for a few days.

Stepping out of the kitchen, he hesitated. On the floor by the lounge wall was a screwed-up piece of paper. It would have been no big deal in anyone else's home, but here, where nothing was out of order, it stood out. Recognising the blue page, he picked it up, opened it. And roared with laughter.

'Tell Harrison to stick his head where the sun don't shine.'

So he'd got to her. For some reason that made him feel damned good. Sienna Burch had got under his skin, so it was only fair he'd returned the provocation. They could continue brushing each other up the wrong way for as long as he was here. Apparently rubbing sticks together produced sparks, followed by flames. Would they do the same with each other? Finding out was going to be fun. There was a fling on offer. Maybe not to him—yet—but he wouldn't be himself if he wasn't at least open to the idea.

It couldn't hurt. Come Christmas he'd pack his bag and leave. For Melbourne? His grin died. Was this what he wanted? To finally return home? No. But if he stayed here he ran the risk of getting too involved with Sienna. He wasn't ready for that—and never would be.

Shaking away those irritating thoughts, he headed down the hall to Sienna's bedroom.

'Sienna?'

She stared up at the apparition filling her doorway. From where she sat on the edge of her bed Harrison looked impossibly big. She rubbed at her eyes to remove the sleep grit and looked again. Still large, and gorgeous. 'Hello?'

'How're you doing?'

'Could be better,' she admitted, feeling a little over-whelmed with his presence and the way her body ached from all the bruises while also coming awake in places that had been dormant for so long. This man did the strangest things to her, no matter how hard she fought him.

'Never thought I'd hear you say that.' His smart-alec grin undermined her further.

'What are you doing here?' she snapped.

'Dropping in on the lady next door, seeing as how her heart's working. I can already guess her head's not so flash.'

'Nothing wrong with my head.'

Nothing you need to know about. As for my heart, that's strictly out of bounds.

'Good, then I'll take your pulse and BP reading before we have dinner. Together,' he added with a certain satisfaction.

'In case you haven't noticed, I haven't spent the past hour in my kitchen cooking up a storm.' But she might've if she'd known he was dropping in.

That grin only increased. 'Ahh, but *I* have.'

'Damn it, you cook as well?'

'As well as what?' Harry slid the BP cuff he'd brought with him around her arm, those long fingers warm where they touched her skin. 'Sienna?'

'Sienna what?' Had she said something? Oh. 'You're good at swinging down to rescue people, and even better at taking charge and bossing someone around when they're not up to speed.'

The cuff was in place and yet his hand remained on it, his fingers still touching her as he pumped the bulb with his other. 'You don't like me helping out?'

'Liking and needing are two different things.' Locking her eyes onto his, she saw the black lighten as if she'd made him happy, which sent her stomach into a tailspin. There was no air in the room. Making Harrison happy was not a good idea. He'd get the wrong idea and she'd never be rid of him. Now there was a plan. Put that on the list.

He appeared to have to drag his gaze away so he could focus on taking the BP reading. 'I think I can make you like what you need.'

Sienna gulped, stared around the room. Her bedroom. Harrison was in her bedroom, supposedly taking obs and yet he was also flirting with her. Inappropriate? If it was she wasn't about to tell him off. It had been so long since a man had paid her attention. Make that, since she'd allowed one to. 'You probably think you know what I need as well.'

Harrison read the BP result, let the air out of the cuff, and pulled it off. When his eyes met hers again he was smiling in a teasing kind of way. 'I read your list, remember?'

Far out. He didn't hold back any punches. Or was he teasing? 'So you want to go shopping for a tea mug with me?'

'If we're starting at the top of the page then I guess I'll have to. Or I could drive you to the mall and wait in the car while you find what you're after.'

She'd already found what she was after—for the fifth thing on her list, that was. 'I'm not up to wandering around a crowded mall just yet.' Not up to energetic sex either, but that one she was more than willing to try.

The cuff was being mangled in his hands. 'We can always come back to that one later. Flying's out too, so you're making your way down the page without doing anything.'

But soon she'd reach the one thing she could act on—now. No. Too soon. But what was she waiting for? Here was a hot man, in her bedroom, available as far as she knew, apparently open to suggestions, and she was stalling. She needed air, space to think. Thinking, that was what she always did. Overthought things until the fun had gone out of them. Sienna shot to her feet. 'I don't...' The room spun. Strong hands caught her shoulders, held her steady. Everything around her was moving in circles. Everything except Harry. He was rock-solid, reliable, dangerous, exciting. Go for it. Lifting her head, she found Harrison watching her with resignation flattening that smile and darkening his eyes again.

'When you're ready, sit down again so I can take your pulse. Then we'll have dinner.'

Reluctantly Sienna withdrew from his hold and stepped around him to leave the room. The moment was gone. They were back to Harry helping her out as a neighbour who'd had an accident, not as a woman he might want to bed. 'My pulse is fine.' He was not going to find out it was off the wall. 'It's my stomach that needs attention now.'

CHAPTER SIX

'WHERE ARE YOU GOING?'

Harrison's question interrupted Sienna's concentration. He was standing in her garage looking cross.

'Or should that be, where have you been? You're not meant to drive yet, *Doctor*.'

She leaned out the window of her SUV. 'I've been nowhere.' *More's the pity.* 'And I'm going nowhere, *Doctor*.'

'You felt like hanging out in your car for a bit?'

Sarcastic so-and-so. 'You should mind your own business.' He was always interfering. Shoving her door wide, Sienna placed her feet carefully on the ground, not prepared to show him how much she still hurt in most muscles. Nor was she saying what she'd done. Being laughed at would crank her temper up something shocking, though that would be the perfect outlet for all the frustration brought on by a long, tedious day at home.

Those hands that fascinated her beyond reason were now on his hips. Narrow hips on the vee from his wide chest to his— She jerked her head high and clashed with his gleaming eyes.

'You've re-parked the SUV.' There was a lot of amused twitching going on around his mouth.

Too damned shrewd for her good, he was. 'And what

if I have?' Wait for it. He was going to burst out laughing any second.

'I didn't park dead straight,' Harry grinned. How was he managing not to laugh?

She hadn't known anyone's eyes could get quite so wide. She hoped it hurt because the way he was looking at her suggested he thought her bonkers. He was probably right. Heat suffused her neck and up into her face. But control was so important. 'No, you didn't.' And that had driven *her* crazy every time she'd brought clothes for the laundry basket out here. She glared at him. *Please don't say anything more.*

Of course he did. It wouldn't be the Harrison she was coming to know otherwise. 'You never just drive in and stop?'

'Every time.' She had it down pat. Line up the right front corner of the bonnet with the edge of the cupboard on the back wall and voila. Perfect.

'I'm getting it.' His shoulders were heaving as he turned away.

'You think?' she asked too quickly.

Harrison came back to her and engulfed her hands in those warm, strong ones she still hadn't got over thinking about. 'I'm not laughing at you. I get that you need to have control over your life. What I don't understand yet is why.'

When he was holding her hands as if she was special all her control disappeared, and she had to fight not to lean in against that expansive chest. He'd said *yet*. Did that mean he wanted to spend more time with her, get to know her a little? Hope flared. Have a fling with him. Now. Quick. That'd mean letting go the bonds she'd put around her libido. Huh? They were already snapping apart, one by one, as Harrison spent more time with her. Hard to pull her hands away when she wasn't ready to let him go, but somehow she managed it. 'It's my way of keeping life on track.'

'Sometimes it's more fun going off track.'

'Sometimes it's downright dangerous.'

Harry stared at her for a long moment. 'I hope not.'

He left her with the shattering sensation that he understood her, knew what made her tick better than she did. Now, *that* was dangerous.

'Well, it's fairly obvious Christmas is just around the corner,' Sienna quipped as she walked into the paediatric ward on Wednesday, the large bag dragging from one hand. Staring around at the decorations, covering every available surface and then some, she laughed. 'Has there been any work done in here?'

Julie, a junior doctor, joined her. 'It's a very serious matter, hanging Santas and coloured glass baubles, I assure you. The kids had a ball.'

'Which has to be good for them. So who's here at the moment?'

'Felicity's still around. She got a mild lung infection after that near-drowning but, being her, she's up and about, refusing to let this setback hold her down.'

'Has she got over her anger at missing out on the school trip?' Fliss was one her favourite patients, not that she could ever admit that out loud, but any time the teen had problems she felt bad for her.

'I think so, but check her out for yourself. Here she comes.'

Felicity was running down the ward, arms outstretched. 'Doc Sienna, you're back. Are you all right? I heard what happened. You look pale and wobbly. Shouldn't you be sitting down?'

Sienna braced herself for impact, but Felicity skidded to a halt just short of a collision. 'Hello to you, too.'

Fliss grinned. 'It's not the same around here without you.'

Water filled her eyes. Sniff. 'Thought I was the dragon lady.'

Fliss's cheeks were full of colour and her breathing only slightly laboured. Definitely ready to go home. 'Everyone needs a dragon on their side. We were told you'd be away all week.'

Sienna winced. 'I've only dropped in to see how everyone's getting on.' Her head still thumped intermittently and she didn't want to push it when decisions about other people's health were at stake. At the same time, staring at her four walls had been slowly driving her insane. The only reprieve had been when Harry dropped in to check up on her or bring a meal he always insisted on sharing. 'And to hand these around. Come on, you can help me.' The ward looked warm and inviting, the sterile white walls no longer glaring. It happened every December yet this was the first time she'd taken serious notice. 'Did you have a hand in the decorating?'

'I helped the little kids make paper chains.' Fliss blushed. She didn't like being seen as a softy by other teens or adults, but she could no more refuse a small child assistance than Sienna could refuse to treat a sick person. 'Some of the chains weren't very good but we put them up anyway.'

'That's what it's all about.' Her fingers itched to straighten the large cardboard star with uneven glitter hanging on the wall. Turning her back on it, she looked into the room opposite, not recognising any of the young patients. 'Want to tell me everyone's name as we go?'

The presents were a hit, and the ward was noisy with

laughter and excited shouts. Sienna couldn't stop smiling as warmth threatened to overwhelm her. What a simple thing to do, and yet the rewards were beyond measure.

'Everyone's happy,' Felicity grinned.

'It must be the Christmas spirit.' Something she could do with a dose of at home. She would get a tree and decorations, and it would be a start to livening up her days. The list had come to a grinding halt, tossed in a drawer out of sight. Nothing more had been added, nothing at all completed and ticked off.

Don't sweat the small stuff.

Go away, Harry.

'What do *you* think?' grumped Aiden, fourteen, appendicitis, when she asked how he was feeling, the zing from getting a present gone.

'Definitely ready to go home, I'd say,' she said in an aside to Julie.

'Much to everyone's relief,' the intern smiled. 'Teenagers.'

Toby, ten, another appendectomy. 'Mum's coming to get me after lunch. I can't wait to go back to school.'

'Not this week,' Sienna smiled.

His face fell. 'It's boring at home.'

She couldn't argue with that, so she didn't try. 'Haven't you got some games to play on your computer?'

'Mum'll make me read books.'

'That's really terrible,' she laughed. What was wrong with her? She never said things like that, always encouraged the kids to read and study and not sit around staring vacantly at their electronic toys.

Julie was looking at her as if she was a stranger. Maybe she was. That accident had rattled her. But changed her? Who knew? 'Right. Who else have we got I need to be introduced to?'

Less than two hours later Sienna hated to admit defeat. She was shattered. Every one of those bruises was protesting, her rib cartilage had a lot to say, and her head was spinning, making it hard to stay upright. 'I'm going home,' she told the staff.

'I'll walk you down.' Dale appeared at her side. 'I need a word with you.'

His tone sounded ominous but when they reached the ground floor all Dale said was, 'Go home and do something for yourself for a change, Sienna. You were beyond exhausted before this accident. It's time to rest and relax, get some energy back. You're not pretty when dragging your butt like you're carrying all the responsibility for the ward.'

'I don't need to be pretty to do my job.'

'Make the most of this time out. Come back refreshed.' Then he was gone, striding back to the lifts.

Sienna stared after the man she'd always believed to be a pushover. When had Dale turned bossy? Another dictatorial man in her life. Two in a week was two too many. The only difference being that she had to keep onside with her boss, whereas Harrison she could and did ignore.

The taxi driver had to wake Sienna outside her apartment. Embarrassed, she clambered out, spilling the contents of her handbag on the road edge, gathering everything up before finally handing him the fare. How had she fallen asleep after Dale's bombshell? Inside she opened windows to let the breeze cool the humid air and found her list to scrawl more ideas that she wouldn't ever act on. Next she headed for the bedroom to fall on top without removing her shoes, already asleep as her head hit the pillow despite the stab of pain from her ribs.

She woke hours later to a delicious smell wafting into

her room, and went out to find Harry taking a dish of macaroni and cheese out of her oven. 'Oh, boy, that smells delish.'

'Not bad, eh?'

'You don't do coy, do you?'

'No idea what it means.' He grinned like a naughty boy caught out at something he shouldn't be doing.

'Why am I not surprised?'

'How are you feeling? That was some sleep going on. I could hear the snores out here.'

'He doesn't do diplomacy either,' she muttered.

'Pulling your leg.' He nudged a chair out from the table. 'Take a load off and I'll get the cutlery. This is ready to go.'

'How can I resist such an invitation?' Sienna sank onto the chair, breathing in the rich aroma, and trying to hold her stomach in so it didn't add noise to the scene.

They ate in silence. At least it was companionable. Until Harry said, 'I see you're going to a day spa some time soon.'

Her fork stopped halfway to her mouth. 'You what?'

He shrugged. 'Don't leave it lying around if anything's a secret.' Those full lips tilted up into a wide smile. 'A spa seems innocuous compared to a fling.'

'You think?' Right now a spa was way up there, while a fling wasn't even registering. Not while Harrison was being his usual stroppy self. Setting her fork on the plate, she leaned back in her chair. 'Guess you've never been to a spa, then.'

His eyes widened, and that smile grew. 'I haven't had the need.'

He saw her words as a challenge? *Gah.* Whatever. She was a big girl. 'Another thing to show how different our lives are.' She was backing off, and that surprised her, but then she wasn't used to flirting, usually got cold feet the moment she got close.

Harrison pushed his empty plate aside and leaned back in the chair, his expression now empty of teasing as he watched her. 'We are poles apart, yet we're almost alike in our need to protect ourselves from others.'

The tension that had been tightening over the last few minutes disappeared. Harrison wound her up, softened her down, all too easily. Thoughtlessly she squeezed his hand, and got zapped by an electric current for her trouble. Or so it felt. Her eyes flicked straight to Harry's, saw the same shock registering in that lightening black-grey.

It wasn't as though she could pull away. If she even tried. Which she didn't. It was more as though they were fused together. Her brain had stopped thinking straight, was entirely focused on the current running between them. Her lungs were acting strange, taking in short grabs of air, pushing it out fast. As for the rest of her body—she was leaning forward, getting closer and closer to Harry. They were standing. How had that happened? Their hands linked, fingers entwined. Breathing the same air, hot air filled with tension and sparks and—

Sienna sighed as Harrison's lips caressed hers. Yes. Exactly what she wanted, needed. No. It wasn't enough. As she pressed forward, her peaked breasts touched his chest. Desire fired through her. Her hips found his. Her stomach clenched, relaxed, clenched. Heat pooled lower. The aches and pains of the last few days receded to a dull background throbbing.

Strong arms wound around her, pulling her into that muscular, masculine body, and she was being kissed thoroughly. Harry left nothing to chance. His mouth claimed hers, his tongue forayed inside, his taste sent over more messages of hazy need. His eyes were open, focused on her. She fell into that gaze, gave over control of her mouth, her body. How could she not?

Harry's arms tightened further as his mouth pressed harder. A groan escaped over her lips. Or was that from Harry? What did it matter? Raising her arms to slide around his neck, she held on as her legs no longer had the strength to keep her standing. As she twisted to get more connection with his chest a serious pain stabbed her right side.

This time her groan wasn't about desire.

Instantly Harry lifted his head, set her back without letting go. Just as well or she'd be staggering around finding her balance. 'I'm so sorry. I shouldn't have done that. I don't want to hurt you.'

'You didn't. I moved badly, did it all by myself.' She wouldn't accept he meant he shouldn't have kissed her. That would be humiliating when she'd finally let go completely to kiss him. She did not want to think that for Harry that was an everyday kind of kiss.

He was staring at the point where her finger touched her mouth. Pulling her hand away, she glanced around the kitchen. Back to reality. The kitchen was ordinary. Reality didn't go with sensational kisses. Kiss. They'd only had one. But what a kiss. Right this minute she'd opt for more over keeping her life on track. Her iron-strong control had been stolen in a moment of need. Her eyes sought Harry again, locked on to him. 'Don't be sorry.'

'I think it's time I headed over the fence.'

Her stomach dropped. So that was how he was going to play it. She wasn't going to beg. They'd shared a moment. Not entirely unexpected—on her part anyway. He both infuriated and intrigued her, and for a few minutes that intrigue had won out. Now she knew what it was like to be kissed by Harrison. Shame it wasn't enough. But it was going to have to be. He was already at the door.

Don't show how disappointed you are.

They did not need to get together for a fling. They were opposites. He was all the things she didn't want in a man. Opposites might attract but that didn't mean they worked out long-term. Look at her parents. Not that she was looking for anything like that. Not even short-term involvement. But some fun wouldn't cause havoc on her heart, would it?

With Harry, it just might.

'Sienna, I'm not running away.' He was back, standing before her, his gaze cruising over her. 'But I don't want to take advantage of you.'

Take advantage of her? 'You didn't. I'm an adult. At least I was last time I looked.' But for a moment back in that kiss she could've been a teenager again.

His finger traced her jawline. 'Believe me, I know. I'm playing safe, okay?'

'Why?' She did safe, not others around her. But he had pointed out they were similar in many ways.

Whipping his hand away, he shoved both in his pockets and stared out the window. 'I don't do permanent.'

'One kiss and you're running from commitment? Excuse me, but that was never on offer.'

'There's something between us. It's been there from the night you walked up my drive. I don't usually stall, but I don't want to hurt you, and I think that would be too easy to do.'

'Trust me, I'm on lock-down. You're a man constantly moving, I'm a woman with my feet firmly fixed on my property. We are never going to have more than some fun, if even that.' Disappointment tasted bitter when it should be gratitude for his not roaring in to stomp all over her feelings. What would it be like to make love with this man? Her blood hummed and her head thumped. She guessed she'd never know.

He turned back to her, then said through the softest, most confusing smile, 'You're not as tough as you make out.'

Forget humming. Her blood was racing with longing. A longing for more than having sex. Longing for making love, not sex. Longing for someone to always be there with a smile like that for her. For a man who understood her far too well with so little to go by. 'Only when I want to be.'

Which is right about now.

But she wasn't saying.

That smile lingered, drumming up inappropriate responses throughout her body. If Harry could read her mind he'd be laughing at her weakness, or he'd be disgusted that she was so easy.

'Sienna.' Her name sounded like honey on his tongue.

'Harry.' Where were they going with this? Actually, she knew. He was right. They'd been headed down this track from the moment they met. She made up her mind in an instant of heat and need. Her lungs filled, drawing in confidence, and a heady mix of man scent. Her shoulders lifted as she laid a hand on his arm. 'Harrison.'

'I haven't been called Harrison so much in years.' The smile widened, his eyes filled with—longing?

Please be that.

'Is that good?' Sienna rose on her toes, ignored the protests from battered muscles, and leaned forward.

Then she was being wrapped in those arms again, Harrison's strength holding her still while he moved closer, shutting out the gap between them—physically if not mentally—to tuck her up against him. There was an incredible gentleness about his movements, an awareness of her bruises that he must've forgotten when he'd kissed her.

'Don't treat me like a china doll,' she all but begged.

'Sienna,' he repeated, and put her away from him. 'I can't. We can't.'

She would not give in to the frustration clawing through her. Not in front of him, at any rate. 'Fine,' she snapped and turned away to fill the kettle for something to do with her hands before she wrapped them around him and shook him until he changed his mind.

'I'm attracted to you.' His laugh was terse. 'That's an understatement. But there's the rub. I'm always moving, never stopping in one place for long, and nothing's going to change that. While you…' He stopped.

Turning, she leaned back against the bench. 'I'm in a holding pattern. I go to work, come home, tidy up, eat, sleep and go back to work. Occasionally I throw in a bike ride to change the routine. What has any of this got to do with not following through on what's between us?'

He pulled a chair out from the table and straddled it, his chin resting on his hand, his eyes thoughtful. 'It's all part of how I operate. I sign a contract, move to wherever I'm required, see out my time, and find the next contract. I don't stop for anyone or anything.'

When he put it like that her heart squeezed for him. 'You're so self-contained.' That was lonely. Sad, even.

'Aren't you?'

Not quite as much. Her parents were still there for her if she ever asked for help. 'You don't have family to go back to?' He'd never mentioned parents or siblings. Or children. There was also a squeeze for herself at his warning. He wouldn't stop his nomadic lifestyle for her any more than he would for any woman. While it was too early to be thinking about that, she needed to be strong, ready, watching out for her heart, because deep inside warning bells were ringing. Harrison might be the man who could change her perspective on how she lived. Shock rippled through her. Typical. She found a man to tinkle her keys and he was all wrong for her.

'Sure I do.'

What? Family. Right. 'Sharing isn't your thing, is it?' Her voice was harsher than she'd intended, but he never talked about himself. Had he learned that from his parents? 'Your family not talkers either?' Might as well ask as wonder.

'Most of them don't know when to stop.' It wasn't a joke. When those eyes locked on her she saw anger and bitterness battling for supremacy. 'My mother got pregnant with me when she was nineteen. My grandfather forced her to marry my father by saying he'd disown her if she didn't. Since she had ambitions to take over Granddad's company and the fortune that with it, she didn't argue.'

'Did your father have any say in that?'

'He had plenty of ambition himself. Already working for the company, he saw the opportunities to get to the top and take over. It was a recipe for disaster. There wasn't any love between Mum and Dad.'

'With you caught between them.' She wanted to hug the little boy who'd have been lost in all that, but there was a stop sign blinking out at her. Harry would hate her showing compassion.

'I was stuck right bang in the middle between two warring factions, copping the blame for anything that went wrong. After all, it was my fault they'd had to get married, so it must be my fault the company went through a few bad years; that Granddad wouldn't sign over control to Mum as soon as she wanted it; that the roof leaked. You name it, I caused it.'

Geez, how did any parent do that to their child? Her parents might've given her the craziest start to life but it had been fun and loving, and done with the best of intentions. 'Are you the only child?'

'There's the joke. After my parents married they decided they wanted a family to follow in their footsteps so I have two brothers I adore and would do anything for. My feelings are reciprocated,' he added in a softer voice. 'By them and their wives and kids.'

'So why don't you want what they've got?'

'You seriously think that's going to work? I tried once. Big fail. I refused to be bullied into doing what she wanted.'

'You've been married?'

'Four years and three months. Celia had the same ambitions as my mother—money, power, and never mind who she trod on to get it. Especially me.'

'You didn't see that before you married?'

'You'd think I would've, but no. Celia was so loving and kind, she'd do anything for me. I fell the whole way. Until I wised up and realised I was being played like a salmon on the line. By then we were married and about to move into a mansion I hadn't even seen when *we* made an offer to buy it.'

'Is that when you called it quits?' This was not the Harrison she'd come to expect when she asked questions. This man still hurt, but seemed to want to get it all out there. With her.

'No, I stayed another two years after that, believing that loving someone was for ever and with everything I had. But finally the give, give, give, without anything in return, got to me, wore me down and turned me sour. It seemed the more I gave the more she wanted.' He stood up to his full height. 'I'd read Celia all wrong right from the start, thought she cared about us, not just her own needs. Should've known better with my history.'

She might've felt intimidated by his height and those broad shoulders that seemed bigger than ever if not for that sadness lurking in the backs of his eyes. This big, strong man had problems that made him hurt on the inside. 'Sure you're not hiding behind this to avoid getting tied down again?'

His eyes widened. 'More than likely, but why would I get married again? Some people are meant to be single, and I'm obviously one of them. Guess my expectations are too high.'

'Doesn't sound like that to me.'

'Then I haven't been clear enough.'

Oh, he'd been clear all right. Like a piece of glass. He wasn't prepared to take another chance on love. She couldn't help nudging him a little. 'You believe those close to you will hold you responsible for everything that happens in their lives, yet it doesn't sound like that when you talk about your brothers.'

'They're different, having grown up with me.'

'You didn't find a middle ground with your wife?'

He grimaced. 'Go for the throat. Exactly what I'd expect from you.'

Her stomach sank. She hadn't intended rubbing him up the wrong way quite that much; the words had just popped out. But she wouldn't retract them. They felt right, so she gave something back and hopefully he'd understand where she was coming from. 'I should know. It's why I live this ordinary, safe life. I'm afraid to step out of my comfort zone and take risks.'

'What happened to the girl who demanded her parents stop wandering around the country as though there was nothing to linger for?'

'She got tied up with rigorous hours studying and training, and then she fell in love with a man who woke up one morning and decided he didn't love her any more. Apparently she was too cautious and always questioning why they had to move from city to city to chase the perfect job, the best position, when staying in his first job would've seen him at the top by now. He added insult to injury by dumping her for his high-school sweetheart.'

When Harry took a step towards her she held her hands up, palms towards him. 'Don't.' Now he was giving out compassion and it was too much. She didn't need his sympathy, only wanted the one thing he'd withdrawn minutes ago: desire. For her. She had to be grateful he'd stopped when he did. They were on different paths, and the strength of whatever this need between them was could be devastating. There'd be no happy ending, so best to call a halt now.

Heat in the pit of her stomach told her she was lying to herself. So much for starting over. But having a fling, even with her neighbour, wasn't the only thing on the list. She could try something else first.

CHAPTER SEVEN

Sienna removed her stethoscope from Felicity's chest. 'You're good to go.'

In typical teenage fashion Fliss shrugged her words away. 'Whatever.' She was back in a bad place. It seemed everyone at school would be raving about the wonderful week on Great Barrier Island and she didn't want to hear any of it.

'Doesn't school finish this week?'

'It's not like we'll be doing any work. It's boring.'

'Have you found a holiday job yet?'

'Duh. I've been in here, haven't I?'

Sienna tipped her head to one side. She wouldn't show pity for her favourite teen. 'I think the internet works in here as well as anywhere.'

'You try getting work when you cough goop like I do. People hate it.'

This day had been coming for a while now. Sienna had spoken to the counsellor about Fliss and knew they'd had a session, but obviously there was still a long way to go. 'Not everyone's like that.'

'Really?' All the hurt from previous rejections spilled into that one word and it took everything she had for Sienna not to cry.

Instead she wrapped her arms around the girl and held

her tight. Totally un-doctor-ish, yet about the best medicine she had to offer right now. Anyway, she was off duty this week, and here for a reason. She pulled back. 'What do you want to do when you leave school?'

'Be a lawyer who helps people like me. But I'll be lucky to get work in a warehouse.'

Sienna nodded. She already knew that. This girl had a huge heart and when she wasn't letting her situation get her down was always looking out for others on the ward. 'Okay, Felicity, enough of feeling sorry for yourself. You've shown me your exam results for the year. You are an intelligent girl who can be anything she wants.'

'An astronaut?' There was a lightening in Fliss's expression.

'Since you don't want to be one, I'm not answering that.' Movement down the other end of the ward diverted her attention. Harrison was pushing a trolley with a tiny patient into the ward, and he'd spotted her, his eyes being slits of disbelief. It was none of his business that she was here. Turning away, she tugged her phone out of her bag. 'Don't go anywhere, Fliss. I've got to go make a phone call and then I'll talk to you some more.' She shot into the nearest room and hit Anna's number, and crossed her fingers her friend wasn't with a client. They hadn't been able to set a time for this conversation.

Anna came on the line. 'This still about Felicity or have you decided to sue your bike for taking you over that edge?'

'I could try the manufacturer for a pay-out but I think there'll be a clause somewhere that says any cyclist stupid enough to get distracted by a mental picture of a hot man needs to see a shrink, not demand restorative justice.'

Anna laughed. 'I knew it. He's got to you.'

Sienna closed her eyes and shook her head slowly from

side to side. Stupid. She'd fed Anna enough to keep her busy nagging from now until the following Christmas. Lifting her eyelids, she stared through the door to that gorgeous sight of red overalls hiding a perfect body. At least he'd gone back to concentrating on his patient.

'I haven't got all day,' Anna muttered.

'Are you still okay about talking to Felicity?' Every year Anna *found* work for a teenager who had problems in their background in one form or another, and needed money and support. 'Sure.'

'Right, hang on while I take the phone to Felicity.'

Fliss was still sprawled over her bed looking blankly at the ceiling.

Am I doing the right thing?

'Felicity, I've got someone on the phone I'd like you to talk to. Ms McIntosh is a lawyer, so put on your best face.' She handed her phone over to shaky fingers. 'Go on,' she nudged when Fliss just stared at the instrument. 'Introduce yourself.' Then Sienna walked away, and straight into Harry. 'Hi,' she managed around the lump building at the back of her throat.

'Did you get called in?' It was a demand, not a question.
'No.'

'Getting your concussion checked out by someone else?'
'No.' Amy had done that earlier.

'So why are you here and not dealing with that list?' His gaze dropped, cruised down over her fitted sea-green blouse to her even more fitted white jeans. He blinked. 'You're not working, are you?'

'Nope. I came in to arrange for Anna to talk to Felicity about a holiday job in her legal office.' She really wanted to go eavesdrop on Fliss's side of the conversation.

'Why doesn't that surprise me? You doing something

kind for a patient outside of here? Sorry for being a prat.'
Harrison's gaze turned in the same direction as hers.

'She needs someone to believe in her, someone outside
of this place, and not her mother. A stranger who can tell
it to her like it is and expect her to pull her weight.'

'Anna will certainly do that.' Harry smiled. 'Watch out.'

Fliss flew towards her. 'Doc Sienna, I've got a job.'

Bracing for the slam coming her way, Sienna laughed.
'You're not meant to run around here.'

Warm arms surrounded Sienna with a thump. 'Thank
you, thank you. Ms McIntosh's so nice. She said I can go
see her tomorrow after school and she'll show me what
I'll be doing.'

Swallowing the stab from her ribs, Sienna warned, 'Anna's
a hard taskmaster.' She was also a softie behind that bulldog
exterior, but best Fliss worked that out for herself.

'I don't care. I've got a job.' Fliss danced on the spot.
'Woo-hoo.'

A warm hand spread between Siena's shoulder blades.
'Well done, Felicity.'

'Doc Harry? Did you hear that? I'm going to work for
Doc Sienna's friend. How cool is that?'

'Very cool.' Harry high-fived Felicity with his other
hand.

Slapping his hand, Felicity did a little jig. 'I'm going to
ring Mum. She'll be so happy for me. Thanks again, Doc
Sienna.' She raced away.

'Fliss?' Sienna called after her. 'My phone?'

'Oops, sorry, forgot.'

With her phone back in her pocket Sienna felt a rush of
pure happiness. She'd done something good for this girl
that wasn't medical. Now she really should go and do the
same for herself. What brand of cycle would she buy this
time? She could top up the insurance pay-out that would

turn up in her bank account during the next month and get something swankier than the last one.

'Si?' Harrison stood in front of her. 'Feel like coffee?'

'Haven't you got a helicopter waiting on the roof?'

'We're grounded while the guys fly to the maintenance yard to get something tightened. I said I'd make my own way back to base in an hour.'

'Then coffee sounds good.' Thank goodness she'd put an effort into her clothes that morning, and hadn't chucked on the usual plain skirt and shirt. If the way Harrison's eyes kept giving her the once-over was anything to go by, she'd got her outfit right.

He might be in her life short-term but she would make the most of whatever he had to spare. Starting with coffee. 'Not the hospital cafeteria, please?'

'Wouldn't dream of it, fuss-pants.'

There was a skip in her step all the way to the café along the road from the hospital, but once they were seated with large bowls of steaming cappuccinos in front of them, her excitement died. 'The helicopter wasn't about to fall out of the sky, was it?' Harry being in an accident was not allowed.

'Not at all. We could've operated non-stop all day but it's been quiet and the pilot wanted the job done.'

'What happens if you're needed? When you think it's quiet is usually when the calls start coming in thick and fast.'

Harrison nodded. 'True, but another crew is on standby. They've been doing training exercises all morning so they're up to speed if necessary.'

She could relax. Harry hadn't been in danger. And here he was, sharing coffee in a café—with her. 'I'm going shopping this afternoon.'

'What for?'

'A new bike. Think I'll get something a bit more geared than my last one.'

'So you can fly off the side of a hill faster than last time?' He was laughing but she didn't miss the flicker of concern cross his eyes.

'Good brakes are the first prerequisite.'

'Can you buy focus by the packet?' He sipped his drink.

Heat flooded her cheeks. 'I was focused.'

'Just not on the road.'

'You are such a stirrer, Harrison Frost.' And she liked it despite how he'd somehow figured out he was the cause of her accident, and enjoyed rubbing it in. 'There's nothing wrong with my focus.' Except when he was around. Like now. How long had her phone been ringing? 'Excuse me. I don't usually get calls during the day—it might be important.'

'Go ahead.'

Anna's number showed on the screen, then a text pinged into the box. 'It's Anna, saying she's looking forward to helping Felicity.' Phew. 'Mission accomplished.'

'Go you,' Harry said quietly, all the while watching her with something like care for her in his eyes.

'The humidity has to be at least eighty percent,' Harry grumbled at his own shadow as he slouched up his steps and opened the front door, tipping backward as a wave of hot, heavy air expelled from inside. Heat he could handle, but this humidity did him in. Everyone at work had been complaining while patients had been fractious, unlike their usual grateful selves at being airlifted to hospital.

Opening every door and window wide didn't placate him, nor lighten the sultry heat. Shucking out of his sweaty clothes to pull on a clean set helped his mood a little. The first mouthful of a cold beer helped a lot. He'd been grumpy all afternoon since he'd left Sienna at the café. He hadn't wanted to go back to work and leave her. All because of one kiss.

Kisses weren't meant to unravel a man. At a basic level they were the prelude to sex. At best they were exciting and tempting, and enjoyable. But to knock him off his feet with need and a longing for more—more than sex? It had never happened since Celia; shouldn't be happening now.

He wanted another Sienna kiss.

He needed the follow-through.

He longed to be with her, holding her, touching, talking. Being together.

He had to stay away. Or lose his mind over her, in her. *Sure you haven't already lost it?*

Somehow he had to get a grip or the next few weeks were going to be unbearable. First he'd phone Lance and take up the job offer. A year in Melbourne wasn't what he wanted but it would give him something to focus on, because living in his home city wasn't a walk in the park, and would need constant attention to detail to keep out of his mother's firing line. There wouldn't be time to think about a certain sexy, hot, kind, lost lady.

But he still had time to put in here first.

'Harrison, you in there?'

His stomach dived, while his pulse sped up. Straightening his shirt and running his fingers through his hair, he considered hiding in the wardrobe until Sienna got tired of knocking. 'Be right with you.' How was it she brought the child out in him?

'I'm making good on that wine we promised each other while waiting for the chopper,' she called.

'I thought I was bringing you a bottle when you were off your meds.' He stepped into the hall and nearly gasped at the beautiful apparition filling the front doorway. Slender, curvy in the right places, her long auburn hair brushed out over her shoulders, she looked cool and inviting. Should've gone into the wardrobe. This was going to be the longest bottle of wine he'd ever had the pleasure to drink.

'A girl can only wait so long.' Her head shot up, her eyes widened. 'Sorry, that sounded glib. Not me, for sure. But I wanted to say thank you for everything you've done for me since the accident. I really appreciate it.'

She appreciated it? That set him back. He was only doing what he did for anyone needing help, but doing it for—with—Sienna had been different, had drawn him in in ways he was struggling to understand. He certainly hadn't kissed someone he was *only* helping before. 'I like being there for you.' Damn, this sounded so trite. 'Get inside, woman, and let's open that bottle.'

She perked up at his rough tone. 'Inside? You are kidding me.'

'Make that out on the back deck.' Heat of a different sort was taking over and being outside seemed a wise move. He couldn't act on these rampant urges if the other neighbours were looking over the fence. Putting his beer aside, he dug into the cupboard for wine glasses. 'Half the deck's in shade.' Not that that would lighten the air.

'For the record, I'm off all medication now.'

'That's good news. Make yourself at home while I grab some cheese and crackers.'

The sweetest laughter exploded behind him. Jerking around, he couldn't believe what he was seeing. Sienna laughing so hard her body shook. 'Hello? What's so funny?' She looked so lovable he nearly reached for her. Nearly. The old voice that had played the warning tune all his life— don't get close, don't expect her to love you for who you are—sprang into life just in time. It took a couple of minutes to get a reply and by then mascara had done a number on her face.

'Your Christmas tree.' She wiped her hand across her cheeks.

'I like it. Especially the scent of pine.' They'd never been allowed something so uncontained at home, had had to have the perfect lines that only false trees came with. 'It's random.'

'Not one branch is in sync with another. The ends all droop, pine needles are already covering the floor. There's a bend in the trunk making it look drunk.'

'Probably is, considering I was having a beer at the time I put it up.'

'None of the decorations match, and there are big gaps where more are needed. It's a mess and I love it.' She leaned closer and pointed. 'There's a Santa with only one leg.'

'The reindeer will get him to the chimneys.'

'Come with me.'

His hand was gripped in a vice made of slim, warm fingers and he was being dragged out and down the drive, up the matching one and inside Sienna's apartment. 'See?' She pointed through to her lounge.

His stomach knotted. A fake Christmas tree all perfectly aligned, no branches going in all directions, and the decorations—well—they were gold and red, perfectly matched, placed equidistantly apart. There were no Santas with a leg missing, or bent stars the family who normally lived next door must have made with their kids. It was fake. 'I guess there are Christmas trees and then there's mine.' She so was not the woman he needed in his life, if he ever went off the rails entirely and fell in love. Sienna had some attributes he'd never be able to live with.

Yet Sienna was grinning as if this was the funniest thing to happen to her. 'We are so different, you and I.'

'We certainly are,' he agreed around the lump forming in his throat. He didn't want that, but nor could he deny the truth of it. 'At least we like the same wine.'

'You're showing me up again for the control freak I've become.'

Why was she looking so happy about that? She wasn't letting go because of him, was she? Where would that leave him when he needed at least one of them being sane and sensible in twenty days' time? Because he could feel it in his veins, his gut, his everywhere, that he was losing grip on reality. 'I never set out to do that.'

'Just being you did it. But you know what? It's cool. Today I broke out, bought a tree for the first time. And a new bike. And knocked on your door with a bottle of wine.'

'That's quite a day.'

'Yep, and there's one thing left to do.' She stalked over to the tree.

'No, Sienna, no. That's who you are.' She'd regret this tomorrow and he might get the blame.

Removing three red baubles, she randomly placed them elsewhere. 'Got any Santas left over in your place?'

'There's one I think a dog might've chewed.'

'It's mine for the next three weeks.' Then she hesitated, her eyes going to those three baubles, and for the first time he'd ever seen she nibbled her bottom lip. 'I can do this. I am a mixed-up puppy, for sure, but I can do it.'

Harry had to. He just had to. He could not stand that uncertainty suddenly reflected in her eyes and her voice. Three long strides and he was in front of her, wrapping his arms around her. 'Maybe, but mixed up's better than standing back and not getting involved.' His chin rested on the top of her head, his nose enjoying the apple scent of her shampoo. Then he heard his words. He didn't do involvement, so why had he put it out there that Sienna should?

'You reckon?' she asked against his chest.

Forget involved or anything else that might lead to trouble. Right now, holding Sienna was magic. 'Yeah.' He really, really did. Which led to the next thing he could no longer avoid. 'Mind if I kiss you?'

'You have to ask?'

'Not really.' Her body had somehow moulded to his, her breasts were rising and falling faster than they'd been moments ago. No, he didn't need to ask if she wanted it, but he needed to make sure she'd thought past the desire spiking in her eyes right now. 'Sienna?'

'We didn't even get to open the wine.' Her smile was impish.

'You were planning on seducing me?' For once he couldn't find a reason to argue with that.

A blush crept into her cheeks. 'Sort of. I think. Who cares?' Then she gave him his first full-blown smile and he was lost. He'd give her anything she asked for right at that moment.

'I don't.' His mouth came down over hers, and there was nothing else to be said. It was true—actions spoke louder than words. She tasted wonderful, her lips soft and demanding, her body pressing ever harder against his growing need.

And then there wasn't room for thinking, only feeling, falling into heat and need, wanting more. The kiss deepened, became long and hot and laden with all the things he'd dreamed of kisses being and hadn't found.

In the bedroom—how had they got there? Walked? Crawled?—Harry continued kissing her while his fingers worked at the buttons of her blouse. Her fingers plucked unsuccessfully at the stud of his jeans. Giving up with an exasperated growl, she ran the palm of her hand down over his arousal.

He wasn't going to last the distance if she kept that up. Ladies first. 'Let me,' Harry groaned through gritted teeth. In an instant his jeans were on the other side of the room, his shirt landing on top. Then he was tugging her blouse over her head, and pausing, his eyes scanning her beautiful breasts held in white lace. Breasts that he had to hold, to lick, to… 'Are you sure?' Those bruises may be fading but they were still real. He would not hurt her, would somehow manage to hold on to his almost out-of-control need for her if there was the slightest chance of inflicting even the smallest amount of pain.

Even as she grabbed her blouse from his hand to place it neatly on the chair, she was pulling his head close with her other hand so he had to touch that tormenting cleavage with his mouth. 'Don't you dare stop now. I want this.'

'So do I.' He began to kiss a trail of feather-light touches starting just below her ear, down her neck, and finally reaching that magnificent swell of her breasts. He breathed and tasted and touched. Sienna. Ah, Sienna. From the first time she'd approached him he'd had to have her, and now all his reservations flew out the window on a wave of pure desire and delight and wonder. This went way further than he'd been before. He couldn't get enough contact, wanted his whole body to know the experience of Sienna; her skin, her fingertips, her breath. Her heat and warmth and dampness.

Then her fingers were caressing his skin, moving down to his abdomen, and further down to encircle his manhood, and he was lost against her, his need throbbing as he touched and caressed and finally had her begging for release. He held her at the peak, knew her throbbing need, wanted her to scream her release.

'Harrison.' His name shot across her swollen lips in a long, sexy gasp right before shudders tore through her body, setting his already heated body on fire.

And then they were on the bed, Harry above her, his eyes locked on hers as he touched her again before joining her intimately. When Sienna attempted to pull him down onto her body he wasn't having it, held himself above, aware of those bruises and her ribs. And then he forgot everything else as he lost himself in Sienna.

Unbelievable. His lungs were dragging in short gasps of air, while his blood rampaged around his veins. As for his heart, it didn't seem to know how to cope, just squeezed intermittently. He'd never breathe normally again, never be able to stand upright. Every muscle felt incapable of tightening, his toes unable to wriggle. It couldn't get better than this.

Somehow Harry lifted away to lie on his back and reach for Sienna, to hold her carefully before lowering her over his body as gently as possible, careful not to knock her ribs.

Tears appeared in the corners of her slumberous eyes. 'I'm not fragile.'

Hell, he knew that. She'd just given him the most amazing sex he could remember.

It wasn't sex, Harry. That was making love.

Those short breaths stuttered, stalled, made his chest hurt. He didn't do making love.

Want to take it back?

No. Never. His hands splayed across the soft mounds of her butt. He was a goner. The words leaked from his mouth in a bemused whisper. 'Ah, Sienna, what have we started?'

CHAPTER EIGHT

'I CAN'T ANSWER THAT.' Sienna whispered her reply. Making love with Harrison was out of this world more than she could ever have imagined. 'I only know I want to do it again.' And again. Did she mention again?

'I'm more than happy to oblige, ma'am.'

Elbowing him in the ribs, she laughed. 'Cheeky.' Then she threw herself over him and obliged right back.

'Sun's going down. Let's go over to my deck, open a wine and eat some steak.'

'Spoken like a true man.'

'Lady, if you haven't figured that out by now then I've been wasting my time.'

Another laugh spilled over her lips. She'd been giving a lot of those lately. 'I'll make a salad.' Someone had to make some pretence at being healthy.

After some wine and barbecued steak with fries and salad they made their way inside and down to Harry's room to try out his bed. It worked perfectly. Sienna only hoped the remaining weeks before he left were enough to sate her appetite. And if they weren't? She wasn't going there. Why spoil a wonderful interlude with negative thoughts? At the back of her mind she knew this was a short-term fling and it would come to an end, but only then would she deal with the consequences. Now was about sharing meals and talking about the most ridiculous subjects, like what to wear when on a lion safari in Africa—she had no intention of going to Africa—and making love long and slow into the late evening. She reached for him and forgot everything else.

When Harry got up to go to work in the morning Sienna had headed through the fence to shower and plan her day. Now she was heading back over the harbour bridge to a mall to do some serious shopping after an eventful morning.

On the console of her car the phone hummed. A parking space was only metres ahead, which she snagged. 'Hey, Anna, how's things?'

'Just thought I'd let you know Felicity's working out well. How she copes with that CF all the time is beyond me. She's one tough cookie.'

'I know. It comes from having to be.' Sienna was thrilled Felicity and her friend were getting on well, and that Anna had no complaints about the girl's work efforts. It had been a stroke of genius putting them together, and there hadn't been a moment of doubt.

'So, how's it going with Mr Tall, Dark and Gorgeous?' Anna always switched subjects fast, said it was how she kept the opposition on their toes in court.

Denial was a waste of time. It was this woman's job to see through the most experienced liars. 'Great. And that's all I'm saying.'

'That's all I wanted to know.' Anna laughed.

Sienna wasn't buying it; she knew Anna too well. But she'd go along with her for now. 'You decided what you're doing Christmas Day yet?'

'Is he as good as he looks?'

No such thing as lead-in time. Nor was there any chance

she was answering that. She mightn't be a lawyer but she could play the game. 'You coming to my place or going to your cousin's?'

'Millicent's. Sorry, but the whole family will be there and the pressure's going on already. I'd better make an appearance, but have a spare bottle of wine in case I need to beat a hasty retreat.' Anna adored her family, but couldn't cope with the overwhelming love they dumped on her, saying it made her claustrophobic.

'Your favourite Pinot Gris, no less.' It was also her preferred choice, so it wasn't hard to please Anna.

'Well, is he?'

'Not answering.'

'I'll take that as a yes, then.' Then Anna turned serious. 'I'm glad you're having some fun; just don't get too involved, okay?'

'No chance. He's leaving at Christmas. It takes longer than a few weeks for me to let anyone get close.' Except she was already in deep, wanted more with Harrison than a fling.

Sure this has nothing to do with amazing sex and a hot man stewing your brain? Or has that knock on the head done some permanent damage?

'I'm not so sure about that. You might've met your match.'

Only a close friend could get away with that. 'I think it was the sitting on the side of the hill in the middle of a storm and seeing my life fly before my eyes that made me take a chance, but I'm still in control.' Sienna hung up and stared out the window. Wasn't she? Harrison wasn't into telling her much about himself, and that irked the more time she spent with him.

He hadn't answered when she'd enquired where his next job would be, and, not wanting to upset him, she'd left it alone. It wasn't as though knowing where his next job was would alter what was happening between them. From what she understood, his next contract could be anywhere. That much she did know about the man, and she really knew it as that was how her father operated.

She'd have liked to use Anna as a sounding board as she worked her way through the little she knew, but no matter how close they were, how much they knew about each other, she wasn't discussing Harry's personal life behind his back.

Harrison had issues with relationships and she could certainly understand why, but when he'd talked about his brothers his shoulders hadn't tightened, his mouth hadn't flattened, and there'd been love in his eyes. So he did have some good, honest relationships in his life. Why not try another one with a woman? Whatever had gone down between him and his parents kept him away from Melbourne and his brothers, but there had to be more to it. No one upped sticks and left without good reason.

Dad did it, and has never stopped, apart from my five years' gift.

Her father had been on a mission to get away from his father, to be the artist he was and not the lawyer his parent expected.

But that didn't mean Dad had to keep moving from place to place.

He could've settled anywhere. Couldn't Harry stop in one place, make a home for himself where he'd create a circle of friends, get a job that he'd see through the years, not the weeks or months?

Harry, Harry, Harrison. He was in her head no matter what. She smiled, rolled her shoulders, and tugged her phone from her pocket to call him. 'Hi, how's your day going?'

'Up and down. Four call-outs so far, which is kind of hectic.' Surprise shaded his question, 'What about you?'

Was he worried about why she'd rung? 'I went out to the aero club to make enquiries about learning to fly, got taken on a trial flight, booked my first lesson for Monday, and soon I'll hit the mall. Just thought I'd say hello, that's all.' That's all? It was momentous for her, probably mundane for many people, but then she didn't do hot sex with a man she didn't know very well. That had switched on all kinds of emotions; the strongest being happy.

'You were serious about learning to fly? I thought that was a passing notion to fill in time while stuck on that hill.'

'It's on the list.'

'Yes, I saw that,' he admitted through a laugh. 'Are you going to do everything you wrote down?'

'Seems like it.'

'Have you ticked off the one we've been working on?'

Heat spilled into her cheeks. 'It was tempting. I even had a red felt pen in my hand, but I chickened out.'

Have a fling with a hot man—that had happened. So far a one-night stand, but who knew what the coming days would bring? As for ticking that off the list, it kind of cheapened the experience, so she'd put the cap back on the pen and dropped it in the drawer.

'Got to go. There's been a crash on the Brinduan's.'

'Catch you later.' How cool was that? Talking to Harrison came easily, and as far as she could tell he hadn't been annoyed with her phoning. They'd even talked about last night in a roundabout way and she still felt comfortable with him.

On the footpath a woman was walking two dogs on leads and a pang of longing hit Sienna. Owning a dog would be fun, special, a pet to love and rush home to at the end of the day. And not fair on the animal with the long hours she kept. It wasn't even worth putting that one on the list. Nor was a pet a man replacement.

With all the moving around, then the years of studying, she'd never had a dog or a cat. Not even a pet rock. Her father had always said no when she'd asked for a puppy. They'd lived how he decreed, and that was that.

It's in his bones, the need to continually move, never sit still. You can't change him. Which means you probably can't change Harry. If you wanted to.

She didn't like the idea of losing Harry from her life, but she also wasn't about to make a fool of herself by asking that he change his lifestyle. Nor would she ever go back to the nomadic way of her childhood. She just couldn't.

Despite the sun pelting down on her arms, a sudden chill enveloped her. Had she got in too deep too quickly? Was she going to be able to wave him goodbye and not fall apart?

She had no choice.

She had to make the most of the days and nights she had. That was all. Suck it up and enjoy; laugh and have fun. This was starting to sound as though she cared too much for Harrison. Cared? Loved? Her heart skittered. She loved Harrison? As in give-up-the-life-she'd-made-for-herself-to-be-with-him love? To follow him anywhere? No. All her adult life she'd believed she would never do that for anyone, and that hadn't changed even if her lawns were mown in circles now and not straight lines. This wasn't love. More like deep friendship with benefits. *Gah.* That sounded terrible. Strange how she couldn't come up with a better description though.

Harry simply couldn't get Sienna out of his system, not even after the long, hot night they'd shared. From the moment he'd left her to go to work the hours had dragged, become laborious. He wanted more of what they'd shared throughout the hours in his room. Bad for the future. Good for now.

At least Sienna would be at home when he finished his shift, and they could continue working this *thing* out of their systems. She'd surprised him when she phoned, but he'd also been surprised at how good that had made him feel. Like he was a part of something he had never had. Seriously? A simple phone call and he was all hot and flustered? Who knew where they were headed with this…? This fling? Interlude? Getting together. It wasn't something permanent. They both understood they were opposites, wanted very different futures, so this had to be about having fun and using up some hormones. Right?

'Three minutes to destination.' The pilot's confident voice sounded in his headphones.

'Roger.' Where did Roger come from? Why didn't everyone say okay, or right, or Gerry? Harry shrugged and looked out the window, his head space a mix of the serious and ridiculous since making love with Sienna the first time. And something else he couldn't name. Couldn't, or wouldn't? Afraid to look the truth in the eye? 'What truth would that be?' he asked under his breath.

Connor tapped his arm. 'Over to the left.'

The state highway stretched north and south through dairy farms as far as he could see, with a small school directly below. The playground was devoid of children, while three adults stood on the perimeter, one holding high a home-made wind sock for the pilot. 'No sign of the bee swarm that struck our patient,' Harry tossed over his shoulder.

'Unless it had found a suitable tree, it wasn't likely to hang around. The kid was lucky to only receive a few stings.'

'More than enough to go into anaphylactic shock.'

Harry returned to staring out at the rapidly approaching scene, breathing deep, in and out, slowly, calming the sudden but familiar fear that he wouldn't be good enough for the child relying on him to save his life. Once the rotors slowed he'd be okay and the dread would recede, but until then he had to wait out this insecurity. He'd never worked out where it came from, but presumed it was from never getting anything right for his mother. Now he accepted this aberration as part of who he was when in doctor mode. Could be it had made him stronger as a doctor, helped him to see more clearly the priorities and how to stabilise patients successfully.

Whichever, it made him more vigilant, sharper, more connected with his patient for the time they were together, whether it was minutes or hours.

Hours. On a hill. Together. Time. Sienna. A sleepless night, her messed-up bed, his messed-up bed, a driving sense of time disappearing on him way too rapidly.

'One minute.'

Harry stood up, moved to sit on the edge at the door, his pack at hand, feet planted on the bar used to disembark. 'Here we go.'

The wheels touched the ground with only a nudge. The rotors were already slowing. Harry slipped to the grass and bent over low before running across to the men and woman at the edge of the playground. One man was pointing to a building and running in that direction. Harry charged after him. 'Is this boy known to have an allergy to bees?' he asked once within earshot.

'No, but we have two children who are so we recognised the symptoms and have the means to administer an antidote. One was administered within minutes of our realising what was going on, but Tommy's not reacting as we hoped.'

'Any known allergies?' he asked as they reached the boy, whose face was swollen to the point he couldn't open his eyes.

'Nothing on his records.'

'Hello, Tommy. I'm a doctor and I came on the helicopter to help you, so don't be afraid. Have you ever had bee stings before?' Find a country kid who hadn't, but Harry liked to start softly with little ones. He asked over his shoulder, 'Have the parents been told?'

'Yes, but, as luck would have it, they're in town. They're waiting there to see if you're taking Tommy to hospital.'

Harry nodded. That wasn't the best-case scenario. He preferred a parent to accompany children but it was what it was. 'Tommy, I'm going to give you an injection to help with the bee sting. Is that okay?'

'Will it hurt?' the boy asked in gasps, his shortness of breath another confirmation of an anaphylactic shock. 'The other one did.'

'If it does I'll buy you an ice cream when you're better.' He'd set himself up to fork out for a treat but that tiny smile the kid was giving back was worth it. 'First I'm cleaning your skin with a wipe.' He tore the packet open and sterilised Tommy's upper arm, then prepared the dose of epinephrine. 'What's your favourite flavour?'

'Chocolate with extra chocolate buttons.'

'That's mine, too.' Done, and not a murmur. 'There you go, sport.'

'You did it already?' The kid's face fell, and the gasps were harder. 'I didn't know.'

Harry patted his hand. 'That's because you're brave. Let's make it a double-sized cone.'

'Really? Thanks, mister.'

Harry picked up the boy's hand, began rubbing the back to bring the veins to the fore. 'One more prick, Tommy, so we can get fluid into you.' This wouldn't be so simple. The needle was bigger, but there were good veins to work with.

Sure enough, Tommy howled. 'Ow, that hurts!' His face fell. 'Do—do I still get my ice cream?'

'Of course you do, sport. But first you're going for a helicopter ride. Ever been in one of those?'

'No, but I want to.'

'Then let's get you on a stretcher and we'll go for a fly. I need you to lie still and not talk unless we ask you questions, okay?'

The boy nodded, his breathing still laboured, so the less he spoke the easier on his lungs.

'Do they breed them tough out here or what?' Harry said to Connor when the cannula was in place.

'I reckon. The kid could show some adults a thing or two.'

While Connor strapped Tommy onto the stretcher, Harry approached the teacher. 'Can you inform the parents Tommy has had a moderate reaction, but he's doing fine. We'll take him to North Shore Hospital. They can meet us there.'

North Shore, not Auckland and Sienna's ward. Not that she'd be at work, but even landing at that hospital had him thinking Sienna. An enigma. She managed to wind him up something shocking when no one else could, but more and more he was starting to see behind the control she exercised over herself and everything around her to the kind, fun-loving, gentle yet tough woman she was. As if she was deliberately letting him in one step at a time.

Only that morning when he'd left his bed to get ready for work he'd tripped over clothes lying on the floor. *Her* shirt and skirt. Unheard of. He recalled the first day he'd gone in to make sure she was all right and get her some food, she'd got up and made her bed, every corner tucked exactly the same, not a wrinkle in sight, the two stacks of pillows up against the headboard identical.

Last night had been the antithesis to that Sienna. There'd been no control whatsoever when she made love with him. She'd touched him sensually and with confidence, equally she'd received his touches and strokes, and when she came it was with abandon. Heat was firing in his veins just recalling last night. He needed something else to concentrate on if he wasn't going to look stupid when they landed at the hospital.

Harry checked out his patient. 'The flying's fun, isn't it?'

Tommy nodded, his lips pressed firmly together, not saying a word.

Harry grinned. 'Be better if you could see out, but I don't want you sitting up. You'll have to go flying again another day.' This time he got a bigger nod.

Glancing at his watch, Harry sighed. Four hours before he knocked off, if that happened on time, which often didn't in this job. All day he'd been counting the minutes, checking the time way too often, which only made the day drag ever slower. Last night after making love with Sienna in the early hours, he'd lain beside her until she fell asleep, only to give himself a lecture about letting her fill his head and waken his body in lasting ways. Finally unable to resist, he'd rolled toward her and tucked against her soft skin and nuzzled into her neck—and stayed with her until the sun came up. A first. On their first night together.

Bad move. Impossible-to-avoid move. Scary.

She'd told him very little about herself.

Oh, and he had given her a long account on his family and past, had he?

But he knew enough to believe her desire to hold sway over everything possible had been brought about by her childhood. Waking up every morning wondering where she'd be when she climbed back into bed at night time would be hard for anyone to cope with, let alone a child without siblings or friends to share the disappointments with. It made his blood boil to think of the young Sienna missing out on friendships and stability because her father liked to gad about the country as the inclination took him. Why hadn't her mother stood up to him?

'We're here,' Connor told Tommy. 'Doc Harry will take you inside.'

Good idea. Then he might stop thinking about Sienna for five minutes.

'You joining the gang at the pub tonight?' Connor asked after they'd dropped Tommy off.

It was Friday and a few beers at the end of the shift was mandatory. 'Might give it a miss tonight.'

Connor's head tipped back. 'You coming down with something?'

Lust. Needs. A great woman who looked amazing in black lace knickers and bra. Yeah, he liked coming down with her. 'Just got a couple of things on.' Such as sharing a meal and going to bed, and not getting up until the sun came up because he liked having Sienna's legs wrapped around his all night. 'Oh, forget it. Count me in.' They weren't joined at the hip. He didn't want that kind of relationship. He had to be free to come and go as he pleased, not trying, and no doubt failing, to keep someone else happy all the time. He had to fight this, not give in to the need clawing through him, making him giddy. 'I've got a phone call to make first.'

Back on the ground Harry loaded up with kits and gear and sauntered into the hangar, his phone at his ear. 'Hi, Sienna. You spend all your hard-earned dosh at the mall?'

'Had to take out a loan. You finished for the day yet?'

'Just knocking off and going for a beer with the gang. Not sure what time I'll be home.' Damn but if that didn't sound like a husband tied at the apron strings. 'We might head into town afterwards.'

'Sure. Have a good time. Might see you over the weekend.' If that wasn't disappointment coming over the airwaves at him then he was a monkey's cousin.

But he had to go with what he'd started, as they weren't in a relationship that did the 'where are you, why aren't you home with me?' stuff. 'Okay.' At least he'd told her, not just not turned up even when they hadn't made arrangements to get together.

'Maybe.'

Ouch. Exactly why he didn't want to get in too deep. He'd thought—make that hoped—they were on the same page, understanding there was no future together. Had Sienna got too caught up in the shared moments that she'd forgotten they weren't right for each other outside of a few hours in bed?

Oh, and you're not feeling the pinch? Not starting to wonder how you're going to leave without a backward glance come Christmas?

Definitely time for another phone call. One that'd get him out of the hot water swirling at his knees, his gut, his heart. His heart? No way.

Then do something about it—stop procrastinating.

His finger hit Lance on speed dial. Using his shoulder to hold the phone tight against his ear, he packed syringes into the kitbag and listened to the ringing tone, and waited, and waited, until the answering service came on. Tossing the phone aside, he denied the ping of relief that metallic voice had brought him. He needed to get his next job sorted, and the Melbourne position was excellent, would look good on his CV. He could make a life outside the hospital knowing it wasn't for ever. Face it, he told himself, there still weren't any other jobs waving at him, unless he made the call to go further offshore. Singapore, Hong Kong even. Or the States. He'd never worked that far afield and wasn't that keen. He liked Australasia, felt he belonged in either country. But getting away on or before the twenty-fifth was essential. Christmas with Sienna would be going a step too far, cementing another foundation in their relationship that suggested there'd be more foundations to follow.

Christmas was a time for family and close friends. The speed with which he and Sienna were approaching this *friendship* was frightening and there didn't seem to be any brakes in sight. It could go further than he wanted. Hurting her was not an option either, though the pressure was lessened knowing she was of the same thought process. Not that it had been put in words exactly, but they both *knew*.

Damn it all. He was a mixed-up bag of needs. 'You taking your heap of metal to the pub, Connor?' he called through the door into the staff kitchen.

'Yep. You want a lift?'

'Too right.' Better to leave his vehicle in the security of the flying rescue base than parked outside the pub all night. 'I feel a bender coming on.' Anything to drown out images of Sienna sprawled beneath him, her head tipped back in ecstasy. Her blistering smiles. Then the picture of her laughing over the differences between their Christmas trees. Oh, yeah, he had some serious forgetting to do.

But when Connor offered him the use of his beach house and fishing boat in Coromandel for the weekend he forgot all about forgetting and instead began dreaming of two whole days—and a night—away with Sienna doing things he enjoyed, and hopefully she did too. 'Thanks, man, I'd like that.' Fishing was his favourite occupation outside of work, and boats, being a part of the scene, were up there too. But higher on the scale for his excitement was Sienna. When he was meant to be remaining uninvolved, all he could think about was getting closer. He had it bad for her. Not that he was admitting that. No way.

CHAPTER NINE

'GET UP, LAZYBONES.'

'Harry?' Sienna forced her eyelids up.

'Don't tell me there's another man you allow to walk into your bedroom when the mood strikes him.' Gentle fingers teased at her hair, lifted it off her shoulder, ran strands over his palm.

'I wasn't aware I allowed you to do that. You kind of made yourself at home.' She reached for his hand. 'Not that I'm complaining.'

'Good. Now get up, will you?'

'Where did you come from? I didn't miss something, did I?' Like kisses and hands and making love? He hadn't called in when he returned home last night—at five past ten, and she'd been miffed—but he was here now and she didn't want to waste time complaining.

'Maybe.' His wicked grin sent a shiver down her spine.

'What time is it?'

'Five thirty.' He was dressed in shorts and a tee shirt that did nothing to hide the muscles underneath. His hair was a mess, and stubble highlighted his stubborn chin.

Reaching for him, she growled, 'I'm not getting up at this hour.' Not when she'd read an unputdownable book till two in the morning. 'Climb in here with me.' It was good she'd never asked for her key back.

He took three steps back. 'Uh-uh. No can do.' There wasn't even any regret in those dark eyes. Make that not much. 'We're going away for the weekend, and the sooner we're on the road the better.'

Now she was fully awake. Did Harry just say *they* were going away? Tossing the bedcover aside, she sat up. 'Tell me more.'

'Do you like fishing?'

Her nose screwed up. 'As in, getting all stinky and icky?'

'Yes, that kind of thing.'

'Not really.' Hold on. An image of her and Dad in a dinghy with lines over the sides while they talked about anything and everything came to mind. Warmth trickled through her. A good Dad moment. The meal of battered snapper afterwards hadn't been bad either. 'Okay, maybe a little bit.'

'Good, because we're off to Coromandel, where we have the use of a bach and boat for two days, starting now. Let's go.' He was already heading out the door. 'I've thrown some food in a chilly bin and we can stop in Thames township for anything else.'

'I haven't said I'm coming.' But she was already on her feet, heading for a quick shower to wash the sleep out of her eyes. A weekend away with Harry was right up there, was already negating that residual sense of let-down from last night.

Harry turned at the end of her hallway, a grin on his far too handsome face. 'But you are. Even if I have to toss you over my shoulder and haul you out to the four-wheel drive.'

Oh, yes.

Sinking against the wall, she laughed. 'Come on, then.'

He stepped towards her.

She beat a hasty retreat to the bathroom. Her body

needed a wash, while her head needed time to absorb this sudden change of plan. Not that she'd intended doing more than going to the market this morning.

Amazing how quickly a girl could shower, apply make-up and pack an overnight bag when she put her mind to it. Make that when she was excited about what might lie ahead. Lie, as in bed, and having out-and-out fun without the restraints of having to remember to go to work or clean the kitchen.

Harry must've been feeling the same as there was a load of humming going on as he backed down the drive. 'Five to six. I like your action, woman.'

'I'll need a caffeine fix before too long,' she warned while suppressing a smile. Couldn't let him think he could charge into her house, take over her weekend, and not have to pay in any way. 'Probably breakfast as well. Not a pot of yoghurt on the run, either.'

'Some women are so darned demanding.' He said that without a trace of annoyance. Further progress, and promising. This weekend was going to be something else.

Laughter bubbled up Sienna's throat. 'You wouldn't want a wimp, would you?'

'Sometimes they have their advantages. But mostly, no.' His hand touched her thigh briefly before returning to the steering wheel. 'So here's the deal. This bach's in Coromandel township itself, and there's a boat ramp near by. The weather's meant to be perfect for fishing. And if it's not we have other ways of making the most of our time.'

She could only smile through the images that that conjured up, none of which had anything to do with fishing.

'I hope you packed shorts and more of that sexy underwear, and little else.'

'Spoil all my surprises, why don't you?' There'd been a lingerie shop in the mall that she hadn't been able to walk past yesterday, so she'd added to the one decent set of black lace she owned with a red set, a cream one and a black chemise that had *her* blushing. Probably overkill, but she was making the most of having Harry in her life for this short time.

'To hell with fishing. Let's go straight to option two.'

'It shouldn't have been second anyway,' she gave him with a nudge in his ribs with her elbow.

'Good point.' Harry drove onto the southern motorway. 'Do you know the way or should I use the GPS?'

'I haven't been to the Coromandel since I was ten, but it's straightforward. Should be signposted all the way, since the peninsula is popular with locals and tourists alike.'

'You can recall your age at every place you and your parents stopped?'

'All part of keeping control over my life.' Had she always been a control freak? Mostly. It wasn't an adult habit she'd learned after settling in Auckland. Waking up every morning as a child reciting the name of the latest location they were staying at, reminding herself of her age, the plans for the day: all part of dealing with whatever would come her way over the next twenty-four hours.

'So when you lived in Thames, did you go fishing?'

'Down there everyone goes fishing.'

Breakfast in Thames township was long and leisurely. Sienna hadn't felt so relaxed in for ever. It was as though she and Harrison had always been together, the conversation easy and ordinary with no hidden agendas. She had to keep pinching herself to know it was real, that she wasn't dreaming. What residual tension still hovering in her system disappeared somewhere between the eggs Benedict and the strong coffee.

Finding their accommodation was straightforward, Coromandel having one main street. The bach was small and simply furnished. 'It's got everything we need,' Harry said as he dumped their overnight bags on the floor of the bedroom, his gaze fixed on the not so large bed. 'We can make this work.' He reached for her.

Sienna stepped close, plastering her overheated body to his, her nipples tight and sensitive against his chest, her thighs taking in the heat of his, her core hot and moist as his hardness pressed into her belly. 'We don't need a bed,' she whispered.

'Not every time,' Harry whispered back against her ear, his sharp breaths setting the skin on her neck alive with desire.

Sienna closed her eyes and tipped her head back to expose her throat for those lips that could send her into a frenzy with little effort. Harrison was irresistible. When he made love to her it was as though she became a different woman, one who could let go the locks on her self-control; could just enjoy; was able to give and take without questioning herself about everything, about if she was doing the right thing. Desire rocked throughout her as she gave herself over to Harry.

'So much for an early start to the fishing.' Harry grinned at her as he pushed the boat off the trailer into the water.

'Don't for one moment think I'm ever going to come second to a fishing rod and bait.' Sienna wagged a finger at him. 'Just remember there are more lacy pieces to keep your mind off that.' The simple but creative cream bra and G-string she'd put on back at home had had him agog earlier.

'Get in, woman,' he growled. 'Before I change my mind and haul your sexy butt back to the bach.'

Again she laughed, and clambered aboard the aluminium boat and used the pole tucked in the side panel to hold the boat in place while Harry parked the four-wheel drive and trailer on the roadside. Even going out fishing with Harry was fun. He was making her see everyday life in a totally different light, and that was special, if not a little scary. But she wasn't going to let the scary encroach today. It would spoil a wonderful time with someone she was caring about maybe a little too much.

Harry headed for the spot marked on a map by a cross that Connor had given him when he'd handed over the keys for everything. 'A GPS would be handy,' he muttered as he stared back to shore to line up the points marked in blue on the map.

'Excuses, excuses. If you don't catch a fish you're going to blame the lack of a GPS.' Sienna laughed as she dropped her baited hook over the edge, let the line out firmly and moved quietly so as not to disturb any cruising snapper, before sitting down on the edge of the boat to wait. 'Let me show you how it's done.'

'I'm told catching snapper takes patience and skill.' Those wide shoulders lifted and fell back into place.

Even out here in the hot sun, bobbing on the water, holding a rod, she could get distracted far too easily by his physical attributes. 'You think I don't have either requirement?' she asked with her tongue pressing out a cheek. One way of holding some control over the feelings watching Harry engendered.

'I am so not setting myself up for that fall,' he chuckled. 'I've never caught one before.'

'I might have. I don't remember, but I do recall being told not to drop things on the bottom of the boat as the sound will reverberate through the water and scare them away.' She also remembered her father catching fish. 'Dad got a massive eighteen-pounder once. I tried to reel it in but couldn't hold it.'

A gentle tug at her hook had her sitting up straight. 'Come on, take the bait.'

'You got one?'

Sienna grinned. 'I might have,' she teased, though it was only an inquisitive fish checking out what was on offer.

Harry was working from the other side of the boat. 'More than I've had so far.'

Sunscreen was smeared roughly on his face and arms while a wide-brimmed hat shadowed his cheeks. Knots formed in her stomach. This was the life. A day on the briny with someone she cared about. Now all they needed was a big, fat snapper.

An hour and a half later Sienna landed her second brim of the day. The fish had finally started biting in earnest on the turn of the tide, resulting in Harry having three in the chilly bin already.

'Not the big snapper everyone wants to catch, but young ones are juicier,' she said, now remembering catching a fish with her father. Those were his exact words. 'Thank you for bringing me here. I'm having fun.' The past and the present were melding, bringing together both her lives, making her feel a little bit more whole than she had done since she'd become an adult in charge of her life. All because of this man. Which meant he had the power to wreck it too. She shuddered.

'So you're glad I dragged you out of bed early?'

'There wasn't much dragging going on.' And that was what she had to hold on to now, not spend precious time thinking about what could go wrong. 'But if you'd thrown me over your shoulder and taken me away then, well, we mightn't have made it to Coromandel.' Not until they'd had time in his bed first.

Harry grinned. 'Let's head in. We've got more than

enough fish for dinner, and I'd like to go for a drive over the other side of the peninsula, mosey around some.'

'Sounds perfect.' More time getting to know Harry better, and better. The more she learned about him, the more she had to know. It was as though she had an insatiable appetite for all things Harry.

They moseyed and talked, drank a beer at a pub and talked, before Harry suggested they head back to their accommodation.

'I can run with that. In fact, I'm salivating about barbecued fish with fresh bread for dinner.'

'I'm disappointed.'

'Oh, all right, I'll dribble about testing out that bed again before the fish.' It wouldn't be hard to delay a meal for making love. There was hunger to appease her stomach, and then there was downright hungry for Harrison. No contest.

Later that night, Sienna fell into the deepest sleep the moment her head hit the pillow, only to wake when Harry wound his arm around her and snuggled into her back. Of course, she wasn't going to miss out on any touching time. Touching which progressed so that they weren't lying quietly for long.

'What made you want to become a doctor?' Harry asked when their heart rates were back to normal and their bodies languishing in after-match stupor.

Where did that come from? Sienna wondered. 'When I was eleven I had an appendectomy and according to my dad I didn't stop asking questions about why an appendix could get infected, what would happen if it wasn't removed, why it had happened to me. I know I wasn't satisfied with some of the answers nurses fobbed me off with, so when I got home I tried to find out everything I could. I was becoming a science nerd.'

'That was enough to make you want to do medicine?'

'Not at all. The nurses were kind and did everything to make me feel better—apart from answer my questions—and I planned on being a nurse when I grew up.'

'But that science nerd took over?' Harry's fingers were making soft circles on her skin.

'Yes, thank goodness. I can't think of being anything else.'

'Why paediatrics?'

Ah.

'I've always liked kids, especially the little ones with their inquisitive minds and willingness to try out anything before they learn they might get hurt or make a mistake.'

And I was never sure if I'd be lucky enough to have my own family.

'What made you take up emergency medicine? Apart from being an adrenalin junkie,' she asked.

'Not so much the adrenalin rush as the need for action, the urgency, putting things to rights as soon as possible. Not that I always save my patients, but I put everything on the line in the attempt.'

'How's that related to your past?'

'Don't hold back, will you?' Those fingers didn't hesitate with their circles.

'Sometimes it's the only way to find out what I want.'

They lay there for a while and Sienna knew he wasn't going to answer her. Disappointing as that was, she accepted his choice. They might be getting along better than ever but, since it wasn't a permanent thing, he didn't owe her details of his past. Unfortunately.

Then his hand stopped, his fingers splaying across her waist, holding her lightly, as if he was acknowledging they were together, however temporarily. 'As an emergency doc, I go in, do all I can to fix up a patient and discharge them, or get them stable to move on to a specialist ward where they'll get the care they need, and I move on to the next person needing immediate attention. In and out. Done and dusted. It works for me.'

'None of the long-term involvement.' Like his relationships with women by the sound of things. Like his connection with his parents. Short and sharp. Was everyone the result of their childhood? Their adolescence?

'Yeah,' he sighed, and his fingers went back to making those relaxing circles on her skin, making her sleepy again.

As Sienna drifted into sleep Harry stared at the darkened ceiling, trying not to admit the day had been one of the greatest he'd known in a very long time—if not the best ever. They'd been so comfortable together it was as though they'd known each other for a lot longer than a few weeks. Yet they knew next to nothing really, not the deep, hurtful reasons for being who they'd become. Sure, there'd been some give and take about family and growing up, but they'd only scratched the surface, yet still this felt different, like a real friendship. Friendship with benefits? No. A true, deep and meaningful relationship had to have it all. Was it possible that Sienna would give him that and more? Had they found a connection because they were both marked by their pasts? Did the reason even matter?

She flung an arm out, clobbered him lightly on the chest and muttered incoherently before settling further into her pillow.

He waited, breathing deep the scent that was Sienna. And knew hope. Knew they were special together. Knew this fling would still have to run its course because he wasn't prepared to take a risk again.

Sunday brought more of the same: sex, a leisurely breakfast, fishing… Except instead of driving along the coast

to visit other towns, the excursion drew to a finish. Reluc
tantly Sienna climbed into the four-wheel drive, sensing
that more than the weekend was over. If not today, then
soon. In one sense she felt happier than she had in a long
time, in another way she'd been given a taste of something
that was not long-term. 'That was fabulous. Thank you so
much for taking me along.'

'It wouldn't have been half the fun on my own.' Then
Harry gulped and went all silent on her. Realising he did
like sharing his time with someone? With her, even?

She wasn't asking. The answer might be confronting
and that was not how she wanted to end this interlude.
While the kilometres ticked over and the Coromandel
Peninsula disappeared behind them before the Bombay
Hills on the outskirts of Auckland began to fill their vision, she refused to dwell on anything but how enjoyable
these two days had been, not on what she'd been missing
out on. Finally she told Harry, 'I'd forgotten how much
fun doing something simple like fishing could be. Dad
and I used to go out quite a lot in some places we stayed.'

'You'd do it again?'

'With you?' She winced. Wrong thing to say. 'Yes, if
the opportunity arose, but then it's not likely to, is it?'

'I can't imagine I'll get another chance before I head
away.' Definitely reminding her he wasn't here for ever.

Then slam. Out of nowhere it hit hard.

*I am like Dad. I do enjoy wandering about with no
timetable to adhere to.*

Putting emphasis on keeping her life orderly all her
adult life was designed to make her feel normal. Other
people went fishing, played sports or partied, had lots of
friends around them, and stayed in one place. This past
week had opened her eyes, and she'd hardly started on that
list. All she had to do was find a balance between who she

needed to be and the girl who wanted to toss caution to the wind and have a ball every day. It did not have to mean reverting to the girl child on the road. Yeah, sure. 'I've been fooling myself all along.' A shiver rattled down her spine.

'What are you talking about?'

She'd said that out loud? See, already losing control. 'Nothing.'

'Sienna? What's going on?'

'Nothing,' she repeated. When had she become such a fool? It had taken nothing more than a wonderful weekend to loosen all the restraints she'd spent her adult life putting in place.

'You're shutting down on me.'

How could he think that? 'No, I'm not. Because of this weekend I'm starting to understand all that I've been missing out on, and that I can't let go entirely if I don't want to be like my father.'

Harry clenched the steering wheel. This couldn't happen. Sienna needed to live life to the full. She'd missed out on too much already, and he didn't want to be the one who showed how it could be if she wasn't going to follow through. That'd make him feel guilty, like waving chocolate in front of her then eating it himself. 'You've got another week's leave yet. Plenty more time to catch up on some of those things you want to do.' He also wanted this Sienna to become stronger. They'd got on so well he'd miss her if she reverted to her old self.

Like you're hanging around to notice?

His heart dived to his toes. No, but he could get something from knowing she was succeeding with moving on.

Not good enough, Harry.

It was the best he could come up with right now. He was not putting his heart on the line again, even if it had taken a hit these past couple of days. 'There's nothing to stop you carrying on with your list.'

Her gaze was fixed on something beyond the front of the car. 'I hope you're right. I've had a blast this weekend. But it's also brought back memories of a past I've strived hard to keep under lockdown.' Her finger was picking at the hem of her denim shorts above her knee.

'You're frightened?'

'What if I can't get myself back under control?'

'Would that be a bad thing if it's what you truly want?' What was an out-of-control-out-of-bed Sienna truly like? Exciting? Enchanting? Infuriating? Guess he'd never know.

I'd like to know.

Again, his heart did a dive. Again, he ignored it.

'I might not know where to stop. My father has never let me forget the time I said I wanted to take to the air and swoop over the world observing everyone and everything. It was a child's fantasy that had nothing to do with real life.' Pick, pick. There'd be no hem left if she continued.

But Harry kept on his own scratching. 'Do you really want to live in a way that doesn't make you happy?' He needed to know this. It would explain Sienna better.

Sienna swallowed hard. Why was Harry pushing her? It wasn't as if he'd done much more at sorting out *his* life. 'Being a doctor is more important to me than going off for a day on a boat or driving to another town for a week.' So was finding the love of her life and settling down to raise a family with him, but that was definitely under lock and key. Not going on the list. Her eyes slid sideways. No, Harrison was adorable, too easy to fall in love with—if she hadn't already. He *was* the man she'd like in her life for ever, but he wasn't available because of his own issues. Going there would be too frightening. But equally tempting.

'You've been happy these past few days. Keep pushing yourself, Sienna.'

'You're great at handing out advice, aren't you? Tried following any yourself?'

'Yeah,' he drawled. 'I took you away for the weekend.'

'You enjoyed it?'

'You have to ask?'

Sienna shook her head. 'No, I don't. But that frightens you. You're as messed up as me.' But nor did she want to stop being with him, while Harry might walk away from her when they got home. Which was moments away.

Harrison nodded. 'True, but there again, we went into this knowing there's a cut-off point, and to make the most of our time together.'

That was what was starting to frighten her. D-day. If she didn't want to stop seeing him now, how would she feel in a couple of weeks? Would her heart withstand the pain of letting him go? There were risks involved with living a well-rounded life.

Turning into his drive, Harry told her, 'I'll unpack and prepare some of that fish for dinner.'

'Sure. I'll take my bag home and grab some wine.' She eased out of the four-wheel drive and, hands on hips, stretched up on her toes to relieve the tightness in her back from the ride, while ignoring the bands of worry in her head. Enjoy the moment, seize the night.

Minutes later she walked around the corner of Harry's apartment and heard him saying, 'When's the start date?'

She paused, her heart nearly deafening her.

But not enough. Harry was saying, 'That'd work in perfectly with me finishing here at Christmas. I said I'd never return to Melbourne, but there's nothing else out there at the moment, and I need to leave Auckland.'

Sienna closed her eyes, trying to block out those words.

Too late. They were pummelling her from inside her skull. He *had* to leave Auckland. Because of her?

Harry hadn't finished. 'It might be time I gave the old city a try.' A pause, obviously listening to his caller. Then, 'You know if I say I'll take it on I'll see it through.'

Wake-up call, Si. Harry's moving on.

He'd never led her to believe differently, but hearing it for real hurt, and proved she'd been living in la-la land for the past few days. But what days they had been. The best. Couldn't complain about that. Would she do it all over if she'd heard this phone call beforehand? Yes. Without a doubt. Harry had been good for her. Could be better, but that wasn't going to happen.

'Okay, Lance, I'll give you a call after I've read the contract. I'd have done it earlier but I've been busy. See you.'

Busy. With her. Like she'd been a mission now completed. Two could play that game, and save her heart along the way.

Go home and tick off the fling early. Try not to let this get to you.

There were always going to be knock-backs but this was the one she really, really didn't want, even when she'd known it was coming.

At Harrison's back door she paused, drank in the sight of him as he put down his phone and began on the fish. Dressed in his knee-length shorts and a tee shirt that hugged his pecs, he was every inch the man of her dreams. How was she going to turn her back on him now that she knew every part of that body, the pleasure he gave? He took?

Harry looked up from the plates he'd filled with flour, breadcrumbs and a bowl with egg to coat the fish. 'Come in and pour yourself a glass.'

Suddenly her appetite for food fled, leaving her sagging—

yet still hungry for Harrison. She could stay for another night of wonderment, or she could go while she was able. 'I'll forgo dinner, thanks.'

'There's plenty of time tomorrow to do whatever's bothering you.' His words were straightforward, but the shutters were coming down in his eyes. He knew she was pulling out early. 'Don't end a great weekend this way.'

'Sorry, Harrison, I really am, but it's how it is.'

Turn around and walk. Now. Don't step closer to him... don't reach out to touch him.

Jerking about, she carefully trod down the steps and onto the path that'd take her back home to safety and control. Every time her foot moved forward she fought not to spin around and rush into his arms.

'Si,' Harry called softly, then said no more.

Sienna was relieved. There wasn't anything he could say. They were always going to break up, it had just come about quicker and sharper than expected. Hearing him discuss his next job was a timely reminder. She had to look out for her heart. She paused to draw a breath. But she'd continue her leave this coming week and start learning the intricacies of flying. It was time to find the middle road for her future. It mightn't end up being perfect, the man she might've begun falling in love with wouldn't be there to share it, but there would be more than medicine to keep her going. So sensible. So darned awful. Lonely. Heart breaking, if that cracking, aching sensation already going on in her chest was an indicator.

Back inside her apartment Sienna wandered through to the lounge and studied the Christmas tree. Her fingers itched to tidy it up, balance the decorations, make it all perfect—make her life perfect again. Turning her back on it, she went to poach an egg for dinner. Having no appetite didn't mean not eating.

Silence weighed down on her. The weekend had been full of laughter and chatter. She and Harrison saw eye to eye on many things, and argued like stink on plenty of others. That was one of the best things about their relationship. Huh? Before the mind-zapping, body-melting sex? Yes. No. Oh, whatever. It had all been magic, and now it wasn't. There was a quick fix—go back over the way and apologise and enjoy being with Harry until he left at Christmas. And *then* go through this indecision and pain.

It hurt now. It would only get worse if she made love to Harrison for days and nights all the while knowing she was snatching at moments. He was leaving Auckland. Putting distance between them. Guess it was better than him staying here where she ran the risk of bumping into him through work.

Under the hot shower she rested her head against the glass wall and let the warmth relax the tension in her back, her arms and legs. Unfortunately, the heat did nothing for her heavy heart and the sadness swamping her mind. This was reality. It was over with Harrison. Overhearing that phone call had been the catalyst to protect herself, making her understand that a fling wasn't done in isolation. It involved head and heart, new needs and longings she hadn't known before and didn't want to let go; and afterwards none of the emotions could be switched off with a single flick.

The coming days with him right next door were going to be difficult. Painful. Filled with temptation to rush across and pick up where she'd left off.

But I will get through them. I have to. Please.

Starting with ignoring the dull thud going on behind her ribs, constantly reminding her of what she was walking away from.

CHAPTER TEN

'HARRY...'

Sienna's sweet voice broke through the clouds in his head.

Timing was everything, apparently. He could've checked the mailbox ten minutes ago, instead of sitting staring at his feet thinking of what might've been with Sienna if he had the guts to give it a go. He could've prepped the steak he'd bought for dinner before he came out here. By then surely she'd have gone inside. 'Hey, there. How's things?' His hands gripped his hips. It wasn't that he didn't want to see her, more that he already knew the pain that would follow as he watched her walk back up to her apartment alone.

Sienna swung around the end of her drive, a large smile splitting her face. 'You've got to see this.'

He did? What was so important she wanted him to take a look? It could be her report card from primary school and he'd willingly read it. 'What've you got?'

'My very own pilot's logbook.' She skidded to a halt in front of him and opened to the first page. 'See, those are my hours, and that shows what the lesson was about, and that's the type of plane.'

'Whoa, that's awesome. You've done one-hour-five in total over two days?'

'The lessons are intense and, therefore, not very long at first. But, Harry, it was fantastic. I'm learning climbing and descending.' Her hand rose and fell in gentle waves. 'Tomorrow I'm starting on turns.'

'Who'd have thought you could get so excited about making a turn?' His laugh was low and a little sad. Had she been excited when she did an about-face on him?

'I know.' She snapped the book shut. 'Sorry, I got a bit carried away.' Stepping away, she drew her shoulders back, determination now covering her beautiful face. 'How're things with you?' Determined to be polite, not excited and happy?

That hurt. He didn't deserve it. They had both agreed to a fling, not for ever after. He just hadn't been ready for the finish, was all. Was still getting used to it. 'I've left a chilly bin by your back door with some fish fillets on ice. You might want to eat them tonight or put them in the freezer.' He began to walk away, unable to stand there and not haul her into his arms and kiss the daylights out of them both. Yeah, he still wanted her. And that was something that had never happened before, not in a long time at any rate.

'Thanks.' Then, 'Harry, are you all right? Why aren't you at work?' She sounded concerned.

Unfortunately he couldn't use it to his advantage. 'I'm fine. Got today and tomorrow off as I'm working the weekend.'

'I'm glad nothing's wrong.'

Oh, believe me, plenty's wrong.

How to fix it was another story. He stomped up the drive and inside to unpack groceries, open every window in the place, hang out the washing. Oil and season the steak. Mundane, meant to distract the picture of Sienna seared at the front of his brain, and not working. Now what? He'd been on the go since six and it was only ten and he didn't know how to fill in the rest of the day. This was when living in a town where he didn't know anyone other than colleagues sucked. No one to ring and say 'Want to go for a run, or a beer, or a game of squash?' At least returning to Melbourne would change that, if nothing else.

No point looking over the fence. Sienna had gone out again, probably headed to the aero club and another lesson that got her all wound up in a ball of barely contained excitement. He'd never seen her so happy. Or maybe he had when they made love, or when she'd caught her first fish the other day. Long may it last. She deserved it. If only he could find the tenacity to hang around and share her happiness. Harry shivered. This wasn't about doggedness. It was about risk-taking, and where his heart was concerned that wasn't happening.

So he needed to find something to fill in his time.

The lawns could do with a cut. He got a sweat up fast in the heat. It felt good, worked some of the hurt out of his system. Hurt he shouldn't be feeling. They'd had a fling, and now Sienna had beat him to pulling the plug. If he'd done it. The weekend in Coromandel had shown him another side to Sienna, and to himself. It had woken up those old dreams of love and family and settling in one place.

His legs ate up the lawn as he raced round and round. The middle came way too fast. He needed to expend more energy. Sienna's lawns could do with a cut. She wouldn't thank him. Too bad. He didn't need thanks. Just a kiss.

No, not a kiss, you idiot.

She could ignore him for all he cared. But he would mow the lawn for her.

Round and round and round until he reached the centre.

She'd go ape—no straight lines to be seen, but there was nothing she could do about it, just as there was nothing he could do about her calling off their fling before he was ready.

Now he'd earned a beer. But who to call? Everyone was at work. Except his neighbour, and he was not calling her. Grabbing a glass of icy water, he went to find his laptop and cruised the medical sites for jobs that didn't involve Melbourne, and his parents, and all the things he'd spent years avoiding. More importantly, he had to find one that wasn't in Auckland, because he needed to avoid Sienna more than anything. She'd pressed some buttons, kick starting emotions that he didn't want to admit to. So he'd go for broke and do his usual—he'd move on.

On Wednesday afternoon Sienna indicated to turn into her driveway but the old man in the wheelchair kept on going right into her path. 'Watch out.'

Clunk. The wheelchair bounced off her bumper, teetered on one wheel before banging down on the other and rolling on down the road.

'What?' She quickly pulled into her driveway and hauled the brake on before leaping out and running after the man.

He was out of control and heading into the path of another oncoming car. 'Stop,' she shouted. 'Look out.'

The driver of the car couldn't hear her with her windows closed, and if the old man had he didn't understand or was incapable of acting on it. She ran, her breath stuck in her throat as she waited for the inevitable, and hoped impact wouldn't be too nasty.

It was worse. The chair slammed square on the front grill and the man was tossed out and under the engine.

The car wheels squealed as brakes were applied, then the driver screamed. 'What happened? Where did you come from?'

Sienna reached them. 'Turn off the motor while I check out how the man's situated under there.'

'Shouldn't I back off?'

'No,' she all but shouted. 'The gentleman might be caught on a part of your car and we don't want you dragging him along the road.'

The woman blanched. 'Just as well you're thinking straight. I'd have injured him even more.'

Deep breath as she kneeled down. 'It's all right. We've got this.'

'Is he caught in the wheelchair?' came a familiar voice.

'He's strapped in,' she told Harrison as she took in the odd angle of the man's arm and the blood pouring from the side of his head. And the lax mouth. 'I wonder if he had a medical event. He wasn't controlling the wheelchair at all.'

'I heard a bang and came rushing out to see what had happened.' Harry lowered onto his stomach and pushed forward, his head disappearing under the car, still talking. 'Did he hit your car first?'

'Bounced off the bumper.' She squatted beside Harry and looked at how to disentangle their man. 'This isn't going to be easy.'

Wriggling out, Harry stood up and pulled his phone out. 'I'll call 111 and then get my medical bag. Do you have one in your apartment?'

Shaking her head, she admitted, 'Only the basic bandages and creams.'

'Our man needs a lot more than that.' Harry rattled off details and the address to the emergency service.

Sienna straightened up. 'I'll get your gear. Emergencies are more your strength.' She could do what was required, but why not give the old man the best chance they had available and right now that was Harrison?

'See if there's a crowbar in the garage, would you? I'd like to shift this bumper off his chest if I can.'

'On my way.' Ducking inside the apartment, she retrieved the medical kit before heading into the garage to search through the biggest collection of tools she'd ever encountered. Everything but a crowbar. Would a hammer be large enough? Snatching the largest one, she spun around to head outside and stopped. A crowbar hung from a nail on the far wall, half-hidden by a raincoat. 'Yeah.'

Back beside Harry she opened the kit so he could get at anything he needed. Then she began checking over the man's legs, searching for broken bones.

'I think he's had a stroke,' Harry said quietly.

'That would explain the loss of control over the wheelchair.' At least he was still breathing. 'Lack of consciousness?'

'There's an impact injury to the skull, but the stroke might've caused him to lose full consciousness before. Did you notice anything out of the ordinary?' Harry was working at stemming the bleeding.

'Only that he didn't seem to see my car, nor hear me when I yelled to watch out.' Shuffling closer, she put her hand over Harry's where he pressed against the wound. 'Let me do that while you try and shift the bumper.'

Harrison handed over immediately and studied the bent and buckled wheelchair. 'It's stuck hard. We've got the fire service coming. Those guys will have cutting equipment. I doubt the crowbar will be of any use without hurting our man further.'

'There's a siren now,' a woman said in a trembling voice.

Sienna glanced up to see the driver of the car watching them worriedly. 'You okay?'

'Not really. I could've killed him.'

'He is alive, but we think he's had a stroke, so don't go

blaming yourself.' She turned back to their patient and with her free hand began checking his pulse again.

'Can you move left a bit?' Harry asked as he bent back some broken wheel spokes.

'Sure.' Working alongside Harrison felt right. They just clicked. As they did with most things. Except her lawn. Even in her new, slightly relaxed state, those circles drove her nuts. 'Thanks for mowing the lawn, by the way.'

He didn't look her way, so focused was he on the bolt he was trying to undo, but his grin was obvious. 'No problem.'

She wouldn't give him the satisfaction of knowing he'd annoyed her. If he hadn't already guessed. Plastering on a big smile in case he looked her way, she continued checking her patient.

Her smile faltered. She dragged it back in place. Harrison was a problem, but that didn't mean everything else was stalled. By starting to do things outside work she might become better prepared for a man in her future, whether it was Harrison or not. In her chest her heart slowed, unhappy about the idea of any man other than Harry. Okay, it seemed Harrison owned her heart. But for now she had to concentrate on getting her act together, becoming a rounded person with more to her bow than medicine.

If she had to pretend to be happy, then she'd keep pretending until it became real.

'Harry, got a minute?' the base director called as he made his way out of the changing room, dressed in light shorts and an even lighter shirt, the Santa suit he'd started wearing this week hanging on the peg for tomorrow. Seemed the kids loved Father Christmas turning up to save them.

That blasted humidity was doing a number on Harry again. 'Sure, Derek.' It was Friday night and he'd prefer a cold beer with the crew than what was probably going to be a discussion about how he thought the past three months had gone for him.

A chilled wine with a certain lady as company would be even better.

Yeah, well, that was not happening. Wine hadn't been his favourite drink until a little over a week ago and he needed to move past that. The door had slammed shut on that particular relationship.

Sienna was busy getting on with her life and he was still in his nice, comfortable holding pattern of work, drinks with the crew, and avoiding everything else. Except the more he saw Sienna going out or arriving home well after him, the angrier he got with himself. Doing the same old same old wasn't working any more. He wanted more, wanted to partake in living, not remain on the sidelines. In other words, he wanted to watch trees grow. Just as Sienna was doing. If she could sort herself out, surely he could manage the same?

'Take a load off.' Derek nodded to the chair on the opposite side of his desk and handed across his dream libation.

'You read my mind.' Hopefully only about the beer.

'It's stinking hot and we're both off duty, so why not? This will hardly touch the sides.'

Harry poured beer into his mouth, savoured the chill, the flavour, then swallowed. 'You softening me up for extra shifts?' Some of the medical staff were trying to get days off for Christmas shopping and other pre-season stuff that needed doing before hordes of family descended upon them. He didn't have that problem.

'There is that, but what I want to ask is—what are your plans once you're finished with us? Have you got another contract lined up?'

'Sort of. I haven't dotted the i's and crossed the t's but there's a contract in my inbox.' It needed signing and returning, fast. The days in Auckland were running out and he didn't want to be left languishing. Definitely not in Auckland, where there was every chance of bumping into Sienna. Time to put this little glitch behind him and pull his finger out. He had to or go spare with need. He had to get away. Siberia wasn't quite on the cards, but desperation did strange things to a man. 'I've been offered the HOD's position at Melbourne General for a year.'

The man opposite him nodded. 'That sounds too good to turn down.'

'It is, but for personal reasons I'm hedging my bets.' Which wasn't fair on Lance. He'd get on to that the moment he got home tonight.

'Then you might be interested in staying on in Auckland. Working with us,' he added quickly.

He'd walked into that one, hadn't he? Too busy thinking about Sienna. 'I'm not interested in continuing to live here either.' But even as the words formed he was weighing up everything for and against. Getting away from being next door to Sienna was right up there, but there were other apartments or flats in this city that he could rent. On the plus side it meant not returning to Melbourne. Harry continued. 'Tell me more about this position. How long do you need someone? What's the role?'

'This is confidential, you understand.'

'You have my word.'

'I'm going to Europe indefinitely with my wife. She's Italian and wants to spend time with her relatives over there. There're also lots of other countries we'd like to visit for more than a day or two crowded amongst millions of tourists, which is possible if we're there out of peak season.'

'Sounds fantastic.' Harry drained his bottle. That sort of trip wasn't something he'd do but then he didn't have anyone to share the experience with, so he'd never given it much thought. It wouldn't be half as enjoyable doing it alone.

Do you want to travel, Sienna?

The beer choked him. Wiping his mouth with the back of his hand, he stared at his white knuckles. He'd got it bad. Perhaps he should go abroad, work in faraway places, and get over what ailed him.

Derek got two more beers from the small fridge shunted into a corner out of the way of medical packs and equipment. As he handed over a bottle he looked around his cramped office and then outside to where the helicopters were parked. 'This would be a permanent position.'

'Has this been approved by the board?' There was no way the base director could make the offer off his own bat. The board would want a say in the matter—*all* the say.

'They know and have agreed for me to approach you. You've impressed everyone with your cool, calm way of approaching patients and staff alike. If you don't want to accept then we'll have to go through the laborious process of advertising.'

'Laying it on thick, aren't you?' Harry chuckled.

'Of course. Tell me you're not a little bit interested.'

The guy was good at this. 'You already know the answer to that. I am thoroughly enjoying working here.'

'But you're not so keen on our great city.'

'A city is a city.' *Saying too much, Harry.*

'So there's someone in this particular city you want to avoid? Don't you know the population is well over a million and a half?'

Yes, he did, but there were only so many hospitals and paediatric wards to go round, and in this job he visited all of them one week or another. 'I'm not going to give you an answer today.'

'Fair enough. That's better than I'd expected after you said you wanted to get away. But don't take too long, eh?'

'I can shake on that.'

'No need. Your word's good enough for me.' Derek shoved his chair back and stood up. 'Feel up to a couple more beers at my place along with a barbecue and meeting Lisa?'

He knew when he was being set up. All part of the conditioning process, and no one could blame this man for trying. 'I'd like that.'

'Good. Hans and his wife will be there too.' As in board-member Hans.

Too late to pull out—if he wanted to, and right this moment he wasn't sure. Something about staying on in this particular service, this city, was pulling at him. Something he suspected revolved entirely around Sienna and what they'd started. She might've finished it but his heart still had to catch up, let her go. Or dive in deep. He shivered. 'No problem.' He'd buy a bottle of wine for Lisa on the way. Which promptly reminded him of the last bottle he'd bought and who for. Which in turn underscored exactly why he had to say no to this opportunity. Or did he?

Sienna would tell him where to stick that thought if she knew. She'd feed him back his own line about avoiding life. Damn, but they were alike, yet acting out their lives in opposite directions. Or had been until she cycled off that hill. The thought of signing on for a position with no end date in sight no longer frightened him as much as it once had. Getting old? At thirty-six? He grunted a sour laugh. No, but this constant moving around was getting old. The idea of waking up to the same possessions around him, the same people every day, the same town or city, was starting to become a persistent nag in the back of his head.

I planted trees I want to see grow.

Sienna. Of course. Damn her.
Get out of my head, will you?

'I need wine.' A glance at her phone told Sienna it was well after nine. Hardly wine o'clock. Too bad. Her last glass of wine had been on the lawn of the bach in Coromandel, with Harry beside her telling some embellished story about a road trip he'd done in outback Australia. She'd poured one the first night home after the weekend, and ended up tipping it out, unable to face it on her own. Wine was for enjoyment, for sharing, for laughter and chatter.

And for celebrating spreading my wings. Tick.

There was a bottle of champagne in the back of the fridge, put there yonks ago when a grateful parent had given it to her for saving his daughter's life. Normally gifts from patients and parents went into the staff pool, but Dale had insisted she take this one home—the patient had been his niece. The bottle had languished in the fridge waiting for the right occasion. Well, tonight she'd finally found one.

The sound of the plastic cork popping made her smile, but as she poured the liquid into her glass the smile drooped. Champagne wasn't made for drinking alone. New life, remember? The list was making things happen. Celebrate.

A vehicle pulled into the drive next door, making her pause. Harry was late home. Friday-night drinks with the crews? But his arrival was perfect timing if she had the courage to invite him in for a drink. He'd say no. She'd apologise for everything she'd said. He'd still say no. Did she need that?

Yes, if she was going to keep moving forward. No, because rejection stung.

'Harry,' she called over the fence. 'I've just opened a bottle of champagne. Would you like a glass?' He was probably thinking she had an alcohol problem, given the time of night.

His head appeared around the back of his four-wheel drive. 'I've already had a couple of beers.'

'Fair enough.' She turned away. At least she'd tried.

Call that trying? Come on, Si.

Turning back, she drew a shaky breath. 'I'm celebrating a grand total of three hours ten minutes' flying time.' Nerves warred with jubilation. 'I don't really like drinking alone.'

His sigh was loud enough to be heard across the fence. 'Pour me a glass. I'll be right over.'

She headed inside so she couldn't hear when he called out his change of mind. Champagne spilled over the bench as she tried to fill a glass for him.

'So you're still getting a buzz out of heading up into the sky in a tiny flying machine?'

Sienna whirled around to stare at him standing in her doorway. 'Absolutely. I should have done it ages ago. Right from the first time rolling down the runway it's been thrilling. Very different to anything I've ever done before. Exciting, scary, demanding.' Slow down. Harrison could still disappear on her if he thought she'd lost her mind.

He stepped inside. 'So your fear of heights hasn't raised its head as the hours go up?'

Handing him the glass with champagne inside and on the outside, she stared at him. Wow, he was gorgeous, but she already knew that. Now that she'd experienced his lovemaking there was no going back on her feelings for him. All she could do was rein them in while he was close. 'Not one moment of trepidation.'

'So no jumping off a building needed.' That couldn't be disappointment in his voice, surely?

The bungee-jumping idea still rattled her. 'No.' Not even with you.

'I'm impressed.' Harrison moved across to the table and pulled out two chairs, tilting his head at one.

Sinking onto the seat, she sipped her drink, needing the false sense of courage it gave her. If only he'd smile at her, turn her insides to mush. Then what? They had fallen out; he was here out of politeness, not because he wanted to make love with her.

'Thanks, so am I. I haven't been scared once. Honestly, when I hold the controls and the instructor tells me to pull back slowly and steadily and the nose of the plane comes up and then we're off the ground and the plane's flying because I did that—along with a lot of help—it's the most incredible sensation out there. I can't get enough of it.'

A bit like you. I can't get enough of you, and yet there are times when I want nothing to do with you.

Harry sat, stretching his legs half across the dining room. 'Go you. What's next? Going onto the bridge of a cruise ship and taking that out to sea?'

He'd seen her list, knew everything that was on it. Including having a fling. Tick. She hadn't written 'end the fling quickly' but mentally she gave that a tick too. 'I might plan a short trip to South America to see Dad some time in the new year.' Since when? Since right this moment. It wasn't her preferred option but it was a load better than not continuing to push the boundaries. 'I'm getting the hang of this.' Hopefully not so much that she turned into a clone of her father.

'You won't want to return to the ward.'

His ability to read her mind still flummoxed her. 'Yes, I will. I'll always be a doctor at heart. That's who I am before anything else.' The wine was top-of-the-range yet she wasn't getting the buzz she'd expected.

'So you'll start using up some of the leave you've got accruing.' He swirled the champagne around in his glass, staring into it as if he was looking for something. But all he said was, 'Are you heading back to work on Monday?'

'Yes. The body's back to normal, no aches or bruises.' Though sometimes if she moved suddenly her ribs would give her grief.

Harrison's eyes widened when she said body, but he didn't give her the once-over. There certainly wasn't any lust going on in his expression. He had got over her—very fast. 'That's good. I saw you coming back from a ride last night. The new bike looks like it's got every bell and whistle going.'

Had he been looking out for her? Can't have. He was giving off vibes that said he wanted nothing more to do with her. 'I upgraded.' Damn this. 'What have you been doing since the weekend other than work?'

His shrug was eloquent, and really annoying. 'Not a lot. The job takes most of my time, as you know.'

'Sure. But there's more to life than work,' she gave back, tired of being the only one who had to sort out her life. 'You could find a permanent job somewhere and stop running away.'

Rolling his glass back and forth between his hands, he glared at her. 'You don't pull any punches, do you?'

Her chin jutted forward. 'I'm learning. And guess who taught me?'

The glare faded, replaced with something like longing. 'Glad I've been some use.'

'Some use?' Harrison hadn't pushed her off the road that night, though he had distracted her enough to lose concentration, but he hadn't let her get away with her need to keep everything under control either. 'That accident woke me up to certain things.' Be honest, if nothing else. 'But your irritating habit of rubbing me up the wrong way has helped. A lot.'

His eyes widened again, and his fingers relaxed their dangerous grip on the glass. 'Even when you didn't agree?'

'Mostly when I didn't agree with your damned fool suggestions.'

'None of them were foolish, just backing up what you really wanted to do in the first place.'

Man, he could be such a know-it-all.

'You—'

No, stop.

Playing *You said... I said; if I can do this, you can too* wasn't going to get her anywhere. He was going to head back over the fence shortly, leaving her to her sad heart.

'This is crazy.' Draining her glass, she reached for the bottle. 'More?'

He'd barely started the first glassful. 'No.' The glass started twirling between his fingers again.

Silence fell between them.

Sienna sipped her wine, trying to enjoy it. This was a celebration, after all. Not that anyone was dancing or singing.

'I got a job offer today.'

Great. Not. No denying he was leaving now. Melbourne here he comes. 'When do you start?'

'I haven't said yes.'

He'd been cagey the night she'd overheard his side of the conversation. Might as well pretend she knew nothing about that. 'Is it too close to your current one?' As in, right here, staying in the apartment next door and having to see her most days of the week, close?

'It is my current one.' Now he emptied his glass in one long swallow.

That got her attention. 'Seriously?' Definitely as in right

here, staying in the apartment next door and having to see her most days of the week, close. Her heart whacked out of rhythm, unable to absorb this news.

'As I told you, I haven't said yes yet.'

He didn't have to sound so down about it. Sienna pushed the bottle across. 'So my neighbours aren't returning?' She wanted to be excited at the chance Harry might be next door for a while to come, but how could she be when the dark expression on his face told her it was the last thing he wanted? She might love him, but she didn't want him at any cost. He had to feel the same about her and obviously that wasn't the case. Had never been.

'Okay, not quite the same job. Yes, your neighbours are returning, but the base director is leaving and his job's mine if I want it.' The darkness was still there in his eyes, his mouth tight, his cheeks pale.

'You're not exactly leaping in the air with excitement so I'd suggest you turn it down.' How she managed to get those words out was beyond her, but they had to be said, and in the long run this was about protecting herself. Draining her glass, she struggled to swallow the now less than wonderful liquid for the lump in her throat.

Don't let him ruin your day.

With grim determination she refilled both glasses and raised hers to tap the rim against Harry's. 'Here's to making the right decision.'

He didn't return the tap. 'How does anyone know they've got it right? You hear so often about people at crossroads and selecting one way when it turns out the other would've been best.'

'Or worse.' This time it was easier to swallow. 'Like you've told me, don't let the past hold you back. Work out what you want and go for it, boots and all.'

'Where do you want to be in six months' time?' There

was genuine interest in his eyes and face, and his voice had lightened from that dark huskiness.

Living with you.

But that wasn't something she could share. It was so new and raw, so fragile, she could break if he didn't treat her with care. And he had no reason to. She only had herself to blame for falling for him. 'It's still a work in progress.'

His face shut down, and he stood up, setting his glass aside. 'Time I headed away. It's been a long day.'

The fingers holding the stem of her glass whitened. 'Sure. Good luck with the decision about the job.'

'Yeah, it isn't easy.' He stood looking down at her, something very like need in his gaze, making her heart whack harder. But then he took a step away. And another, aiming for her back door. 'Thanks for the drink.'

The door closed behind him with a soft click. He was gone. Again.

No way would Harrison take up the offer of a permanent position with the rescue service. 'He's just like my dad.' Gulping a mouthful of champagne didn't ease the pain, even as bubbles tingled on her tongue. 'Never stopping in one place long enough to make friends.' This had been a celebration that had turned to mud, but she wasn't giving up. After pouring the last of the wine into her glass she leaned back on her chair and stared at the door, hearing that click over and over. Harrison had gone. She'd been the one to leave him on Sunday, and the result was the same. It hurt beyond what she'd ever known. Worse than when her parents broke up and her dad left for good. This was closer, was her pain. It broke her heart, that was what it did. Smashed it to smithereens, and there wasn't a glue in the world that could hold it together now. 'I want to follow you to the end of the earth, Harry, but I can't. I would destroy both of us, living your way of life. It's in me to move around non-stop and yet I hate doing it, hate the consequences. So I won't do that, no matter what the cost.'

Si. Harry had called her Si. Tears welled up and spilled over, to run down her cheeks and drip off her jaw. She liked that. 'I love you, Harrison Frost. I love you like I've never loved before. And won't ever again. You are the one.' She whispered these final sentences, afraid to say them too loud in case they ricocheted around the room for ever.

CHAPTER ELEVEN

HARRY PAUSED AT the gate in the fence they'd begun using this past week. Sienna was still talking. To him? Couldn't be. Had to be having a yarn with herself, or one of the Santas on her tree.

'Just like my dad.'

The pain and sadness wound around him, made him cross his arms to keep her away.

'Never stopping in one place long enough…'

Harry sank to his haunches, unable to stop listening when he knew he should. Eavesdropping wasn't gentlemanly. Or polite. But how did he turn off from that longing, that despair? He couldn't. Every word dug into him, twisted his gut tighter, smacked his heart. He understood her need for control; she had to hold on to what was around her, to keep her life on the straight and narrow. She believed she had her father's genes, but he didn't accept that. She was too grounded, just didn't know how to let go a little. Though these past two weeks she'd gone some way to achieving that.

He didn't want to hear any more. Sienna's sadness was too hard to deal with. It resonated with his. He leapt up and headed for his deck, where his shoulder slumped against an upright holding the roof above, the light drizzle he hadn't really noticed until now making the warm air heavy and his skin uncomfortable. As far as days went, this one had been a doozy. Make that, the worst in a long time. Confusion reigned supreme. Two jobs in two cities. The rescue position was his preference, even if permanent. Melbourne would be safer on his heart, but still filled with difficulties.

Both positions offered security in one way or another. Both would give him time to settle a bit, possibly buy a home, not a house to rent out to some ungrateful tenant. Both came fraught with problems—big problems. His family versus the woman who'd stolen his heart and wasn't letting go; who'd just tightened the hold over him.

Decisions, decisions. He didn't know where to start. So he wouldn't. He'd take his usual out and sleep on it, see what popped up in his mind when he woke in the morning.

He didn't wake, because he didn't go to sleep. At four thirty he crawled out of bed and pulled on running shorts and a grey singlet. The colour suited his mood. Downing a glass of water, he debated where to go for a run. The roads would be quiet but didn't appeal. There were beaches to choose from or the hills if he could be bothered driving for an hour first. Mission Bay won out. Handy and easy to negotiate the way around to the next bays. He could head straight into work afterwards. No need to return home and risk seeing Sienna outside.

The sun had begun its climb up the sky as he locked his vehicle and did some stretches, trying to ease the kinks gained during the restless night spent tossing and turning in bed.

Bed. Sienna. The two fit together perfectly, and gave him lots of memories he'd given up trying to banish. She was one stubborn woman who refused to go away, even when there were kilometres between them. What was he going to do about her? About them?

Crunch, crunch, crunch went his shoes on the wet sand.

Swish, swish went the small waves as they unfurled at the edge of the tidal line. *Thump, thump* went his brain as he focused on nothing more than the beach ahead and getting to the end without thinking about Sienna.

Or which job to take.

Or settling down.

Or whether to become a monk and hide with a religious sect living on some mountain in a far-eastern country.

Splat. His foot had snagged a small log, tipping him sideways to land spread-eagled on the hard sand. Great. Just perfect. Concentrating on trying not to concentrate on Sienna had dumped him hard. His ankle throbbed. A cut on his hand from a shell trickled blood. Double great.

Sienna Burch, this is all your fault.

Scrambling to his feet, he tentatively tried out his ankle. A dull ache, and when he shifted his weight onto that leg it was good to go. After rinsing his hand in the salt water he started for the end of the beach again, this time jogging at a slower pace, not trying to outrun everything in his head.

Strange, but it was quieter in there now, as though acting calm made him calm. He breathed deep, lifted his eyes to take in the blue sky with a few clouds scudding around the top of Rangitoto Island. The harbour waters were tossing up small whitecaps, and pleasure craft were already heading out from downtown Auckland, no doubt aiming for the fishing grounds. Gulls squawked overhead before diving deep into the water.

He couldn't fault the place. At moments like this he felt at home.

Harry tripped, righted himself. At home? Get away. This was not the city he wanted to stop in to put roots down. So he'd made one decision. But then that negated the job on offer here. Didn't it? Returning to Melbourne wasn't exciting him either. This wasn't working. He turned and jogged back to his four-wheel drive and a towel. After wiping himself down, he threw on a shirt and crossed the road to a café for an early breakfast and lots of very strong coffee.

His phone rang loud in the near empty café. 'Hi, Derek'

'Connor's down with gastro. I'm switching crews around. Can you come in now?'

'On my way.' He'd shower at the base before pulling on the stuffy red suit that the kids adored. Funny, but they were easier to handle when he was dressed up as their favourite character. 'Can you put my coffee in a take-out mug, please?' he asked as he paid the guy behind the counter. 'Those eggs were delish.'

'Thanks. Come again.'

Harry took his change and the coffee and headed for his vehicle, a bounce in his step. The day ahead was sorted, leaving no time trying to find ways to fill in the hours.

All he had to do, and that wouldn't be until later, was to figure out why he was really holding out on spending more time with Sienna when he adored her and couldn't get enough of her. Not that she'd welcome him in her life with open arms. He would have to earn that right.

There were the 'don't want to be pushed around' and 'lack of trust' issues, but there was something else ticking at the back of all this. It rose whenever he considered the jobs he'd been offered. Again when he compared cities, and the friends he had through work in both those places. It always came back to Sienna and why he was afraid to love her.

Um…actually he already did love her.

That's why I can't decide. Holy moly.

He was stumped. Now what? It wasn't as though he could rush in and tell Sienna. She was too vulnerable, and their lifestyles were still poles apart. He swallowed the sudden pain gripping him. To admit his love to Sienna was impossible if he was to remain strong and invulnerable and not hurt her.

Why, damn it, why?

Sienna bounced back onto the ward on Monday morning feeling happy to be there and knowing she had other things to look forward to at the end of the day. 'Morning, Dale,' she smiled as she picked up patient notes from the desk. 'I've had the best break, thanks to you nagging.'

His face fell. 'We need to have a word. Grab a coffee and meet me in my office.'

Why did that sound ominous? A chill ran down her spine. 'You want one?'

'Already got it.' He started down the corridor in the opposite direction.

What was going on? Opting for a double-shot long black to keep the sense of unease at bay, she headed into Dale's office and at his instruction shut them in. The apprehension increased. 'You're freaking me out.'

'Do you remember Wendy Hall?'

'You took over from her about six months before I came on board.' Her reputation as a determined woman for getting her own way hadn't been kept quiet even after she'd gone.

'She's coming home from London next month and is making it known she wants her old job back.' Anger rode off Dale in waves. 'I have no intention of letting that happen. I am here for the long haul.'

So where did she fit into the picture? 'You think I need to be concerned for my job?'

'Yours is the next one up for renewal and somehow she knows that—I suspect from a certain board member she's always had under her thumb.'

Sienna slumped back in the chair. 'But I don't understand. Am I going to have to compete for my position?'

'It probably won't come to that. I'm just giving you warning so you can make sure you're up to speed with all the changes going on in the hospital.'

'I need to know what shifts the cleaners are doing now that their new contract has gone offshore?' This was payback for having fun last week, for spreading her wings and living life outside of here. For *getting* a life. So much for planning how to use those other weeks' leave owing. She'd never use them now.

Dale balanced a pen between his thumbs. 'Not quite, but be on your toes all the time. Just in case.'

Just in case. Those words followed her around all day. She could lose her security, her sense of worth, her control—all because Wendy Hall wanted to take her job as a stepping stone on the way to the top. Just as well she had walked away from Harrison. There was no way she could fit into his lifestyle now. She needed to hold on to her job to know who she was. Didn't she?

Of course she had to hold on to this position. She worked too hard to let it go now just because someone else thought they could snatch it off her. Thank goodness for emergencies or she'd have hidden away and spent the rest of the day trying absorb that idea.

'Jonty Brooks is on his way down from the rescue chopper,' Julie told Sienna a little after three.

'Get the mask and oxygen set up in Room Three.' Sienna flicked through the computer files until she had Jonty's before her. The six-year-old was a regular with severe asthma who lived on a remote island. 'He was in here last week with a severe attack.'

'Time of the year, I suppose,' Julie said. 'Here he is.'

Sienna looked up and directly at Harrison—dressed

in an oversized red outfit with white fluff at the neck and cuffs. She smothered a laugh. 'Hello, Santa. How's Jonty today?'

'His condition's not as severe as it was last week, but he needs attention.' Harry handed her the patient notes he'd filled in. 'How's your first day back?'

Hell on wheels. 'Wish I'd stayed away.'

He stared at her. 'Never thought I'd hear you say that.'

She'd never thought so either. She shrugged and stepped up to the stretcher. 'Hi, Jonty. Hello, Mrs Brooks.' His mother looked tired, probably due to some major seasonal work happening on the farm. This family never stopped working, including all six children, right down to the five-year-old. Sometimes Sienna wondered if that contributed to Jonty's recurring asthma attacks, exhaustion taking away his ability to fight physical blows. The boy was pale despite spending most of his days outside. She'd add a CBC to his requirements while here to see if he was anaemic.

'Jonty had two minor attacks during the night apparently,' Harry, standing beside her, said quietly so as no one else heard. 'How minor is of concern. It took some time for the nebuliser to help his breathing.'

'The family's usually pretty good at calling for help if they're worried.' But once they'd been too busy with shearing and Jonty had been very ill that time. 'I'll look into it.'

'Good. I'll head away. The chopper's waiting.' But he didn't move.

Sienna looked at Harry properly, and had to bite down on the wave of need swamping her.

I miss him all the time.

No doubt about it. She loved him. And if she hadn't had two weeks off work it would never have happened. That was what came of stepping outside her comfort zone. 'Love the outfit,' she told him while thinking, would she do it again if she could go back to the night she came off her bike and rerun the days differently? Or would she turn up here every single day and work all the hours that came her way so as not to get thrown under a bus by Wendy Hall?

Flying had turned out to be one of the few things that she couldn't line up in straight lines all the time, wasn't in control of all the factors affecting flight or the engine or what other aircraft were sharing her space in the sky. And she loved it. Got so much pleasure from learning how to master a plane that she felt alive in a way she hadn't since she was a child going down to the river to catch eels with her dad. That hadn't stopped her doing school work. She'd done both. And coped, been more rounded than she'd become as an adult.

'Doctor?' Julie was waiting on the other side of the stretcher. 'We need to get Jonty offloaded onto a bed.'

Cripes. She'd been completely distracted. Harry had said he was on his way, in other words needed his stretcher back. 'Let's go.' Taking one corner, she began pushing the stretcher towards the room he'd be in. Jonty needed her concentrating on him, no one else.

In very little time the boy had been transferred and Harrison was taking his stretcher to the lift. Julie was listening to Jonty's chest and reading the monitors noting his heart activity.

'Give Jonty another corticosteroid injection, Julie. And then we monitor him. I'm also wondering if we might get a CBC and renal functions done in case there's an underlying illness going on.' A gut feeling there was more going on than what they were used to with Jonty had her tossing up other ideas and rejecting them.

'You think anaemia? Or worse?' Julie asked away from Mrs Brooks.

'Hopefully neither, but Jonty is paler than usual, and

Harrison thought his previous two attacks might've been more severe than the family let on. I'm playing safe, really.' But listening to her gut had saved patients in the past. 'I'll talk you through my thoughts once we've got him stabilised.'

'Haemoglobin's nine-point-five,' Julie told her an hour later. 'Severe iron deficiency. Renal function normal.'

The lab had added iron studies after getting that haemoglobin result. 'Right, now we know what we're dealing with. All we have to do is find the cause.'

'At Jonty's age it'd be diet, wouldn't it? Or celiac disease.' Julie's brow creased in thought.

'Most likely, but we need to check for internal bleeding anyway. He could've been kicked in the stomach by a calf, though I'd have thought he'd have been brought in if that was the case.'

Thank goodness for busy. Knock-off time came around fast and for a minute Sienna tossed up whether to stay or to hand over to the night team. She was afraid of losing her job to Wendy Hall but the past two weeks had shown her more to life, and maybe she could take a chance on what the woman might do to her. What was the worst that could happen? Losing her job would break her heart but it wouldn't destroy her.

'This is where we're at with Jonty,' she told the head paediatrician coming on for the night shift. After running through the notes she walked away, fully expecting the roof to fall in on her.

By the time she pulled into her drive she was beginning to relax. Then she noticed Harry climbing out of his four-wheel drive and the tightness returned.

'How's Jonty?' he called over the fence.

After filling him in and trying to not gaze into his eyes like a lovelorn teenager she closed the garage and went inside to pour a wine. Yes, she'd decided one glass on her own wasn't going to turn her into an alcoholic.

There was a lot to think about, but instead she immersed herself in the theory of flight, and weather patterns.

Tuesday was busy with three serious admissions leaving little time for anything other than hastily downed lukewarm coffee at intermittent moments, but Sienna didn't hang around when it was obvious the staff didn't need her. By the time she got home all she wanted was to put her feet up and enjoy a wine while eating dinner and reading the flight training manual. It was her new passion. Not that it cancelled out the passion that was Harrison. Sussing out the apartment next door, looking for him, was not an option. But want to or not, she still did it. Often. Finally, to distract herself, she put the manuals aside and wrapped the few Christmas presents she'd bought a couple of weeks back and placed them under the tree, including one for Harry.

Staring at the green-and-red paper covering the long, narrow box containing a fishing rod, she knew it was a mistake. He wouldn't drop by on Christmas Day. For one, he'd probably be in Melbourne, and two, even if he wasn't he wouldn't call in to see her ever again. She'd wrecked two chances, one more than most people got. But she hadn't been able to resist buying the rod. It had had his name on it. Of course, why she'd even gone into the hunting and fishing shop in the first place was a mystery.

Retrieving the parcel, she took it out to the garage and leaned it against the cupboard in a corner out of the way. Out of sight. Back in the lounge she sank into a chair and let the tears fall for a few minutes before straightening her back, plastering on a reluctant smile and turning on the TV. She could be happy. Her life was changing, not necessarily how she'd envisaged entirely, but one step at a time she'd make it work out.

Except for Wendy Hall creating waves, that was. Dale had set up a meeting with two board members, himself and Sienna that afternoon, and she felt more confident that they'd do all they could to renew her contract. When she'd suggested they draw it up a month early there'd been some hesitation, so she'd had to drop the idea. But what was bothering her more than anything was that she wasn't losing sleep over the whole idea of her job being in jeopardy.

Not that she was planning on going hooking up with Harrison and traipsing around after him. He'd have to love her for her to do that, and there'd been no sign of love coming from him.

Wednesday brought Santa to the ward, handing out presents and good cheer, and generally causing mayhem with the kids. Sienna watched the excitement with a lump in her throat and a knot in her heart. She wanted this. Kids, presents, Santa, the whole shebang.

With Harrison. In Melbourne? Or Auckland? Or the back of beyond? No, she hadn't progressed that far.

Her smile slipped. She pulled it back, getting used to wearing one even when she felt like curling up in a ball and crying. When a little boy rushed up to her waving the toy aeroplane he'd unwrapped, Sienna got down on her knees and played flying games with him. 'This is the best medicine out,' she told Julie.

'We should bottle it,' Julie replied as she worked to remove sticky goop from a toddler's hair. 'Though I'd be leaving this stuff out.'

That night Sienna and Anna hit the town for cocktails followed by dinner to celebrate the season as they did every year. 'To us.' Sienna knocked her glass against her friend's after they'd been yakking for a while.

Anna took a large mouthful of her drink, looking as though she was about to cry. 'To another Christmas without husbands and kids.'

'Whoa. Where did that come from?' Shock rippled through Sienna. Anna never sounded sad about her lot. Angry, sometimes, yes, even nostalgic, but sad?

'Did you hear yourself when you were talking about your day on the ward? Did you feel the longing that was in your voice when you mentioned those kids and their excitement? We are missing out on all that.'

No denying she'd felt it earlier in the day, but Sienna hadn't realised it was still in her system, and worse, had let her yearning rise to the fore. 'Sure we are, but we're also living how we choose.' Harrison appeared behind her eyes, and he was waving, like she needed reminding of her love for him and how she'd like that to unfold.

'We're both so tied up in our careers I sometimes wonder how we function in the real world.'

'Who ticked you off today?' This so wasn't her friend talking.

'Your Felicity's making me take a look at myself. She's gutsy and determined to get ahead with school and friends and everything that comes her way despite the cystic fibrosis ruling her life. She never stops talking about you and how wonderful you are, yet she only knows half the picture.'

'My Felicity? She's a patient I've got to know well over the years and am trying to help in other ways than medical.'

'Of course. Nothing to do with your loving side, your need to be engaged with people, your caring nature.' Finally Anna's smile was back in place, and she sipped her mojito. 'You going to do anything about Mr Sexy?'

The warmth drained from her face. 'We're not really talking at the moment.'

'You should do something about that. Don't let the problem get so big it can't be managed.'

If only it were that simple. 'No point. Harry heads home to Australia in a couple of days.' Which had to be a good thing, right? He wouldn't take the position at the rescue base. Permanent wasn't a word in his vocabulary.

'Damn it, Sienna, stop making everything so hard. Take some risks, have some fun.'

'Oh, like you do, right?'

'Well, one of us has to break the mould first. Why not you?'

Good question, and one that kept blinking on in the front of her mind for the rest of the evening, and all through the night, and on the way to work next morning. Unfortunately, an answer wasn't so quick or determined to make itself known. Or was she hiding from it? Afraid of the consequences of taking further risks?

'There you go, sport.' Harry nodded farewell to the thirteen-year-old lad the rescue helicopter had just delivered to North Shore Hospital. 'Take care. No more riding your cycle on one wheel over the cliff onto the beach ten metres below.' Luck had been on the kid's side. His arm was broken but otherwise nothing more serious than a few bruises. About as lucky as Si had been.

Si. He wished he could stop calling her that. The abbreviated version of Sienna had slipped into his vocabulary one day and refused to disappear. Si meant warmth, excitement, hurt, longing. And a load more.

Including taking the biggest risk of his adult life.

Connor sat opposite him in the chopper and reached for his safety harness. 'What time's your flight out?'

'Midnight.'

'Want to have a farewell drink with the gang before you go?'

A farewell drink. 'Probably not. I've got to see Derek, and then there are some things I have to do at the apartment before I head away.'

The look he received from over the top of Connor's sunglasses told him he'd let his friends down, but it couldn't be helped. There were more important details to attend to. He could only hope everyone would understand when it became general knowledge on the base. 'I'll put some money on the bar.'

'Wish you were hanging around.'

Harry's eyes widened. 'Thanks. It's been a good number, this one.'

Connor got busy writing up case notes, leaving Harry to contemplate his navel. He checked his phone. No messages. Sienna was still cold on him. Like he'd done anything to crank up their relationship. The time read five forty-two. By the time the chopper landed and they'd restocked the kits it would be knock-off time. His final stint over and done with. Auckland had been a lark. The job one of the best. The people—he'd made some good friends he'd miss.

He tapped the photo icon and up came all the reasons he should stay. Sienna laughing at his Christmas tree. Sienna winding in her first snapper. Sienna sound asleep on the outdoor couch in the shade at the bach in Coromandel. Sienna—

Tap. Stop it.

'You won't change your mind about leaving?' Connor asked, a guarded expression on his face.

Did he know there was a position on offer? It was a small base and word got around fast at times, though Derek said no one knew his plans. But that wasn't the question. Would he change his mind? He looked out at the harbour below and the rapidly approaching city centre with the ferries at the quays, the workers on their way home or to the bars. The Sky Tower where he'd challenged Sienna into agreeing they should leap off and take a chance on a piece of rope. Should he remind her they had yet to see that through? What was the point when they weren't about to become an item? But if he stayed they might. Might not, either.

What did he have to lose by staying? His heart was already entrenched here, and his chance at a future that included family and roots and friendships he wasn't always walking away from was also here.

What did he have to lose by leaving? All of the above.

Man, oh, man. Just like that, he knew. Harry leaned forward. 'Thanks, mate.'

'Pay me later.' There was a small smile twitching at the man's mouth.

Harry squirmed in his seat, stretched his legs out, drew them up again, folded his arms around his waist, dropped them onto his thighs. It never took this long to reach base.

'I'll do the stock,' Connor announced as they finally dropped out of the chopper right outside the main hangar.

Was he that easy to read? 'Thanks, again.'

The day had dragged. Gone was the small spring in Sienna's steps, gone was the enthusiasm for everything. That there were fewer admissions only added to her gloom. 'It's as though people are refusing to get sick because of Christmas.' Hopefully no one was staying away when it was imperative they see a doctor.

Once Sienna was away from the ward and back at home changing out of her work clothes into shorts and a tee shirt, Christmas loomed larger than ever in her mind. Unheard of. It rattled her stoic, professional front. Her mother and

Bill had arrived early yesterday and promptly taken over her kitchen. Nothing unusual there, except for the tingle of excitement sneaking under her radar. The traditions set in place over the last few years were claiming her as never before. Previously she'd held on to them as a way of keeping the past out of the way. This year they gave hope for the future, and yet she couldn't see how that would really change the way she'd like it to. They certainly didn't include Harrison—or those children she wanted to have.

There were the same number of presents under the tree. She wasn't counting the one languishing out in the garage. That would go to a charity shop in the new year.

Harrison seemed to be out all the time. If his attire of those in-your-face overalls were anything to go by, he'd made himself available for every shift. His body had been slumped with exhaustion as he'd walked up the drive half an hour ago. Presumably he'd be heading to the airport any time soon to catch a flight home.

So you're going to let him go without a word?

She was hardly going to attempt to get onside with him a third time. She might be a novice at the dating game, but she wasn't entirely stupid. She understood it wasn't working between them, and that there were too many reasons why it never would.

Yes, and you are one of the biggest reasons.

Gasp. What?

You're afraid.

Yes, she sure was. Unwilling to take more risks than she'd already managed. Didn't want to end up being her mother, never settling when it was her greatest wish, all because of love.

But you're more than willing for Harrison to stop moving from a job he enjoys to another he'll enjoy just so you can be happy.

Was she being selfish? Harry didn't know she loved him. She had no real idea what he felt for her; guessing games didn't cut it. There was risk number one, laying her heart on the line without knowing the outcome.

Third time lucky.

Now, where did that come from? He was leaving. Better he knew the truth than have him go away totally unaware she loved him.

'Sienna?'

'Yes, Mum?'

'Is that man in the other apartment the one you had such a wonderful time with in Coromandel?'

'He sure is.'

Her mother's sigh had Sienna turning to stare at her. 'Mum.'

'Just remembering, that's all.'

'Dad?'

'Yes. It wasn't all bad, you know.'

'You two used to tuck me up in bed and go walking, hand in hand along the beach or the river bank or whatever was there. I'd follow sometimes and you were completely oblivious to anything but yourselves, laughing, talking, kissing.' She'd forgotten those times.

'You followed us?' Her mother's face coloured up. 'How often?'

'Often enough. Relax. I always knew when it was time to disappear back to my bed.' Suddenly the hesitation was gone. She and Harrison had shared some wonderful days and nights. It hadn't only been about the lovemaking, but all the conversations and laughter, and the fishing. Togetherness. It had been the best two days of her adult life. And she wanted more of them. Would Harrison? With her? Only one way to find out.

But first she'd brush her hair out the way he liked it,

and put on that blue blouse he liked so much. Cosmetic changes, sure, but why not? This was the man she loved and would do anything for. Anything? Yes, anything.

She snagged a bottle of wine on the way through the kitchen.

Harry saw Sienna coming up from her apartment as he headed down his drive. They met at the letterboxes, each with a bottle of wine in their hands. That had to be a good sign. 'Hey,' he said.

'Hey, yourself.' She didn't hesitate, or blush; her eyes didn't turn frosty. She kept on coming, her empty hand reaching out to him. 'I wanted to see you before you left.' Then she stumbled. 'There are things I need to tell you.'

Catching her, Harry slipped his fingers through hers and held tight. 'I was on my way to tell you I'm not leaving.'

Her head jerked upward, her gaze searching his face before finally locking onto his eyes. 'You're not?' Some emotion made her voice squeaky. He thought it might be hope. Or that could be wishful thinking on his part. Sienna swallowed hard and tried again. 'You're not going back to Melbourne tonight?'

'Not tonight, not for a long time, other than briefly to visit my brothers and friends in a few weeks' time.'

'Where, then?' she whispered.

'I'm staying here. I've accepted the base director's post. It's a job I'd like to own, to be able to make changes as I see fit, train more volunteers and look after the paid staff.'

Her fingers were gripping his. 'Wow. That's quite a change of direction for you.' He could almost fall into her eyes, they were so large. 'Glad I brought the wine.'

'You want to celebrate me hanging around to annoy you?'

'Is that what you intend doing?' She was holding her breath, as though the next thing he told her would be the most important ever. Was she aware her fingernails were digging into his palm?

'If you'll let me.' Then Harry couldn't breathe either. Had to be something in the air to be affecting them both in the same way.

Damn but he was a fool. But he wasn't used to opening up his heart.

Just do it. Put it out there. Deep, deep breath.

'Sienna, I love you. I didn't want to. I fought it hard, but there was no stopping you getting into my heart. You're changing me, making me stand up for those things I have been denying I want for so long.' There was no stopping him now he'd started. It was as if a cloud had finally evaporated, to be replaced by sunshine. 'I want the whole caboodle with you. Love, laughter, tears if we have to, kids, even. What do you think?' His chest hurt as air stalled in his lungs. If she didn't answer him fast he might drop in a heap at her feet, gasping like a fish on the sand.

She tried to pull away, but he increased the pressure to keep contact. 'Tell me,' he said with as much constraint as possible.

'I...' Sienna paused, looked around them and returned to watching him. 'I want you to know our weekend away was extra-special and I'd like to repeat it. Not necessarily doing the same things in the same place, but repeating the togetherness.'

Harry's heart beat hard against his ribs. 'I hear you. I even agree. But—' A finger from the hand holding that bottle pressed his lips, effectively shutting him up.

'I've gone and fallen in love with you.' Her eyes lightened, and that mouth that could do wonders on his skin curved upwards. 'I love you, Harrison. End of story.'

Knots in his stomach and around his heart dropped

away. A weight lifted from him. 'Or the beginning of a whole new one.'

That smile widened. 'I didn't want to push my luck saying that.' Then she stared at him, her finger now worrying *her* lips.

Wrapping his arms around her waist, he picked her up and swung them around in a circle. 'We'd better not drop the bottles. We've got some celebrating to do.' Then, placing her on her feet, he proceeded to kiss her until he lost all cohesive thought, only Sienna stealing into his mind.

Then she pulled back. 'There are some problems on the horizon. I might lose my job due to someone wanting to use it to get to the top in a hurry, but I think I can live with that if you're with me.' She hesitated, doubt beginning to fill her eyes, darken her face. 'In fact, I wouldn't mind less hours at work if it meant doing other interesting things.'

'All the way, sweetheart.'

'I've learned that I'm ready to take some chances, to let go some of my hang-ups—all because of you. To the point that—' she locked her eyes with his '—I will go wherever you want to go. I no longer need to stop in one place for ever, Harry, as long as I can be with you.'

'I won't ask you to do that.' As she started to say something he held up a finger. 'I am stopping running away. Yes, that's what I've been doing for so long now it's a habit, a bad one that needs banishing.' Swallow.

'Don't be rash. There might be times you want, need, to move on. Take your version of a road trip. I'll be there with you.'

Then Harry knew what to do. Reaching for her free hand that had got away from him, his fingers slid between hers again as naturally as opening his eyes when he woke in the morning. 'Come with me. I'll show you the only road trip we're doing.' Turning her around, he tugged her down his drive and back up hers, around the corner to her back yard and onto her deck, where he gently pushed her down onto a chair before pulling another close and sitting beside her. Then twisted the lid off his bottle of wine and held it up. 'This is what we'll drink to. Our way of keeping the world moving at our pace, keeping us safe from the past and moving into the future.' He nodded at the two magnificent rhododendrons. 'Together we will watch those trees grow bigger and stronger.'

Sienna squealed and leapt up. 'You're serious.'

'Very.' He placed the bottle on the nearby table before it was knocked out of his grasp as Sienna clambered onto his lap, her legs on either side of his thighs, her hands taking his head and drawing him close for a kiss. A kiss that ignited every point in his body and fused his brain until he knew nothing but Sienna.

Until, 'Oh, dear. I think this is the moment we disappear, Bill. I'm not going to bed, like Si used to do, but I think we need to buy some more pine nuts for that salad I'm planning on making.'

Who the hell…? Harry pulled his mouth away from that kiss and stared over Sienna's shoulder at an older version of his woman. She looked very amused about something. No doubt them kissing. The older man at her side wore the same expression. Oh, boy. Talk about caught. Why this sensation of being a naughty teen snogging the girl from class? Kissing his woman was allowed. Yeah, but not in front of her mother before he'd even met her.

As Sienna wriggled around on his lap, nudging that obvious reaction to her kiss and causing him more distress, he went for light-hearted and silly. 'Hi, I'm Harry Frost. Sienna's neighbour. Do you think you could get me a packet of…?' *Not condoms.* 'Um…a box of chocolates while you're there?'

Sienna gasped out a laugh. 'Guess we're even, Mum.'

The lovely woman stepped forward, her hand out to

him. 'I know exactly who you are, Mr Neighbour. I'm Katie, Sienna's mother.' As her warm hand wrapped around the one he hadn't realised he'd put out she nodded to the man with her. 'This is my friend Bill.'

Still with Sienna on his lap, though now facing her mother and hopefully hiding the bulge she'd caused, he shook Bill's hand too. 'I'm glad to meet you both.'

Katie laughed that light, tinkling sound he knew from Sienna. 'I doubt that very much, Harry. Timing is everything and you've got it a bit messed up tonight. So, which brand of chocolates shall I get?' Even her eyes twinkled like Si's. 'I think we'll walk to the supermarket, Bill. That should fill in time before dinner,' she spun back to Harry, 'which you're invited to, by the way.'

Did he tell her he could just take Sienna next door for that hour to continue what had to be finished or he'd combust with need, and that no one had to go shopping for things they didn't require? Somehow that might earn him a swipe across the arm from the younger version of the woman standing before him.

The younger one was speaking up. 'Do I get to say anything?'

'Nope,' replied her mother. 'Not a word. See you shortly.'

'Not too shortly,' Harry whispered in Sienna's ear, and yep, got the swipe on his arm.

'I'll get the glasses and we can take them back to your side of the fence. Just in case we forget to stop whatever we're getting up to in time.'

EPILOGUE

CHRISTMAS DAY DAWNED bright and clear. Just like her head and heart, Sienna mused as she stood under the shower. Harrison's shower. Last night they'd made it over to her apartment for dinner with her mother and Bill, and spent a couple of hours chatting and laughing. Lots of laughing, actually. Most unusual. And wonderful...freeing.

'You going to use all the hot water?' The shower door swung open and Harry stepped in. He filled his hands from the liquid-soap dispenser and rubbed it over her shoulders, down to her breasts. 'Merry Christmas, sweetheart.'

'Same back at you.' She kissed his chin, his cheek, then his mouth, hunger rampant in an instant.

As it very obviously was in Harry. Leaning against him, she rubbed her belly across that hot reaction, needing him in her—again.

Harry pulled his mouth away. 'We probably shouldn't. We were expected for breakfast five minutes ago.'

'You don't do quick?' Her hand wrapped around him.

'Oh, yeah. Watch me.'

'I think you mean feel me.' And before she knew it her body was falling apart under the onslaught of heat and need.

Within minutes they were towelling themselves dry, grinning at each other as if they'd just unwrapped the best

Christmas present ever. Which she had. 'Harry, thank you for being you.'

When he reached for her, that level of intensity in his eyes spelling more passion, she ducked away. 'We really should to go next door.' And there was another present she had to put under the tree. 'Mum will be clock-watching.'

But her mother surprised her. 'Coffee's just made. I thought we could open presents while we have that. Breakfast will be thirty minutes.' She looked from Sienna to Harrison and back again, the acceptance of him warm in her eyes, and adding to Sienna's glow. 'I allowed extra time for you to get here.'

'Thanks, Mum,' she growled around a swallowed laugh. She and her mother didn't talk about things like this. But other than Bernie, whom Mum hadn't liked, there hadn't been men in her life to talk about. And now there was. The most wonderful man she'd known. 'Harry, can you pour the coffee? I've got something to get from the garage.'

The fishing rod was a hit. 'Does this mean we're going to Coromandel again?' Harry asked with a grin. 'You won't grump about smelling like something the cat left in the back of the cupboard last week?'

'Of course I will. And I'll get you to gut the fish I catch so I don't stink for a week.' That grin drove her crazy. If her mother and Bill weren't here she'd be dragging Harry down the hall to her bedroom right now. Christmas breakfast or not.

Harrison handed her an envelope, and sat back waiting, his eyes full of amusement.

'What?' Slipping her finger under the flap, she opened it and tipped out the card inside. And swallowed. 'The bungee jump. I was hoping you'd forgotten about that.'

'A challenge was made and accepted.' He grinned. 'You're not chickening out, are you?'

Unfortunately not. 'Don't push your luck.'

Harry laughed. 'You'll enjoy it, sweetheart.'

'I hope so.' Then she relaxed. She'd be fine. So far everything she'd done on her list had worked out. Why wouldn't this challenge? 'Bring it on.'

'Only if you want to.'

'Contrition doesn't suit you, Harry Frost.'

'Right, are we done?' Her mother looked under the tree. 'Who are these for?' She prodded the last three parcels.

'Anna, Fliss, who is a young friend working for Anna, and I don't know about the other one,' Sienna answered.

Harrison stood up and reached down for the red square packet with a huge gold satin ribbon. Then he dropped to one knee in front of her. 'For you, Si.' He held on to it. 'But first, I need to ask you something.'

Thud, thud. He'd better shout it because her ears were deafened by the pounding of her heart. 'Harry?'

'If we're going to watch those trees grow and raise some kids, and settle in one place, do you think we should get married to start the whole thing off?'

Her mother clapped.

Bill chuckled.

And Sienna—well, her eyes filled up and tears streamed down her cheeks. 'Absolutely,' she croaked. 'No other way to go.'

Then she was being wrapped in her favourite arms and kissed thoroughly.

In the background she thought she heard her mother laughing as she said, 'You'd better be quick. I'm not putting off breakfast for a second time.'

* * * * *

CHRISTMAS WITH HER BODYGUARD

CHARLOTTE HAWKES

MILLS & BOON

To Mum,
for all the hats you wore!
You're my inspiration xxx

CHAPTER ONE

'REALLY, RAFE.' GRITTING her teeth to stay calm, Rae hurried behind her half-brother's long strides as he burned through the Rawlstone Group's UK headquarters. 'I appreciate you're only looking out for me, but I really don't need a bodyguard. Especially around Christmas.'

Her stomach roiled at the mere thought of another bodyguard. Even after all these years.

'I'm sorry, Rae.' He sounded genuinely regretful. 'If there were any other way...'

'There has to be,' she pleaded. 'Please, Rafe, you know the press will take any excuse to rake up the past. They never believed in my innocence as it was, and I couldn't bear it. Not again.'

Another stomach lurch. It was hard enough putting up with paparazzi dogging her daily life, pretending she didn't care what lies they wrote about her, or how little the public thought of her. She certainly didn't need to give them a reason to rerun all those stories of her utterly spectacular plummet into shame almost fourteen years ago.

No matter what she'd done to try to redeem herself, they had refused to believe that she'd known nothing about the sex tape, let alone leaked it. It had taken her ten years and a career in medicine to get them to finally stop linking her—usually scandalously—to every Hollywood A-lister, every rock musician, or every trust-fund kid in whose presence she was spotted.

It hadn't mattered that she'd barely even exchanged a word with some of them, let alone dated them. Sex sold. Scandal sold. That was all that mattered to them for so, so long. Only in the last four years had they finally, reluctantly, begun to come around to her side.

A bodyguard would undo all that good work. She could just read the headlines now.

Scarlet woman Raevenne Rawlstone finally takes a new bodyguard. Will he be as undercover *as the last one?*

And that would be one of the tamer offerings.

Hot shame flooded her body as X-rated images, intimate moments that never had been anything but private, filled her brain.

'I can't have another bodyguard,' she choked out. 'I won't.'

Abruptly, her legs gave out and she just about made it to the wall for support, the old stonework rough beneath her hands. She'd trailed her fingers over their cool surface many times in the past, but tonight they seemed colder than usual, sapping her body heat as unseen edges cut into her skin. Rae withdrew her hand abruptly.

She usually loved visiting Rafe here. The offices might be as super high-tech as every other square millimetre of real estate in the company's portfolio, but Rafe's flair for restoring vast, old buildings, with their inspiring architecture, always had her gasping with admiration.

Today, however, she barely noticed the glorious stonework or vaulted ceilings. December was in a matter of weeks and yet she couldn't envisage the festive lights and decorations that would go transform this place into something infinitely magical. She didn't even think about the fact that, when the offices closed their proverbial business doors for the Christmas shutdown, Rafe would open the physical doors to the house and feed the homeless, the way he always did for those ten days.

Her half-brother was moving back to her, reaching out to cup her shoulder, the closest he came to a hug. None of the Rawlstone clan found it easy to show emotion— an overhang from their mutual father, the cold and remote Ronald Rawlstone—but she and Rafe both knew they cared about each other.

'We'll deal with the press if we need to. You won't be alone, Rae. But I told you, I received a death threat the other day.'

'We always receive death threats.' She waved her hands desperately. 'We're Rawlstones.'

Or at least *her* side of the Rawlstone family always received death threats. Her limelight-loving sisters and mother had made it their mission with their *Life in the Rawl* reality show.

By contrast their half-brother, Rafe, CEO of the Rawlstone Group and former British army officer, was generally universally adored. At least by the press and public.

'This one is credible,' he replied simply. 'So, it's precisely because it *is* Christmas that I need to know you're safe. Especially with all the festive fundraisers and seasonal socials you'll no doubt be compelled to attend. Your sisters already have bigger personal protection details than even *they* need, as does your mother. It's *you* I worry about.'

She stared miserably at some fixed point on the stonework that her eyes didn't even see. 'They'll bring it all back up...what happened with Justin.'

The images flashed up again and she squeezed her eyes shut. It didn't help. She could still see it. The moment she'd lost her virginity played out on social media for the world to see.

She might have gagged, she couldn't be sure, but suddenly she was wrapped in a tight, if awkward, embrace.

'The guy was a piece of scum.' Controlled fury laced his voice along with a thread of guilt, and she hated that her half-brother felt even slightly responsible for the mistakes she'd made so many years ago. 'I'll never let anything like that happen to you again.'

'You can't promise that.' Her voice sounded more strained than she would have preferred.

'I can.' Releasing her slightly, Rafe took a step back. 'I personally requested the guy I've chosen to be our bodyguard. I trust him. He's a major from my army days.'

Her heart actually stopped beating for a moment.

And another.

It took everything she had to tell herself not to be so foolish. That it couldn't possibly *be*. And still her throat was thick, constricted, her tongue too big for her mouth, when she replied.

'He's some major or other from your army days?'

'Not *some* major,' Rafe disapproved. 'Myles is one of the best officers I had the pleasure to serve with.

Everything receded. Went black.

She had no idea how long she stood there but when she came back, squeezing her eyes closed, she was eternally grateful that Rafe was too busy marching along to have turned around to look at her.

There seemed little point in trying to soothe and corral her skittering heart but she made a valiant effort nonetheless.

'Myles.'

As if, perhaps, it could possibly be a different *Myles*.

'That's right, Major Myles Garrington.' She could practically hear Rafe's eye-roll. 'I mentioned it was him before. Keep up, Rae.'

'You didn't,' she managed feebly.

Myles. Numbness crept over her, but she had to hold herself together. Especially in front of Rafe. Her half-brother's opinion was the only one that mattered to her these days; she certainly couldn't let him know how she'd thrown herself at his best friend all those years ago.

She managed to stumble after him.

'Oh, well, no matter.' Rafe was oblivious. 'Myles is a decent bloke—you'll like him. You might not remember but you even met him once. He came with me the one and only Christmas holiday I spent with your family...oh, probably fifteen years ago now.'

Actually, fifteen years and two months ago. Not that she was counting. Much.

It was the only Christmas that Rafe had come to his half-family's home. It had been at their mutual father's insistence. As though the shocking death of his first wife had made Ronald Rawlstone suddenly remember the son he'd had little contact with—other than sending monthly financial support—for the best part of two decades.

She still didn't know why Rafe had agreed—duty, probably, her half-brother had a strong sense of duty—she only knew that he'd brought his best friend, a fellow junior army officer, with him.

Myles Garrington.

He had changed her life in so many ways. Not all of them good.

And how humiliating that the numbness was only now beginning to recede because her traitorous body was already tingling at the memories of Myles that began to lace their way into her brain. Memories she'd spent fifteen years trying to bury.

The attraction between her and Myles when he'd walked into the Rawlstone family home with Rafe had been instantaneous. Its intensity had side-swiped her, and at seventeen—barely a few months off eighteen—it had been long overdue. Myles had just turned twenty-one, a medical student at uni, and already a junior officer in the British army. He'd seemed so much wiser and more mature than the American boys from her high school, and she'd fallen so very hard, so very fast. She'd genuinely believed him to be her first love. With the benefit of hindsight, of course, she recognised it for what it had really been...her first intense crush. Nothing more.

But still, when she looked back over that Christmas holiday she knew she'd acted wantonly. Then again, he hadn't exactly beaten her off him.

Except for that last night.

'Anyway,' the usually astute Rafe continued, his pace unrelenting, 'Myles was one of the best officers the British army had.'

'Had?'

A sense of foreboding crept over her. Being an army trauma doctor had been Myles' sole focus in life. She couldn't imagine him ever leaving of his own volition.

'He left six months ago.'

'Why?'

To most other people it would have been indiscernible, but Rae didn't miss Rafe's uncharacteristic beat of hesitation.

'There was a village. A fire. One of the riflemen protecting Myles' medical team...died. Myles was injured badly, too... His hand. He couldn't operate for a while but he couldn't stand the idea of getting stuck behind a desk. Possibly there was a degree of survivor's guilt, too. He'd been going through the process of coming to the States anyway so taking a clinical observation post under your supervision means he can still do that whilst also protecting you around the clock.'

'Round the clock?' She gasped. 'He can't live with me.'

'Do you want to stay safe, or would you prefer to pander to your sensibilities?'

'Rafe—'

'Relax.' He cut her off with a half-smile. 'I don't mean to needle you. For the moment it seems this threat is UK-based, so he'll accompany you to your lecture tonight and on the private jet back to the States tomorrow. But he won't need to live with you... I've purchased the property next door.'

There was no reason for her to feel so panicked. No reason at all. And if there was, she told herself firmly, it was at the idea that people had been hurt. Not at the thought of being in Myles' company twenty-four seven.

'Wait, you said Myles was hurt?'

Clearly there was more to it than that but it was little comfort to know her instincts had been correct. Still, since Rafe hadn't stopped pounding along the corridors leaving Rae's legs burning as she tried to keep up, this wasn't going to be the ideal time to press him on it.

'Wind your neck in, Rae. I didn't say that.'

It was so far from Rafe's usual lexicon that there was no missing his agitation. Which perhaps helped to explain why he apparently hadn't noticed she'd gone from pretending not to remember Myles to showing fear he had been hurt.

Ironically, that only stirred her up all the more. Still, she needed to be more careful. More blasé.

'Wind my neck in?' She fought back her agitation to teasing him, shedding her American accent in order to imitate his vaguely plummy English pitch. 'My dear brother, I do believe you're the one who had me practically frogmarched from my thirty-six-hour shift at the hospital onto your private jet and flown across the Atlantic. Yet *I'm* the one who needs to "wind my neck in"?'

'Funny, Rae.' She could almost hear him roll his eyes at her. 'Your impersonation leaves a lot to be desired. You could take the Dick Van Dyke award for abysmal cockney accents. I'll warn Myles.'

She forced a laugh and told herself she wasn't getting anxious. She had to pretend that his existence meant absolutely nothing to her.

Which, of course, it did.

It was only galling that she didn't find herself remotely convincing.

'Fine.' She forced a dazzling grin even though her half-brother couldn't see her. 'You try my accent. I bet you can't sound like a New Yorker.'

'Rae,' he cautioned.

'Seriously, give it a try.'

'Raevenne.' He stopped at last, turning around to face her, his hands on her shoulders. 'Stop panicking.'

Her stomach somersaulted again. Her half-brother *knew*? Surely that was impossible.

She was only relieved she'd slept most of the plane journey and her shift at the hospital had been so busy that she hadn't eaten more than a biscuit for the last eighteen hours. At least it meant there was nothing to regurgitate.

'Who said I'm panicking?' Her shrill voice didn't help and she stopped abruptly.

The silence was practically pressing in on her as she nonetheless followed Rafe up the stairs to his office in the panoramic suite on the tenth floor. He never took an elevator if he could take the stairs. One of the few overhangs he couldn't conceal from his years in conflict zones as a frontline officer in the British army. Thank goodness for her own daily cardio sessions at the exclusive gym uptown.

And for the fact that they weren't in the Manhattan office with its sixty-five storeys.

Then, all too soon, they were standing in the anteroom to Rafe's office, her heart threatening to pound out of her chest at any moment.

Myles was on the other side of the door and she wasn't ready for this. She wasn't ready to face him. To see even a shadow of disgust or condemnation in his expression.

Rafe's hand reached for the door handle.

'I can't…' she choked out, stumbling backwards.

'Well, if you can't do it for yourself, or even for me, then do it for Myles, Rae. He'd never say it but I think he needs us. The firefight was bad, Rae, it took Myles out for months whilst he wasn't able to operate.'

A surgeon who couldn't operate? *Myles* unable to operate? It didn't bear thinking about.

She'd been ready for Rafe's cajoling, even for him to order her in. But she hadn't been prepared for him to lay such a perfect trap. It was her Achilles heel. If someone needed her help, she could never deny them. Rafe had known it, and he'd baited her shamelessly.

'What's going on, Rafe?' She glowered at him even as she was compelled to ask the question, but Rafe simply shook his head.

'It isn't my story to tell.'

Frustration rushed her, but she was determined to hold her nerve. At least, outwardly.

'If you want me to agree to this—' she was amazed she managed to make it sound as if she were actually in control—as though her body hadn't been turning itself inside out, caught between longing and sheer terror, from the moment she'd discovered that Myles was even in the building '—then you'll tell me exactly what's going on. Now.'

Myles could hear them, out in the corridor. Talking quietly.

He couldn't make out the words but the context was unmistakeable. The higher, female voice, clearly Rae's, was demanding. Rafe's deeper voice was firm but uncharacteristically urgent. Myles gripped the sides of the plush chair and shifted awkwardly.

Why the hell had he ever agreed to this?

An image of Raevenne hovered in the back of his mind but he pushed it easily aside.

Ridiculous.

He wasn't here for her. He was here because he had no other choice. Because he needed a job that took him away from battlefields and death, and Rafe, his former best friend, had offered him exactly that. And because his painstakingly constructed life had unravelled so incalculably these past six months.

Almost seventeen years in the British army—where he'd thought he would stay his whole life—over. Just like that.

Guilt pressed in on him.

Heavy.

Suffocating.

He blocked out the images—the smell of burning flesh, the village burned to the ground, young Lance Corporal Mike McCoy—which threatened to overwhelm him. Blackness closed over him and for a dangerous moment he swayed on the spot.

Only his subconscious fighting to lock on the familiar, feminine voice, muffled as it was through the door, provided him an anchor to the present.

He grasped at it gratefully.

One day at a time. Wasn't that the advice he'd given out, time and again over the years, to soldiers in his position? Never imagining that one day it would be him standing there, his life having imploded and now lying in tatters around him.

But this wasn't the army. Or what had happened *out there*. This was simple, uncomplicated, repaying an old debt to a good friend. Playing bodyguard whilst Rafe tracked down exactly who was threatening his family.

And right now, being a bodyguard beat being a surgeon hands down. True, part of Rafe's plan included clinical observation but he could handle that. Observation was one thing. It was staying an active surgeon right now that certainly wasn't an option.

An operating room with a body on the table in front of him and a scalpel in his hand was no place for a man who suspected he was on the edge of mild PTSD. His heart hammered angrily at the mere thought of it. At such an obvious sign of his own weakness. But those tours of duty had taken so many men and women he knew, so many innocent kids, so many helpless civilians, particularly that last week. And especially that last mission.

When perhaps he could have…*should* have…made different choices.

All those women, those kids. Mikey. It had taken them all.

Did it have to have taken part of his soul, too?

The sounds in the hallway provided a sudden, welcome distraction from his uncharacteristic moment of self-pity.

Ten operational tours in the past twelve years alone, sometimes back-to-back, and never once had he allowed himself to look back and dwell. Everybody knew that was the road to self-destruction because it wouldn't bring anybody back and it was a waste of time.

Galvanised, he pushed himself out of the seat and stalked across the floor just as the door swung open and the familiar form of his former army buddy strode in. But it was the figure slinking in behind Rafe—her head resolutely down—that arrested his gaze.

Raevenne Rawlstone.

He hadn't thought about her in years.

Liar.

He ignored the silent accusation.

But he *had* shoved memories of her, of that one Christmas together, to the back of his mind. Yet now, having heard Rae's muffled yet nevertheless unmistakeable voice through the door, he found he couldn't stuff her back into whatever cold corner of his mind in which she'd been lurking all these years.

It was insane. Objectionable. Unacceptable. And yet, it seemed, here he was.

He wasn't aware that he'd crossed the room towards her until she lifted her head—those unmistakeable laurel-green eyes with their perfect, moss-green edging that had haunted him far more than he had ever cared to admit—and finally met his stare full-on.

His breath lodged, as though he were winded, as though seeing her for the first time in fifteen years. Innocent and fragile. So far removed from those gossip columns, those entertainment channels, that awful *Life in the Rawl* reality show.

He'd tried to escape them but it hadn't been easy. When you were out in a conflict zone it was amazing what light escapism soldiers found entertaining. And still, it made him grit his teeth so hard he was surprised his jaw didn't break.

'Ma'am,' he ground out stiffly before his brain got into gear.

It was ridiculous given how they'd once known each other, and he wasn't surprised she hesitated before sliding her smaller palm against his and managing a stiff handshake.

'Major.'

Was that a jolt of…*something*…surging through him? *Impossible.*

So why was he having to fight himself not to snatch his hand away?

Myles glanced back at her.

He had no words to articulate why he felt so upended. Or even what it was. Which was when she opened her mouth and bit out, 'I don't want you as my bodyguard.'

Not quite that fragile, then.

Something else tipped sideways within him and suddenly, bizarrely, he found himself fighting a faint smile that toyed on his lips.

He thrust the odd sensation aside, reaching instead for his more familiar cloak of dispassion and finding something slightly less reassuring. It was all he could do to school his features.

'Something wrong?'

She cocked her head to the side as if actually contemplating it.

It occurred to him that he hadn't had anyone *evaluate* him like this in a long, long time. Ever since he'd been a desperate recruit, prepared to leopard crawl from Fort William to Cape Wrath if it meant winning an army bursary to study medicine.

'I think I might prefer someone who looks like they could handle a shoving, unruly crowd. Someone *more…*'

Belatedly, he realised she was deliberately trying to insult him.

'More?' He arched one eyebrow as though indulging a silly, petulant child, which, he reminded himself, was exactly how he saw her.

'Yes, you know, *more...*' She waved her hand airily. 'Bigger, more intimidating.'

'Is that so?'

'That's....so.' She flicked out her tongue and the movement snagged his gaze. Inexplicably he couldn't seem to draw his eyes away.

'Indeed? Well, if you're worried that you aren't going to be...safe enough with me, I can assure you that I have no intention of letting anyone go near you.'

Including himself, he concluded haughtily, and it felt like an odd kind of triumph. Almost as if they were sparring again, the way they had done all those Christmases ago.

What the hell was going on, here?

'That aside,' she stated primly, 'are you always this high-handed and condescending? Or is it just because it's me?'

The flashes of the Raevenne he used to know weren't doing much to help his sense of self-control. Oddly, it was as if a light were suddenly glinting through him, casting tiny spots of illumination and colour on a darkness that had been growing for too long.

A part of him wanted to lean towards that light.

A bigger part of him wanted to extinguish it.

'Not usually. Then again, I don't often come across someone so infamously flippant and disparaging.'

She glowered at him, and instead of it confirming every last, negative rumour he'd ever heard, he found himself oddly drawn to her. Still, he held his ground.

He wasn't sure who was more startled when Rafe cut in, clearly amused.

'Glad you still remember how to handle my sister's prickly side.'

It was testament to how much his old friend thought of his half-sister that he dispensed with the *half* part of the title.

Interesting.

'Seems so.' Myles forced a lightness into his tone. He wasn't sure why, but he couldn't allow Rafe to see there was any issue between him and Rae.

'Good, then there's an urgent business call I really need to make. I'll see you both tonight at the conference. Good luck, Rae. I know your lecture will be incredible.'

Then Rafe was gone, leaving the two of them alone in the plush office suite.

For several long moments neither of them spoke.

'So,' Myles finally broke the silence, fighting the urge to clear his throat, 'you're a doctor now?'

CHAPTER TWO

HE HADN'T INTENDED the emphasis on *now*. Hadn't meant to sound so disparaging. But the storm raging in his head wasn't letting him think straight.

'I am. Obstetrics and gynaecology.' She lifted her head proudly and something kicked in his chest. 'And I'm a good one, too. I'm also a maternal and foetal medicine specialist.'

She was actually sparkling. That moss-green edging in her eyes seemed more like a deeper navy blue right now, which had always meant her emotions were running high. He'd learned to read Rae through her eyes long, long ago.

'So Rafe said.' He wrenched himself back to the present.

'Right.' She bit her lip and it did something to his gut that it had no business doing.

'He also told me you were giving a keynote speech at the World Precision Medicine Conference tonight.'

Her cheeks flushed again.

'I am. And I heard you gave a brilliant lecture there a few years ago. I was meant to attend but…there was a medical emergency and I missed my plane.'

She offered a rueful grin and suddenly it occurred to him that whatever stories the media told—however they touched on her medical career but focussed on her personal life—Rae was utterly invested in her career as a doctor.

This, Myles realised with a start, was more like the Raevenne he remembered from all those years ago.

The rest of the world might know her as the girl who had catapulted her despicable side of the Rawlstone family onto the reality scene with a sex tape of her eighteen-year-old self and her twenty-eight-year-old bodyguard.

But that wasn't the girl that he'd known. At least, not back then.

It wasn't the sweet, blushing seventeen-year-old with whom he'd felt an attraction from the moment Rafe had introduced them. He'd tried to fight it, of course—Rafe had been his best mate, but even at seventeen she'd seemed far older, far more mature, than her years. The three years between them had melted away and, cooped up in that house trying to stay away from the rest of Rafe's god-awful half-family—from the self-serving mother to the callous father so wretchedly similar to his own—he and Rae had forged a bond.

And then, despite his best intentions, the heady glances had evolved to fleeting touches, stolen kisses, and something so much more intense. He'd wanted her with such a ferocity, as he'd wanted no other woman before.

Probably as he'd wanted no other woman since, either.

It had taken a supreme effort to eject her from his room that night, even as he'd been physically *aching* to do something altogether different. It might have been legally acceptable, but it was still wrong in Myles' mind. She'd been too young besides being Rafe's sister. Neither argument had gone down well with Rae that night.

And all the while she'd been standing there in the flimsiest scraps of lace and his body had been under no illusions about how much he'd wanted her.

Even now, at the mere memory, his body tensed, coiled, like steel bands cinched tight on machinery, barely harnessing hundreds of pounds of pressure. The chemistry between him and Rae had been instantaneous. He'd tried to fight it, but it had been like nothing he'd ever experienced before. Its intensity had rocked him and it had only been the fact that she was his best friend's half-sister that had enabled Myles to walk away from her that last night when she'd offered herself to him completely. When she'd offered him the precious gift of her virginity.

That and the fact that he'd thought she deserved better than someone like him who might sleep with her once or twice and then would be gone. He'd thought *she* thought more of herself than to want someone like that.

And then she'd gone and not only thrown her virginity away on some wide boy like that bouncer, but she'd filmed it and leaked it to the press, as well.

Instantly he shut down the quiet doubt that had always nagged in the back of his mind.

Rafe had always claimed his half-sister had been innocent, but if that were true Rae herself would have told her side of it a long time ago.

He'd fallen for that innocent act once before. Surely he wasn't stupid enough to let himself be taken in by it a second time?

'I'm here because your brother asked for my help.' He injected a deliberately harder tone into his voice, reminding himself that nowadays he was immune to that look of hurt that skittered across her face. 'Not to blow smoke up each other's backsides.'

She blanched, but he had to admire the way she jutted her chin out that little bit more.

'I was merely complimenting a colleague. I had no idea it was so offensive to you.'

Her self-assurance was heady. He hadn't been prepared for quite how much of a woman Rae had grown into. But he could resist her, he'd proven it that night when the temptation had been immense.

So why, after all these years, did something still scrape away inside him making him feel raw and...*edgy*?

'I'm not here for you.' Was he repeating it for her benefit, or for his own? 'I'm here because Rafe asked me to be.'

'The same way you came to our home all those Christmases ago, because Rafe hadn't wanted to spend the holidays alone with his new stepfamily after his mother had just died?' she challenged.

'Rafe and I were recruits together. We did officers' training together.' Myles shrugged. 'They break down the individual and build up a team.'

'Is that why you tried to talk Rafe out of leaving when the stipulations in my father's will forced him to leave the British army and move to America to take over the Rawlstone Group instead?'

'Being an officer in the army was the one thing your old man knew Rafe truly loved. It was a power play from the grave.'

'Obviously.' She let out a humourless laugh. 'But why did you care so much?'

For a moment, Myles almost didn't answer.

'Because when I was on a medical mission that went south, Rafe's infantry unit was there. I owe my life to your brother.'

'Which is why you couldn't refuse his request to play at being my bodyguard.'

Something skittered over her features, too fast for him to read.

'Yes,' he bit out, instead.

He just hadn't banked on that old attraction roaring into life at the mere sound of her voice through a door. A chemistry like a volcano that had lain dormant for so long that it had fooled even himself into thinking it was extinct, but which now rumbled and heated and swelled within him.

And she was looking at him as though she felt exactly the same way.

'I'm glad it's you,' she whispered suddenly. 'I don't think I could have gone through with this if Rafe had found anyone else to play the part.'

Dammit, she was creeping under his skin and he didn't think she even knew it.

He couldn't allow her to know he still looked at her like that. That he still thought of her the way he had done fifteen years ago. That he still thought of her *at all*.

He tried reminding himself that his career as an army surgeon was all he'd ever needed.

But then he remembered that was gone, now—blown apart in an instant—and he had nothing.

Nothing to be proud of any more. Nothing to offer. Not to any woman, but certainly not to Rae. So, if he couldn't keep his tone even, controlled, neutral, then he was going to have to go the other way.

He was going to have to ensure that the last thing Rae wanted to do was revisit old haunts best left to rest.

'I owe Rafe. And if that means taking on the role of discreet bodyguard to his half-sister—' the words were deliberate, as if to wedge even more distance between them '—then I will. But believe me, Rae, as soon as it's over I'll be back out of your life faster than you can even turn around.'

Rae couldn't move, could barely even breathe, and she had no idea how she'd managed to answer him. Caught in a fist so tight that it felt as though it was crushing her soul right out of her chest.

She swallowed hard and plunged in.

'Fine. Then…we keep it strictly professional.'

'That would be best.'

He didn't blink, didn't even move. There was no trace at all that he even remembered the kisses they'd shared. The way he'd made her body come to life as no man ever had before.

Or since.

'Rafe mentioned that you've already completed the necessary qualifications and that you and he have been discussing a clinical observation role for some months already?'

'I'm weighing my options,' Myles confirmed curtly.

A coldness crept over her skin; the sense that he was trying to shut her out as much as possible. It shouldn't hurt. But it did.

She fought to peel her eyes off the man who stood, more imposing and mouth-watering than ever, in front of her. She failed.

He looked well.

Actually, he looked more than *well*. She wasn't sure when they'd closed the gap between them again, but he was so close now she had to tilt her head right up to maintain eye contact. To prove she wasn't really as intimidated as she felt. To pretend her heart wasn't doing odd… *flippy* things.

Myles was tall. She'd forgotten quite how tall. She wasn't exactly short to start with, but even wearing heels as she was, he still towered above her. Six feet three with shoulders wide enough to block out the view from even the expansive picture window behind him, but then a V-shaped chest tapered to a narrower waist, more athletic-fit than body-builder-fit, and powerful thighs encased in dark trousers. Familiar, and yet at the same time different.

His body itself looked like a weapon—precisely honed

and utterly lethal, but it was more than that. He'd grown up, she realised with a start, and now he was more honed, more powerful, more...*dangerous*.

He positively exuded dominance, strength, control. As they stood there glowering at each other it was as though the last decade and a half toppled away without warning.

'I'm sorry.'

The apology was out before she even knew the words were on her tongue. But his scowl only deepened.

'What for?'

Rae hesitated. What *had* she meant? That night? Justin? Whatever had happened to Myles' distinguished army career?

Ultimately she shook her head, unable to articulate the thoughts that lurked in the fog of her mind, and the fringe that she'd been growing out, which was too long to be bangs but too short to tie back into her trademark ponytail, fell forward from behind her ear.

For a split second she thought his hand moved, as though about to tuck the hair back into place. And then she realised he was merely lifting his arms to fold across his chest, even as he took a step back. Putting more space between them, leaving her inexplicably bereft.

Had she imagined that instinctive, smouldering gaze from Myles? She must have, because the look he was casting her right now was, at best, one of distaste. At worst...

God, she still wanted him.

Realisation crashed over her like an icy wave on a scorching day. Because if she still wanted him, after everything, then she was as much in danger of making a fool of herself in front of the man as she had ever been.

And that simply couldn't happen.

Heat scorched her cheeks as Rae remembered the way she'd crept into Myles' room practically naked that last night and offered herself to him in the most intimate way she possibly could. He'd responded so urgently, so demandingly, so loaded with intent, she'd been lost in the moment and totally unprepared when he'd wrenched himself away, bundled her up into the quilt from the end of his guest suite bed, and pushed her unceremoniously back out into the corridor, slamming his bedroom door in her face.

He'd rejected her. Without a word of explanation. And she'd felt as though her world had crashed around her. The fact that he and Rafe had left the next day for some army exercise had meant that there had been no chance for her to get answers, and so for months she'd shut herself away wondering what was wrong with her. If she wasn't pretty enough, or sexy enough, or experienced enough.

Nonetheless, a bruised self-confidence didn't excuse the fact that she'd been stupid enough to fall for lies from a piece of trash like Justin. How had she ever thought that he could make her feel like an attractive woman again?

'You're sorry for what, Rae?' he repeated, his voice harsher than ever.

But if she couldn't explain it to herself, how could she explain it to Myles?

In all these years she'd never once explained herself to the press. Never once tried to put forward her side of that story. Not least because she knew no one would listen. Or if they did, they would spin it so that somehow she ended up coming out even worse.

Stupid, as well as scandalous.

More than that, if she'd told the truth, said that she'd known nothing about the camera, then it would have been a criminal offence and there would have had to have been a legal case.

Inevitably there would have been a character assassination of her, and even back then Rae had known that if the police and press had delved into her, then they might have found out about Myles.

She would have ruined his friendship with her half-brother, dragged his reputation through the mud, and even harmed his army career. All because she hadn't seen Justin for what he really was…a lying, scheming lowlife who just thought he could use her connection to *Life in the Rawl* to get his own fifteen minutes of fame.

Plus, she'd figured the less drama, the quicker it would all die down.

She'd been wrong. It had been too juicy for the press to let go of. It was only in the last few years of her becoming a fully-fledged doctor and OBGYN that they had finally begun to leave her alone and stop trying to connect her to any decent-looking male with a healthy pulse.

The silver lining, if she could call it that, was that she'd long since learned to *own* her mistakes. *Own* the woman those awful experiences had moulded her into. It had become her armour, her best emotional defence. And right now, with her head swirling wildly and thoughts jostling impatiently, she needed some way to buy herself time before she blurted everything out to him without first preparing the ground, and inevitably ruining her one opportunity to make him understand.

She needed something familiar. She needed some kind of anchor.

Even if a part of her knew that anchor was actually a tub of cement shoes ready to drown her at any moment.

She tipped her head almost coquettishly and pulled her shoulders back in the kind of deliberately provocative move her sisters executed to devastating effect on practically a daily basis, but which she hadn't used in years.

'Forget it.' She even managed to force the beginnings

of a wicked little smile, even if her cheeks did feel tight and unwilling. 'I wasn't really thinking.'

Myles locked his jaw and she could practically see the tiny pulse flickering away.

'Of course not,' he ground out. 'Because why change the habit of a lifetime?'

'Why indeed?'

She didn't care that he was staring at her as though she were a fleck of contemptible mud on the toe of one of his polished army boots. Really she didn't.

Not, she imagined, that he would *ever* tolerate any form of dirt on his parade boots.

And it didn't twist inside her to know that he, like pretty much the rest of the world, actually believed that she had ever had any part in that vile sex tape. There was no reason for this shameful heat that spread over her cheeks. She'd long since mastered the art of pretending that it didn't get to her. If she could fool the press, the public, then she could certainly fool Myles.

Tilting her head that little bit higher, Rae forced herself—however many knives stabbed into the dark hollow where her soul had once been—to meet his glower.

As if she were simply playing the game he evidently thought she was playing, although her voice damn near cracked when she answered him.

Myles narrowed his eyes but she ignored it.

'Well, now we have those *pleasantries* out of the way—' she rolled her eyes to make her point '—I think it's time for me to go. I have a lecture to get ready for. Doctor or not, I find the press prefer glamorous photos to dowdy shots.'

'Is that so?' Myles pursed his lips and she knew he was thinking of the sex tape.

Just as she'd intended, she told herself.

It was the only way.

Other than Rafe, Myles was the only other man alive who she'd ever wanted to impress. She couldn't explain it, but in some perverse way she would prefer he hated her for the choices he thought she *had* made, than know she was so pathetic that she'd let someone like Justin play her.

She scowled at him, and in that moment something crossed his face, pulling his features and making her look again.

She realised abruptly that he didn't look as well as she'd initially thought. Or, more accurately, he looked physically incredible, but *non-physically…*?

Her heart kicked before she could stop it and it was all she could do not to reach out and touch his tense, strained face. His eyes were darker than she remembered. Bleaker. Grim and laced with pain.

Her head swam with echoes of her half-brother's words outside the doors just before they'd entered the room. That Myles needed their help.

She had known that Myles had spent most of his career as a battlefield trauma surgeon with a specialty in plastic surgery—specifically with burns from bombs, IEDs and mines. But hearing that Myles had been caught up in it, injured so badly that he'd chosen to leave the army altogether rather than fly a desk, was sickening.

It had been awful hearing Rafe tell her that Myles, having been authorised to return to operating, had turned down lucrative job offers with hospitals up and down the UK, as well as opportunities in multiple top US hospitals.

It had taken her a while to understand what Rafe had been suggesting.

'I think that right now Myles needs to see other specialties of medicine.' Rafe's caginess had snagged her attention. 'I need you to help him, Rae.'

It was the closest she'd ever heard her half-brother get to a plea.

'Let him see a different side to being a surgeon. One which doesn't involve suicide bombers, and maimed kids, and putting your closest buddies in a body bag.'

She'd felt sick on Myles' behalf.

She could have told her brother that being an OBGYN wasn't all hearts and flowers; that death touched this area of medicine, too. But somehow it didn't seem the same. Especially when she remembered the look on Rafe's face when he'd told her that a lance corporal, a mere kid, had taken his own life that day, and that he feared Myles blamed himself.

'Is he right to?' Rae had asked abruptly.

She hadn't meant to, but she'd suddenly found that she was shaking and this was the only way she could stop it.

'Of course not.' Rafe had looked momentarily annoyed, before making a clear effort to soften his tone. 'Please, Rae? You'd be solving two problems for me. You would be getting a bodyguard we can both trust. And you would potentially be helping the man who showed me how to be the best leader and soldier I could possibly be.'

The pain on his face had got to her. But it was nothing like the expression she was looking at right now on Myles' face. Fifteen years ago she would have ached to steal that pain away for him. *But not now*, she told herself firmly. *Not now*.

Rae wasn't sure she believed herself or why the words sounded so hollow in her head.

But still, she would do what Rafe had asked her to do. Not just because it was her half-brother asking, but because, deep down, they both knew she liked to fix people. She couldn't fix her own life so she concentrated on others'. It was probably one of the reasons why being an OBGYN suited her so well. There were always dark moments but in this field the outcome was more often positive, especially when it entailed bringing a new life into the world, and into the arms of an ecstatic mother.

If that couldn't shine some light into whatever dark pit Myles was in, then surely nothing could?

And the fact that she was the one helping him—that maybe she could prove to him she was a skilled, professional OBGYN and that the incident with Justin, for which she'd become infamous, was nothing more than a brief, shameful moment in her past—had nothing to do with it.

'You know you can talk to me, Myles,' she began impulsively. 'I'm a good listener…whatever you're going through.'

She knew immediately it had been the wrong thing to say.

'Did you manage to sleep on the flight?' he asked abruptly.

How she wished she could take her words back. Swallow them. Instead, she tried to regulate her breathing enough to answer.

'Yes.'

Seven hours of blissful, uninterrupted sleep in the company jet's bedroom suite had inarguably been more comfortable than the doctor's accommodation at the New York clinic where she'd snatched the odd hour or so whilst pulling her second thirty-six-hour shift of the week.

'Clearly it wasn't enough—you still look tired.' He peered at her, concerned.

It was hard to ooze the nonchalance for which she was so ironically well known when her whole body was going into overdrive at the mere suggestion of solicitude from him.

'Gosh, thanks for the compliment.'

She even managed to keep her voice from shaking, but Myles ignored her dry tone.

'You should look after yourself more.' He apparently felt the need to hammer home the point.

Rae chastised herself for hoping for something more praiseworthy from him.

'Says the man who, if you're anything like my brother, exists on four hours' sleep a night.' She kept her laugh deliberately light.

He shrugged as though it was okay for him.

Her chest cracked.

So much for Myles being her bodyguard, meant to protect her, to ensure she didn't get hurt. As far as Rae was concerned, he was the one person who could wound her more deeply than anyone else ever could.

Just as he had done before.

Clearly fifteen years had taught her absolutely nothing.

CHAPTER THREE

'CASE C CONCERNS emergency foetal intervention at twenty-five weeks and four days into the pregnancy, for a sacro-coccygeal teratoma. That is, a congenital tumour growing at the base of the foetus' spine. It is one of the most common tumours amongst neonatals, occurring in approximately one in every forty thousand babies. But because it arises from stem cells it can be made up of any kind of tissue from anywhere around the body.'

It took a while for Myles to realise that he was as caught up in her lecture, her enthusiasm for her subject matter, as everyone else in the ballroom.

She looked magnificent up there on the stage and holding the entire conference in silent rapture. He had hugely underestimated her. Underestimated the residual feelings that still ran between them, and now he was here. Paying the price.

He tuned back in, unable to help himself.

'Ultrasound. And because the teratoma has a blood supply, the baby's heart was pumping much harder. It was as if they were in competition and the tumour was winning, resulting in a significant risk of the baby going into cardiac arrest.'

Myles shifted his position.

He'd been a battlefield trauma surgeon for so long. He'd never imagined doing anything else. Never wanted to.

But that was before.

In seventeen years, nothing had quite got to him like that day with Mikey, and what had happened in that village. And, suddenly, he'd found himself never wanting to pick up another scalpel for the rest of his life. Not because he was afraid of what he might do. But more he was afraid of what he might no longer be able to do.

Ever.

PTSD. Not uncommon after so many back-to-back tours, and so many atrocities, but that didn't make it any easier to accept. It didn't make the idea of going back to operating any more appealing. Which was why accepting Rafe's suggestion of clinical observation—a sort of halfway house—had made sense, even if he hadn't actually *liked* the idea.

He had his qualifications. And it wasn't as though he was doing anything else. The death threats to Rafe's family had been the proverbial added bonus. The tie-in with Rae almost like fate. He focussed back on Rae.

'The de-bulking of the tumour on the actual foetus usually takes less than half an hour,' she was telling them. 'The majority of the five-hour operation is spent opening up the uterus in the first instance, and then stitching it closed again. Our biggest concern is to avoid compromising the health of the mother, and we have to make sure the uterus is sealed and watertight.'

Fascinated, he allowed himself to be absorbed by her presentation. Her care for her patients shone through her excitement for the skilled procedure. She handled the questions well, informing without patronising, always happy to elaborate or explain.

For a moment, Myles forgot everything. Who he was. Where. Why. And just let his old enthusiasm for medicine begin to slowly unfurl. Then the ballroom erupted into applause, and Myles made his way backstage to meet her.

It hit him even before he turned around. The shift in the atmosphere, the way the air seemed to close in on him. When he turned around, she almost stole the breath from his lungs.

It wasn't Rae's looks that struck him, although she was certainly attractive. She'd always been attractive, and that hadn't changed. But this was something more. A presence, an aura, for want of a better term. She carried herself better than she once had, but with none of the arrogant hauteur he'd been expecting.

Unsettled, he could only stare in silence for what was a split second but felt more like a minute; fighting the sensation that he was actually drowning in his own lungs.

When had they closed the gap between the two of them? And why did the unexpected proximity send a slew of memories cascading through his brain, all of which centred on the chemistry that had arced between them that Christmas, the hot glances and the bodies brushing against each other in the long corridors of that old house?

And now those shrewd eyes were assessing him. Judging *him*.

'Good lecture. I'm glad to see that you've finally found something for which it's worth being well known.'

It was a low, cruel blow, and he loathed himself for it. As though he was deliberately trying to goad her. To remind her of the girl who had leaked a sex tape, which Rafe had only found out about when some of his men had been watching it online, in the middle of a tour of duty.

To remind her of the girl who had offered him her virginity first.

What was he angrier about? That she hadn't waited for

him? Or that she'd rubbed his face in it by doing it for a sex tape for the world to see?

Or maybe he was trying to remind *himself* of that girl, since his body appeared to be reacting to her in a way of which his brain unquestionably disapproved.

She blinked, a faint stain spreading across her cheeks, and if he hadn't known it to be impossible he'd have thought he saw a flash of shame and regret in those forest depths. But then it was gone and she eyed him with distaste.

'Which is fortunate for you, since you're to be shadowing me.'

He tried to pretend her voice didn't tremble a little at the end. That she was still as strong as she was clearly pretending to be. Because otherwise it might make him soften all the more towards her.

And that wouldn't be acceptable. There was clearly more wrong with his state of mind than he had feared.

Then she crossed her arms over her chest as if it could somehow provide her with some degree of armour, when all it really did was highlight the generous breasts Myles was unexpectedly having to fight to pretend he didn't notice.

Lust barrelled through him. As shocking and unwelcome as it was unstoppable. Making his body fire up like a mark five thunder flash.

In some perverse way, he almost welcomed it. Ever since that last mission he'd been numb. Unable to feel, to want, anything. In the six months since he'd left the army he'd been existing, not living.

At least this—whatever *this* was—made a change from the hollow, empty *nothingness* that had swirled around his chest for so long now, like the dark waters moving perniciously beneath the blue marble of an ice road, ready to claim a life the moment that sheet barrier grew too thin. Ready to erupt in a blowout at the first opportunity.

It was time to open the memories on the girl he'd once known. To finally acknowledge that he might have been mistaken in what he'd thought about her all these years.

Almost against his better judgement, he found himself employing one of the skills he'd perfected so well throughout his career.

The ability to re-evaluate.

Her hair, as long, thick, and glossy brown as he remembered, was pulled back into an attractive yet practical ponytail thing. Her clothes were professional yet subtly sexy and she wore no false nails, or eyelashes, or caked-on make-up. In fact, he couldn't be sure she was wearing any make-up at all, her face was so clear, so soft.

Horrified, he realised his fingers were actually itching to touch her, to see if she was as smooth as she looked. He balled them quickly and resisted the urge to shove them in his pockets. Yet her eyes flickered, as though she somehow knew.

His head was already a mess without the complication of attraction. He felt like that angry, desperate twenty-one-year-old all over again, not knowing where his life was heading but knowing he needed to take the only chance he had to get away from the nightmare childhood that had made nasty Ronald Rawlstone look like Father of the Year.

That Christmas with Rae had been the only time he'd ever stopped, and wondered, and wanted. Even if she'd never known it.

He needed to understand if he really had been a gullible idiot to have lain there that night and wondered if he should just walk out of his room, down that hallway, and risk it all to be with her.

'I was with Rafe on his last tour of duty when your father died. When you leaked that ignominious sex tape,' he said quietly. 'I was with him when we walked in on men, soldiers under his command, watching you...frolic... on-screen.'

She blanched but he forced himself to go on. Pretending it hadn't seared him as much as it had seared Rafe, if for very different reasons. Pretending he hadn't harboured secret fantasies of returning to the US after his tour of duty and making good on the offer she'd presented him with on that crazy night.

If he pretended it was just about the way she'd let down Rafe, and not about his own hurt pride, then maybe it could be true.

'Your brother...half-brother, had to command those men. Up until that moment, he'd been respected by those men. After that, things changed.'

'I didn't...' She faltered, then stopped.

'You didn't what?' Myles echoed.

But she didn't answer. She simply shook her head.

And what galled him the most was that suddenly there was a small, hitherto non-existent part of him that desperately wanted to hear her say something, anything, to make it less unpalatable.

It made absolutely no sense. And yet he *ached*.

They were standing close. Too close. He could feel her breath on his chest, rapid and shallow. The temptation to step forward, to lift his hands to her face, to...what? *Kiss her?* That couldn't happen.

He had no idea how he managed it, but, abruptly, he took a step backwards. Was the distance a blessing or a curse?

Rae stood motionless, silently willing Myles to stop moving away from her, though she couldn't explain why.

Her eyes were still locked with his, which were the same intense colour as the most turquoise-blue waters that lapped at her favourite Caribbean island. Eyes that had plagued her darkest dreams for the last decade. He might as well have weaved some kind of spell over her at that first encounter all those years ago.

But, more than that, she'd seen the respect when he and her brother had approached each other, she'd heard the fondness, and suddenly she found herself craving it, too.

To be on the receiving end of a warm look from Major Myles Garrington, instead of a look that suggested he considered her on a par with the dirt on the sole of his shoe.

He'd changed so much in the last fifteen years. He was now so solid, so unyielding, so authoritative. And yet, in some way she couldn't put her finger on, he hadn't changed a bit.

It left her feeling strangely rattled. Undone.

'You didn't what?' Myles pressed again.

She wanted to tell him that she wasn't the woman the press made her out to be. That the only man she'd ever been intimate with had been Justin. That she'd thought herself in love. That he'd assured her *he* had been in love.

She could almost taste the words on her tongue, sweet syllables that could free her.

Or condemn her.

Because she knew what her reputation with the salivating press was. Knew what the public thought of her. And even if none of that were true, hadn't she thrown herself at Myles that New Year's Eve? Of course he was going to believe she was capable of doing exactly the same thing with Justin only months later.

He would never believe that wasn't at all how it had happened that night.

The best thing she could do would be to forget any history with Myles. But surely it was impossible *not* to notice the man now looming in front of her? The man who had always been *good-looking* but who now made that term seem flimsy and two-dimensional.

His handsome qualities had long since segued into something more brooding, more weathered. His strong features now had character. They told a story. She was already spellbound, and it frightened her. Just like the lines etched softly onto his skin, which suggested he'd been places, seen things, *done* things. He was a hard, autocratic, lethal kind of handsome.

'I didn't *frolic*,' she bit out abruptly.

His mouth curled ever so slightly, his antipathy surely evident. Yet inexplicably it only made her traitorous fingers twitch to reach out and touch those unusually bow-shaped lips; the dimple gave him the most glorious cleft chin.

Would it still feel the same as it once did beneath her fingertips?

Before, when she'd said she'd been *expecting someone... more*, it struck her that what she'd really meant was someone *less*. Someone who didn't affect her anywhere near the way this one man affected her. Someone who didn't make her feel as though she were searing from the inside out. Cauterised by his every mocking look, desiccating from his indifferent tone.

Just as she always had been.

'Of course not,' he replied silkily. 'Because you're the steadfast, quiet Rawlstone sister, with no press reputation at all. Forgive me but I forgot.'

She flashed her brightest smile.

The one that she had long ago learned best concealed all the hurt inside her.

She knew exactly what the press said about her, every

line, every lie. Which made it a hard reputation to shake. Although, by God, she'd tried.

But whilst Rafe might appreciate how she'd struggled to distance herself from her mother and sisters all this time, the press weren't always as understanding; the public not completely forgiving.

Neither was Myles, standing there, judging her as he was. She felt weighed and she felt measured, but what bothered her more was the shame flooding through her body at the realisation that this man...*this* man...found her deplorably wanting.

How was it that his opinion of her mattered so much more than that of hundreds, even thousands, of other people? The way he'd got under her skin with barely a word was shocking. Frightening. Not least because of last time. What was the matter with her? She wrinkled her nose in self-castigation, blurting words out before her brain had the chance to engage.

'Why are you doing this, Myles? Just so you can taunt me?' Her pitch was rising but she couldn't seem to control it. 'Just so you can remind me of the fool I made of myself when I crept into your room practically naked, stupidly— so stupidly—imagining that the kiss we'd shared earlier that evening meant you wanted me?'

'This isn't about that night,' he rasped, his voice so unrecognisable that it took a moment for her to realise it really was him.

'It isn't?' she whispered.

'No, Raevenne, it's definitely *not* about that night.' There was no mistaking the look of utter disgust that contorted his features now.

She tried to rearm herself but it was too late, and his loathing smashed over her with deadly force.

'I try not to remember that night. It isn't difficult. It isn't something I ever care to think about. I thought you were different, Rae, I thought you were someone else, someone worth being honourable for.'

'Yeah, well, having a door slammed in my face certainly didn't feel *honourable*.'

She didn't know why she was fighting back. What she was hoping to achieve.

'You offered me your virginity.'

'I know what I did.' Her whole body felt as though it were on fire. 'And I know you practically laughed me out your room.'

'I believed I was doing the right thing. I thought…' He paused as if having to catch himself. 'I thought your innocence meant more to you than it obviously did. I was leaving, as soon as that Christmas break was up and Rafe felt as though he'd done his duty. I felt you deserved more than someone who slept with you once or twice and then cut out, never to be seen again.'

'It did mean something to me—' she began.

A brash, humourless laugh, which she barely even recognised, cut her off.

'Of course it did. So much so, in fact, that you not only slept with the next guy you dated- and I use that term very loosely- but you filmed the whole thing and leaked it on the Internet all in the name of fame.'

Nausea crashed over her and it was all she could do to fight it back. Still, she couldn't stop herself from crying out.

'I didn't know anything about it. I didn't know he was filming me. I certainly didn't leak it. My God, is that really how little you think of me?'

'That's bull,' Myles growled, ignoring her question. 'If you hadn't known anything about it then he would have been filming a sex act without consent. That's a criminal offence. You would have said something. He would have been convicted. He *should* have been convicted. But instead you stayed quiet. You protected him. Why do that unless you were in on it, too?'

She wanted to tell him. She'd imagined this moment so very many times over the years. But the words wouldn't come. Something seemed to be stopping her.

'I was pathetic, naïve, desperate and I didn't want to look any more of an idiot than I already did.' The words tumbled out inelegantly.

The harsh bark was about as far from a laugh as it was possible to get.

'Oh, come on, Rae. You can't seriously expect *anyone* to believe that. You weren't protecting yourself, you were protecting *him*.'

She shook her head, hating the very idea of that.

'I wasn't. I never protected him. I hate him. I…' She bit her lip and then decided she had nothing left to lose. 'I was protecting you.'

The silence that descended on them was so instant, so heavy, that for a moment she thought her eardrums had burst and all she could sense was a ringing in her head. For long, long moments they stood, eyes locked, perfectly still, and then Myles spoke.

'Say again?' Dark, forbidding. It wasn't exactly the response she'd been hoping for.

Rae drew in a deep breath, her voice quaking unrecognisably.

'I was protecting *you*,' she practically whispered. 'Just like you protected me that night when we were kids. You were so principled even though you were only three years older than me. Telling me I was too innocent, too young emotionally, that I might hate myself when you left, that I was Rafe's sister.'

Not that it had made her feel any better, and less *re-*

jected, at the time. Even now she couldn't shake the knowledge that if she'd been sexy and worldly like her sisters, even at seventeen, he couldn't have walked away from her however principled he was.

But that was a truth she would always hug to herself. A truth too embarrassing to voice aloud to anyone. Ever.

He didn't answer, but the locked jaw told her that he was barely containing his fury. She hurried on before he could say any words she didn't want to hear.

'If I *had* told people that I hadn't consented then there would have had to have been an investigation. It would have been my word against his. They would have looked at my sexual history. And they might have found out about you.'

'We didn't do anything,' Myles growled, his obvious contempt slicing through her more deeply than she could have thought imaginable.

In all her scenarios over the years, she'd never once considered that he wouldn't believe her. How foolish that seemed now.

'But *they* might not have believed we didn't do anything,' she cried. 'And you know what they say about mud sticking. Your name would have been dragged into it whether we liked it or not. The press would have loved any whiff of scandal concerning a supposedly principled British army officer. The truth wouldn't have mattered. Your reputation would have been tainted for ever.'

'You really want me to believe you let people think and say everything they did about you to protect me?'

Disgust, and what looked terrifyingly like hatred, clouded his face. It was all Rae could do not to shrink away, even as something tore at her heart.

'It's the truth.' She had no idea how she held her ground. 'But it wasn't just about you. Like I said, it was about me, too. Whatever I said wouldn't have undone what had happened. That video would always be out there...*will* always be out there. And there would have been no guarantee they'd have believed me over Justin. So I tried to make the best out of it. I figured it would die down when the next scandal came along.'

She could never have imagined what a miscalculation that would be.

Probably about as gigantic a blunder as blurting out the truth now and allowing herself to think, even for a moment, that Myles would believe her.

Even forgive her.

Instead she found herself staring into the glacial depths.

'Myles—'

'I don't want to hear any more.' He cut her pleading off abruptly.

'I really—'

'I said *enough*, Raevenne.'

She bit her tongue. She could refuse to be cowed by him but what good would it do to force the issue? It would only make him shut down all the more.

If that was even possible.

So instead she stood still, too afraid even to shift her weight from one foot to the other, as if they were teetering on the edge of some abyss and the slightest movement could send them plummeting down.

She wasn't even sure if she remembered to keep breathing.

And then, finally, Myles spoke.

'This was a mistake.'

She opened her mouth to reply but he silenced her again.

'You don't want a bodyguard and I sure as hell don't want to play one.'

Somehow, incredibly, given the maelstrom raging inside her chest, she stayed standing. Stayed...impassive.

'I'll tell Rafe this isn't going to work.'

She should be pleased. Relieved. Wasn't this what she'd told her half-brother less than twelve hours ago? That she didn't want a bodyguard again, reminding the press of her past.

So why was a part of her silently screaming out to Myles not to do this?

'I thought you said you owed him.' She had no idea how she kept her voice from breaking.

'I'll find some other way to repay him,' Myles bit out.

She opened her mouth, then closed it again.

She had no idea how long they stood there after that. It felt like a lifetime but it was probably no more than thirty seconds. Until the shrill sound of a mobile cut through the air, making Rae jump.

Was it her imagination or did Myles hesitate for a fraction of a moment before answering it?

'Garrington.' As his eyes lifted back to hers, his expression utterly impassive, something Rae couldn't identify snaked through her. 'When? How? Understood. Follow the SOPs, keep me apprised.'

He terminated the call, his focus still locked onto Rae. She ran a tongue over suddenly inexplicably dry lips.

'What is it?'

'Change of plan.' His voice still gave nothing away, although for a brief moment something skittered across his features before it was gone. If she hadn't known better she might have thought it was concern. 'I'll be your bodyguard for the foreseeable.'

She tried to control the panic rising inside her.

'What's going on, Myles?'

He paused for a moment before dipping his head in a ghost of a nod.

'Your Manhattan home has been broken into. There's a fair amount of damage.'

She was going to be sick.

'Opportunists?' she managed to get out.

'At this point I don't know. It could be coincidence, but I can't rule out the possibility that it's related to these death threats.'

'Myles—'

'Rafe has the company jet ready. You'll need to get home to confirm as soon as possible if anything is missing so we have a better idea if it was a directed attack.'

'I can't.' She shook her head frantically. 'I can't do this alone.'

Vaguely, she was aware of Myles taking her hand.

'You won't be alone, Rae.' His voice sounded gritty, lower, but her head was spinning too much to be sure. 'I'm not going anywhere. I won't let anything happen to you.'

And with that he erased the confrontation of the last twelve hours as if it had never existed.

The tears came without warning, silent and hot, but suddenly she was stepping towards him, a part of her desperately needing his warmth and strength. And then his arms were around her and she was drawing comfort from him.

'I can't stay in the house,' she muttered against the solid wall of his chest.

'We'll go to a hotel. I won't leave your side.'

'Promise me?'

He paused, and when he spoke again his grave voice rumbled deep inside her.

'I promise, Rae.'

Later, much later, when she was alone in the company jet bedroom, she would remember that moment. The way he hadn't exactly enfolded her in his arms willingly, but he hadn't exactly pushed her away, either.

She would wonder at the sanity of staying in a hotel with him whilst her emotions seemed to be so scattered, so fluttery, and she would conclude that sleeping in the hospital's on-call rooms would be infinitely safer, both mentally and physically.

And yet she would wonder if, after all, she might finally be able to convince him that she wasn't the woman the world all too often made her out to be, but more like the girl he remembered from that Christmas all those years ago.

CHAPTER FOUR

'COME ON. EMERGENCY C-SECTION.' Rae spoke crisply as she hurried down the stairs to the operating rooms, taking the steps two at a time.

They'd barely spoken since that night she'd given the lecture back in the UK. The night when he'd come so close to letting her see just how easily she could wrap him around her little finger. Still.

The night he'd hit back the only way he'd known how, but which had given him no pleasure and had, if anything, made him feel like a complete bastard. Since then, he'd accompanied her to her home to check what had been stolen, all of which had confirmed his suspicion that the break-in wasn't opportunists but was somehow connected to the death threats.

He'd stayed with her at the hospital whilst a team cleared up her home, but otherwise they'd only conversed on a medical basis.

He should be pleased. He should feel victorious. They had sidestepped the inappropriate attraction that, as ludicrous as it was, lurked between them even after all these years, and put things on a purely professional footing.

Instead he felt oddly deflated. Oddly…at sea.

It wasn't just concern for her personal safety and the knowledge that Rafe's fears weren't entirely unfounded.

Although he had to admit, both of these facts had affected him far more than they had any business doing.

It felt somehow more personal than it should do.

'Veronica is a thirty-six-year-old parturient,' Rae hurried on, forcing him to pull his head back into the game. 'She arrived on the labour ward a few hours ago, five centimetres dilated and progressing nicely. However, she's subsequently developed heavy bleeding and the baby's heart rate began to drop dangerously low. Suspected placental abruption, which an ultrasound has appeared to confirm.'

He might have been an army surgeon for his whole career, but he could remember back to his training enough to know that when the placenta detached from the uterus wall prematurely, it could be life-threatening for the baby, who could be deprived of nutrients and oxygen. Not to mention the bleeding. But Rae had said the baby still had a heart rate.

'Partial abruption?' he verified.

'Yes, but it could turn severe at any time, which is why we're going in for the baby.'

'Understood.'

Dr Raevenne Rawlstone, his mind wandered again as they moved swiftly through the corridor.

She wasn't at all what he'd been expecting and, as galling as it was to admit it, over these last couple of days, she'd thrown him. Perhaps even more than she had back in the UK less than a week ago.

And it had been one thing reading about her success and skill as a doctor from afar, but it was quite another experiencing it first-hand. She was also a surprisingly generous teacher.

And he could only admire the fact that she'd pushed some society gala—due to start in an hour—in order to extend her thirty-six-hour shift into something even more inhuman.

She was more like the army surgeons he'd worked with, shoulder to shoulder, for so many years, and it was beginning to make him...*homesick*? Homesick for operating.

It was entirely unsettling.

And that was without the added complication that he'd been pretending hadn't existed ever since that first meeting in Rafe's offices, of that ridiculous attraction that still smouldered between them.

Wholly incongruous and utterly inappropriate.

Yet, there it was. Still sizzling in every unguarded look, hastily smothered into a deep scowl, every careless brush against the other, which was instantly replaced by a deliberate step away, every time they came to the same medical conclusion only for the moment of connection to be immediately severed by some imaginary scalpel.

He could recall with all too startling clarity the occasion her hair had grazed his forearm at some point when they'd been examining the same chart, and a jolt of electricity had snaked its way up his biceps, across his shoulder and right through his chest. Or the deep shiver that had run through Rae's body when she'd reached across him for the ultrasound machine and his breath had lifted the hairs slightly on the back of her neck.

She'd lingered just that fraction too long and he, foolishly, hadn't been able to help himself repeating the action.

He caught himself shortly after that; tried to remind himself of exactly who Raevenne was, and precisely why Rafe had employed him.

These moments of weakness wouldn't be happening again. He refused to let them.

'Which is why we need to deliver the baby by C-section before the abruption is complete.' Rae shouldered the door open as they hurried to scrub in. 'I'm guessing you didn't do many C-sections in your time as an army trauma surgeon?'

'It wasn't really a common procedure, no,' he demurred. 'Although I have assisted in a couple. All of the field hospitals I worked in treated civilians as well as allied and enemy soldiers, although usually for injuries. But some of the civilians were pregnant women and sometimes the injury meant the baby was coming out whether we liked it or not.'

'Okay, well, now you get to see it day in and day out. Then it's up to you to decide whether changing speciality to OBGYN is for you.'

Something unexpectedly hot wound through him at her clipped tone.

How much of his recent events did she know?

Tucking the question to the back of his mind, Myles scrubbed up and followed her into her operating room. He knew that, even after this, she still wouldn't go to the ball until she'd checked on her last patient, the seven-months-pregnant woman who had been admitted with significant bleeding after falling off a ladder while trying to decorate a Christmas tree for her three-year-old daughter.

Exquisite.

Her fitted dress showcased every delectable curve to perfection without being too revealing, her dark hair swept off her neck and piled artfully on her head like the rich, chocolate mirror coating of the dessert he already knew was her favourite indulgence after a long, gruelling shift.

It was only one of a multitude of insignificant facts he should not have taken the time to learn about her at all. He'd told himself that moving into her house with her was a sensible precaution after the break-in. That it was his job, that Rafe was paying him to be as vigilant with his sister as they'd always been *out there*.

Deep down he suspected there was something far less noble—and something far more primal—behind his decision.

He had never understood Rafe's misplaced sense of protectiveness towards Rae after the tape had come out. Yet now, here he was, watching Rae circulate the ballroom, with something reeling and circling his chest that he feared was all too close to that same protectiveness.

Her passion for the charity shone out of her like a glorious, golden light, buoying the guests and instilling them with the pre-Christmas spirit on what was otherwise a dreary November night.

A night which was all about raising enough money to buy Christmas gifts for displaced and refugee children, and ship them worldwide in time for the special celebrations.

Though why Rae needed anyone else to help her was beyond him—surely her enthusiasm alone could have filled up this ballroom ten times over.

She was charming guest after guest as though she didn't know that they would delight in making vicious, cruel comments behind her back as soon as she'd left. He watched them do it.

Could practically hear their ugly, bitter laughter from across the room.

His hands clenched in the pockets of his tuxedo. Forget two-faced, most of these people were more like forty-faced. They didn't deserve so much as the time of day from a woman who had, up until an hour ago, been delivering triplets in the most complicated birth he'd seen to date.

There were women here he could well imagine had been primping and preening all day, at least, just *to be seen* at this supposedly philanthropic event. Rae, however, had shucked off her operating garb, dashed in and out of the shower and dried her hair courtesy of a quick blast crouched under the hand-dryers, and had been in the car ten minutes later applying her make-up and dictating medical notes.

Yet she eclipsed every single person in the room.

She shimmered amongst them, delicate and breathtaking. Like the most glorious butterfly flitting amongst a deadly cluster of predatory dragonflies.

The army had honed his observation skills to perfection over the years, yet it had felt as fascinating, as *game changing*, as it did right now. He took in everything, his mind processing it and trying to make sense of it all. From the close-knit team back in the hospital who, to his surprise, clearly adored their hard-working Dr Rawlstone, to the guests who barely retracted their claws as they fawned over Rae at this ball.

Only one thing stopped them from being rude to Rae's face. They might feed off her long-time bad-girl reputation, but she was still a Rawlstone and these people knew the value of that. Which was why they laughed and fawned over her, and pledged hundreds, thousands, even tens of thousands in some cases, of dollars to the charity that Rae so earnestly promoted.

And all those vainglorious men, who laughed so uproariously when their jealous partners sniped about Rae, all the while not so secretly coveting her. Men who took every excuse to touch her, who undressed her with their eyes, who would sleep with her in a heartbeat only to, he was sure, turn around and plead they had been involuntarily seduced by her.

There was no reason whatsoever for him to feel aggrieved on Rae's behalf.

Certainly not for the shards of possessiveness that

lanced through him when he was least expecting them. The way his hands itched to run over her unequivocally sexy, feminine form. Or the way he felt altogether too hot, too wired, too greedy, as he struggled to drag his eyes from the way she sashayed around the floor.

But he didn't try too hard. Myles reminded himself that it was his job to watch her, to ensure she was safe. It was what Rafe had brought him in to do. He firmly quashed any other thoughts in his head.

Abruptly Rae stiffened, her expression becoming that little bit frozen, her movements less fluid. He followed her line of sight, ready to move, although he knew from the silence in his earpiece that she was in no physical danger.

It wasn't hard to spot what had unsettled her.

Her sisters were making their way towards Rae, along with the matriarch of the Rawlstone Rabble, their tight expressions and false smiles evident even from this distance. From the way they were bearing down on her, they weren't intending to merely compliment her on a successful charity gala. Or at least, any compliments would most certainly be like roses. Beautiful on the surface but with well-placed barbs designed to draw blood if one was foolish enough to forget to look out for them.

He started forward, only to stop himself. Rae's family was *her* problem. He was here to protect her from any maniac stalker, he wasn't here to protect her from her *tiger shark* relatives. If her sisters ganged up to feast on the weaker one, then surely that was for Rae to deal with herself. Wasn't he forgetting that at one time they'd all been as bad as each other?

Yet since when had he thought her the vulnerable one? Only a week ago he'd thought of her as a highly skilled predator herself.

What was the matter with him?

And then she looked up, her gaze snagging his, the frantic glimmer in her eyes tugging at him even across the vast ballroom. He knew it wasn't his situation to resolve—he should stand his ground, continue observing the guests. But suddenly he was moving again, parting the buzzing throngs with the same ease with which he had parted villagers in the crowded towns when on patrol. Gaps opened up for him and closed behind him without him having to say a word, without him even having to look twice, so that before he had time to talk himself out of it he was there.

Standing next to her. Pretending his body hadn't just gone up in flames the second her arm had slipped around his in a grip that was too tight to even attempt to conceal her anxiety; the second she'd edged closer to him as though she thought he was some kind of protector.

'Who would have thought that you would object so vociferously to a bodyguard when your life might be in danger from a stranger,' he murmured darkly, 'yet leap at the chance to have one when you're in the sights of mere family.'

'Given that you've done little to hide your opinion that my side of the Rawlstone family is trashy, I can't imagine you're really all that surprised.'

Her response might have been pitched only for his ears, but its unexpected feistiness rippled through him. Something he might have mistaken for *pride*, if he hadn't known better, swirled around the two of them.

'Clearly I was mistaken in thinking your look from across this immense room was a plea for help. You can obviously look after yourself.'

Her grip tightened on him.

'Of course I can, I've been doing it long enough. But, since you're here, you might as well stay.'

A week ago he might not have recognised the faintest of

tremors in her tone. What did it say that he recognised it, now? That it made him nudge that little bit further forward with his body, as though to shield her that fraction better?

And then her family were there, and her grip on him loosened only long enough to accept their greeting.

'I hope you're working the room properly, *pug*.' The fake air kisses set his teeth on edge almost as much as the deliberate slur. 'This is quite an event we're championing here tonight.'

Pug. How had he forgotten the cruel nickname her sisters had given her? Because she'd followed him around that Christmas holiday just like their neighbour's ugly old pug.

'I expect it to be a massive success if I'm putting my name to it,' another sniffed.

As if it were *their* victory rather than Rae's, Myles thought. As if they'd done more than simply show up having been made-up and coiffured to within an inch of their inconsequential lives.

'It's already a success,' Rae tried to assert.

'Front-page-news success?' Her mother arched one condescending eyebrow. 'I don't think so. You need to do better, Raevenne.'

'I am—'

'Six-figure sums, child,' the older woman snapped.

'That only happens when someone gets the ball rolling. Like the Jenning family. And, after all, Mariella Jenning is one of your best friends, Mother.'

'I lunch with that woman.' The feigned shudder was purely for dramatic effect. 'You can't possibly ask me to stoop so low as to ask her for money.'

'For charity,' Rae cried before appearing to catch herself as her sisters laughed scornfully.

'Don't be absurd, *pug*.'

'Fine, well, how about Rowena Kemp? You don't lunch with her.'

'Are you insane? You expect the first time I speak to a member of the illustrious Kemp family to be asking for handouts?'

'Donations.' Rae gritted her teeth.

'I'm not talking to anyone about something as vulgar as money, Raevenne.'

The contempt was cutting enough to slice a person in two. It was credit to Rae that she managed to hold her ground, even if she did conceal a shaky exhale of frustration.

'It's a charity gala. You do understand that asking for money is *exactly* what we're supposed to be doing?'

'We're not doing anything so humiliating,' her mother snapped. 'So you'd better pull your finger out and sort it out yourself. I will not allow you to associate us with a failure.'

'I didn't ask you to associate yourself with it at all,' Raevenne bit out. 'In fact, I don't remember talking to you about it even once. You just decided to throw your names in when Rafe set up the gala and you realised anyone who's anyone in Manhattan was going to be here.'

'Don't whinge, Raevenne. It doesn't suit you. And for that matter, neither does that hideous get-up you're wearing.'

'Oh, I don't know if that's fair, Mummy,' her other sister cut in with the kind of saccharine smile that set Myles' teeth on edge. 'Maybe she's *deliberately* trying to remind the world that she's still that whore from the sex tape.'

He could feel the strength drain out of Rae in the way she sagged against his body, her grip dropping from his arm. He didn't think, didn't hesitate, he simply turned around and wrapped his arm around her to keep her upright.

'I think we're done here, Rae. Let's dance.'

Then, without waiting for a response, he propelled her through the crowd and away from her jealous, vindictive family.

'Put your arm on my shoulder,' he muttered as soon as they were a safe distance away.

It made no sense that her pinched white face should make him feel quite so murderous.

'Raevenne,' he commanded, his voice low and direct. 'Put your hand in mine and your other on my shoulder and dance. Or do you want those witches to win?'

She hesitated, then, as if on autopilot, obeyed his command.

'Good,' he murmured approvingly. 'Now, dance. And smile.'

She managed the first but not the latter.

'Is that what I look like?' her voice finally came out, strangled and quiet. 'Like some kind of…*tart*.'

'You look beautiful,' he growled before he could even think twice. 'Sophisticated, smart, elegant. All the things your grotesque family can only dream of being.'

The twist of her lips could hardly be described as a smile.

'That's the most hypocritical compliment I've heard all night, and, trust me, I've heard a lot of them tonight. I know you hate me, but of course you'd say that. Rafe is paying your salary.'

'That's not why I said it.'

'Of course it is.'

'Look at me, Raevenne. I don't like games and I've no time for people feeling sorry for themselves, so I'm only going to tell you this once. *Look at me.*'

And then she did.

It was like a punch to his lower gut. He wanted to erase

every ugly thought she had in her head right at this moment. He wanted to make her see her hideous family for what they were and realise that she was no longer the eighteen-year-old who had made that life-changing video.

He knew his reaction made no sense. He couldn't explain it; worse, he didn't want to. He wasn't sure exactly who *this* Raevenne Rawlstone was, or even if she could really be trusted. All he knew was that he no longer felt as though he was talking to the girl who had humiliated Rafe all those years ago.

'Tell me what, Myles?'

Her voice was barely recognisable, its quiver seeming to mirror all the emotions he was trying to deny were jostling inside him, desperate to get out. He refused to let them, but then she flicked out a tongue to moisten her lips and he was powerless to stop his eyes momentarily dropping to track its progress.

'I didn't want to take this job protecting *you*. I admit it.'

Her expression flickered, like a flame on the verge of being extinguished. He felt even more of a cad.

'Then why did you?' she managed.

'I needed the job,' he stated flatly. 'And Rafe asked me to.'

It was close enough to the truth. How could he tell her that a part of him had welcomed the offer when he'd been ashamed of such a reaction?

'Well, you don't need to worry about it for too much longer,' she managed bitterly, before she could stop herself.

'Which means what, precisely?'

'Forget it. So that's what you wanted to tell me?' Disappointment crept into her voice. 'An admission of something I already knew? That you never wanted to play bodyguard to me?'

He hesitated, assessing her. Evaluating. Or maybe he

was evaluating himself. He couldn't be sure. 'Not entirely,' he conceded after a long moment. 'I wanted to apologise.'

'You did?'

'Rafe told me a long time ago that the stories…the stories about you…weren't true, but I didn't believe him. I just couldn't understand why you wouldn't go to the authorities.'

'I told you why the other night.' She was clearly trying not to sound bitter. 'You didn't want to hear it.'

'Would you?' The challenge burst out before he could swallow it. 'Hearing that protecting my reputation and my career was the reason *you* allowed someone like that to use you?'

'So…you believe me?'

Did he? Evidently he must do.

'It isn't easy to change what I thought to be true all this time,' he hedged.

'You're not the only one. It's hard to shatter people's perceptions, especially a bad one they simply love to hate.'

Why did it feel like a victory that he'd swept that sad expression from her features and now a small smile toyed at the corners of her mouth?

Too late, he realised he was bending his neck, almost ready to claim that soft, inviting mouth with those perfectly pink, plump lips. Jerking his head back, he caught himself in time.

'Your family taints everything they're associated with, even a charity event. It's time you distanced yourself from them, Rae, the way Rafe did.'

'I've spent years distancing myself from them,' she cried out.

'Then you need more distance.'

'Trust me, soon enough I won't be able to get any more distance.' She stopped abruptly, biting her lip.

As if she hadn't intended to say anything, as though the admission had tumbled out before she could stop herself.

'Rae?' he prompted, using the tone he'd perfected as an officer. The one that made his men talk to him even when they might have preferred to keep it all inside.

'There's a woman here—' she wrinkled her nose awkwardly '—Angela Kaler, who helped me to organise this charity event. I'm joining her worldwide health programme abroad.'

'Angela Kaler?' he frowned. 'I know her. A few years ago the army sent my unit, a logistics unit and some engineers to join her organisation on one of the hearts and minds missions in a former warzone.'

'Yeah? Well, now she's running humanitarian programmes sending doctors where they're needed, whether conflict zones, or just a remote area in need of a school or a hospital or a well; or where there's been a natural disaster, or maybe an epidemic. I volunteered.'

'*You're* going? What does Rafe say about it?'

'Rafe doesn't know.' She jutted her chin out defiantly, voicing the one thing he didn't want to hear.

'Rae—'

'No.' This time, she refused to cow to him. 'This is something I want to do. I've done all the courses, all the tests, all the evaluations. I passed them all. I got my mission a while ago. Myles, I've been planning it for months... long before he made you shadow me, and long before this latest death threat.'

'Yet you must see that's exactly why you can't now go,' Myles pointed out.

She shook her head wildly, her eyes suddenly dancing with the same kind of light as when she saved a baby. Only now, it was even brighter, even more mesmerising.

'Surely that's even more of a reason to go? If that break-in wasn't opportunistic, and if my life *is* in danger here, they definitely won't be able to get to me where I'm going. I'll be safe, Rafe will be happy, and you'll be free of baby-sitting me. Everybody wins.'

Only, for a moment, he wasn't sure it felt like a win for him. And he couldn't help feeling Rae felt the same. This…*thing*…still shimmered and rippled between them, however much they pretended to ignore it.

But what was the alternative? That he joined her out there? An invisible band tightened around his chest, making it painful even to draw breath. Images of that village, those bodies, flashed in his brain like flicking through a photo album too quickly to dwell on any single photo, but recognising the images all the same.

His heart picked up its beat, and he fought off the urge to stick a finger between his stiff white collar and his skin. He wasn't ready to go back to a conflict zone. He still hadn't processed what had happened that last mission. The people he'd been laughing with only hours before…

Not to mention the decision he'd made to ignore his gut when he'd discovered that Lance Corporal McCoy—Mikey—was part of the squad that final, fatal time.

It was all he could do to keep looking at Rae, to keep dancing, to keep upright. If he could get through tonight, buy himself enough time, experience told him it would be a lot easier to work things through in the light of the morning. Maybe Rafe was right. Maybe he should have talked to someone.

He just had to get through one night.

Just tonight.

Abruptly, he stopped dancing.

'Where's Angela now?' he demanded.

'Why?' She was understandably guarded and nervous. 'Myles…we've stopped dancing. People are watching.'

'Let them watch.' He didn't care. 'And I'm coming with you.'

Sliding his arm around her, he whisked her around, a weave and a turn and they were back into a decent space.

'That's insane.' She was trying to stay light in his arms, following his lead and floating like a feather. He could tell she felt anything but. 'You can't come. You don't have clearance.'

Something deep in his chest thudded with apprehension. Old fears slowly resurrecting themselves, but he stamped them down.

They had no business in the here and now.

'I was a trauma surgeon in the field six months ago—I have clearance.'

He'd just hoped to never use it again. And yet...

'You can't go into the field within twelve months of being in the forces.' She sounded panicked.

'Some organisations say that,' he acknowledged. 'But not Angela's. Her criteria are different and I fit it. I know that for a fact.'

'You need evaluations.'

'Shall I say it again?' He had no idea why a part of him actually seemed to be thrilling to the concept whilst another part balked. Loudly. 'They're all covered.'

She stared at him, her green eyes wide and shooting sparks.

'This is nonsense, Myles. You have to have a special training for contagious diseases and tropical medicine.'

'I did a year with the Liverpool School of Tropical Medicine in the UK.' He held her tighter, and he couldn't work out who was holding whom upright. 'You can't get rid of me, Rae. I'm coming with you and that's decided.'

'But...'

It was done. He couldn't afford to second-guess. He'd

made a commitment to Rafe and he was seeing it through. He wasn't about to let his buddy down. Not even if that meant going back out to hellholes like those with which he was all too familiar. And there was no other reason for his change of heart.

None at all.

'Now, shall we see about getting those donations for you? Let's make this event the best fundraiser these social climbers have ever had the privilege of attending. And as for the rest of your family, they can go and jump in their new handmade rock pool.'

CHAPTER FIVE

HOURS LATER RAE still hadn't processed what Myles had said.

He was coming with her?

It had sounded surreal. But she'd decided that if she just clung to Myles, if she simply stared into those eyes that were so hot, so searing that they seemed to cauterise each lash and wound from the tongues of every single person in this room tonight, then maybe she could emerge from this gala miraculously unscathed, after all.

And so she'd clutched him, physically and mentally, as she worked her way around the room, inch by inch, making sure the night was an unequivocal success. Whether her family tried to take credit for it or not, this night had to be a triumph by securing eye-watering donations from even the Jennings and the Kemps and telling her that the charity deserved nothing less.

Enough to buy container loads of medical supplies, clothing, and heaving toy boxes for the kids. Christmas several times over.

So why did it continue to needle her that he'd shut her out so abruptly back there?

And why did it thrill her when they worked together as though they were some kind of team? Her and Myles against everyone else. Certainly against her family. Gravitating towards each other as they had done a decade earlier. As though it was the most natural thing in the world. As though it was more than just a situation engineered by her half-brother. As though she and Myles were the kind of real couple that everyone who had seen them had assumed them to be. And so she was still clinging onto Myles when he walked her through her door several hours later—the first time she'd returned since the break-in, more relieved than she would ever admit that he and her brother had agreed it wasn't safe enough to leave her alone. Not until they could identify the reason for the break-in.

Still, it didn't stop her from grumbling as she walked along the corridor half an hour later only for Myles to step out of the bathroom. Her nerves were jangling in an effort not to let her eyes drift down the naked, solid, mouth-watering chest. Or to linger on the soft white towel that teasingly just about went around his hips but stopped halfway down his thighs.

She tried to shift. The air seemed to have closed in on her, almost stealing the breath from her lungs. The strange magnetic draw that she'd spent the last few days denying was impossible to ignore now they were stuck in a room… well, a corridor…together. Alone.

All of a sudden her clothes felt too tight for her body and she was sure her tight nipples were visible through the soft tee.

'I still don't understand why this particular death threat has Rafe so rattled. It isn't like we aren't always getting them. He's head of a global company where, no matter how environmentally friendly the design is, new construction is always angering some group or another. My two sisters— not the nicest of people to start with, I'm afraid—live off income from their substantial shares and flaunt it in people's faces via their reality show *Life in the Rawl*, and, as you've reminded mc on multiple occasions already, I've got a sex tape out there, which won't go away no matter how many babies I deliver or how many lives I save.'

Something flashed across his features—too fast for her to put a label on it, and less muted than that first day, but she might have guessed it was disdain.

She told herself it didn't cut through her. That his opinion of her didn't matter any more than that of hundreds, even thousands, of other people out there.

'And is your brother always getting into cars where the brakes have been tampered with?' he asked bluntly.

She reached out for the handrail to steady herself.

'They tampered with Rafe's brakes? He never said.'

'He didn't want to scare you.'

'Whilst you, of course, don't care about that.'

He shrugged, and peered at her and she had the oddest sensation he was trying to see right down to her soul.

Her body and her mind were spiking with desire, and for a moment they stood there, watching each other, not moving. She was desperate to say something, anything, to fill the silence. To give him and his ridiculously tantalising towel a reason not to leave. It made no sense.

Or more worryingly, it made perfect sense.

'You didn't have to do that, tonight,' she managed. 'Help me get donations, I mean. I know I'm not your favourite person.'

'I wanted to.'

'Thank you.'

They stood again, silent and motionless. The tension cranking up a notch. Something inched down her spine and, if she hadn't known better, Rae might have wondered if the thermostats hadn't been set a touch too high. It was paradoxical, then, that she shivered.

She might have known the ever astute Myles wouldn't miss it.

'Cold?'

He hitched one eyebrow. *As though he knew it was pure molten heat burning though her.* She narrowed her eyes.

'A little.'

'Liar,' he whispered.

The wry smile tugged at the corners of his mouth, snagging her gaze, pinning it, and doing things to her insides that he had no business doing. Her stomach couldn't have been more fluttery if it had turned into the lepidoterarium where last year's fundraiser had been held. But infinitely worse than that was the way a fire was roaring deep inside her, much, *much* lower down. The smouldering embers making heat, and desire, and *need* pool between her legs.

What was the matter with her that she was so incredibly attracted to this man? Even after all these years. He was like an insect that had crawled under her skin and was itching her from the inside out. It made no sense.

She would be wise to remember that Myles had never said that he believed her explanations as to what had happened with Justin, just that it was *difficult to change his perceptions.* And the truth was that he'd never even tried to explain his *own* actions that night he'd rejected her all those years ago. Yet she still felt as if she weren't herself. That she hadn't found herself. Worse, there was no denying the electricity that sparked and arced between her and Myles.

So many years later and she was pretty much in the same position she'd been in all those years ago.

'You know my sisters will give me the third degree next time I see them?' She swallowed hard, trying to loosen her dry tongue. To find something—anything—to say to break the silence. 'They'll want to know exactly how I came to be in contact with you again. And how you came to escort me to that ball.'

'I can't say I give a damn what that lot want to know.'

He took a step towards her, his voice unbelievably husky. Sexy.

She should back away. The idea of something happening between them was insane. And yet she couldn't bring herself to move a muscle. All she could think about was how much she longed to tell him the truth. But that was madness. The whole world had already decided what they knew about her to be true. Whatever she said, Myles wasn't going to believe her.

And did it even matter? In a few days she'd be gone. Thousands of miles away on the month-long posting that she'd told him about earlier that evening.

By the time she returned, Rafe would have resolved the issue of the death threats and life would be back to normal. No more bodyguard. No more Myles.

The last thing she needed to do was complicate it now.

He took another step towards her.

'I'm not who you think I am, you know,' she choked out in panic.

She hated that he pulled a face. She was suddenly so desperate for him to know the truth. As if, if she could convince him that she wasn't the girl the media had set her up to be—had never been that girl, not really, not intentionally—then maybe there was hope she could one day convince the rest of the world.

'Stop, Rae. You were better off when you didn't play that game.'

He was so close now she could almost feel the heat bouncing off his body.

'It isn't a game,' she managed shakily.

'I've seen enough about you over the years to know it's always a game with you lot.' The words were ground out almost as though he was acting against his own will.

And he still didn't step away. He didn't break eye contact.

'Myles—'

'Stop talking,' he bit out.

There was no reason at all for her to obey. *So why did she?*

And then he'd closed the gap completely and they were standing there, in front of each other, and she had no idea what to do next.

Myles, by contrast, suffered no such doubts.

He reached over, thrusting his fingers into her hair and hauling her to him, to his mouth. Then he kissed her.

And, oh, how he kissed her.

He didn't just press his mouth to hers, he claimed her, invaded her, branded her with every slide of his tongue and every graze of his teeth.

Her entire being exploded, like the most dazzling firework display on New Year's Eve. She wasn't sure when she'd lifted her hands but somehow they were on his shoulders, her fingers biting into the thick, corded muscles, revelling in Myles' strength, his size.

Like coming home.

Briefly, images of that awful tape, and the way she'd been with the press those years immediately following the most humiliating year of her life, flooded her brain.

She should tell Myles the truth, she thought weakly. Surely basic pride, self-respect, should mean she'd want him to know who she really was.

But what if he didn't like it?

He'd claimed to despise the brash, indiscreet, classless girl she'd reinvented herself into those years immediately after the sex tape had come out. He'd told her that she epitomised everything he despised. He'd been only too quick to accept the media lies that this was the girl she still, albeit to a moderately lesser extent, was.

Yet here he was. On the one hand telling her that he loathed her. On the other, kissing her as though he couldn't get enough of her. Would *never* get enough of her.

He certainly hadn't kissed the quiet, innocent, pure Raevenne like this.

Which made her wonder which girl he was *really* attracted to.

And then there was the fear that she would tell him what had really happened, and he wouldn't believe her. Sadness spiralled down inside her like the helicopter seed from a sycamore tree.

As much as people were all too eager to accept her first, scandalous reinvention from innocent girl to man-eating, party-loving vamp, it had never suited their salacious appetites to see that only a few years later she'd reinvented herself again into a focussed, private, junior doctor.

It was too deliciously scandalous to keep seeing her as the girl she'd been for those few brief, lost years. The girl who had made a sex tape with her bodyguard to boost her ailing family name, to bring in *money*, after their father's death.

And yet she put up with it. All the press' lies and all the public's feigned shock, because, frankly, she'd wasted enough years trying to win her father's approval when he'd been alive. She'd be damned if she was going to waste more years trying to win over a public who thrived on the perceived drama.

But if Myles did that…? If he refused to see past his prejudice and only saw her as that girl, she feared it would torment her far worse than anything else. *Better not to try or know than to try only to be disappointed.*

Placing her hands on his chest, she braced herself. It was distracting, how little strength she suddenly seemed to have. How instead of pushing him away, her fists were curling around his lapels, and pulling him closer.

Briefly, she wondered where all this was leading.

Would it shock Myles to know that, even though she'd slept with Justin that night because she'd imagined herself to be in love, believed him to be her soul mate, she'd never once felt as *alive* as she had with Myles?

Probably.

Probably worse.

Yet still she clung to Myles, his mouth crushing hers so exquisitely, and hers responding so completely. As though every part of her had been waiting for him to do it all night.

As he kissed his way down her body, searing her skin with his mouth as he dropped kisses down her neck, across her breasts and nipples, which were so tight they ached, and over her belly, she closed her eyes and let the shivers of pleasure ripple through her body. He might as well have been worshipping every inch of her, and as she stood there, practically naked and otherwise exposed, she realised that he didn't make her feel ashamed, or small, or cornered, the way Justin had.

On the contrary, Myles made her feel powerful, desirable, all woman. It was a heady experience. She'd never ached for *anyone* the way she ached for Myles.

If only she knew how to act on it. How to *show* him.

He was kissing her to prove a point, Myles told himself fiercely. A point to himself. To her. It didn't matter. All that mattered was that he understood that he wasn't kissing her because he hadn't been able to bear another second without doing so.

He wasn't kissing her because his entire body had

ached for him to do so ever since they'd walked into that ballroom.

No. It was ever since she'd walked into Rafe's offices back in the UK last week.

He couldn't acknowledge that the truth was altogether less complicated and more primal. He mustn't. Because he didn't want to give himself any reason to stop.

'Myles…' She murmured the objection against his lips even as her arms tightened around his body.

A better man would have listened to what she wasn't able to say. A better man would have stopped. A better man would have walked away.

Up until tonight, Myles would have imagined himself to be that man. But right here, right now, he couldn't tear himself away from the kiss. More to the point, he didn't want to,

'Tell me to stop,' he ordered, his lips barely leaving hers. 'Tell me, and I will.'

But it was a safe assurance, because they both knew she couldn't do it. They both knew that she was as consumed by the kiss as he was. As powerless to put an end to it.

Myles' skin prickled. *What was it about this woman that allowed her to get under his skin the way she did?* She was the epitome of everything he despised. Or at least, she had been. The woman he'd been watching these last few days was so different from the caricature he'd thought he'd known. And he certainly hadn't allowed for the inconvenient chemistry that arced undeniably between them.

The chemistry that meant that he was now standing— and he had no idea when or how this had happened—right in front of her with his hands gripping her upper arms, his face dangerously close to hers. A delicate, faintly floral scent filled his nostrils, making his pulse race even faster.

'What…are you doing?'

Her voice was altogether too hoarse, too raw, too…
everything, but she didn't pull away. He wondered if she
could. Was she as helplessly trapped in her body as he was
in his, right now? He could taste her on his lips the way he
had back in that ballroom. God, but he wanted to taste her
again. His body tightened painfully. His head pounded.

He pulled her closer. She didn't exactly resist.

'Myles…' It was little more than a breathless whisper.

'Tell me I'm wrong. Tell me you haven't been looking
at me like this, all night.'

It might sound like a command but it felt like a plea.
As though, for the first time in his entire life, Myles didn't
feel in control of himself, and knew that he wasn't going
to be able to walk away from her this time.

'I…' She faltered, her gaze flicking from his eyes to his
mouth and back again.

Her tongue darted out to wet her mouth and the last of
his resolve began to crumble. Desperate need gripped him.

Without warning, Rae crested up onto her tiptoes and
pressed her lips to his, the grudging mutter vibrating on
his mouth.

'You can pretend all you like, but you want me just as
badly.'

And everything else tumbled. Need and desire ripped
through him. As lethal an ambush as any he'd known out
of the battlefield, almost dropping him where he stood.

He hauled her to him, revelling in the way every inch
of her delicious body moulded itself to every inch of his,
her hands reaching up to wind around his neck, her head
angling to allow him better access.

He tasted her, plundered her mouth, losing himself in
the maelstrom of desire that had been swirling inside him
from the first moment they'd met again in the Rawlstone
Group's HQ, however much he'd tried to deny it.

Slowly, carefully, he ran his hands down her body, over the rough, metallic beads of her slinky, sexy dress, until he reached the high slit on her thigh. He should take it slower, take his time, but he couldn't. He was driven by the primal need to divest her of her clothing and bury himself inside her, so deep, so tight, that neither of them would know where one ended and the other began.

So, instead, he slid his hand inside, easing the dress enough that when he lifted her up, she could wrap her legs around his waist, her perfect heat pressed against the very hardest part of himself. And then he released the clasps that kept the halter neck in place, letting them drop, and it felt as though the very air were sucked from his lungs as he took in the soft swell of gloriously creamy skin; the deliciously hard, brown buds that strained as if in a greeting meant only for him.

Briefly he recalled the images he'd seen of her, a lot more naked than this, a lot more compromised than this. With any other woman it would have been enough to stop him. To put him off. It should concern him more that it didn't. But Rae was such a different woman from the girl in that sex tape. So far removed from the girl who'd been linked to more men than he'd had ration-packed army meals.

He desired her, ached for her, and there wasn't a damned thing he seemed to be able to do about it. He looked into her eyes, all the longing and the need he felt reflected back at him. He shifted and her breath hitched, making him feel more powerful than he'd ever felt. So, for once in his life, Myles shut his brain off, stopped trying to tell himself that he should know better, and instead let his body do the thinking.

Why not? What harm could it do?

He backed them against a wall, her legs still locked

around him and one hand still cradling her pert backside, whilst the other explored. His palm grazed her skin as his thumb raked over one taut nipple. She gasped, her eyes slightly hooded, her cheeks slightly pink, but not breaking her gaze from his. He tried it again, and this time she rocked her body so that it pressed harder against him, sending need pulsing all through him.

He cupped her tighter, letting his mouth take over from where his hand had been. His tongue swirling gently around the nipple, revelling in the way her breathing shallowed, then sucking hard until she cried out with pleasure.

Rae opened her mouth to speak only to find she couldn't say a word. He was cupping her, her sex chafing on the lacy material that he hadn't even bothered to remove. She gasped and rocked against him, his palm raking over her wet heat. His eyes not leaving hers, he twisted his hand, and suddenly he was on the other side of the lace, tracing her swollen folds with almost lazy ease. She shivered and moved against him, desperate to intensify the pleasure, but he shifted his hand away, his mouth curling into a teasing smile.

'I'll be the one setting the pace, I think, Raevenne, not you.'

And she groaned and gasped, her fingers biting into his solid shoulders, trying to obey him, yearning for him to begin again. The way he was taking his time was like some exquisite torture. It hadn't been like this her one time before. As if she could go on for ever, yet simultaneously couldn't wait another second.

As if he could read her mind, Myles drew his finger around her again, but this time, as he closed the pattern, he moved his finger straight across her core, stroking the most sensitive bud. Fast then slow, then fast again, repeating it, deepening it, until she felt dizzy, almost mindless. This time, when she surged against his hand, he didn't stop. Instead he matched her, pulled her along with him, her body clenching and fizzing and burning with this fire he was building, as his mouth now paid homage to her neck, his teeth nipping at her earlobes, pressing kisses into the sensitive hollow behind her ear.

Without warning, he moved his hand away, and it took Rae every ounce of strength to lift her head.

'Don't stop,' she gasped, not realising she'd uttered the words until Myles answered her. His voice was thick with desire, his thumb pressed to his lips.

'I have no intention of stopping.'

'Please…'

'I have no intention of this night ending any time soon.'

Suddenly his hand was back, his cold thumb pad taking up where his fingers had left off, the pace every bit as powerful, as intense as before. The sensations were cresting now, threatening to crash down over her, like nothing she'd ever known before. She was gripping his shoulders tighter, barely recognising the sounds escaping her as she began to buck against his hand. And as everything began to explode in her head, throughout her body, he slid his finger inside her, then another, his thumb maintaining the deliciously punishing pace. Rae shattered.

She was only half aware of burying her head in his shoulder to keep from crying out his name so loudly that anyone outside her room might hear. And still Myles didn't stop. Without warning, he twisted his wrist and the last of the explosions sounded in her head, and then she was soaring and tumbling, and there was silence. Pure, blissful silence.

She finally came back to herself to find him watching her. The unguarded look in his eyes pierced straight through her, making her heart do strange looping things in her chest.

You're falling for him, you little idiot.

The voice sounded remarkably like the sharp, bitter mocking of any one of her sisters.

You're a fool if you think this is anything more than just sex to him.

She blanched, hating it, and tried to thrust it aside. But not quickly enough, it seemed, and before she could think twice she was bracing against him, pulling away.

'Rae.' The warning was unmistakeable, but she pretended she couldn't hear it.

She couldn't afford to hear it.

She wanted him inside her. So much that it was almost painful. She wanted him to take her, to show her all the things she'd read about, heard about, but which Justin had ruined for her. The reason why she couldn't bring herself to utter the words aloud, however much they hovered on her lips, or hummed through her body.

'Is that it?' she heard herself demand, her cool, brittle voice nothing she'd ever sounded like before. 'The best you've got?'

'Say again?'

Something dark and lethal moved between them but she only jerked her head up higher and ignored it. There was no other way. She couldn't have sex with Myles. If that was how much he made her come apart just from touching her, if that was how easy it had been to break her defences and remember just how much she'd loved him in her girlish, naïve way, then she could only imagine how intense it would be to have full-on sex with him.

She couldn't risk it. She couldn't be hurt again by him. Not like last time.

'I must say, I've had better.' Every word scratched inside her. 'I was expecting more from you.'

'What the hell kind of game are you playing, Raevenne?'

His low voice was like a physical blow but she stood her ground, though she would never know how.

'Talk about an anticlimax.' It was amazing how still her hands were as they made a great show of sorting her clothes out, deliberately, unashamedly, with no indication of just how much she was shaking inside.

'Well, as…enlightening as that was, Myles…' *think airy, think breezy, don't think needy* '… I really don't feel we need to revisit it, do you? And, for both our sakes, let's never speak of it again.'

CHAPTER SIX

'WHAT HAVE WE GOT?'

Rae barely had time to glance at the interpreter, Clara, as her colleagues brought in a heavily pregnant young woman, clearly in pain and looking generally unwell. She gazed at the doctors with a mix of fear and hope.

Just like the hundreds of pregnant women and babies Rae had already seen in the five days since she'd arrived at the camp, none of whom had ever been under the care of a doctor in their life before.

It was a never-ending flood of desperate women, all with pregnancy or labour complications. But then, that was the issue out here. Lack of nearby medical services, lack of money for medicine, or being a displaced person meant that non-complicated pregnancies were dealt with at home. They either never came into the clinic in the first instance, or they only came in when they realised there was a problem—often, sadly, when it was too late.

And so the place was heaving with pregnant women who needed medical attention. Rae was already beginning to realise that an average twenty-four-hour period here meant sixty or seventy women giving birth and many of them—so many of them—needing emergency C-sections at the very-least.

She felt as if she was stretched so thin she was terrified of missing something.

There was one silver lining, though. And that meant the shifts were so long, so exhausting, that it was all Rae could ever do to stumble back to her room in the compound and flop onto her cot bed and into sleep—a deep sleep, not plagued by memories of that night with Myles. Certainly not reliving the excruciating awkwardness of the flight over here, when they had scarcely been able to look at each other, let alone exchange a civil word.

Even now she could feel her cheeks heating at the memory of that night together. Or, *not together*, depending on how she looked at it. The way he'd touched her, made her come alive in a way no one ever had before... Her heart skittered slightly in her chest. And then the way it had all unravelled in those final, humiliating moments...

'This is Fatima.' The interpreter mercifully drew Rae back to the present. 'She's twenty-six. She has severe pain on her right side and has suffered some blood loss. She's about eight months pregnant and she has been walking with her husband for several days, almost non-stop, to get here.'

'Is this her first baby?'

Rae carefully examined the young woman as Clara translated the question and Fatima replied earnestly between her gasps of pain.

'Yes,' Clara passed the information on, 'although she's had a couple of early-term miscarriages in the past.'

'I take it Fatima hasn't seen a doctor throughout this pregnancy?'

She knew the answer, but she still had to ask the question, just as Clara had to check.

'No one,' Clara confirmed after a moment.

'There's a strong foetal heartbeat.' Rae nodded, using

the handheld Doppler device. 'That's a good sign. Still, I'd like to take her through for a proper ultrasound.'

No need to mention her concern over the solid mass under Fatima's ribs. Not until the ultrasound confirmed her suspicions that it was the baby's head, and that the baby was lying transverse, instead of head down.

As she waited for the only machine they had to become free, Rae watched the couple as the man held his wife's hand. Caring, loving, tender. It was touching, not least because it was so different from many of the cases over the last few days.

Back home, she was so accustomed to talking to the mother-to-be, ensuring the woman gave consent for herself. Yet out here she was already beginning to learn that the women rarely made their own choices. So many times already she'd found herself conflicted when she'd spoken to the woman only for the woman to look straight to her husband or even her husband's mother, to be told what she could or could not do.

If Rafe were here, she could have talked to him. She hadn't realised quite how much she'd come to rely on bouncing ideas back and forth with her half-brother over the last few years. She could talk to any of the other volunteers, of course. She knew that. But instead her thoughts came squarely back round to Myles.

As they so often had since that night.

Since before that night, a voice echoed in her head. *Since the moment you walked into Rafe's offices and saw Myles standing there.*

It was impossible to escape him. Not physically, since he'd clearly been keeping his distance this last week, but mentally. Neither of them had mentioned the kiss, the... sex, but memories of it pervaded her thoughts constantly, even when she didn't want them to.

Especially, it seemed, because she didn't want them to. And even those mere echoes were enough to make her body shiver and pulse, and feel more alive than she had done in such a painfully long time.

Or ever.

Which was as terrifying as it was thrilling since it called into question everything she'd thought was true the night she'd let Justin convince her that she was ready to lose her virginity to him.

The night she'd told herself that if she was in love with Justin the way she thought she was, then she shouldn't keep holding herself back from sleeping with him. The night she'd told herself that if she didn't want to then perhaps she really was as frigid as her sisters and Justin mocked her for being.

She'd spent the years afterwards believing that was the only explanation. And then Myles had come along and she'd physically ached for him in a way she'd never known was possible. That night she hadn't had to talk herself into anything with Myles. She'd wanted him with such a wanton intensity that surely no one could ever have felt before.

She should have been ashamed—living up to every last false image that had been told about her over the last decade. But Myles had made her feel so...*alive*, so *free*, so powerful. It had been like nothing else she had ever imagined. Nothing like Justin. How could she regret that?

So she'd spent the past few days here desperately ignoring him. She'd got away with it so far, but she couldn't avoid him for ever. Not if she didn't want the other volunteers to notice and start wondering. She and Myles had arrived together; it would be obvious if she avoided him for the entire month.

As she'd heard at least three times already this shift, even in a place as hellish as this it couldn't be all work, *all* the time. There had to be at least a few moments of snatched private time, or else one would go truly insane.

Which meant once her shift ended, she was going to have to go and find him and come up with a solution.

She told herself that it was purely apprehension that made her chest spin like the triple-axle she'd learned to execute as a youth champion ice-skater.

'Machine's free.'

Rae stared blankly for a moment, the words taking their time to sink in, to push away the unwanted thoughts of Myles. And then she was moving, grateful to be able to focus on her patient.

The ultrasound confirmed her suspicion, and since the baby was clearly intent on coming out that night, one way or another, there was nothing else for it but to carry out an emergency C-section.

As Clara translated all the information and gained consent from the mother, Rae looked around for one of the senior surgeons to brief.

'I can join you, if you like,' offered Janine, a sixth-time volunteer and one of Rae's mentors. 'I've just cleared a clinic of the usual diarrhoea and urinary tract infections. I have a free half-hour.'

'That would be brilliant.' Rae nodded gratefully. 'I knew the lack of healthcare out here meant complicated pregnancies were more common than I was used to, but I don't think I was prepared for sixty to seventy women giving birth in a twenty-four-hour period. And many of them to twins or triplets because of the unregulated fertility pills out here.'

'No one is ready that first time.' Janine laughed. 'But you'll get used to it and be a dab hand before you know it. And wait for a busy night when north of ninety women give birth and there are a couple of quadruplets thrown in for an added kick.'

'Oh, well, thanks for that.'

'Any time. Seriously though, Raevenne, you've already settled in well these last few days. You'll be fine. Come on, you take the lead on this one, I'll just assist.'

And then it was time.

Sucking in a steadying breath, Rae lifted the scalpel and began.

'I'm going for a transverse abdominal incision, given the position of the baby.' She cut carefully until she could see the uterus.

But it wasn't what she'd expected and it didn't make any sense. She stopped, frowning. A glance at her equally baffled mentor didn't help. They began a quick set of checks.

'It *is* the uterus,' she breathed a few moments later. Half a statement, half a question.

'It is,' Janine concurred.

'But it looks like a normal, non-pregnant uterus? Yet I felt the baby. I saw it on the ultrasound?'

'Try extending the incision upwards. Until it's T-shaped.'

Dutifully, Rae cut until she was where the gallbladder might usually be. Only it wasn't a gallbladder.

'It's an abdominal pregnancy,' they both gasped at once.

Rae shook her head in awe. How was it possible that this baby had developed entirely outside the uterus? Entirely inside the abdominal cavity?

Ectopic pregnancies might occur one or two per cent of the time, but in pretty much all those cases the pregnancy was usually in the fallopian tubes, and would be terminated because of the high risk to the mother. But to see a baby—an almost full-term baby—still alive, outside both the uterus *and* the fallopian tubes? Rae had been prepared for the high number of complications out here, but she could never have imagined she would ever see something like this.

'I've only ever read about this in my medical journals back home,' she marvelled. 'And even then there was only a sketch to accompany the condition. It's just extraordinary.'

'Once in a lifetime,' agreed Janine. 'And if we're somehow able to get this baby safely out whilst keeping Mum well, I think it will stay with me as the most incredible birth of my career.'

'Do you think we can?' Rae bit her lip. 'Save the mother and the baby?'

'We can certainly try. The baby is crying, so I'd say that was a good sign. We're going to have to get it out as quickly as we can. You see that mass there? That's the placenta. We need to remove it carefully so as not to cause bleeding.'

They worked swiftly, carefully, with one eye on the baby and another on the mother. Both of whom seemed to be doing remarkably well.

Rae wasn't even sure she was breathing during the entire painstaking procedure. But suddenly they were closing up and it was all over and she and Janine stared at each other in disbelief. Tired but elated.

'We'll still have to keep a close eye on them. The mother is at risk of both bleeding and infection, and I don't know how the baby is going to develop, but you should be very proud of yourself, Rae. That's an incredible job tonight.'

'Thank you.' She smiled, not sure whether it was the baby they'd just delivered or her mentor's praise that was filling her with such an incredible sense of euphoria.

'Right, now didn't your shift end an hour and a half ago? So go and get something to eat, get some rest, and we'll do it all again tomorrow. Well, maybe not *this*, exactly.'

'No.' Rae laughed, feeling exhausted but insanely proud. 'Not exactly.'

She wasn't sure whether she crawled, walked or floated to the doors of the clinic but she might have known her escape wouldn't have been that easy as a frantic-looking colleague from the general hospital on the other side of the courtyard came racing in.

'We've got an old guy hauled out of the river. Don't know how long he was down but he was in a bad way. We've run out of stuff. Have you got any blankets and fresh trousers over here?'

She should keep walking. Her shift was over but her next one would start in a matter of twelve hours.

Rae glanced over her shoulder. Everyone was hectic, as always, and time clearly wouldn't be on the old man's side if he had hypothermia.

'I'm just coming off shift. If you fill out one of your department's authorisation slips I'll run it to the warehouse for you.'

The issue sheets were a precious commodity around here. There was no way the women's clinic could afford to use one of their own for goods from the main hospital, and the warehouse staff couldn't release anything—clothing, food, toiletries—without a paper trail.

'Oh, would you, doll?' the older woman breathed gratefully. 'I'll fill out a slip now. We're swamped over there.'

Rae followed her back across the courtyard, the paperwork in her hands within a minute, a quick, tight hug almost squeezing the life out of her.

A quick run to the stores and back, and then that would be it. Bed. Sleep. And a good breakfast. Then another non-stop twelve-hour shift would start. To so many people, this would be their idea of hell.

Yet somehow, Rae had never felt so settled. So right.

As if this was somehow her calling, she just hadn't realised it before.

Her first week would soon be up. Already. Another three and she'd be home. In time for New Year, Rafe had said.

Why did she already get the feeling that one month out here simply wouldn't be enough?

'Oh. I didn't know you'd be here.'

Myles stilled in his task as her voice carried in the quiet, cool air, its faint quiver hitching curiously in his chest.

He battled to keep images of that last evening at her house out of his head. He couldn't afford to go there. Each time he did, something else kicked lower, harder, and eminently more forcefully.

He'd spent five days—seven, if he included the flights over here—pretending he hadn't given in to the temptation of kissing her, tasting her, touching her.

But it was impossible. Rae was always there, tempting him in gloriously vivid Technicolor, whether in his nightly dreams or his waking hours.

He supposed he should be grateful. If he wasn't dreaming of Rae then it was other memories that pervaded his head. Nightmares that infiltrated his sleep like an unwanted invader. Images he could never, ever bury, and which would haunt him for ever.

The longer he'd been out here, the worse they'd become. But he couldn't speak to anyone. He would not talk about it. He was just waiting to get home.

This month out here couldn't end soon enough.

'What are you doing in here, Rae?' He deliberately made his voice unwelcoming, forbidding even, brutally calling to mind every scurrilous thing he'd ever heard or read about her. He couldn't fall for her act again. He *wouldn't*. 'The warehouse is off-limits.'

'I need a couple of blankets, and a pair of trousers for a patient.'

'Authorisation slip?' He held out his hand, taking care not to let their fingers come into contact as she handed it over.

Rae looked exhausted...but elated. He peered at her whilst appearing to be focussed on the paper in his hand.

He'd spent the last week overseeing her from afar, making sure she was safe just as he'd assured Rafe he would do, but he'd kept away. Waiting for her to finally admit that this latest stunt was a step too far; that she was out of her league with the game she was playing with the media; that she'd overestimated her hand in trying to improve her image by coming out to a place like this to volunteer.

Because a place like this ate into your soul. The poverty, the sickness, the pain. He recognised it only too well from his years of operational tours. Indeed, this was tame compared to some of the horrific places he'd visited; missions he'd been a part of.

But it was still eating him alive.

For someone as pampered as Raevenne Rawlstone, it should certainly have been enough to send her screaming back to New York, and the best, cushiest, private practice posting that Rafe's contacts could buy her.

Instead, she was fitting into life out here in a way he'd never anticipated. She hadn't folded, crumbled, or run to contact her brother to get her a way out of here because she couldn't cope, but rather she'd taken a deep breath, rolled her sleeves up, and thrown herself into chaotic camp life.

Which only made it all the more difficult for him to keep his distance. She was like some kind of breathtaking, beautiful angel. But a beauty, he had to remind himself, that only went skin-deep.

'I still don't understand why the clothes have to sit in this place under lock and key, when there are people out there who need them.'

He told himself not to react to her sad expression.

'Because there aren't enough to go around,' he answered simply. 'If we hand them out now to some families and not to others, we'd have fighting on our hands. That's why all this stuff stays here. Trousers, shoes, tees, whatever. Once we have enough for each family, we'll distribute them.'

'I guess.' She chewed her lip. 'But some families are clearly in greater need than others.'

'Which is why the forward camp near the border gives a basic package to every family coming through their gates.' He shrugged as he located the crate, taking out a couple of pairs of trousers. 'It's the best we can do. Certainly the fairest way we can do it. Which one is closest to his size?'

'Probably that one.' She pointed. 'Have you got a belt?'

He snorted.

'You're not shopping in one of your designer stores now. There's some twine over there. Cut a length off, that will have to do.'

He told himself he didn't notice when she wrinkled her nose and offered him an involuntary sheepish smile. Nor did he notice when she shifted awkwardly from one foot to the other with that little finger-twist tell of hers.

'Myles, I… I wanted to apologise for…you know…that night last week. I—'

There was no reason whatsoever for anything to lance through him the way that it did.

'Forget it,' he cut her off briskly, deliberately focussing on the task in hand.

He tracked across the warehouse.

'Myles…'

He thrust the blankets at her before getting her to sign the authorisation slip and giving her the bottom copy. Then he moved off, ostensibly to find a new bag of donations to sort through and filter into pallet boxes, but she shuffled along behind him.

'I don't want to hear it, Raevenne.'

For a moment he thought she might have stopped. Turned away. And then she spoke again, quietly, urgently.

'I *need* to apologise for that night, Myles. I wasn't…it wasn't…that wasn't me, that night.'

'Don't you need to get those blankets and trousers to your patient?'

She stared down, as if she couldn't remember how the garment had got into her hand in the first place. Then she jerked her head in some semblance of a nod and, muttering something he couldn't catch, hurried out of the repository as quickly as she could.

Which was a good thing, he repeated. Over and over. As if somehow he thought that might make it all the more believable.

He certainly wasn't prepared for her to walk back into the place minutes later, trouser-free.

'Raevenne,' he cautioned, but this time there was no hesitation.

She strode up to him, so close he could smell her unique scent. Whatever objections he'd been about to make erased themselves from his brain.

'Everything is at the hospital where it needs to be, so now I'm back here and you have no more excuses to push me away.'

'Then how about I'm more direct?' he growled, but she stood her ground.

'Please, Myles. I need you to know that I'm not the woman you think I am.'

'You said that once before. I was even ready to believe you, even to believe that maybe your refusal to defend yourself all these years really was out of some kind of misguided loyalty. And then you turned around the other night with that…*stunt*, and proved to me you were *exactly* the woman I'd thought you were.'

He tried to sound hostile. He hadn't thought he'd succeeded but then she swallowed once, twice, squeezing her eyes closed as if to summon up all her courage.

'What happened the other night…my reaction…was in part down to the mistake I made all those years ago, with Justin.'

Some unidentifiable emotion surged through him.

'We've already been through this, Rae. I don't want to hear it again.'

'And I don't particularly want to have to say it.' Anger flared in her unexpectedly. 'But I can't seem not to because, frankly, I'm sick of you treating me like I'm some kind of nineteenth-century fallen woman whilst you're completely blame-free.'

'I don't believe either of those things,' he said through what felt like a mouth full of gravel. 'But need I remind you that you were the one who reacted to intimacy between us by telling me that you'd had better?'

'Like I just admitted, I reacted badly, for which I've spent the last few days trying to apologise,' she bit out. 'Which you'd know if you stopped ignoring me for one moment. So I'm just going to keep making these ugly little scenes, which are embarrassing the both of us, until you shut up and listen.'

He eyed her curiously, telling himself that it wasn't hope

that made his heart thud in his chest. It wasn't desire that whispered down his spine.

He believed in loyalty and principles, and discretion. She believed in living larger than life, and in letting every last detail of her life be played out in full view of the press and the public. There wasn't a thing about her that the entire world didn't already know.

And yet he couldn't help it. Despite every fibre of his being bellowing at him not to show any weakness, not to cave, the whisper of need infiltrated his head, scraping around in there, like metal on dry ice.

A traitorous part of him wanted to listen to her.

'Fine, you have my full attention.'

She inclined her head a fraction, all elegant grace. Only the red stain creeping up her neck betrayed her.

'I panicked, pure and simple. What happened between us the other night happened so fast and I was embarrassed, because the truth is that I haven't actually slept with anyone since Justin.'

CHAPTER SEVEN

HE WASN'T SURE how long they stood in silence. He only knew that he could barely get a word out for the jumble of questions tripping over themselves on his tongue, and that his heart seemed to hang in his chest. Whether it had forgotten how to beat, or simply didn't have the strength to in that moment, Myles couldn't be sure.

'Say that again?' he managed at last.

'I think you heard me the first time.'

Her soft voice electrified him. He had to take another few moments to get his head around what she was saying.

'You're telling me,' he began huskily, 'that aside from the other night, the only time you've been...*intimate* with a man was the night you made the sex tape with your sleaze of a bodyguard.'

His needling was deliberate. He couldn't seem to help himself. But when she flinched he felt like a heel. Still, she held her head up.

'That's exactly what I'm saying, yes.'

'And you expect me to believe that?'

Something flashed through her eyes for a split second before she shut it down. It shocked Myles to realise that he recognised it as regret.

'I expect that you probably won't. But I didn't ask you to. I simply asked you to listen to me.'

'So you could make out that I was no better than that pervert bodyguard of yours?'

But what really rattled him was the realisation that, if what she was saying were true, then it was all too accurate a description.

Her face might as well have been on fire but to her credit she didn't drop her gaze. If anything, she tilted her head a little higher.

'That's not at all what I'm saying. You're nothing like him. I knew exactly what was happening between you and me, but I didn't have a clue what he was doing.'

'He was making a name for himself,' Myles snarled. 'That's what he was doing.'

'Yes, thank you. Well, that became clear *after* the fact.'

She threw her hands up in the air, her composure slipping, and to Myles' shock he realised that his fury was aimed more at the slimy Justin than at Rae.

'Did you love him?' He didn't know why he even asked. It didn't matter. He didn't care. It was just some morbid curiosity, surely?

'I… I wanted to love him.' For the first time she allowed her eyes to slide away. 'He told me he loved me and I believed him.'

'Why?'

She snapped her gaze back up to glare at him, making Myles feel as though he was missing something obvious.

'Why do you think, Myles? Because I *wanted* to believe him. The idea of someone loving me, *me*, was so thrilling. For years the boys I'd known had only ever been able to talk about my sisters, how glamourous, or sexy, or hot they were. And then here was Justin paying attention to me, and I fell for it.'

He wanted to tell her that not everyone she'd known had been so taken with her superficial sisters that they'd overlooked the real thing standing right in front of them. To point out to her how close he'd come to being with her that New Year's Eve.

But voicing something like that would be tantamount to knowingly walking out onto quicksand. The consequences were inevitable. So instead he bit back the words and stayed silent.

'I suppose I found it flattering,' Rae continued with a self-deprecating laugh. 'And hearing someone tell me they loved me was like balm to my battered ego. Not least after I'd humiliated myself the night I offered myself to you only for you to throw me out of your bedroom.'

'Christ, Rae, you blame me for humiliating you simply because I had enough respect for you not to sleep with you when you were my best mate's seventeen-year-old kid sister?'

'That wasn't what you said, though, was it?' she fired back. 'You said that I was insane if I thought you were ever going to sleep with me.'

Instantly, shamefully, he recalled his harsh words and the way he'd thrown that handmade quilt from his guest bed over her practically naked form and bundled her out into the corridor in wholly ungentlemanly fashion.

Ironic then, that he'd thought he *was* being gentlemanly by not sleeping with her.

'You were seventeen. I was twenty-one.'

'So? That's perfectly legal. Plus, I was a few months off being eighteen and you were only just twenty-one. There's barely three years between us.'

'It might not have been illegal but it still wouldn't have been a good idea,' he bit out stiffly.

Which made it sound logical, and well thought-out. But the truth was that his decision back then had been less about logic and more about convincing himself to keep his hands off her than anything else.

At twenty-one, he'd never before experienced such a heady, all-consuming attraction before. His teenage years had been too focussed on dragging himself out of the hell-hole of his childhood, trying to build some kind of real future for himself. He'd had a couple of girlfriends but nothing that had amounted to anything much.

And then he'd met Rae and their attraction, their chemistry, had been instantaneous. Overwhelming. Even despite the handful of women with whom he'd been in relationships over the years since then, none of them had equalled the same intense heat he felt with Rae.

Not that he was about to tell her that now. He could already feel that familiar desire stoking up his senses. But he was here under her half-brother's employ to look out for her. He wasn't here to revisit old temptations.

'And you think I'll buy into all this?' He let out a bitter laugh.

Anything to cover the fact that he pretty much already had.

'I know how it sounds, but it's true. I swear it.' She stepped towards him, her hands reaching out instinctively to lie flat on his chest before she caught herself, no doubt expecting him to back away.

He probably should.

He didn't.

And when she tentatively made contact, it was like throwing a match on a pile of dry, petrol-doused leaves. His whole body ignited in an instant. He remembered everything with startling vividness. Her scent, her taste, the way she'd come apart so perfectly with him. He wanted to make her lose herself all over again. To take back every lie that had slipped from her lips. To make her admit she was as hungry for him as he was for her.

He wanted to bury himself inside her, so deep that neither of them would know where one ended and the other began, and he wanted to make her climax all around him. His name the only thing in her head.

But he couldn't do any of that. He couldn't allow himself such a weakness. And it was all he could do not to let her see his reaction.

'What about the *not living up to expectations*?' he growled, trying to remind himself as much as remind her.

She flushed, a deep, scarlet stain spreading over her skin.

'I was embarrassed, Myles. You'd just made me…you know…'

'Orgasm?' he supplied.

If it was possible she flushed an even richer hue. It didn't help his self-control one bit.

'From just a touch,' she muttered.

Awareness rippled through him. He shut it down.

'Which you're now telling me was the only time you've been intimate with a man since you made that vile tape?' he stated flatly, belying the uproar in his head. His chest.

She jerked her head up and down.

'Really? Raevenne Rawlstone, the woman who changes her man along with her always up-to-date seasonal wardrobe.'

Sarcasm was etched into every syllable of the well-bandied media quote.

Rae stared at him for a moment, her eyes dulling.

'You don't believe me.'

He wanted to believe her. With an urgent, *primal* drive he'd only ever felt with this one woman; with a voice that roared that she was *his*. That she'd always been his.

Ever since he'd made her come apart in his arms barely a week ago. Even then hadn't he wondered at her sweetness, her naivety, her lack of experience? Right up until the moment she'd pulled her *'is that it?'* charade and it had been easier to despise her for that than to consider she might have been saving herself all these years? For him?

'You surely can't believe for a second that I'll buy into this *prim* act of yours?' he bit out icily, hating himself for the less than proper thoughts racing through his body.

Taking up residence in his sex as surely as if she'd skimmed her hand over him.

'Why not? Because you know me so well?' Her boldness was a delicious challenge. 'Are you really so entrenched that you can't begin to even consider that there might be some truth in what I'm saying? Or is there a part of you that can't allow yourself to believe me because then you might have to finally acknowledge that we're attracted to each other? Still.'

'This conversation is pointless, Rae,' he warned, but she ignored him.

'Just as we were attracted to each other over a decade ago. Only back then I was gullible enough to believe you when you said you didn't want me. This time, I think we both know the truth.'

He stood immobile, rooted to the spot and unable to move even if he'd tried. Never mind his legs, though, it was all he could do to get his mouth moving.

'I'm your bodyguard, Rae.'

'That didn't stop you the other night,' she whispered. 'Besides, did you really need to come to this with me? We still don't know if that break-in at my house was merely opportunistic, but even if it wasn't, surely no one is going to reach me thousands of miles away?'

'Actually, we *do* know about the break-in.' He hadn't

known whether to tell her or not before she'd brought it up herself. 'From their investigation at the house and everything that you confirmed was taken, they've concluded there is more than likely a connection between the break-in at your home and the tampering of Rafe's brakes.'

'Which means whoever it is is operating on both sides of the Atlantic?'

She paled, her scratchy voice worming into him and making him wish he could do something, anything, to take away her fear.

'There is an upside.' He would never know how he sounded so detached, so in control, when every word felt clunky and awkward, as though his brain was trying to work out how to piece words together. How to make a sentence. 'In that it also narrows the field considerably. Not many individuals have that kind of reach.'

'You're thinking competitors to Rawlstone Group? Were they trying to get to Rafe through me?'

The idea of Rae being in danger, of him having to voice it aloud, filled him with something he didn't care to evaluate too closely.

'It's too early to say for certain, but that's certainly one line of investigation we're currently following.'

She swallowed.

'Which means they *could* reach me here. If they really wanted to.'

'It's unlikely.' He forced his voice to become lighter than he really felt. 'But it can't be ruled out.'

'We have three more weeks here. Together,' she managed. As if she could somehow pretend that the last half-hour hadn't happened. 'So we have to get past this. Get along with each other.'

'You do know I will protect you, Rae?'

'From any external dangers, yes.' She looked as though

she wanted to say something else, something more, but eventually she offered a resigned shrug.

'We've managed to keep our distance up until now. Perhaps we can just carry on like that?'

'It won't work. The last few days have been hectic but as the new teams settle in we're going to have to spend more time together. It would look odd if we didn't.'

Her body slumped as though suddenly leaden.

'What are you suggesting?'

'That we find a truce. Any animosity between us would quickly filter through the camp and bring the rest of the volunteers down. So perhaps we should…forget our history. Start again.'

'Start again?' She looked dubious. 'How, precisely, are we supposed to do that?'

He hadn't thought that far. His whole adult life he'd had a plan, had mapped things out in advance. He liked it that way. He thrived on being prepared. But now his mind cast around wildly until, eventually, it touched on a potential solution and grasped it as though it were the last life jacket and he were on a sinking ship.

'Christmas. Come on, I'll show you.'

'Christmas?' She frowned.

It was galling how contained, how unaffected Myles was whilst her heart was skittering around her chest and her thoughts were a chaotic mess.

Just like that New Year's Eve back when she'd been seventeen.

She forced the past from her head and fought to concentrate on the here and now.

'Yes,' Myles was announcing, his tone clipped. 'Your Christmas toy boxes have arrived.'

'Really?'

She hadn't expected his tactics to work, but suddenly

a thread of excitement rippled through her as she hurried after him across the warehouse. And then she saw the pallet boxes, the contents wrapped in a transparent film, and she stopped dead.

It was almost surreal. The same red, white and green boxes that had been filled in New York were now out here, and her fingers longed to reach out and lift the pop-up Christmas tree on just one of them.

'I can't believe they're here,' she murmured. 'I can't believe *I'm* here.'

The excitement rippled again. And then something else. She wasn't prepared for the apprehension that suddenly overcame her, like a fire blanket thrown down to smother the flames.

'Everything okay?'

As if he could read her thoughts.

Her eyes flickered to his almost against his will.

'What was I thinking?' she murmured.

'Rae?'

'There I was, back in my sheltered life in New York, going on and on about these boxes, encouraging people to come to a charity gala just to donate for more boxes, for toys, for Christmas, when the kids out here don't need that. I was naïve. I didn't have a clue what it was really like to be a kid out here. I've wasted so much time on stuff which doesn't matter.'

'It *does* matter, Raevenne.'

'Of course it doesn't. I was such an idiot, telling people how important those toy boxes were, back home. Making such a big deal out of getting people to buy them or fill them.'

'You're not an idiot.'

'Of course I am,' she cried. 'As if Christmas means the same thing out here. The kids out here don't need stupid toys, they need real solutions for real problems, like where their next meal is coming from, whether the water is safe enough to drink, if their mother is going to get through her next childbirth without a fatal complication.'

She was so caught up in her own frustration that she didn't notice Myles reach out until he'd snagged her hand, holding it tightly in his.

'What are you doing?'

'Come with me.'

It was a command rather than a request. And one that, despite everything, Rae found herself obeying.

'Have you actually been around the camp since you arrived?'

'A little.' She wrinkled her nose.

The truth was she'd been so caught up in getting herself up to speed medically that she really hadn't had time to go anywhere but the clinic, the mess and her bed. But the last thing she wanted right now was Myles taking her around and proving to her everything she'd just said. Proving to her how much of a naïve fool she'd been thinking stupid toys made a difference.

'Have you seen the classrooms?' Myles pressed her, not letting her pull her hand free.

Not that she tried too hard.

'No, why?'

He didn't answer as he left the warehouse, locking it quickly behind them, still not letting go of her hand. She told herself she didn't feel the surges of electricity racing through her at his mere touch, making her burn up even though her breath was visible in the freezing night air.

They crossed the compound, away from the hospital and the mess and through the warren of dusty roads to another set of prefab, community-style buildings.

'They have Christmas trees,' she exclaimed in surprise.

And over on the other side of the square, a nativity scene had been painstakingly created.

'It *is* Christmas time,' Myles pointed out wryly.

'But it's a *nativity* scene.'

He laughed, but Rae got the feeling it was with her, not *at* her.

'Why not? Just because we're thousands of miles away from home doesn't mean some of the people out here don't have the same Christmas story that we have. They might not celebrate it quite the way we do, with eggnog and turkey, but it's still Christmas. They'll be feasting and dancing and singing.'

'I... Right.' She dipped her head, feeling a little foolish. Myles seemed to understand how places like this worked so easily, whilst she struggled with even the more basic concepts.

'Wait, according to the map the charity drew up for us, the schoolhouse must be around here somewhere.' He glanced around. 'There.'

'Where are you going?'

'Inside.' He barely looked over his shoulder, his voice more a command than a request. 'Come on.'

She'd seen the classrooms through their makeshift windows, complete with mismatched chairs and tables and a very old chalkboard by what had to be the teacher's desk, but she'd never been inside. She hadn't dared.

Rae only paused for a moment before scurrying after him, trying to quell her nerves as he opened the door for her to step inside the deserted building, expecting any moment someone to stop them and tell them that they weren't allowed.

CHAPTER EIGHT

IT WAS THE homemade decorations that struck Rae first. Sparkly paper chains, red felt stockings made from fishing nets, and glittery, colourfully decorated, foam Christmas tree ornaments; red-and-white Father Christmas hats lovingly made from scraps of felt, some well, some not so well, were strewn through the two classrooms. Names she couldn't pronounce sewn haphazardly on each of them with obvious pride.

In a bowl sat ornately carved wooden recorders, ready to be played, whilst an old piano with its missing front and its yellowed keys, hunched yet proud, took pride of place. She leaned over to see what they were learning.

'Those are carols.' Surprise rippled through her. 'Christmas Carols.'

'Probably to entertain the volunteers.' Myles nodded. 'You'll likely be expected to sing along.

'Really?'

'*We* will,' he corrected belatedly. 'Especially when they then teach us some of their songs.

'I didn't know,' she breathed softly.

'You weren't an idiot for wanting to give these kids those toy boxes. They might have to worry about food and water and medical care, but they still love toys and gifts and playing, just like every other kid. Perhaps it can be *more* important out here that they have something like those toy boxes to remind them that they're just kids. That they should still have something approaching a childhood.'

She inched around the classroom taking everything in.

'What are these?' She peered at some cans, empty but for the string lacing through them.

'Shakers.' Myles smiled. 'The kids will fill them with different things, some with grit, some with stone. If food weren't so scarce, they would usually fill some with rice. Then the men will tie them to their legs and do traditional dancing to celebrate the festive season.'

'I look forward to seeing you join in with that.' Maybe it was dangerous, pushing this tentative truce they'd established, but she couldn't seem to help herself.

To her relief he offered a wry smile.

'Fortunately for me, I've been to a place like this before, so I'll have an idea of what I'm doing. But don't think you'll get away without learning the women's dance.'

'Oh, I hadn't considered that. Luckily for me I'm a half-decent dancer. At least I can keep to a beat.' She laughed, realising too late that it might be too reminiscent of that night at the ball.

Was it always going to be this way? Talking with Myles as though she were walking on eggshells, not wanting to say anything to cause him to back away.

He was right, a truce was the most sensible option, and it suited her. She didn't want more than that, of course she didn't. Because that would have been insane.

And yet, once again, Myles surprised her.

'I seem to recall that you're more than a half-decent dancer,' he murmured, his hand reaching out to tuck her grown-out fringe behind her ears.

It was so gentle, so intimate, that she hardly dared to breathe, let alone move.

'Do you like Christmas? Back home?' she whispered.

She seemed to remember he didn't. Wasn't that the reason he'd been so happy to accompany Rafe a decade ago? Because he hadn't had a family of his own with whom he'd wanted to spend the holidays.

'I don't remember the last time I celebrated it. At least, not the way you're thinking. If I wasn't on a tour of duty or some exercise, then I usually volunteered to stay in barracks to cover duties to let the men with families go home.'

Why did she feel compelled to ask him the questions she knew he wouldn't care to answer? What was this urge she had to get to know him? To understand what drove him to be a surgeon? A soldier?

'You don't have a family.'

'Not one I'd care to waste my time going to see.'

At least he wasn't shutting her down outright. Then again, it probably would be wise to let it go.

'Why not?'

He glowered at her, his eyes almost glittering with unspoken distaste. If he'd turned and stalked out of the classroom she wouldn't have been surprised.

Instead, he spoke. Although it was as though every word were being dragged, kicking and screaming, from him.

'My mother gave birth to me, and she just about managed to drag me up. That's about the top and bottom of what she did for me. She had four more kids, Debbie, Ralph, Ally and Mason, all to different men. She was that desperate for love, for a man, that she did stupid things. She was pretty pathetic.'

The accusation sliced through Rae. It was all too horribly familiar. Was that why Myles had been *so* very disgusted by her sex tape? With her?

'What about *your* dad?' she managed to choke out.

'Never knew him. Only Debbie knew her dad, not that

it did her much good. Ralph died when he was a baby, cot death. Ally was on drugs by the time she was sixteen. Possibly Mason made it out, but I was gone by then, I'd joined the army, got them to sponsor me through a medical degree.'

'Oh.'

'Wishing you hadn't asked?'

She shook her head but didn't dare answer. Perversely, it felt more like an honour that he'd even told her that much.

'They make your family look like the Waltons.'

'You already met my family,' she countered. 'Aside from Rafe, who grew up with his mum in England when my dad left them for my mum, they're hardly the most... loving people.'

'Love is overrated.' The humourless laugh made her feel sad, as though she wished she could steal away some of his obvious pain.

Pain he would deny if she was foolish enough to try to point it out.

'Is that why you devoted yourself to the army instead?'

His eyes bored into her and, for a long moment, she thought he wasn't going to answer.

'Maybe. And now I'm out and I have nowhere else to go.'

'You could be a surgeon out here, or places like it.'

She shouldn't feel so hopeful. So keen.

'This isn't the life for me.' He shook his head and she felt oddly deflated. 'Not any more.'

'Do you really hate being out here?'

'It brings back memories.'

She didn't know who was more shocked. Her, or Myles himself. Tentatively, she spoke.

'Rafe mentioned that you might be dealing with some level of PTSD.'

She wasn't at all surprised when this time he didn't answer, deflecting instead with a question of his own.

'Do you really love it?'

Despite her disappointment at Myles shutting her out, she found it impossible to stop the smile from cracking her face.

'I do. I didn't expect to, and I know it's only been five days but it feels…good. I feel good.'

'I can see that,' he murmured softly, surprising her.

'You can? I thought perhaps I looked out of my depth?'

'You don't,' he assured her. 'And it isn't just how you appear. It's what people are already saying. Seasoned volunteers who have done multiple medical missions are talking about your skill, your adaptability, your compassion.'

Her skin prickled at his words, making her feel unexpectedly proud. Ten feet tall. So why did the confession come bubbling out of her?

'Sometimes I feel lost. Well…every day, if I'm honest. Back home I might deal with lots of straightforward pregnancies and labours, with a handful of complications thrown in. Here, they're all complicated, and some multiple times over.'

'I know that feeling.' He nodded. 'I found that it worked to approach it a bit at a time, doing a little bit and then another little bit, and then another, until there was nothing left to do.'

'I know. But sometimes that's easier said than done.'

'It's daunting, but you just have to be confident. You need to remember that even if you haven't ever seen any multi-part complications before, you've probably got all the pieces in your head from doing them at different times. Maybe a C-hyst here, or identifying uterine arteries during a bleed there. It's just a matter of putting it all together for one patient, here.'

* * *

'I was worried I wasn't good enough. As much as I'm loving it, I'm also finding it a lot harder than being back home. Here almost all the cases are complications, especially obstructed deliveries and UTIs but there's very little for us test-wise. There just isn't the equipment to work things up so we have to treat empirically and I'm always hyper aware that if I make the wrong call, if I draw the wrong conclusion—especially since so many of the symptoms could be any number of things until it's too late— the patient can die.'

'Every mortality rate is high out here. Maternal mortality, infant mortality.' He nodded gently. 'It's a fact of life out here that we don't have to worry about the same way back home.'

'Your home or mine?' she joked weakly.

'Both.'

'So I just muddle along, and I try to do the best I can, but I can't help wondering what I'm bringing these kids into.'

'You can't think like that. You just have to know that you're giving mother and baby a better chance than they would have if you weren't there.'

'And being alone can be frightening,' she added after a moment. 'Sometimes exhilarating but sometimes frightening. I'm used to having other obstetricians around me to bounce ideas off, but there are so few of us and so many women in labour that we usually don't have time to stop and discuss cases, or possible diagnoses, or whatever.'

'You're the only one who can decide what to do.' He nodded.

'Exactly. And what if I make the wrong decision? Or hit a vessel? Or—'

'Shh.' He stepped forward abruptly, his hands reaching out for her shoulders. 'You might think you're the only one with these fears but you're not. Everyone is feeling the same but, like you, they just have to get on with it. And like I said before, you're a good doctor, Rae. Everyone values your contribution. What's more, they all like you.'

'Thank you.' Her brain scrambled for words. He was so damned close that her body was going into overdrive. But she couldn't ask the one thing that she really wanted to know.

'Especially me,' he added brusquely.

Almost as though he could read her mind and couldn't help but answer her unspoken question. Even though he hadn't wanted to admit it.

Rae stayed silent, not wanting to break the spell. Not when his hands moved from her shoulders to cup her face, not when his thumb dragged deliciously slowly across her all too sensitive lower lip, not when he lowered his mouth to claim hers with an intensity that thundered through her body and to her core.

He kissed her over and over. Hot and wild and uncompromising. And she couldn't get enough. Standing in that deserted building, clinging onto Myles in much the same way she'd clung onto him the night of the charity gala, and dreaming of doing more—so much more—with this man.

But more of anything with Myles was too dangerous. She knew that. She should pull away now, end things before they went too far.

In the end, however, it was Myles who broke the moment. His expression was stern but his eyes were still dark with desire, and his voice was too husky, too fractured.

'We can't do this.'

'No,' she agreed, her throat closing up.

He hesitated another moment, then walked them out, wordlessly. The sun was not yet up and their matched strides were the only sound in the silent camp. To Rae, it felt as though they were almost slowing down as they walked, as if each wanting to prolong the time together, yet neither of them prepared to admit it.

And then they were at the door to her room with Myles inching slowly backwards and her standing on the threshold, unable either to put her hand out to stop him or to go inside.

'Myles…that is…would you like a coffee?' It sounded so naked and vulnerable out there that she found herself babbling on. 'It's good coffee. Proper coffee beans. I brought them over with a little hand-held grinder…you know…as my luxury item.'

'Good choice,' he endorsed stiffly, but she noted he took another small step away from her. 'I brought a guitar.'

'Oh…yes… I can imagine you with an electric guitar…'

Like some kind of rock star. It suited Myles perfectly.

'Acoustic actually.' He smiled suddenly. 'The electric sounds better with the amp and stuff, and I didn't fancy lugging all that paraphernalia all this way.'

'Right. Of course. Make sense.'

Abruptly, he glanced up and down the corridor before stepping back towards her, sweeping her inside and closing the door behind them.

'Actually, I think a coffee would be nice.'

The metallic *click* charged through her, as though they were suddenly locked in their very own Faraday cage. It was thrilling and terrifying all at once.

Awkwardly, she moved across the room to make the drinks, moving between the metal cupboard where she kept the beans to the desk where the hand-turned grinder took pride of place. And all the while she didn't dare to turn around, afraid that he'd be right behind her.

Afraid that he wouldn't.

And as she made the coffee and then they sat and made excruciating small talk, she hoped he couldn't read her mind. All she kept thinking of was that moment, back in that classroom, where he'd almost opened up to her. When he'd told her that being out here brought back those memories.

'I'm sorry, you know, that I made you come out here. I didn't know it would be so difficult for you.'

'How could you have?' His tone was clipped but at least he was answering. 'Besides, it wasn't as though you decided to come out here on a whim. You'd already gone through the process with Angela, long before I came along.'

'But when things changed, when Rafe got those death threats and asked you to be my bodyguard, I could have explained things to her. Got my mission postponed.'

'Well, it's done now.'

No blame, no censure, just matter of fact.

'I'm still sorry if this is hard for you.' She swallowed, knowing she was risking angering him again, but not able to stop herself. 'There's no shame in talking about what happened...out there, you know.'

The silence was so heavy, so loaded, it seemed to compress the room down. The ticking of the wind-up alarm clock echoed louder and louder, making her heart pound in time to its ominous beat.

Tick. Tock. Tick.

'I understand that.' Myles broke the silence unexpectedly, his tone a little too even, too bright, to be genuine.

As if his head knew it to be the truth, but his soul wasn't entirely in accord.

She waited a little longer but he didn't expand. She hadn't really expected him to.

'So...' she licked her lips '...would you like to? Talk, I mean? I'm a good listener.'

'I'm sure.' He looked at her but she had the distinct impression a part of him didn't even see her. 'But no. Thank you.'

'Myles—'

'How about you tell me about what happened with Justin? And that tape.'

He just about managed to keep the sneer from his mouth.

'I thought you didn't want to hear it?'

'I've changed my mind.'

He was distracting her. She knew that. But he was also offering her a chance to finally give someone her side of events. Someone other than Rafe. Someone who mattered.

Still, she shifted uncomfortably.

'If you don't want to,' he began, but she cut him off.

'I *do* want to. It's just that…it wasn't exactly my finest hour.'

'No, it wasn't.'

Her temper flared and somehow it gave her the impetus she needed.

'Fine, then how about you tell me what you want to know and I'll give you all the gory details to satisfy yourself that I'm as wanton and easy as they like to say I am?'

'I don't want the gory details.' Myles just about kept from snarling. It was madness how he'd spent so many years schooling himself to stay calm in the most incendiary of situations and yet this woman set him off like a match on an oil spill.

'I get the picture, Rae. You got talked into bed by a guy who should have known better than to take advantage of you and during one of your, shall we say, intimate sessions, you decided to film it.'

He had no idea how he managed to act as though it didn't rip his insides out just thinking about her with that sleaze, the man who was supposed to protect her in the aftermath of her high-profile father's death.

'That's exactly what I've been telling you. There weren't multiple sex sessions. I only slept with him that one time. That was it.'

'You only had sex with the guy once?' He was dubious.

She nodded her head, her body slumping slightly where she stood. Only her hands still on his chest appeared to hold her upright.

'I only had sex with Justin once,' she repeated, coughing awkwardly. 'And the only person I've ever had sex with is Justin.'

'You've only had sex once in your entire life?'

She'd said it earlier, or at least alluded to it, he couldn't remember clearly; his head was still a jumbled mess.

'Ironic, isn't it? Given the reputation the press have given me.'

'You did give them a sex tape.'

He regretted the words the instant they left his mouth. If he could have swallowed them back up then he would have. He didn't even know why he'd said such a cruel thing. If he hadn't known better he might have thought it was jealousy.

But that was impossible.

Wasn't it?

'I'm sorry. That was uncalled for.'

Her woebegone smile only made him feel worse.

'Not entirely inaccurate, though, was it? Of course, my sisters played up to it as soon as they realised they might be able to gain from it, not that we knew it would become something as big as *Life in the Rawl*, and they fed the press all kinds of leads and false stories.'

'Why didn't you object? Why didn't you defend yourself?'

'I was embarrassed. Ashamed. Rafe would have been

the only one I could talk to, and, as you already pointed out earlier, he was away on a tour of duty. I had no intention of contacting him. I didn't want him to find out that way. I certainly didn't know soldiers out there—*his* men—had access to it.'

She looked physically ill. It took Myles an inordinate amount of time to process what she was saying.

'So that really was your first time?' he asked eventually.

'Are you listening to me at all?' She scowled at him but eventually nodded her confirmation. 'My first time. My only time.'

'Which brings me back to the question I asked you earlier: why the hell did you film it?'

A look of pain twisted her face.

'I didn't. At least not intentionally. I had no idea the camera was even there. I trusted Justin. I told you, I thought I loved him. I thought he loved me. He told me he did.'

'He was using you.' Myles did little to disguise his clenched fists.

If the guy had been standing there, in front of him, he wasn't sure he wouldn't simply have knocked him out with a single punch.

'Why the hell didn't you tell me this when we met again in Rafe's offices?'

'Would you have believed me?'

Probably not.

So what had changed?

The fact that she was an incredible, dedicated, focussed doctor, or the way she'd felt in his arms, her body wracked with the climax *he'd* given her?

'Why not tell me that night?'

He didn't have to clarify which night he meant. They both knew. Desire was beginning to move around the room, like molten hot lava threatening to consume her whole. She shifted awkwardly, trying to keep her head, trying not to give into these primal urges that seemed to flood her every time she was with this man.

'What could I say, Myles? That what you did that night was like...nothing I've known before? I didn't want you to know how inexperienced I was. I felt raw, and exposed, and I didn't want a repeat of that night all those years ago.'

She tried to keep the pain out of her voice but the hoarseness was all too revealing.

'So you rejected me before I could reject you again?'

'I guess.' She chewed her lip and he fought the urge to capture her mouth with his own. 'I spouted all those lies. But you're the one who believed them.'

'I'm not sure I believed them. Not deep down. Not entirely. Not after the way you came apart at my touch.'

'Is that true?' she whispered.

'You were too honest, too giving, too guileless. It was like a completely different person from the manipulative Raevenne of the press.'

Frustration poured through her.

'Then why did you walk out as though you were so repelled by me?'

'Perhaps my disgust was aimed as much at myself as at you. Your brother entrusted you into my care. I was supposed to be protecting you, not taking advantage of you. I was acting no better than that last no-mark bodyguard of yours did.'

Rae stepped towards him, her head swinging wildly from one side to the other, unable to begin to tell him how many things were wrong with that assessment.

'You're nothing like Justin. *Nothing.* You didn't take advantage of me. I was a gullible and foolish eighteen-year-old back then, wanting to believe the first guy, the only guy, to tell me he loved me.'

'Especially after I'd just made you feel about as desirable as a Christmas sweater knitted by a well-intentioned aunt?' he offered with a touch of guilt.

'I'm not trying to make excuses, Myles. I knew I hadn't imagined the chemistry between us but you seemed to find it so easy to reject me whilst I'd just thrown myself, practically naked, at you.'

'I was trying to do the right thing.'

'I'm beginning to understand that. However, I'm a grown woman now. I might not be experienced but I'm also not imprudent enough to be pushed into things I don't want to do any more.'

Myles raised his eyebrow at her, his dark expression doing little to calm her racing pulse.

'Except when your brother talks you into having a bodyguard you don't want?'

She hesitated, then shrugged her shoulders with as much nonchalance as she could muster.

'Who knows?'

However honest they were being right now with each other, she still wasn't about to tell him that a traitorous part of her had thrilled at the idea of having Myles in such close proximity again. Contrived or not.

Had it been anyone else, would she have capitulated to Rafe's request as easily? Or at all?

She had a feeling her response to her brother would have been curter, more direct, and have culminated in her racing out of there before the doors had even closed to the office suite.

'At least I know I'm not frigid.' She plastered a bright smile onto her lips.

'Say again?'

His dark tone had an edge, a sharpness, which she didn't understand but which dug at her nonetheless.

'That is… Well, I didn't feel like I was,' she stammered. 'I thought I was quite…responsive?'

'Why the hell would you think you were frigid?' Myles demanded.

She wanted the ground to open up right where she stood. A sinkhole that would allow her to escape this new humiliation that she'd brought down on herself.

'Forget I said anything…' she began to plead.

'Did that sleaze call you that?'

What was the matter with her? Drawing attention to all her shortcomings?

'I wasn't exactly…as *responsive* to him as I was with you.' She echoed her earlier words awkwardly.

'Because he couldn't satisfy you he called you names?' Myles was incredulous and, she realised with a start, angry on her behalf.

It was a heady experience.

'It was my first time,' she hedged. 'But that night with you I wasn't as bad.'

'You weren't *bad* at anything. Just as you aren't remotely frigid. He had no right saying that to you.'

'No. But I'm not exactly…' She licked her lips. *What was the opposite of frigid?* 'Not exactly passionate either, am I?'

'Oh, but that's exactly what you are.'

The statement was accompanied with a dark, intense look. Her stomach kicked. Hard.

'Do you need me to prove it to you?'

His words were so low, so loaded. They slid over her skin, into her body, down to her core. She couldn't even answer him.

'I want to hear the words, Raevenne,' he growled.

It seemed to Raevenne that she was summoning all her strength to answer him, yet when she eventually spoke she barely recognised the seductive, sensual invitation in her voice.

'I shouldn't have to beg you to prove anything to me.'

'You just did.' He smirked.

And then he was hauling her to him, her suddenly putty-like body moulding easily against his solid, unyielding one, her arms moving apparently of their own volition to loop around his head, his mouth claiming hers.

Branding her.

His, something whispered through him, *after all this time.*

But he stamped out the sound and told himself this was just about sex. About giving into a temptation that had haunted him for over a decade. It was nothing more than that.

They both understood that it never could be.

CHAPTER NINE

RAW, MASCULINE POWER blasted through Rae, like a towering, cresting wave, and if she didn't learn to ride it, then she would surely end up drowning in it. He was so much. Too much. She felt intoxicated, reckless, lust-fuelled.

The kiss went on for ever, demanding, insistent, unrelenting. Every slide of his tongue against hers made her body pull in and ache for him.

His hand glided smoothly down her spine, caressing her, and making her tremble. When he trailed his touch over her hips she couldn't help but shudder, and when he spanned her waist she stopped breathing.

She thrilled to him. To the way he was taking his time, acquainting himself with every inch of her, stoking a fire inside her that she feared would never burn the same way for anyone else. Never had in the past.

Need pooled within her as her nipples grew tighter, strained. She pressed herself harder against the wall of his chest as though that could offer her some relief, but it only heightened the ache. Then he was moving his hand around, his palm against her ribs, his thumb grazing the underside of one breast and she was helpless to swallow back the moan that escaped her lips.

'Myles...'

'We have all night,' he murmured.

She shifted against him.

'I don't think I can last that long.'

She shifted as he hooked his fingers under the hem of her tee, pulling it over head and letting it drop…somewhere… Neither of them cared, her bra quickly following. And then his eyes, greedy and dark, were focussed on her naked chest making her rethink the breasts she'd always thought too heavy, too full, to be attractive.

She didn't realise she'd voiced as much until he jerked his head to look at her with an incredulous expression.

'Are you mad, woman? My God, you are incredible,' he breathed.

When he said it, she actually considered it might be true. But when he trailed a finger down the generous valley, cupping a breast in each hand as though testing them, worshipping them, before lowering his head to suck one hard nipple into his clever mouth, she *knew* it to be true.

As his tongue drew lazy swirls over the tight peak, one hand caressed the other, and all Rae could do was drop her head back and arch her body into him, pressing herself into his hands, his mouth. She wanted more, but didn't really know how to go about getting it.

She should *do* something. *Show* Myles how much she wanted him. This time wasn't going to be like the first time when she'd been with Justin, when she hadn't known what she should be doing, hadn't known how to ask for what she wanted.

This was *Myles*. And she knew exactly what she wanted to be doing. *Where* she wanted to feel him. The urge was so deep inside her, as if it was meant to be. As if it was *right*.

Reluctantly, she drew herself back, creating enough of a gap between them that she could divest him of his T-shirt as he'd removed hers. The fact that he let her, that he held himself so still whilst her inexperienced fingers fumbled a few times before succeeding in their task, only helped her to feel more in control. He boosted her confidence without saying a word.

Rae trailed her hands down that incredible torso, her knuckles deliberately grazing every muscle as they went, enjoying the ride, delighting in every sensation that cascaded through her. Until, at last, she was reaching down between them and feeling for his zipper; then there was the deliciously naughty sound of it sliding open, and the shake of her hand as she carefully eased him out.

He was magnificent, proud, and hot against her palm as she assayed the solid weight of him against her hand, which suddenly felt so very delicate in comparison. As if she could make him believe she knew what she was doing. His low groan of response was guttural, so primal, that she felt it in the apex of her legs, like a Molotov cocktail to her desire.

'Rae...'

Hot need pooled, pulsed, ached, and she heard the sigh that slid of its own volition from her mouth as something pulled tight within her. She moved her fingers up and down his length, revelling in the way it flexed against her, making her feel insanely desirable. Powerful. She coiled her fingers around him, at least as far as she was able, and increased the pressure. Another groan from him reverberated through her, pooling at the apex of her legs.

He grabbed her wrist around the same time he choked out a strangled command.

'Don't tell me that wasn't good,' she offered mildly, as though her heart weren't hammering in her chest for fear of getting it wrong.

'I think you know it was,' his voice rasped over her skin, making it tingle. 'But I want us to take our time, and if you carry on like that, it's going to be over embarrassingly quickly. At least for me.'

A wicked shiver rippled down her spine, bolstering her, making her voice so husky she barely recognised it.

'I think I'd like to see that.'

'I can assure you that *I* would not,' he growled.

He rammed his point home by pinning her arms behind her back, one hand circling her wrists, whilst the other moved back around to cup her breast, to graze his thumb over its straining, aching peak, before lowering his head and drawing it into his mouth. He was playing with her, toying with her. And she, for her part, seemed incapable of doing anything other than arching her back and offering even more of herself to him.

Then, suddenly, his hand was grazing over her abdomen, sliding beneath the waistband, hooking it down. His other hand let go of her wrists so that he could slip off her ballet-style pumps and her soft trousers in one easy movement. And when he grazed his hands back up her legs, his hungry, dark gaze locked with hers, his fingers inching their way up her inner thighs until she could barely keep herself from wriggling on the edge of the desk in anticipation, she stopped breathing, couldn't even remember how to start again.

'Myles...'

And then he was scooping her up, carrying her across the room as she hooked her legs around his hips, his sex pressed, like an iron rod, deliciously against her. She shifted, revelling in his groan, rocking into him, making her objection heard when he lowered her to the bed and moved away.

'Stop grumbling,' he teased, hauling off the rest of both their clothes in a couple of all too slick moves, leaving her naked but, for the first time in her life, not remotely self-conscious.

Instead he made her feel beautiful, desirable, proud. It was an empowering experience, lying there and watching his eyes sharpen with desire as he took her in, his breathing growing shallow and his body...*growing*.

Rae almost giggled, but the sound caught in her throat. For a long moment she could only gawk at him. He was so impossibly hard, like the most revered, chiselled marble sculpture, from his wide, strong shoulders, to his broad chest and athletic torso. Even those muscled, pumped legs. Her fingers ached to touch him, to trace those hard planes and edges, to lower her mouth and taste that tempting skin, but she didn't know where to start.

It didn't matter anyway. Suddenly he had moved down her body, his mouth scorching a trail on the insides of her thighs, working his way higher and higher with deliberate laziness, teasing her, toying with her, heightening her senses.

She found her fingers had worked their way into his hair at some point. Her legs had fallen that little bit wider to welcome his touch. And when he finally skimmed over the centre of her need, she heard the most impossible carnal sound escape her lips.

'Tell me what you like,' he murmured.

'Myles...'

'Tell me.'

'I...like that,' she whispered.

'And this?' He slid his finger through her wet heat, flicking the tiny bud, which had her bucking in response.

'And that,' she confirmed, her voice almost too thick to be her own.

'And this,' he muttered.

And this time she wasn't prepared for him to press his

mouth to her core, licking into her, branding her as his. She cried out, possibly an acknowledgement, possibly his name, possibly any number of glorious things, her body helpless to do anything but rock against the perfect rhythm of his tongue, losing herself with every stroke and every suck, feeling herself sinking beneath the waves of lust until they were finally closing in over her head.

When she was writhing in the bed, unable to believe she could take any more of this exquisite torture, he anchored her down with his hands, and feasted on her some more. As though he could never get his fill of her. As though he never wanted to.

Her release came so swiftly, so forcefully, that everything seemed to go black in Rae's head moments before an explosion of colours filled her mind as she cried out his name. She might as well have been catapulting through them, soaring, gliding, with no sign of gravity ever pulling her down again.

But slowly, so slowly, it did, as she came back to herself.

'That was…' She shook her head, searching for the right words but none seemed adequate.

'It's not over yet,' he assured her.

And then he was moving over her, his body coasting slickly over hers, fitting to her as if they were each two perfect parts of a unique, bespoke design. She didn't think, she just reacted, looping her legs around his hips, thrilling in the sensation of his blunt head sliding through her wetness, her hands acquainting themselves with the muscled contours of his arms.

Need poured through her. She recognised it so perfectly, had traced and retraced it almost every night in her dreams since the first time they'd been intimate, but it hadn't remotely compared to the reality of touching him again. Of lowering her lips to his skin. Of tasting him. Salt and sin, maleness and magic.

'Easy,' he murmured as she lifted her hips to press against him.

'It's fine.' Rae slid her hands over his shoulders and down his back. 'I'm ready.'

She didn't know what made her do it—instinct, not experience—but she suddenly twisted her body and lifted her hips again, drawing Myles inside her, gasping as he stretched her, faster and wider than she'd imagined. She had no idea how much self-control it took him but she felt him brace himself, holding himself back, allowing her time to adjust to his size.

'That's why I said easy,' he berated her softly.

She shook her head.

'I didn't realise.'

'No, but I did.' He dropped a kiss onto her forehead, still careful to hold back. 'You can stop frowning now.'

'Am I? Sorry.'

'Does it hurt?'

She wrinkled her nose. It had, for a moment, but not now.

'No,' she confirmed, experimentally rolling her hips.

He groaned and she couldn't help but grin.

'This time, I set the pace,' he warned.

He began moving again, slowly at first, with gentle pressure, sliding himself in and out, a little further each time, his eyes not leaving hers, and it felt to Rae as if she were the most precious thing in the world.

She couldn't have said when the tightness eased completely, she only knew that she had moved her hands lower, gripping him tighter, moving with him as he began to pick up the pace, sliding deeper and harder, their breath mingling as they rode the wave together. Her body lifted up to meet his, to match his, with every perfect thrust. It drove them both on, making need pound through them.

And then her hands dropped lower, clutching at him, pulling him deeper than ever, and this time when he slid inside she shuddered and then she heard his groan of release and everything ignited, like a glorious blaze all around them, consuming them both.

Devouring them alive.

The blow came from out of the blue, pain jolting her awake. As if someone had just body-slammed her to the ground, winding her. Temporarily paralysing her. And then suddenly Myles was growling at her, his tone brutal, dangerous, making her heart pound in her chest with fear even though the words seemed to make no sense.

'Myles? What's going on?' She could hear the rising panic in her voice, but she still couldn't move. She certainly couldn't get up.

It took her another few unnervingly long moments to work out that Myles wasn't really engaging with her at all. And then she realised that he was actually asleep.

Nightmares.

Or night terrors.

The demons of the night that so often came with PTSD.

She'd almost forgotten what her half-brother had told her about Myles' last mission.

Her brain raced. There was a safety protocol associated with this, wasn't there? Something Rafe had once mentioned to her in passing, neither of them ever imagining she'd be in this situation. And that included not waking him whilst he was in this state. At least, not by shaking him awake.

God, what must he be going through? Her chest tightened, and she had to fight every instinct to go to him, to wake up. To stop this nightmare for him.

But that wouldn't work.

Besides, hadn't Rafe once said that some doctors advocated letting the nightmares play out, just managing their effect? Wasn't there a line of thought that suggested that, as long as the individual wasn't a danger to themselves or others, it could be beneficial to allow sleep to play out the fears, to allow the brain to process whatever traumatic event had occurred? Especially if a conscious Myles wouldn't talk about what had happened?

But she needed to get out of the bed. Out of his range. Right now, it seemed, she was too close. He could actually touch her. *Had* touched her, not that he would have realised it. But by being in contact with him she was putting herself slap-bang in the middle of whatever trauma he was reliving right at this moment. And that was pretty much the last place anybody should be.

Carefully, gently, she slid out of the bed and moved away from him. The loss of contact immediately seemed to take the edge away from Myles' actions, although it was clear he was still in some horrible, terrifying world. Her stomach clenched for him.

Would he hear her if she talked to him? Could that help to remind him of where he was? Or at least that he was no longer wherever his mind had taken him?

'Myles,' she murmured quietly. 'Myles, can you hear me?'

She watched the figure but there was no indication that her voice was having any effect. Still, she couldn't leave him like this, not when he was so clearly troubled. She sucked in a steadying breath.

'Myles, it's Rae. Raevenne. Can you hear me? We're at Camp Sceralenar. We're volunteers at a hospital for pregnant women.' Still there was no response. 'You're dreaming. You're safe. Myles, everything is going to be okay.'

She had no idea how long she kept talking, repeating the same things over and over, her voice as quiet and steady and soft as she could make it. Tweaking here, adding there. And slowly, bit by bit, it began to take effect.

Finally—she couldn't have said how much later it was—Myles settled, his sleep becoming more regulated. More relaxed. Deeper. She stopped talking but sat still on her chair in the corner, allowing him to rest. Then, eventually, she stood up, padding slowly around the room as she located her discarded clothing from earlier.

She didn't realise he was awake until she heard him sit up.

'Raevenne?'

She spun around with relief.

'You're okay?'

'Say again?'

He sounded curt. Almost forbidding.

'You were dreaming.' Why was she the one sounding apologetic? 'Well, having a nightmare.'

'Did I hurt you?' He was out of bed and across the room before she could move.

She hated that she couldn't stop herself from taking a step back. Trying to keep some distance between them.

'It doesn't matter.'

He stopped abruptly. Hands that had been reaching out to her dropped to the side with a heavy sound. His expression was heart-rending.

'I hurt you.'

'What were you dreaming about?' she asked.

She knew it was a mistake the moment the question fell from her lips. Even before his body shuttered down.

'I don't remember.'

She should stop now. No good could come from pushing it.

'I think you do,' she said softly. 'And I think you need to talk. Bottling it up can't be helping you.'

'I think I've overstayed my welcome.'

'Myles, please. I want to help. Let me help.'

'I'm leaving. Now.'

She stood immobile, her mind desperately searching for the words that would change his mind; wondering how she could prove to him that she meant what she said. She *wanted* to help.

But his forbidding expression bit into her. An icy shiver rippled down her spine. This was a battle she wasn't going to win.

Wordlessly—helplessly—she dipped her head in acknowledgement as he gathered up his belongings, and left her room.

CHAPTER TEN

MYLES HEFTED ANOTHER crate onto his shoulders and carried it from the four-by-four to the supply room in the compound, his eyes trained on the steady stream of people crossing the river.

He told himself he wasn't brooding. That his head wasn't still stuck back in Rae's room last night. That his mind wasn't still full of her words, her scent, her taste. But mostly, that his heart wasn't full of self-loathing for whatever he'd done to her in his hellish sleep.

He should have known better.

He should never have gone near her, never have let his desire for her overwhelm logic. He was supposed to be looking out for her, not sleeping with her. However undeniable the attraction between them. However intoxicating.

Because, ultimately, where could it ever lead to? What did he have left to offer a woman like Raevenne?

He'd lost his career in the army, he couldn't function as a surgeon, he didn't even have control over his own head. He was broken. Damaged. Defective.

And she deserved so much better.

He could scarcely believe that last night he had come so astonishingly close to telling her what had happened that last mission. That he had been on the verge of spilling every last regret, and fear, and anguish that had been crowding his head—making him feel as though he was inevitably going to implode at some point—for far too long.

So, instead, Myles concentrated on the tiny figures stretched out for miles on the flat plains on the other side of the river. They travelled fast or slow, in groups or alone, as far as the eye could see. Just like hundreds of thousands of caribou migrating annually across the arctic tundra. Only they weren't wild animals. They were humans. Wretched and frightened, involuntarily displaced from their homes.

His eyes followed the straggling groups as they got closer, became more tightly packed, until they were swarming and grouping, and all desperate to cross the single rope and plank bridge. It was sheer madness how being on one embankment rather than the other would make such an incredible difference to their lives.

In other camps they might be alone because of an earthquake or a flood, or some other kind of natural disaster. But here, over a day's drive from the Camp Sceralenar, the people weren't coming for those reasons. They weren't coming for the women's hospital that Rae ran so smoothly.

He knew what *these* people were running from.

Only too well.

For a brief moment, flashes of other images played in his brain like a horror show he never wanted to watch.

He shut them down. But not before he heard Rae's voice in his head telling him there was no shame in talking about it. Logically, he knew she was right. He'd spent the last six months trying to stuff it back down, pretending the memories didn't exist.

And look where that had got him.

'That's the last of it.' Pushing the thoughts from his head, he approached the camp leader. 'Where do you want me now?'

She eyed him up and down with a grin.

'Take a break. Get some water. You must be exhausted. You were like a machine, lifting three crates to everyone else's one. Talk about a man on a mission.'

'I just want to work.' He forced himself to sound pleasant.

There was no need for everyone to know how preoccupied he was. How he wished he weren't here, but back at the main camp. Back near Rae, where he could make sure she was okay. Happy.

Or, at least, happier than he'd made her last night.

What the hell had he been thinking, telling her all that stuff? Things he'd never told anyone else. Never *wanted* to tell anyone else. Because outside the army no one else's opinion of him had ever mattered. Until now.

Until Rae.

He clenched and unclenched his fists at his sides. Why couldn't he get her out of his damned head?

'Well, I'm not going to look a gift horse in the mouth.' The camp leader laughed. 'They're starting to build a couple of new buildings. It's more a matter of putting prefab wooden panels together. Fancy giving us a hand?'

'Not a problem.' He even dredged up a smile. Hard manual graft would be more than welcome. 'Just point me in the right direction.'

'Right around that wall over there.'

He was heading off before she'd even finished talking. Anything to distract him; to help smother the fire he feared was smouldering in him, ready to consume him from the inside out. The embers that he was very much afraid Rae had begun to fan.

Myles looked at the kit, like a flat pack on an enormous scale. The panels were pre-insulated, lightweight and easily assembled, designed to be thrown up quickly to enable rapid erection of refugee camps in times of emergency, especially for geographical disasters like earthquakes or volcanos when rapid reaction times were essential.

He was a few hours into the build when they heard the explosion. For a moment he was sure the very blood had frozen in his veins. He couldn't move, couldn't even breathe.

And then that split-second reaction was over, and Myles was heading for the door, racing out of the compound and towards the noise, his senses taking in everything. Ready to stop, to regroup, if there was any unexpected danger.

And then he rounded the corner.

It was the smell that hit Myles first. The unmistakeable stench of burning flesh. It lodged itself in his nasal passages, reminding him, taunting him. He swayed, momentarily overcome by the flashbacks he'd been trying so hard to thrust aside, dangerously close to reliving that night. His body flushed hot, then cold, the seat making him feel clammy and helpless.

There was screaming and shouting all around him, but experience allowed him to phase it out. He couldn't let cries of pain pierce his emotional armour. Not right now. Not when he was so close to the edge as it was.

Something battered his chest and it took him a moment to realise it was his heart, hammering so fiercely he was convinced it was going to ram its way out. His lungs strained with the effort of trying to draw a breath, desperate to suck in deep lungsful yet struggling to allow in even a trickle. He reached his hand out but the canvas tent offered scant support.

He'd dealt with this before. Too many times, adults and soldiers with devastating, often fatal, burns. But this was a non-combat area, and these were civilians. The tiny kernel of logic that was fighting to make itself heard warned him that it was likely to have been a domestic cooking explosion. It wasn't unusual for a substandard pressure cooker to explode, or for a gas canister, used to make the family meal, to get too close to an open flame.

They might not be used to it in this camp, but he'd seen it too many times over the years.

He glanced around; the chaotic scene in front of him seemed to confirm his suspicions.

And then he saw the child. A young girl with burns on her face and arms and whose leg had clearly been crushed by something landing on her in the explosion. He couldn't tell if she was alive or dead, but if he just focussed on her, if he shut everything else out—the all too familiar cries of pain and pleas for help—maybe he could just deal with her.

Maybe he could save her.

Racing across the room, he dropped to the ground and began to crawl carefully through the debris, his hand reaching out to try to take a pulse.

It was faint but weak, yet even that felt like a powerful victory.

'What's her status?'

A voice dragged him back to reality and he managed to crane his head over his neck enough to see another volunteer, a doctor, had arrived and was trying to get to him. Movement around them suggested other volunteers were trying to reach the other victims. Good, this once he could let others triage, he could just deal with this one child.

This one echo of his past.

'She's alive. Just,' he managed. 'Time is going to be critical. We'll need to get her out to intubate and secure central venous access.'

He had dealt with enough to know that burns victims were usually those who required the most surgical inter- ventions, with multiple trips to Theatre. Not to mention even when burns victims were kids, their surgical procedures were often in line with battlefield trauma surgery usually reserved for adults and soldiers.

'You're a doctor?'

'Army trauma surgeon,' Myles replied automatically, before qualifying it. 'Well, I was up until I left six months ago. That was my last tour of duty.'

This was what he'd been trained for. This was what he knew best. Yet his six months away from the operating table could only have left him rusty. Then again, how many doctors out here with this group would have his particular field of expertise? How many of them would have operated, night and day sometimes, on such cases in such basic environments like this?

The main question was whether the length and intensity of all his operational tours of duty meant that, even rusty, he would still be the best chance this little girl had.

His head was still swirling as the two of them worked quickly and efficiently, clearing enough rubble to get to the girl, who mercifully began to regain consciousness on her own as they worked. Then whilst Myles performed a routine check and pulled her out, the other doctor prepared to intubate, and to take over pain management.

'You have a blood bank?'

'Yes. I'm guessing she's going to need a transfusion.'

'Possibly multiple,' Myles confirmed. 'You're not really geared up for skin grafting here, but we can do something.'

And then his mind clicked over, like turning on a light switch, and the past six months faded away and it was as though he'd never stopped operating. Never stopped thinking about medical solutions.

This was who he was. This was what he had been built to do. How had he forgotten that? But could he begin to separate his army career, which was now over, from his medical career, which didn't have to be?

He'd been an army surgeon for so long, were the two inextricably linked in his mind?

He was so preoccupied with his thoughts that Myles didn't realise they'd been working for almost an hour, and the girl was finally freed, and they were loading her onto a gurney and rushing her into the single, makeshift operating area, where the only surgeon the forward camp had was hastily going over the triage lists.

He checked the girl as quickly as he could.

'Leg's too far gone.' The doctor pulled a sympathetic face. 'We'll have to amputate.'

'She'll be ostracised.' Myles barely recognised his own stiff, raw voice.

A hand appeared on his arm and it took him a moment to realise it was the doctor.

'I'm sorry but we simply don't have the equipment out here, certainly not paediatric.'

'I can do it.'

He heard the words but didn't remember saying them.

'Sorry?'

'I'm a surgeon. Trauma. Ex-army.' Why did it sound so jolted? So staccato? 'I can try something.'

'I thought you were a manual work volunteer?'

'I haven't operated in six months. Ever since I came out.'

'I can't authorise that. Besides, she'll need a skin graft and all sorts.'

'Multiple operations and skin grafts over about a month to six weeks, I would imagine.' He was beginning to warm to it now.

Beginning to feel a little more human.

A little more...*real*.

'Give me some plastic tubes, some wires, maybe some aluminium rods and I can cobble together some kind of external medical scaffolding. A homemade mechanical construction device to realign the bones and hold the leg in the right position.'

'I don't know...'

'Speak to whoever you have to speak to,' Myles commanded, his voice sounding much more like his own. 'Get whatever authorisation you need... *I* need. I can do this. But you amputate without even trying and you've condemned a six-year-old kid for life. You know how harsh their society can be.'

'Yes, but—'

'Starting with early insertion of a subclavian line. Get me an eight-point-five-gauge trauma line.'

'You didn't say your man was a surgeon, too,' Clara accused jovially as she came on shift to find Rae moving back and forth between two mercifully non-complicated deliveries.

'My man?' She commanded her stomach not to somersault at the idea. There could be little doubt who Clara was talking about.

'Myles, of course.' Clara rolled her eyes. 'Or should I say *Major* Myles? Army trauma surgeon.'

Rae's head snapped up from the chart she was filling out to look at the woman.

'Has something happened?'

'Apparently there was a gas explosion near the forward camp—'

'Was he hurt?' She gripped the edge of the table, her knuckles white with the effort. Relief flooded through her as Clara shook her head.

'Not him. It was in the refugee camp. A couple of families were cooking over a gas stove when the canister exploded.'

'Serious injuries?' She fought to stay focussed, in control, as she glanced between the two mothers in labour, never more grateful for a quiet lull in her shift.

'Multiple.' Clara pulled a face. 'But one of them was a kid with a crushed leg. The docs there deemed it unsalvageable, and then your Myles stepped up and apparently had some battlefield skills he'd picked up, which enabled him to save the limb.'

'He's not *my* Myles,' Rae muttered. 'Anyway, he operated?'

'Don't know, he didn't come out here as a surgeon so possibly not. But he went into the operating area with one of the surgeons and I'm guessing if he couldn't operate himself then he at least talked the surgeon through it.'

Myles, operating again? Even by proxy, it was a huge step forward.

'So, the kid's okay?'

'They're transferring the casualties here as soon as they're stable, maybe tomorrow. I think someone said the little girl will need more surgeries over the next few weeks, including skin grafts.'

'How do you know this?' Rae stepped forward as she thought one of her mothers might need her, then stopped as the girl was tended to by her mother.

'The other volunteers are back and it's all they can talk about. The mess hall is buzzing. Figured you might want to know.'

'Thanks.' Rae nodded; for the first time since she'd been here she silently cursed the never-abating flow of women ready to give birth.

Maybe when she finished her on-call shift, she could swing by his room.

Maybe.

'Myles…' she knocked tentatively '…are you there?'

Silence, and then, just as she was about to leave, he pushed the door open then backed into the room wordlessly.

The pre-planned teasing quip died on her lips and, in the absence of a verbal invitation, she took that to be the only encouragement she was going to get, and followed.

'I thought you might be asleep.'

It felt like an eternity before he answered.

'I can't sleep. That is… I can't bring myself to.'

'Are you okay?'

She braced herself for him to brush it off. To dismiss her. So it was a surprise when he sat down, his elbows on his knees, his hands clasped between, and his body leaning forward.

'I don't know.'

Carefully, Rae turned the other chair around, sat down, and waited. The quiet swirled around them, almost peaceful.

But opposite her Myles was too silent, too still. As though there were a storm raging in his head that only he could hear. As though it were buffeting him whilst leaving her untouched, only a few feet away.

He looked…*broken.*

'Myles?' She spoke softly. 'What happened?'

For a moment he didn't answer and the silence pressed in on her, far more brutal than the oppressive heat outside.

'You already know what happened,' he ground out when she'd almost given up hope of him speaking to her. 'Or else you wouldn't be here.'

'I came to congratulate you,' she admitted after a moment's hesitation. 'They're calling you a hero out there.'

He made a sound that might have been a bark of laughter but for the fact it was possibly one of the most chilling sounds she'd ever heard.

'A hero is the last thing I am.'

'You saved a little girl. You fought to save her leg when no one else was going to. Out here that's the difference between her having a family to go back to, a home—wherever that may actually be—and being cast out for ever.'

He didn't answer. It was all she could do to resist the urge to pull her chair closer, to run her hands over his bent back, to try to soothe him. To take his pain away.

But she couldn't be that person. She could barely even sort out her own mess of a life, how could she possibly imagine that she could be enough to help someone else?

Besides, Myles would never want her help. Sex was one thing, a simple physical act. But intimacy, actually laying oneself emotionally bare to another person, was a completely different thing. He'd made it clear time and again that he would never want her in that way. She would be a fool to keep repeating the mistake, hoping for a different outcome.

And still, she didn't move.

Which meant she *was* that fool.

So she could scarcely believe it when he started to speak again.

'The smell was almost unbearable.'

He had fastened his hands together, lacing his fingers tightly, around the back of his head, and if she hadn't strained to hear his agonised voice she would have missed what he said.

'What smell?' she asked, tentatively.

'The smell of burning flesh. Once you've smelt it you can never forget it. It scorches itself into your nostrils. Brands itself into your brain. There's no escaping it.'

She wanted to answer, to ease his obvious torment. But what could she possibly say? So instead she waited, her hands balled in her lap to stop her from reaching out to touch him, to comfort him, the way she wanted to. To stop herself from lifting his head to look at her, as though that could somehow break this terrible spell he was under.

But she couldn't risk it. He was only talking now because he was caught up in his own head. If she reminded him of where he was, of the fact that she was there in front of him, he might realise who he was talking to and shut down altogether.

Now, more than ever, she knew how close to the mark her half-brother had been when he'd told her that he thought Myles was suffering.

And so she sat still, quiet, waiting. It felt like an eternity before he spoke again.

'That's what I smell…in those nightmares.'

He lifted his head abruptly, to look at her, to connect with her. And suddenly she wished he hadn't. It was as though something were wrapping itself around her lungs, preventing them from expanding, from drawing in any breath.

The torment that laced his voice was magnified tenfold in that bleak expression, dark torture roiling in his eyes. She wanted him to talk and yet the idea of making him relive it was almost unbearable. She yearned to be the one to take away his pain. To be the one who could make it all right for him.

'From a mission?' she pressed gently, smothering the guilt she felt at knowing more than she was prepared to reveal.

But she wanted it to come from him. She wanted him to be the one to tell her. He dipped his head in what she took to be a nod.

'One of the last missions I went on.' He stopped again, and she held her breath. 'I was on a medical mission, going from village to village treating a number of medical issues. I was looking at a cleft lip, with and without the cleft palate in paediatric cases. There were a few of us, from medics to surgeons, and we had a rifles team with us when we went into the less stable regions.'

She offered an encouraging sound, not wanting to risk speaking and interrupting his thoughts.

'We'd been to a village in the foothills. Whilst I dealt with a couple of surgeries, others tried to resolve some of the more common issues such as diarrhoea and vomiting. There's a general lack of education, poor nutrition, no access to medical care out there. They were mostly farmers so there wasn't a lot to go around, so, other than that, we played some football with the kids and provided some materials and labour to help with general repairs around town.'

'Football.' She risked a soft laugh. 'The universal language.'

Relief coursed through her when it worked.

'Yeah, I guess. Though I'm usually more of a rugby guy, myself.'

She laughed again but didn't push it by saying anything more.

'Anyway, we left the town and went on to the next. A few days later we were heading back to our main army camp when we saw these plumes of black smoke. I don't remember anyone saying anything, but we all knew where it was. Our convoy changed direction and we went to investigate.'

She didn't dare to speak. Not even move.

'When…' He clenched his jaw so tightly, she expected to hear it crack. Shatter. 'When we got there, we saw it. Men, women, children. The enemy forces had been in to kill everyone. And they'd left the bodies where they'd fallen before setting the town alight.'

Hence the smell, Rae realised, forcing herself not to speak.

'We tried to save those few people who were still alive. But it was too late. Plus, we had to go slowly. There was still the fear that some enemy had stayed behind in case we returned, and we didn't know if we were going to come under fire at any time.'

'Which is when Michael McCoy died.'

The words were out before she could stop herself.

He froze as if she'd slapped him. So unmistakeable that she actually had to check herself to make sure that she hadn't.

'Say again?'

Abruptly, Rae wished she hadn't started the conversation. It was as though Myles had the power to control the very air around them. A few minutes ago, she'd been walking out in the hot, dry, dusty camp. Now, it felt as though there were a storm rumbling ominously around the darkened room, a chill tiptoeing over her skin leaving her whole body shuddering.

And yet, she wanted to know. She needed to hear it from Myles himself.

'I heard about Lance Corporal Michael McCoy.'

His jaw tightened. Dark. Lethal.

'Mikey.'

'Sorry?'

'Michael McCoy. Mac, or Mikey, to his friends.' His voice sharpened. 'To me.'

'Right.' She swallowed hard.

'What did you hear? *How* did you hear?'

'Rafe mentioned it. Once,' she added hastily. 'In passing, the night you and I first met at his offices. He said you'd lost a good buddy on that last mission, that you'd taken it hard and that he didn't know the details but he thought you were suffering... PTSD.'

'Is that so?'

It wasn't really an answer. Certainly not the response she'd hoped for. Something tightened around her heart, like an invisible thread pulling it in, painful and constricting.

'I think he thought maybe I could…talk to you. Help you get over it. I'm good at that…listening. Helping people talk.'

Her voice was raw. It made her throat ache.

She might have known he wouldn't answer. Instead, he simply turned the tables on her as though he was the one who deserved answers, not her. The way he always did.

'Is this a game to you?' Without warning, Myles advanced on her. Too big, too powerful, too *everything*. 'A typical Rawlstone Rabble stunt for your own twisted amusement?'

His dark expression should have frightened her. It didn't.

'I don't know what you think you're doing, but I don't want to talk to you about it.'

It took everything she had to stamp down her instinct to object.

She drew in a discreet breath. Then another.

'I understand,' she acknowledged quietly, when her voice was calmer. 'And you don't have to talk. I just wanted you to know that I'm here. If you ever want me.'

'I don't,' he ground out.

But, surprisingly, the rejection didn't hurt her the way she might have expected. With a rush of something she couldn't yet name, or maybe she just didn't want to, Rae realised she trusted him. Perhaps it was because Rafe trusted him, but she didn't think it was that simple. There was something inherently dependable about Myles. Something *she* believed in just as much as her brother did, or, at least, she wanted to.

If only it weren't for that cruel, taunting voice in the back of her head reminding her what had happened the last time she'd trusted a man who wasn't her brother. How her most intimate moments had become public property all because Justin hadn't wanted to give up his grasp on fame.

Maybe if Myles could just give her something, *anything* to show that he needed her. There was more—she knew that…but this felt like a start, a real step forward. She could work on this.

Not that she knew what it was she thought she was working on.

CHAPTER ELEVEN

'WHAT'S THAT FOR?' Myles frowned at the kit bag Rae had just thrown into the back of his four-by-four.

'What does it look like? I'm coming with you.'

Light, breezy, airy. She clearly had no idea how dangerous it was closer to the border. He considered telling her, but then knowing Rae she would only use the information against him later.

'Most of the work up there is sorting out displaced people, triaging medical cases, and administering basic injections that they've never had before, like polio. I can't imagine this camp can spare your expertise.'

'Now that's where you're wrong.' She grinned. 'There are several of us here at the moment, but apparently the forward camp only have two OBGYNs and one of them has just gone down with a vomiting bug. They asked me if I wanted to go up there for forty-eight hours and take up the slack.'

He felt restless. Frustrated.

'Forget it. They can get someone else.'

'They have me, Myles.'

'Not a chance,' he bit back. 'This camp is so far back it's relatively safe, but the forward camp isn't.'

'Is that a note of concern I hear? I'm touched.'

She was teasing him again. What was more, he *liked* it.

'Don't be,' he growled, his voice far more loaded than he would have liked. 'It's just my job.'

She arched an eyebrow and he wondered how, after last night, he could possibly expect her to believe such a blatant lie. He grunted and stalked around the vehicle and carried out his first parade.

He should regret last night—his weakness in talking to her, in telling her all the things he'd never told anyone before. And yet he couldn't regret it. He'd felt something like relief—he could barely tell, it was such an unfamiliar sensation these days—seeping out of him with every word he'd uttered. As if she were rescuing him from quicksand he'd thought he would be trapped in for ever. Or at least until it pulled him under.

But wasn't that part of the problem? He was supposed to be the strong one here. He always had been, all through his military and medical career. *He* should have been the one helping *her*. Saving her.

What kind of a man was he that he couldn't look after himself? What did he have to offer a woman like Raevenne?

He glowered at the dusty, barren landscape beyond the compound and offered a bitter laugh. It couldn't have been a more apt vista.

'I want to be with you today.' He startled as she touched his arm gently. He hadn't even noticed her approaching him. 'I thought you might appreciate it, especially when you're talking the other surgeon through the second operation.'

His jaw was so tightly locked he was shocked it didn't crack or crumble under the pressure.

'I'm not totally inept.'

'I never thought you were,' she cried quietly. 'I just wanted to offer you a bit of support. The way you have for me so many times already.'

'You mean, you think I might lose it, after spilling my guts to you last night. You think I might not be able to handle walking someone through this operation.'

'Nonsense,' she snapped. 'I think you'll switch into the same calm, professional mode you always do and talk them through it flawlessly.'

'Which is why you think I need a chaperone,' he bit out icily.

'Which is why I think you need someone there who knows that you aren't as calm inside as you appear to everyone else,' she corrected. 'You bottle it all up, Myles. That much is clear. And that's what is making your PTSD worse.'

'I don't have PTSD.'

Shame thundered through him at her words, at her assessment of him. He wasn't that man. He wasn't that weak. He refused to be.

And then she placed her hands on his chest, palms flat, rooting him to the ground. He tried to move but he was incapable.

'You have PTSD, Myles. And there's no shame in it. God knows it's understandable after all you've been through. What you had to deal with out there is unimaginable to most people, including me, but you can deal with it. I really believe that. And I believe in you enough to know you can overcome it. But you have to stop feeling as though you're alone in all of this, because you aren't alone.'

He lifted his hands to remove hers. To push her away. Instead, he found himself covering her delicate fists with his own bear claws. She glanced at them, then back up at him, and he would have sworn he saw her eyes glistening.

For him.

As though she really did care.

'There are people you can talk to, Myles. I'm here and

I'll always listen but of course I realise you might not want me. Besides, there are those who will understand this better than me. But please, talk to *someone*. The longer you try to ignore it, pretending you're fine, pretending you don't need anyone, the worse it's going to get.'

'You don't know what you're talking about.'

But his words lacked any real bite. The truth was, she made it sound so easy. So appealing. Almost more convincing than the voice in his head telling him to keep quiet. To deal with it himself.

He was out of his depth. Floundering. No one had ever slipped under his skin the way that Rae had. She made him want her; made him *feel* things he hadn't felt in a long time, possibly ever. At least about women. His career had devoured all his time and energy, with the few relationships he'd had sinking because the female in question hadn't understood it. He'd been perfectly okay with that. But now, this one woman made him wonder what he might be missing.

Which was madness.

'We had sex, Rae. It doesn't mean we know each other. It doesn't mean we're suddenly in some kind of a relationship. It was just sex.'

She blanched, just as he'd known she would. Just as he'd intended. But it didn't make him triumphant that he'd made her back off. It just made him guilty. And sad.

Probably because he knew it wasn't true. Sex was one thing. It was a physical, chemical reaction to each other. But what he felt for Rae went beyond that, as ludicrous as it sounded in his own head.

Still, a relationship? Raevenne Rawlstone was the last person in the world with whom he could imagine having a relationship.

Except that he was.

Even if he pushed her out of his thoughts time and again, she crept back into his subconscious. She dominated his dreams. He could still feel the slickness of her skin against his, hear her soft laugh, taste her need. She was wholly intoxicating and he still wanted her.

Right now she was staring at him as though she could see right through him, right into his soul, and she was gathering herself up, squaring her shoulders and readying herself for a fight.

With a start, he realised that she was near livid.

'You think being strong means never leaning on anyone else, always being there for *them*. You think talking to me about what happened to you out there is a sign of weakness. Well, let me tell you this, Major Myles Garrington, you couldn't be more wrong.'

'Raevenne—'

'I bet you you've told this to men time and again. I bet you've even encouraged them to go and speak to someone, a therapist or something. But I bet right now you believe that if you do that, it's you admitting you can't cope.'

'It *is* admitting you can't cope,' he bit out, suddenly.

She snorted scornfully. And loudly. Not even attempting to supress it.

'Of course it isn't. Stuffing it all down and letting it eat at you like some kind of acid from the inside out is weak. Refusing to talk about it when it's clearly killing you is weak. Deliberately putting yourself through night after night of hellish nightmares is weak.'

'You think I *want* to have those nightmares?'

'I think you hate them. I can't imagine anyone would want to live their life in such pain. I think you're a good person who deserved better. But I can't stand by and watch you tough it out as though that's a sign of strength. Please listen to me, Myles, a truly strong man would acknowledge his limitations. A truly strong man wouldn't take the easy way out, stuffing things down, he would make the incredible step of facing his problems, of voicing them.'

He couldn't answer her. Couldn't even begin to get his head around the jumble of emotions crowding him in this moment.

A part of him recognised what she was saying, the same part that so desperately wanted to grab her and hold her and let her ease his pain. But then there was the other part, the monster inside him that taunted and sniped in his ear. Who told him that he had nothing to complain about, given that he had survived when so many of his friends hadn't.

That he'd got off lightly.

That the least he deserved was to suffer a little.

And so he finally found the strength to break free of Rae's touch, and he climbed into the vehicle, started the engine and drove in silence, whilst neither one of them said another word.

But, for the first time he felt cowardly and alone. As though she was somehow slipping from his grasp and, whatever he tried to do, he couldn't tighten his grip.

How was it possible to lose someone he'd never had?

Rae awoke with a start.

'We've been driving all day?' She glanced at her watch.

'Pretty much.'

Another day down and she was already a fortnight into her month-long mission. It was flying by and she had the oddest sensation that every time she slept she was squandering this incredible experience.

'You should have woken me.'

He didn't deserve the accusation in her tone, but it was out before she could stop it. But Myles, in true form, barely even had to shrug it off.

'You've been on call pretty much twenty-four-seven, since you arrived—all of you OBGYNs have been—so I figured if this was your once chance for some uninterrupted sleep then I was damned well going to let you get it.'

Plus it meant he didn't have to listen to her badger him again. She wrinkled her nose in frustration, but this time kept her mouth firmly shut.

'If you want something to eat, there's something which passes for a lunch in that container over there.'

'Thanks.' Not that she was really very hungry. 'We must be close. Isn't that the Kurkshirgar River? Janine said once the road, such as it is, runs alongside it—we just follow it down to the border camp.'

'Yeah, should be a few clicks further downstream.'

Rae reached for the map, trying to work out where they were in relation to the landscape when the young kid seemed to come out of nowhere, frantically trying to flag down their solitary vehicle.

Her heart thudded as Myles began to slow down.

'You're not supposed to stop anywhere,' she reminded him nervously, glancing surreptitiously around for any signs that they were about to be attacked.

She might have known Myles wouldn't miss what she was doing.

'I've already checked, Raevenne. The ground around is too low, too flat, there's nowhere anyone could be waiting to ambush us here. But would you prefer me to play by the rules and leave the boy here alone?'

She scowled at him, but she could still feel the flush creeping up her neck. She waited impatiently as Myles listened to the boy for what seemed like for ever.

'What's he saying?'

'I think it's his mother. Possibly pregnant, collapsed on the other side of the river.'

Rae's head jerked up.

'Well, how did he get here?'

'I'm guessing the bridge. He mentioned that no one at the camp could help unless his mother got to the bridge herself.'

'If she has collapsed then surely she won't make it.'

Half a statement, half a question. Myles simply shook his head curtly.

'Probably not.'

Rae already knew the answer to her next question, so it was pointless to ask it. Still, she couldn't keep it in.

'There's no way we can drive up there? Cross the bridge?'

'Not a chance. Not going against all those people. It's like a swarm. That's why no one at the forwards camp could. Besides, anyone crossing in that direction risks getting shot by border patrols.'

'We can't leave her.'

'No,' he agreed grimly.

'What are you doing?' She hurried after him as he vaulted into the back of the four-by-four and methodically began to open supply boxes.

'Looking for a rope.'

'Why?'

When he didn't answer, she peered around, her mind spinning. The dirty, wide river frothed angrily as it raced across the land.

Her heart lurched sickeningly.

'Oh...no. You can't possibly be thinking of that.'

'It's the only way.'

She mustn't panic. She *mustn't*.

'That current is far too dangerous.'

'Which is why I'm going to tie the rope around my waist and then attach it to the truck.'

'Myles.'

What else was she to say? How could she possibly convince him that this whole idea was insane? That he was risking his life. That she didn't *want* him to risk his life. Not now. Not ever again.

Because the possibility of losing him hurt too much.

Which was insane, because she didn't even have him to lose. And she never would have.

'Do you want me to help this woman, or not?'

She shot him a look that was anger mixed with pure fear.

'That's not a fair question.'

'Perhaps not, but it's the only question there is.'

Rae stared helplessly, her mind raging as out of control as the torrent in front of her.

'Fine,' she snapped at length. 'But if you're going then I'm coming with you.'

She had no idea how the hell she was supposed to do it. All she knew was that she wouldn't, *couldn't*, let Myles go alone.

She was reaching up and grabbing a second rope for herself when his fingers locked tightly against her wrist, stilling her movement.

'I can't let you do that, Raevenne.'

She pursed her lips, if only to keep them from shaking.

'If you can, then I can.'

He leapt down in one easy movement, coming to stand in front of her, his fingers beneath her chin to tilt her head up. Forcing her to meet his eyes.

'You aren't coming, Rae,' he repeated softly.

She blinked back the hot, prickling sensation behind her eyes, which had no business being there.

'You can't go on your own.'

'I can. Besides, we can't both leave the truck.'

'Myles.'

'Stop, Rae. Just listen to me. This is what's going to happen. I'm going to tie up and get into the back whilst you drive back upstream until I say to stop. Then I'm going to get out and start to cross the river. As the current pulls me downstream the truck will hold me fast. But you keep the engine running and if anyone, *anyone*, approaches you, I'll untie my end of the rope and you'll drive as fast as you can to camp.'

'No!' She wasn't sure if she actually shrieked. 'I won't leave you.'

Was it really possible for a heart to race and hang simultaneously? What Myles was saying was preposterous. If he wasn't tied up, that current would pull him under and smash him against whatever rocks lay on the river bed. His body could end up so far downstream they would never find him.

'Yes, you will. You have to.'

'Myles—'

He cut her off.

'This woman needs our help, Rae. This kid needs our help. So I'm going to cross and you're going to stay with the truck.'

'And wait for you to get back?'

'No, just until I've crossed. Then I'm going to release the rope and you're going drive to camp. Just like if someone approaches you.'

She opened her mouth to object but he pre-empted her.

'And the longer you argue, the less chance his mother has.'

'But, Myles…'

'Get a team and wait for me at the bridge. If I can get her down to you, I will.'

'And if you can't. If the baby is coming?'

'Then I'll try to deliver it. I watched you enough times

in your clinic, I can make a decent attempt. I might not be you but if I'm all she has then I'm better than nothing.'

She wanted to say *no*, but part of her knew it could be the only chance this woman had.

'What about the boy? You can't take him with you—it's too dangerous.'

'Far too dangerous,' Myles agreed.

'And I'm not supposed to take him in the truck, but I can't leave him here.'

'I don't think you'll have a choice.' Myles jerked his head to where the kid was fixed on the river bank. 'I don't think he'll leave this spot as long as his mother is on the other side. He knows what I'm trying to do.'

'Will he be safe?'

'Safe is relative in these parts,' Myles offered grimly before putting his hands on the tailgate to jump back in. 'Okay, I'm tied up. Take us back upstream.'

Rae saw the boy before she saw Myles.

She'd been pacing the compound for several hours when she saw the kid heading down the road, his face as pinched and frightened as before. But whilst his body had been stooped with desperation before, it was now straighter, taller, more hopeful.

He was keeping a steady pace, but this time there was no shouting, no drawing attention of any kind. Still, his eyes were trained across the river, and Rae could only follow his gaze, something which might possibly have been her stomach lodged in the vicinity of her throat.

Myles.

His gait was unmistakeable, although he had shirked the volunteer garb that he'd been wearing in favour of something closer to the clothing worn by the people swarming across the bridge. And in his arms, the unmistakeable fig-

ure of a pregnant woman, a bundle in her arms that, Rae realised with a jolt, looked suspiciously like a newborn baby.

There was clearly an issue.

It felt like an age as he reached the bridge, joining the
throng who were already jostling to cross the narrow
planks. She could see him moving, trying to fight his way
through. All she could do was wait, and pace, knowing
that every minute was crucial to the baby and the mother,
but unable to do a single thing about it.

And then he was close enough for her to call a couple
of local volunteers to bring out a gurney, which arrived at
the same time that Myles did. There was no missing the
blood covering the woman's clothing, and Myles'.

'You delivered the baby but the mother's haemorrhaging?'

'Yes. There was no choice, that baby was coming out.
The heartbeat was weak but it was there, I had to clear its
lungs and nose of fluid. It will need to come back with us
to the neonatal team. However, it's the mother I'm most
concerned about. She hasn't delivered the placenta and
now she's haemorrhaging.'

'Okay, let's get her inside and check her levels. I'm
guessing her haemoglobin is going to be down so we'll
need to find her some blood—her son would be a good
start—and start transfusing her. Then we can get inside
and try to get that placenta out.'

CHAPTER TWELVE

'YOU'RE VERY QUIET.'

They were almost an hour into the drive back to Camp Sceralenar, the ambulances with the more urgent patients in the convoy, but the two of them alone again in the four-by-four.

She hitched her shoulders, her gaze fixed out of the window.

'You can talk to me, you know.'

'I know.' She smiled sadly but didn't pull her eyes away from the barren landscape. 'I just don't know what to say.'

'There was nothing you could have done, Rae. The baby was born too early and they just don't have the equipment out here to help these babies survive. But you saved the mother. Because of you, the kid who flagged us down isn't an orphan right now.'

'I know that.' She turned her head slowly to look at him.

'It just doesn't help,' he supplied.

'No, it doesn't. I just… I'm not sure how I feel.' She drew in a long breath. 'When I first arrived here I was shocked at how brusque people were. How cold. How little they grieved, or showed their grief. They were so desensitised to all the death and I couldn't understand it. Now I think I do.'

Was the tight coil inside his chest normal? Like an over-wound clock.

'Do you?'

She shrugged again.

'One in five foetuses don't survive here. That number is so much lower back home, and those that don't survive are often lost well before labour. I might see one death a month. But out here I see them every day. Multiple times. Worse, most of those babies die because of complications during labour.'

'There's no care out here,' he concurred quietly. 'Most of these women don't even know there's a problem until it's too late. And even if they did, what can they do about it? There are so few hospitals, and anyway, what money do they have?'

'Exactly.'

He could see her swallow, desperately trying to hold herself together.

'I couldn't understand how they could be so accepting, so stoic, at first. But these women go into pregnancy knowing the chances of something going wrong are high so they are prepared to lose their baby. Perhaps too prepared.'

'Probably,' he concurred, 'but there's nothing you can do to change that. That's the way life out here is. You just have to find a way to deal with it. To cope.'

'Like you have.' She cast him a sidelong glance before looking away guiltily. 'I'm sorry, I didn't mean that.'

'Yes, you did. In your own way.'

But he was astounded to find that it didn't rankle as it had in the past. It didn't grate on him. He *wanted* to talk to her. To let her into his head. To help her to know him, to *understand* him.

As if he believed she could actually *help* him.

He'd lost his career, his reputation, the life he'd known.

The only thing he had left to give her was his honour. Then it was up to her. She could take him, or she could leave him. His chest constricted painfully.

He'd battled terrible enemies, been in firefights that should only ever have had one outcome, lost too many friends to count. He told himself he'd withstood worse than any woman walking out on him, then ignored the little voice that goaded him that Raevenne wasn't just *any* *woman*.

'And you're right, I haven't found a way to deal with it so I've just been bottling it up inside. But it was always bound to spill over at some point.'

He was aware she'd stilled. She was frozen in her seat wanting neither to look away nor to engage, for fear of breaking the moment. For a few moments, he turned his head from the road and met her clear, direct gaze whilst something rolled through him, low and unstoppable, like a drumbeat, or thunder.

'I'm grateful to you for offering to be the one to listen, but I need you to know that I'm not making any promises. I can't guarantee that I'll be able to tell you everything, or that it will make any difference.'

'I don't need anything from you. I just want you to know that you have that option,' she whispered.

He nodded, unmoving for another moment, finally turning his attention back to the road.

'Part of the reason for not wanting to talk about the night…that we found the village burning…was that I was trying to protect someone.'

He didn't realise he'd stopped talking until Rae spoke up hesitantly.

'Lance Corporal Michael McCoy?'

'No.' He shook his head but then stopped again. When

she reached her hand out to touch him, her fingers resting gently on his forearm, it was oddly encouraging.

'I was trying to protect his daughter.'

'His daughter?'

'Kelly. She was five years old and she was his whole world.'

Rae sucked in a breath, sympathetic but still not understanding. He didn't blame her.

'A few days before that mission Mikey had received a letter from home. A well-intentioned family member telling him that they'd discovered his wife had been having an affair.'

Her hands fluttered against her throat, a shocked sound escaping her lips.

'They wrote a letter? When Mikey was in a warzone?'

'They meant well. I guess they thought he was better finding out with his friends around him than coming back home to his wife knowing nothing about it.'

'God,' she breathed. 'What an impossible choice. But surely… I mean, why did they put him on that mission?'

Guilt, black and familiar, erupted through him like molten lava in a volcano. She gasped, horrified.

'I'm so sorry. That was a stupid thing to say. I didn't mean it at all how it sounded.'

'His OC thought he was okay.' His voice was raw, fractured, barely recognisable. 'When I mentioned my reservations to him, he said that he'd known Mikey a long time and that he was confident. I couldn't argue. I tried telling Mikey he should sit this one out but he begged me not to push it. He explained that he already knew about the affair, that he'd confronted her about it after we'd come back from our previous tour of duty, but she'd sworn it was over.'

'Oh, Myles. What a horrible choice to have to make.'

'He told me it wasn't news to him, that he'd been handling it just fine all this time whilst the rest of his squad knew about it. I couldn't put my finger on why I wasn't so sure, so I let it go. We were days away from the end of his third tour and his rifles squad had been protecting my medical team for eight months. We'd been lucky enough to be together from the start of this tour without any significant casualties, and he didn't want to dip out on the last mission of the tour.'

'He made it sound so plausible.' Rae exhaled.

'He did, and I believed him. With hindsight, I should have known better. The other guys saw what they wanted to see, whilst I was just far removed enough to see the warning signs for what they were. But it was a standard recce and we didn't expect to see anything significant out there so I made the decision to keep his secret. It's a decision I will regret for the rest of my life.'

His voice cracked and for a moment, he couldn't speak.

'What happened, Myles?' Rae prompted softly, and he actually believed she could feel every last drop of his anguish. 'What did Lance… What did *Mikey* do?'

It was as though a dense, black fog had descended over him and he couldn't see, couldn't breathe. Still, he forced himself to push through it.

'We walked through that village, looking for survivors, the stench and the sights worse than any kind of horror film anyone could ever make. I still can't be sure exactly what triggered him,' he began, 'but suddenly he just lost it.'

'Lost it?'

Something roared through Myles, as though trying to drown out the words he didn't want to say.

'He knew they had to still be somewhere in the area. They weren't hard to track. We tried to stop him but… I've never seen anyone move so fast, as though the horror of it had taken him over. We heard the firefight even as we raced in but it was too late.'

He stopped the vehicle, unable to trust himself; needing to step out for a moment, to let the cool night air flow over his skin, to quell the nausea churning his stomach into a quagmire of regret and recrimination.

Wordlessly, Rae got out of the vehicle and moved around it until she was standing in front of him. He had no idea how long they stayed there; it could have been hours, or maybe merely minutes. Then, abruptly, she bowed her head so that her forehead was resting against his, cool and settling. Neither of them moved, barely even breathed, but eventually, *eventually*, the roaring in his head began to abate.

'None of us have ever voiced it, but I can't be the only one to think that Mikey must have known what the outcome would be. That he couldn't have hoped to take them all on alone. That he...didn't intend to come back from it.'

Rae raised her hands to cup his face.

'It wasn't your fault.'

'I should have told someone I thought he wasn't up to it. I should have fought harder to make people listen.'

'You said it yourself, they already knew but they chose to see what they wanted to see. A strong Mikey, not one who was hurting.'

The vision of her swam in front of his eyes.

'You think that makes it easier?'

'I'm not sure anything will make it easier.' She jerked her head lightly from side to side. 'Your responsibility and loyalty to the men you were so close to is strong. I think you'll always believe there must have been something you could have done. Even if there wasn't.'

'You don't understand. It was *my* job to anticipate all of that. If I had insisted on dropping him from the recce, he'd still be alive. A five-year-old girl would still have her father.'

'That's not realistic. And I think you know that, deep down. You did as much as you could with the information you had at the time. Odds are, if you'd left him behind on that mission, you'd have come back to find he'd found another way to do it. Rafe told me a few soldiers couldn't take any more and took their lives in the toilet blocks on camps.'

He couldn't deny it.

'And if Mikey had done that,' she continued sadly, 'you'd have been beating yourself up for *not* taking him on that mission. Thinking that if you had, he would still be alive.'

In the darkest recesses of his head he'd wondered the same thing, too many times to recall, over the years. He'd woken up in a cold sweat, his mind searching to touch an answer that could never be found. He held his head up, his voice sharper than he intended. But at least it didn't break or splinter, the way he felt his very soul was doing.

'We'll never know.'

And that was the worst part about it.

His words hung between them, like a shimmering, electrically charged barrier.

His guilt was palpable. Perhaps he was most guilty that the surgeries he'd carried out on those villagers had drawn the attention of the enemy, made them collaborators. Maybe it was more about Mikey. Probably it was a combination of the two.

She gazed at him, as though silently willing him to keep going, and not to suddenly regret his frankness, and shut her out instead. He hated the sorrow in her expression, almost as much as he hated that flicker of hopefulness behind it. As if she imagined him opening up to her now meant so much more.

Because he couldn't guarantee her more. He couldn't guarantee her anything. He was damaged. Worthless.

'Is that why you walked out on the army? The surgeries? Because you think this is the punishment you deserve?' she asked suddenly.

'You say it like you don't believe it.' He couldn't keep the accusation out of his tone. 'You think it's right that those innocent villagers should die, that I let one man get to the point where he took his own life, that one little girl now has no father, and all the while I get to walk away unscathed? To walk around as though nothing ever happened?'

'But you aren't unscathed, are you?' she pointed out. 'You don't walk around as though nothing happened. You've sacrificed everything: your career as an army officer, your career as a surgeon, even some kind of a decent life. You can't tell me that taking a job as a bodyguard to the vile Raevenne Rawlstone wasn't your idea of punishment.'

'You're not vile.' Anger coursed through him without warning. How dared she talk about herself that way? How dared she even think it?

Rae held her ground.

'But you didn't know that at the time, did you? You thought I was vacuous, and trampy, and spoilt. The perfect penance for someone as culpable and selfish as you?'

The blackness swirled faster, harder.

'You're not that woman.'

'And you're not that man,' she declared triumphantly.

His eyes seared. Scalding and furious. He practically spat the words out at her.

'You don't know what you're talking about.'

'Except that I do,' she announced, ignoring his attempts to intimidate her. 'I've got to know you now. And even if

I didn't, my brother knows you, yet he gave you this job. He entrusted me to you.'

She lifted her hands to his chest. The way she had only a few nights ago. Reminding him all too easily of how it had been between them. How it maybe could still be.

'He trusts me. But I don't deserve that trust.'

'You absolutely do. And that's why I trust you, too.'

He couldn't stop himself. He covered her hand with his, his calloused thumb pad caressing her skin.

Less than a month ago he'd thought she was like some kind of breathtakingly beautiful angel, but that it was only skin deep. But he'd been wrong. She was beautiful inside, as well as outside.

He'd spent the last few weeks humping and dumping. He'd hoped that working out here would soothe his battered sense of self-worth and it made him feel as if he was starting to heal. As if he could be useful again. Worthy.

Worthy of Rae?

He thrust away the taunting voice but he wasn't quick enough. New questions tumbled around his head.

Could he ever be worthy of a woman like her? She was incredible, blending in seamlessly, with no trace of the socialite he'd thought he'd known. She was like a different version of herself out here. A better version. Freer. More comfortable in her skin. The *real* Rae, he realised abruptly.

A woman he could easily fall for.

The thought was like a lasso around his chest. Tight. Constricting. That could *never* happen. Because even if Rae wasn't the woman he'd believed her to be, he was still the man he knew himself to be.

Lost. Anchorless. Valueless.

He had nothing to offer a woman like Rae. He was damaged, and not just physically. He'd lost his body and he'd lost his career, but more than that he'd lost his reputation.

His only worth now was in the work he could do in places like this. Here he felt so much more. *Here he felt whole.*

He didn't belong back in regular civilian life—coming out here had proved that much to him. There was no place for him back there. There was no place for him in Rae's world.

It should have made him want to back away from her all the more. Instead, it made him want to grab hold of the woman he had, enjoy her for the here and now. She'd be gone, moving on from his life, soon enough. The thought terrified him.

Gripping her wrists, he pushed her away from him.

'Confession over,' he bit out as coldly, as icily, as he could. 'We're expected back in camp and you're due on shift in a couple of hours. You don't want to let them down, and start living up to your old reputation, do you?'

And as she flinched he told himself the shattering in his chest was triumph.

CHAPTER THIRTEEN

'YOU'RE GOING TO need to sterilise her if you perform a Caesarean section on her,' Janine, the senior consultant, murmured. 'If it's her third C-section, her uterus will be severely weakened.'

'I know, but I don't see another option for her,' Rae concluded dully, glancing across the room at the patient in question. As if things couldn't get any worse, the girl was on oxygen, still not even stable, and although they'd succeeded in bringing her blood pressure down significantly, it was still elevated. 'Not if we're to save her baby.'

There were times when Rae could feel her limitations pressing in on her, constricting and cruel, but the truth of it, Rae realised with something close to contentment, was that there was absolutely nowhere else she would rather be. She might not have known it three and a half weeks ago when she'd first driven into the camp, but this was where she was meant to be in her life. In places like this, helping women who might otherwise have had nothing.

Perhaps not for ever, but certainly for the foreseeable future. As much as she'd loved her job in her New York practice, it simply didn't compare to how proud, how fulfilled, and, yes, how permanently exhausted she felt out here.

It almost made up for the way things had taken a sour turn with Myles. She'd thought that Myles opening up to her would be a turning point, bringing them closer together, maybe even allowing them to take their physical relationship to another level. One where they could possibly consider actually *calling* it something of a relationship.

She couldn't have been more wrong. Unfamiliar bitterness trickled down her spine.

It was as though talking to her the way he had that night, opening himself up to her and showing her his vulnerabilities, had actually made him push her away all the harder. They'd barely spoken since that day, even before he'd volunteered to return to the forward camp for forty-eight-hour shifts, on two more occasions since.

Folding her arms over her chest and straightening her spine, Rae told herself that she didn't care. Hadn't she told herself years ago that the only person she could rely on to make her happy was herself? Not her family, not her friends, not a man.

And certainly no other man would do for her now that she'd been with Myles. He'd ruined her for life; she knew it for a fact. No one else would ever, *could* ever, come close.

But she had medicine, her career, and that was going to be enough.

More than enough, she chanted brightly, turning her attention back to her immediate patient.

The twenty-seven-year-old woman had come in with such severe pre-eclampsia that her skin had split in some areas and was at high risk of infection. They had battled to reduce her blood pressure, and stabilise her baby's condition and, for a while, it had seemed to work. But now the baby's health was beginning to deteriorate again. They had to get it out.

A third C-section meant a third scar, leaving the girl's

uterus too vulnerable to risk further pregnancies, which meant sterilisation was going to be the safest course of action. It wasn't going across well with the young woman, or her family, who were beginning to turn on the interpreter.

'I'd better get in there and support him.' Rae started across the room. 'This was my other patient I've been keeping an eye on. She came in pregnant with twins and fully dilated. She's with the midwives but she's been pushing for quite some time now, and I think we might need to help things along by delivering the first baby with a vacuum.'

'I'm on it.' Janine nodded. 'You just go and deal with your pre-eclampsia patient.'

'Thanks,' called Rae, already hurrying across the room to where the husband was standing apart from the family, his face etched more with concern than with anger.

Instinctively, Rae summoned the interpreter over, a young man by the name of Lulwar. Her voice was low until she could be sure her suspicions were correct.

'Can you ask the husband what he's thinking?'

The two men spoke briefly, quietly, the family too emotional to notice.

'He wants to know, if this happens, then his wife will be safe?'

'Yes. She won't be able to have any more children, but there's a good chance that any further pregnancies could end up life-threatening for his wife.'

She watched the husband's face as the interpreter passed on the information. Relief pouring through her when he bobbed his head in acknowledgement before a look of determination settled over his features as he stepped forward, silenced the arguing family, and took his wife's hand.

Rae grabbed a local nurse quickly.

'Can you go and secure me the next OR please? Emergency C-section and sterilisation.'

And after that the patients, and the obstructed deliveries, kept coming. And by the time her shift was over, it was all she could do to drag herself to her room and flop down into her bed, asleep somewhere before her body even landed on the mattress.

Tomorrow would be Christmas Day which meant that her month-long mission was nearly over. It also meant that it was the first Christmas she hadn't spent with her family throughout her entire life.

She was almost sad to realise that with the exception of Rafe she didn't miss them, or their inevitable dramas, one little bit.

'Happy Christmas, Raevenne.' His low voice only just carried the couple of feet between them.

Rae swung around, startled, peering into the shadow of the building where he'd been watching her for some time.

'Oh, I didn't see you there. Right. Yes. Happy Christmas.'

She didn't look particularly overjoyed to see him. If anything she looked wary, not that he could really blame her. He'd been avoiding her ever since the drive back to camp when he'd laid himself out there. Logically he knew that it wasn't her fault he'd felt vulnerable, and weak, but that hadn't stopped him from taking it out on her, by avoiding any real contact, ever since.

Mainly because he knew the instant he saw her every regret and reservation he had about talking to her would melt away, replaced instead by the ache to draw her to him, kiss her thoroughly and pretend that none of the bad stuff, none of the baggage, even existed.

'I heard you performed some really impressive procedures over the last few days.'

'Oh?'

'Not least a heterotopic pregnancy.'

He could practically read the internal battle she was waging in every flicker of her expression and he had to fight not to smile. It was typical *heart-on-sleeve* Rae fashion. Or was it just that he knew her better than either of them would probably care to admit?

'Let me guess,' he drawled. 'The private part of you wants to tell me where to shove it, whilst the professional part of you is so geared up by the medical stuff that you're desperate to talk about it.'

She scowled at him. Or she tried to, anyway.

'You can't just flip-flop like this, Myles,' she muttered.

'I know.'

'You open up to me, let me into your most private moments one minute, but the next you're acting as though I barely even exist.'

'I accept that.'

'And now you're pretending nothing even happened.'

'You're right, and I'm sorry.'

He didn't know what he'd expected her to do, but it wasn't to narrow her eyes at him.

'Of course you are. Until the next time.'

Something scraped inside him. He hated the way she was looking at him. As if he wasn't to be trusted. As if he wasn't even someone she liked.

'I wasn't going to tell you this until we had everything squared away and everything accounted for, but we think we've caught the company responsible for the death threats, Rafe's brakes, and your break-in. They're a rival company who lost out on a bid to your brother about a year ago.'

She didn't even blink.

'I know.'

'You do?'

'Rafe emailed a few days ago.'

She was giving nothing away.

'I see.' Myles dipped his head, fighting back some alien emotion pushing within him.

'Rafe also said you'd been working flat out on the investigation even from out here.'

He shrugged.

'I did what I could.'

'Why?' He hated that her voice was so brittle. 'For me? Because you owed Rafe? To appease your own conscience?'

And then he looked at her, and it finally hit him. He understood what it was that had made her fight so hard to distance herself from *Life in the Rawl*, why she'd been so averse to having another bodyguard, why she'd felt compelled to volunteer for a mission like this.

'They really did a number on you, didn't they?'

Rae stopped. Her attempt at nonchalance betrayed by the way her breath had caught in her throat.

'Who did?'

'Your sisters.' He lifted his shoulders. 'Justin. The press.'

'I can handle them.'

She jutted her chin out a fraction, her voice apparently as airy as ever. She looked magnificent and proud, and... something else besides. Something quite different. He'd been watching her closely long enough now to begin to be able to read her, from the way the pretty flush deepened slightly and crept down her neck, to the way she was shifting, almost imperceptibly, from one foot to the other.

And so he knew magnificent and proud were only a

part of it. There was another side to her, and it was fragile, vulnerable.

It was amazing that he hadn't spotted it before. That no one else had spotted it before. Or perhaps people just didn't want to. They preferred the more heinous version of Raevenne Rawlstone, so that was what they believed.

The question was, why had she let them?

'I know you can handle them, but the point is that you don't want to keep having to, do you? It won't matter to them how many good deeds you do, they're going to want to write the lies, because juicy scandal sells papers, not charity work.'

'It doesn't matter.' She flashed a smile, which he now recognised to be too practised, too tight to be real. That realisation gave him a kick. 'I don't care what they write, anyway.'

'Up until a month ago, I used to believe that.' He didn't deliberately soften his voice, it seemed to just…happen.

'And now you believe differently?' The question was almost off-hand, as though his answer didn't matter to her either way.

But she'd hesitated a fraction too long.

'You truly love being out here, don't you?'

She didn't meet his gaze immediately, and when she did look at his face, he got the impression she was staring at a point just on his ear, rather than looking at him directly. As if a part of her was guilty for her answer.

'I find it very…rewarding.'

Surely it didn't actually *hurt* him that she felt she couldn't be honest?

'If they asked you to return for a three-month stint, would you?'

He couldn't explain why his heart was hammering so hard. And then her eyes flickered to his, just for an instant, and she pursed her lips. It was as though someone had dealt him a blow that had punched every bit of oxygen from his lungs.

'They've already asked you, haven't they?'

'Yes.'

'And you agreed?'

'I told them I would consider it,' she hedged.

'But you intend to agree.'

It wasn't a question and she didn't answer it as though it had been one. But working out here had been a good move for her, both professionally and personally. She suited this life. She was good at it. She felt fulfilled by it. That much was obvious.

'I don't see any reason why I shouldn't come back.' Her voice sounded odd, as though she was challenging him. 'Do you?'

And all at once he wanted to grab her and tell her that there *was* a reason. That he wanted her in his life. That when they got home maybe they could start again, perhaps see if they could have a future together.

But then he looked into those laurel-green depths and saw everything that she loved was out here. How could he ask her to leave that behind? How could he ask her to leave herself behind? Especially when she'd only just worked out who she really was.

'You're right, you *should* come back,' he said slowly, realising that he meant it. 'Either here or somewhere else. You can be yourself here, without the media constantly hounding you and fabricating stories about you.'

'I'm not running away.' She jerked her head sharply.

'I never thought you were. But you have so much to offer, both as a doctor and as a human being. And the press won't let you do that. They want to pigeonhole you because it suits their agenda to do so. Out here, you can be the person that I think you've always been meant to be.'

'Really?' Her shy smile abraded against his hollow chest, and he pretended he didn't see the confusing hint of sadness in it.

Just as he pretended that he didn't feel Rae everywhere. Restoring feeling to his body after it had been growing cold for so long. Making him feel alive.

Which left him with a choice. He could continue punishing her for little more than being the one person he had trusted enough to open up to. Or he could set aside all the reasons why being with her was a bad idea, and why it could only end up hurting one or both of them, and he could just enjoy this one perfect day with her. *Christmas* Day.

'Have you eaten yet?'

She blinked slowly at him.

'Not yet. I was just heading over there now.'

'May I join you?'

She slid him a pointed look, her tone dark.

'And if I said *no*?'

'*Are* you saying *no*?'

He refused to bite and after a long moment she sighed, a little overly dramatically for his tastes.

'I should. But this place is too cramped to avoid each other indefinitely. Besides,' she added loftily, 'it *is* Christmas.'

A smile toyed at the corners of her mouth and he had to fight the impulse to kiss it away. This was exactly what Rae did to him. She chased all logical thought, all sense of self-preservation, from his head until it was filled with only one thing. *Her.*

She made him want to tell her all the deep, black thoughts that crept around his head in the still of the night.

She made him want to find a way to cage them so that they no longer plagued him. She made him want to be a better person.

But what did he really have to offer her?

He'd been a good soldier, a brilliant surgeon. Now he was neither. Neither of them had anything to rush home for, yet whilst Rae consequently couldn't wait to get back to another place like this, he couldn't wait to get out of here. But where even *was* home for him?

At least that answered his question, then. He had *nothing* to offer her.

And yet here he still was. Unable to stay away from her any longer. Wanting to spend this day in her company. They were on borrowed time, he and Rae, and he should know better. But right here, right now, he didn't care.

'It is indeed Christmas,' he agreed. 'So let's go and feast.'

It was a Christmas beyond all she could have hoped for. The men dancing, rice cans attached to their legs, their feet practically a blur as women kept time with sticks on the ground. At one point she was even hauled to her feet by some of the women and challenged to match the rhythm; faster and harder and more complex all the time.

It was exhilarating, and incredible, and special.

Not least when Myles looked over from where his own group was taking part in the festivities, the glance they shared so intimate. So unabashed.

Then the refugees sang traditional songs, and when it came time for the volunteers to share their own carols, something akin to pure joy suffused Rae as she turned to find Myles standing there, right next to her.

And then he smiled, and a memory—a decade and a half old—rushed her.

She was in love with him.

All over again. She wanted more with him. She needed more. But if she couldn't help him to face his demons then there was never going to be a chance for them.

Sliding her hand into his, Rae waited for a moment until they could slip out unnoticed, the festivities finally winding down, and led him to her room.

There was no easy way to tell him so she just plunged in.

'I—I've been doing some research into your case,' she announced, trying to ignore the shake in her voice.

'Is that so?'

'It is.' She swallowed hard. 'And I've found out that they think that village was attacked by the local forces in retaliation for the villagers selling some of their harvest that year, instead of saving it all for the rebel soldiers.'

'I see.'

'Which means it wasn't about you or your team. It wasn't because you were there helping people.'

She'd never heard of it at first, but it turned out it was pretty commonplace—farming villages whose crops should have easily provided enough food for themselves and for sale at market, but who were on the brink of starvation because each season almost all their crop was taken by the warlords.

But she knew that didn't mean Myles was about to accept her word for it.

'I have letters, research, if you want it.'

'I've already heard about it. It was a theory.' His clipped tone was clearly intended to end the conversation.

She couldn't give up that easily.

'Whose theory?'

'It doesn't matter.'

'It does to me.'

A month ago his glower would have cut into her. Instead, she found herself sitting up straighter, maintaining eye contact. She had started this. She had to see it through.

'Myles, please… I want to understand.'

'An army theory.'

'You don't believe it?'

Disappointment shot through her but she wasn't prepared for his answer.

'I…don't know. I didn't back then. It felt as though it was an easy answer to salve my conscience. But now, with the benefit of time, of distance, of *you*, then maybe.'

It was like a church full of perfectly pitched choirboys all singing beautifully in her head all at once.

It didn't mean Myles accepted what had happened. But it did at least mean that he was open to possibilities.

'So what does that mean?' she breathed, scarcely willing to break whatever spell they were under.

His fingers laced through hers, his perfect turquoise-sea eyes not leaving her face.

'I can't make you any promises, Rae, but maybe we can just try to enjoy these last few days together—not that work will give us much chance—and see how it goes from there.'

It wasn't declarations of love, but it was better than anything she could have hoped for.

'I wish I had bought you a Christmas present.'

'The only Christmas present I want is you, in my bed,' he murmured, his body tightening as her gaze grew hotter, more intense.

She lifted herself up onto her toes, her breath tickling his ear as she leaned in to whisper to him.

'That's a Christmas present I can give very freely.'

CHAPTER FOURTEEN

'Rae, over here.'

'Raevenne, sweetie, this way.'

'Give us a quick smile, Rae.'

Rae flinched as the photojournalists crowded in on them even as she stepped around the arrivals gate at JFK airport.

Relief warred with regret when Myles slipped instantly out of the intimate atmosphere that had enhanced their last few days together, working hard and playing harder, and back into bodyguard mode.

'Your *fame*?' he asked grimly.

She pulled a face.

'It has to be. Nothing is private, not even going out there to do charity work.'

It made her all the more grateful that she'd already accepted another medical mission—a three-month stint, this time—and would be headed back out before Easter. She couldn't get away from this circus fast enough.

Sticking as close as she could to Myles' impressive body, with which she'd finally become more than familiar, and with which she intended to reacquaint herself as soon as they got to her home, she allowed him to plough a path through the melee, and out of the main doors. The car waiting for them was mercifully in sight, although the press weren't letting her go without a chase.

'Can you tell your fans how it was at Camp Sceralenar?'

'Did you save any lives, Rae?'

'Were you aware that your bodyguard is a British army hero? That he risked his life climbing down a hillside in enemy territory to retrieve the corpse of a Lance Corporal Michael McCoy, who had taken his own life?'

Rae froze, dropping back for a moment as she turned to try to see who had made the last comment. She wasn't prepared for Myles to practically drag her off her feet and to the car.

'Keep moving,' he bit out. 'And don't engage.'

'Did you know that when McCoy defied orders and instigated a firefight with the enemy, resulting in his own death and the injury of several of his squad, Major Garrington told his commanding officers that he was culpable just so that McCoy's young daughter Kelly wouldn't find out that her father died dishonourably?'

She could practically feel the fury rolling off Myles' body, his muscles tense and bunched. She prayed no reporters came too close. But Myles restrained himself, his focus on getting them both to the vehicle.

In a daze, she allowed herself to be bundled inside, pushed across the soft leather seats, her bergens taken off her and the door slammed on the baying pack outside. In slow motion she turned around, watching Myles throw the luggage into the boot of the car and stalk around to climb in the other side.

And then the car was pulling away and the silence might as well have been hemming her in.

She ran her tongue around her mouth. My God, she was so stupid.

'Myles—'

'Forget it.'

It was an icy warning, which she should have heeded. But she couldn't. Desperation clawed inside her.

'You can't really be blaming me for this?'

'I've never told anyone else that information about Mikey's family. Only you.'

'This is the press.' She flung her hands up. 'They unearth all kinds of stuff if they're so inclined.'

His stark look was excruciating.

'No, Rae. You did this.'

'No.'

Her shoulders slumped but she refused to look away from that glare; she would not let him think she was guilty.

'Yes. You engineered it.'

'You can't really believe that.' Pain and disappointment lanced through her.

'You wanted the press to know. All this time you've been acting like you moved away from your reality life, but what was the truth, Raevenne? That you got pushed out for not repeating that bit of TV gold and you've been looking for a way back in ever since?'

'Of course not.' Horror spread through her like wildfire. 'I don't care what they think. Not any more. I only cared what Rafe knew. What *I* knew. What *you* knew.'

'And yet you couldn't let it go. You had to release the story. And now they're running stories about my career, about my missions, about Mikey.'

He didn't mention little Kelly. He didn't need to. She felt sick with the knowledge.

'I didn't say anything, Myles. I never would.'

'I don't believe you.'

Every word, every accusation, was like a lashing to her already broken soul. But still, she made herself lift her chin. She forced herself to meet his eye.

'I can't make you believe me. But I know the truth. Just

as I know that part of the reason you want to hate me now is because you don't know what else to do with the emotions you stuff inside you and never allow to come out. Emotions which are eating you from the inside, Myles.'

'You don't know what you're talking about.'

'I do. And I didn't do this, but I can't say I'm unhappy the press have found out. Because it's time you stopped blaming yourself for what happened. Being an army trauma surgeon has been your life for so long that somewhere along the line it became what defined you, and when you lost that part of who you were, you lost yourself.'

The words shouldn't have penetrated his fury or his misery. Nothing should have.

And yet they did.

Suddenly, he saw the hurt and misery in her expression. He realised he was the one who had put them there. Even as the knowledge snatched his breath away, it wasn't enough to change what she'd done.

The signs for the railway station couldn't have come at a more fortuitous moment.

'I can't do this with you, Raevenne. Or, more to the point, I *won't*. Everything is always drama with your lot and I've seen enough drama to last me several lifetimes.'

'No, Myles—'

'Stop the car, please,' he ordered the driver, before turning to his side and taking one last look at her. 'I'm sorry, Rac. We're done.'

CHAPTER FIFTEEN

RAE PULLED THE baby out, blue, floppy and covered in thick meconium-stained amniotic fluid. If she was going to help it transition to life outside the room she was going to have to work quickly. But, as ever, resources were limited and she had to act fast.

Picking the baby up, she transferred it quickly to the resus table using an Ambu bag to push air into the limp baby's lungs, but the meconium was filling the mouth and lungs, stopping the chest from rising. She checked the pulse.

Decelerating—just as she'd feared.

'Cath, can you grab an aspirator and start getting this meconium out? And just ask someone to see if Janine is still free? The mother is haemorrhaging.'

She didn't wait for an answer, watching instead as her colleague began to clear the baby's airways.

'Okay, that might do it.' Rae nodded after what felt like a lifetime. For the baby, it so easily could be. 'Let's try again.'

She didn't realise she'd been holding her breath until she pushed more air into the baby's lungs and finally, *finally*, heard the faintest of whispers. It wasn't much, but it was better than nothing.

Still, when she turned to the new mother to see her staring over and, despite her own pain, tears of relief spilling freely out at the miraculous sound, Rae felt her own heart swell with pride.

She really did have the best job in the world, she realised, handing the baby over to the mother whose arms were already outstretched. Even out here, where resources were scarce, and maternal and infant mortality was so high, there was still the pure joy of hearing a baby cry for the first time.

It almost made up for the fact that, in order to have this life, this career, she'd lost Myles.

Less than a week after she'd watched him go, a ringing sound had already built up in her ears. Part of her had been desperate to run after him, a bigger part of her had been too paralysed to move. She had almost welcomed the numbness that had been beginning to settle over her, because at least that acted as something of an anaesthetic against the pain she recalled all too vividly from the last time Myles had rejected her.

The ringing had grown louder and more insistent. With a start, Rae had realised it wasn't in her head after all, but her mobile, and she'd heard Angela on the line telling her the next replacement medic had dropped out, and inviting her to jump on a return flight.

She'd opened her mouth to decline, to say that she couldn't possibly return without Myles. But the words hadn't come out. They'd lodged in her throat. And then she'd caught herself.

Myles had gone. She'd had nothing to lose. And besides, she'd loved operating out there, and feeling she was making a real difference. At least she would have that, even if he wasn't with her to share it.

The next thing she'd heard was her own voice accepting Angela's offer.

Could it really only have been five days ago?

It felt like an eternity.

Either way it was time to get over any secret hopes she'd harboured that Myles might step back into her life. Time to accept that he was now well and truly gone. Since he and Rafe had uncovered the source of the death threats there was no reason for Myles to return. She didn't need him now.

At least, not as her bodyguard.

But in the emotional sense?

If these past few days had taught her anything it had reinforced the fact that she loved him. She always would. He had her heart in a way no other man would ever have. Because no other man came close to matching Major Myles Garrington. And that was okay. Some people went through their whole lives without meeting their soulmate. But she had.

And that month she'd had with Myles was hers for ever. She could hug it to herself and no one would ever be able to take it away from her.

'You're done?' Janine barely lifted her head from attending to the haemorrhaging.

'You need some help?'

'No, but the new general surgeon arrived this morning. I was going to walk them through a procedure out here when you called.'

'Shall I take over here so you can get back to her?'

She still couldn't see Janine's face, but she could hear something colouring her expression. If Rae hadn't known better, she might have thought it was excitement mingled with amusement.

'No, I'm happy with this. Besides, might be fun for you to do the walk-through.'

Rae wrinkled her nose, wondering what she could possibly be missing. But there was no time to dwell. Leaving the bay, she quickly scrubbed up and darted around the curtain to the operating area, a bright, welcoming smile on her lips.

'I'm Rae, sorry we have to meet under these circumstances, but hopefully we'll get some time later. How can I help?'

'Apparently you're going to help me identify the uterine arteries.' A pair of all too familiar eyes met hers.

Her heart hung, time seemingly slowing around her. He couldn't be healed, not in a week. And yet he was out here, and apparently the new general surgeon.

'Myles...?'

'Indeed.'

'General Surgeon?'

'I wanted to move away from what I did before. And it isn't as though I didn't do lots of other trauma cases over the years. But maybe we can discuss it later. Before my patient bleeds out internally,' Myles prompted, but there was no mistaking the expression in his gaze.

It promised her all the explanations she could want. Afterwards.

The one that told her everything was going to be okay. He'd healed himself, and he'd come back for her.

Everything else could wait.

Twenty hours, six C-sections, and a slew of both complicated and non-complicated deliveries later and they were in his tiny room, each with a fresh, hot coffee.

She waited for him to start the conversation, afraid to speak first.

'I love you.'

She froze. Her body might as well have stopped working. She stopped swallowing, stopped blinking, stopped breathing.

Something welled inside her and she had the sudden,

frightening suspicion that it was the urge to say the words back to him.

But she mustn't.

A much as hearing him say he loved her was like the most beautiful song in the world piped straight into her chest, she needed more than that. She needed to understand.

'I admit to a level of combat PTSD. You were right. I already knew it but I couldn't bring myself to admit it aloud before now. Perhaps a fear of looking weak, or maybe a fear of losing respect. I certainly lost my self-respect. I didn't know who I was, caught between the army soldier I'd been and this new, terrifying life on Civvy Street.'

'But you're still the same strong, responsible man you always were,' she managed. 'Anyone can see that.'

'*I* couldn't. Not until I met you. You helped me to see that I had a problem, and that I needed to talk about it.'

'And did you?' she whispered.

'Did I talk to someone? Yes. I went to see my old brigadier.'

She stared at him, winded.

'When?'

'After I left you in the car, outside the railway station. When I went into the station there was already a train ready to leave so I bought a ticket and I jumped on board. To this day I don't know where it was headed to. I realised my mistake a couple of hours in, disembarked at the next station and made that phone call to my old unit.'

His wry smile tugged at her. 'You didn't make the entire journey?'

Myles shook his head.

Guilt scraped away inside him. He'd been so caught up

in his own internal battles that he'd wilfully ignored the war that Rae, too, had been waging. She loved him. Just as, he realised with a heavy thud, he loved her.

He was *in* love with her.

He had been pulling the whole macho soldier routine and toughing it out, but even though it had fooled almost everybody else, it hadn't fooled her.

He loved her. A deep, fierce, strong love, which he'd never known he had the capacity to feel, before now. But that also meant recognising that he had nothing to offer her, that he was a shell of a human, and a fraction of the man he used to be. He'd been an army trauma surgeon for so long that he didn't know how to be anything else. Which meant that he was nothing. He was damaged and broken, and Raevenne deserved so much better than that.

And something had begun to untwist inside him.

He'd been existing. But he hadn't been living. And then he'd met up with Rae after all those years.

A woman who seemed to turn the lights back on in his life. She poured warmth—*life*—into even the bleakest, coldest corner.

'Bit by bit, these past couple of months, you helped me deal with a pain I'd been pretending I wasn't wallowing in. You began to save me that month we spent out here last time. But it was time for me to start saving myself.'

For himself as much as for her.

He owed them both that much.

She deserved someone who could give her so much more than he could offer right now. But as that old, familiar, lost grit began to burn inside him again, Myles knew that he was ready to stand back up, to fight, to be the kind of man worthy of a woman like Raevenne Rawlstone.

He had one more shot at living. He wasn't going to mess this one up.

* * *

'So what did you talk about with your brigadier?'

'Too many things to explain now. Old missions. Old buddies. Guys who are no longer here. It wouldn't make sense to you if I told you now. It wouldn't…mean anything to you. But, if you like, over time, I can tell you the stories. Even introduce you to some of the old guys.'

A part of her wanted that, *wanted* to talk to people who knew another side of Myles. But then she thought of her brother, and how closely he guarded some of his stories. Things he knew that she could never fully understand if she hadn't been out there with him.

'That's okay.' She placed her hand on his chest instinctively. 'That's your past. Your memories. Keep them precious. I want your future.'

'And you have it,' he told her fiercely. 'I can't promise that the nightmares are over. Or that I won't have lapses. But I know who I am now, with you, and I know that I can overcome them. I can't control everything, not with the villagers or with Mikey. Or with you.'

'Oh, I don't know about that.' She blushed naughtily, thinking of the nights together when his unique set of skills had controlled her body most efficiently.

The difference was, she was beginning to learn that she had her own set of skills to control his body, too.

'I'm here for you, though,' she added seriously. 'Whenever you want me. To talk to, to distract, or even just to hold.'

'And I promise you, I'll always come to you from now on. I'll never push you away again.'

'I like the sound of that,' she murmured, pushing him down on the bed and moving to sit astride him. 'Starting from now?'

'From now.' He dipped his head in agreement.

'Prove it,' she murmured, lowering her mouth to his.

'Shh… Listen!' He grinned suddenly.

'Ten…ninc…cight…seven…'

'Myles?' she blinked, mumbling against his hot, vaguely salty chest.

'…six…five…four…'

Abruptly, she sat up, finally hearing the muted chanting outside.

'Three…' she chorused quietly with him, her hands resting on his shoulders as she straddled him and felt him begin to grow hard already. 'Two…one… Happy New Year!'

'Happy New Year, Rae.' He lifted up to claim her mouth, his hands gliding up and down her spine to cup her backside. 'Maybe we should make those promises New Year's resolutions?'

'I don't care what you call them,' she moaned gently, 'as long as you honour them.'

'Oh, I will. Trust me.'

And then he obliged, more than happy to begin showing her all the ways he intended to make good on his promises.

For the rest of their lives.

* * * * *

COMING SOON!

We really hope you enjoyed reading this book. If you're looking for more romance, be sure to head to the shops when new books are available on

Thursday 27th December

To see which titles are coming soon, please visit
millsandboon.co.uk

MILLS & BOON

Coming next month

TEMPTED BY HER SINGLE DAD BOSS
Annie O'Neil

Their heads touched, lightly. They both looked up and at each other. He could feel her breath on his lips. He wanted to cup her face in his hands and kiss her. And not just any old kiss. An urgent, hungry, satiating kiss. Something that would answer all of the questions he'd had from the moment he'd laid eyes on her. Something that would tell him if all of this was a hallucination or very, very real.

'Ready, Doc?'

He nodded, not entirely sure what he was saying he was ready for.

Maggie sat back in the chair and detached her prosthetic, their eyes still locked on each other's. He was going to kiss her. Resistance seemed…ridiculous. Why wait for something he'd never known he wanted?

So he did.

He didn't hover nervously. Offer tentative butterfly kisses. No. His mouth crashed down on hers as if he'd been waiting for this moment his entire life.

From the moment his mouth touched hers, he knew that lightning could strike twice. That there was more than one woman he'd been meant to kiss. To hold. To cup her face between his hands. To taste as the water poured over the pair of them, erasing time, history, anything and everything that up until this moment would've kept them apart.

It wasn't a one-sided kiss. Not by a long shot. Maggie's entire body was arching up and toward him. She'd woven her fingers through his hair and was sliding her other hand along his stubble as their kisses gained in intensity.

Just as he was about to slip his hands onto her waist and pull her even closer to him, the bathroom door abruptly slammed open.

Alex pulled himself away from Maggie and turned just in time to see his son walk through the door.

Jake. His little boy. A mop of sandy blond hair, just like his. Brown eyes like his mother's. As if he'd ever forget who had brought this child into the world. His serious, intense, loving son who'd gone through all but a single year of his life without his mother.

'Hey, Dad.' Jakes eyebrows tugged together as he took in the scene then noticed that Maggie was holding one of her legs in her hand. His eyes widened further than Alex had ever seen them.

'Oh....' His eyebrows rose up to his hairline. 'Cool....'

Continue reading
TEMPTED BY HER SINGLE DAD BOSS
Annie O'Neil

Available next month
www.millsandboon.co.uk

Copyright ©2018 Annie O'Neil

LET'S TALK
Romance

For exclusive extracts, competitions
and special offers, find us online: